realms *of*
glory

Catherine Fox is an established and popular author. Her debut novel, *Angels and Men* (reissued in 2014) was a *Sunday Times* Pick of the Year. Her other books include *The Benefits of Passion* and *Love for the Lost* (reissued in 2015), *Acts and Omissions*, which was chosen as a Book of 2014 by *The Guardian*, and its sequel, *Unseen Things Above* (2015). Catherine lectures at Manchester Metropolitan University.

realms *of* glory

catherine fox

Marylebone House

First published in Great Britain in 2017

Marylebone House
36 Causton Street
London SW1P 4ST
www.marylebonehousebooks.co.uk

British Library Cataloguing-in-Publication Data
A catalogue record for this book is available from the British Library

ISBN 978-1-910674-21-5
eBook ISBN 978-1-910674-22-2

Typeset by Lapiz Digital Services, India
Manufacture managed by Jellyfish
First printed in Great Britain by CPI
Subsequently digitally printed in Great Britain

eBook by Lapiz Digital Services, India
Produced on paper from sustainable forests

For
Kate and Vicki
Love, love, love, love, love

Dramatis personae

------◆◆◆------

Bishops

Steve Pennington	Bishop of Lindchester
Vacancy	Bishop of Barcup
Rupert Anderson	Archbishop of York

Priests and deacons

Cathedral clergy

Marion Randall	Dean of Lindchester (the boss)
Giles Littlechild	Cathedral Canon Precentor (music & worship)
Mark Lawson	Cathedral Canon Chancellor, 'Mr Happy' (outreach & matters scholarly)
Philip Voysey-Scott	Cathedral Canon Treasurer (money)

Lindchester clergy

Matt Tyler	Archdeacon of Lindchester
Bea Whitchurch	Archdeacon of Martonbury
Martin Rogers	Borough (and Churches) Liaison Officer
Dominic Todd	Rector of Lindford parish church
Wendy Styles	'Father Wendy', Vicar of Renfold, Carding-le-Willow, Cardingforth
Virginia Coleman	Curate to Wendy Styles
Ed Bailey	Rector of Gayden Parva, Gayden Magna, Itchington Episcopi, etc.
Laurie	Vicar of Risley Hill

| Kay Redfern | Vicar of St Andrew's Barcup, partner of Helene |

People

Cathedral Close

Gene	Husband of the dean
Timothy Gladwin	Cathedral director of music
Laurence	Cathedral organist
Iona	Assistant organist
Sonya Pennington	Wife of Bishop Steve
Nigel Bennet	Senior lay clerk
Freddie May	Tenor, lay vicar of Gayden Parva
Ambrose Hardman	Alto, lay vicar of Gayden Magna
Miss Barbara Blatherwick	Cathedral Close resident, former school matron
Philippa Voysey-Scott	'Totty', wife of the canon treasurer
Ulrika Littlechild	Precentor's wife, voice coach
Helene Carter	Diocesan safeguarding and HR officer, partner of Kay
Kat	Bishop Steve's EA
Miriam Lawson	Wife of canon chancellor
Chad William Lawson	Son of canon chancellor
Tabitha Lawson	Daughter of canon chancellor

Beyond the Close

Dr Jane Rossiter	Lecturer at Linden University, married to Matt Tyler
Neil Ferguson	Father Ed's partner
Andrew Jacks	Director of the Dorian Singers
Becky Rogers	Ex-wife of Martin, mother of Leah and Jessica
Leah Rogers	Older daughter
Jessica Rogers	Younger daughter
Mrs Todd	Father Dominic's mother

Lydia Redfern	Kay's daughter
Chloe Garner	Street pastor, lawyer, lay member of General Synod, cousin of Ambrose Hardman
Madge	Retired midwife, Cardingforth

All Creatures Great and Small

Cosmo	Chloe's labradoodle
Pedro	Father Wendy's rescue greyhound
Dora	Kay Redfern's golden retriever
Amadeus	Cathedral cat
Boris I	Choristers' hamster
Boris II	Choristers' hamster

JANUARY 2016

Chapter 1

It is the best of times, it is the worst of times,
it is the season of Light, it is the season of Darkness,
it is the spring of hope, it is the winter of despair,
we are all going direct to Heaven, we are all going direct the
other way.

elcome to Lindchester. Are you sitting comfortably? If so, then I assume you are at home, rather than in a pew – or (Lord have mercy!) stuck on one of those beastly plastic stacking chairs, knowing you will leave a sweaty bum print whenever you stand for a hymn. Pour yourself a glass of Christmas whisky (a gift from the undertaker, perhaps, if you are clergy). Alternatively, make yourself a cup of that weird spiced Christmas tea out of the hamper your sister-in-law sent. It needs using up. Comfortable?

Then I will begin. I will tell you a Tale of Two Churches. One is the Church in glory, like a bride adorned for her husband; the other – inhabited by the likes of you and me – is the Church incarnate here on earth, ankle deep in the mire of the imaginary diocese of Lindchester. But perhaps, if we catch them in Emily Dickinson's certain slant of light, we may glimpse a bit of glory around the grubby edges of our characters.

What of those characters? How are they faring? More than a year has passed since we waved them off last Advent. It is Saturday night now. The nice Chablis has all gone. Only the yucky coconut ones rattle round the plastic sweet tub. The last clump of Christmas pudding is clenched blackly under cling film like a fist preserved in a peat bog for 6,000 years. We are still telling ourselves someone will eat it. Listen! Can you hear the tiniest tinkle – faint as bells round the necks of nativity oxen on your mantelpiece – of pine needles falling from Christmas trees? Yes, needle-fall is general across the diocese of Lindchester, for Christmas has been and gone. New Year has been and gone, too. We wait, lolled on sofas, remote dangling in slack hand, for the start of term, or work, or whatever comes under the heading of Real Life.

What does the year hold in this best of times, this worst of times; this season of bake-offs and season of foodbanks; this Green spring of muscular theological hope and Lothlórien winter of hand-wringing theological despair? We will peep through many a stained-glass window in pursuit of answers. Once again, you will find yourself dogged at every turn. Your narrator will stand a little too close, breathing in your ear and commenting in the manner of an over-zealous cathedral guide who is not content to leave visitors to wander around looking at things by themselves. I will burst out of vestry cupboards and through the fourth wall right into your face. I will betray my sacred Jamesian office wherever possible. Is this your first visit to Lindchester? Would you like a brochure?

How are your Anglican wings? Give them a shake, and we will mount up, as in days of old. It is dark, but there below is the River Linden, many miles meandering with a mazy motion. There are the water meadows – vast lakes at the moment. Can you just make out the stands of trees, the wooded rises? Give thanks for these boons, O people living in towns further downstream. Without them, the Linden would be in your sitting room by now. As it is, the Lower Town of Lindchester has been flooded twice this winter.

Where shall we go? To the archdeacon's you say? Ah, but *which* archdeacon? There are two – our old friend, the Venerable Matt Tyler, archdeacon of Lindchester, and the Venerable Bea Whitchurch, archdeacon of Martonbury. A *lady* archdeacon, no less! We will save Bea till later (pausing only to report that those scoundrels in the cathedral refer to her as 'the little teapot'). Historically, there have been two archdeaconries in the diocese of Lindchester, but if the new bishop gets his way, there will be four. Four! The multiplication

4

of archdeacons! A terrifying sign that we are all going to Chelmsford in a handcart.

The town of Lindford lies below us now. Let us bend our joyful footsteps to the house of the archdeacon of Lindchester. There are two cars on the drive these days – the sporty black Mini and the knackered old wreck belonging to the archdeacon's—His what? His wife? Has Jane learned to embrace this title? Did she shake her head and smile indulgently as those cards dropped through the letterbox addressed to 'The Venerable & Mrs M. Tyler'?

Let us sneak in and find out. You will see at once that it is a nice house, warm and clean. The archdeacon's taste has prevailed throughout. This was not hard, as Jane's taste is for not giving a monkey's about homemaking. I admit it's a bit generic, a bit like a show house, for Matt is a pragmatist. There's none of that girlie clobber. And no chuffing cushions. Like most red-blooded Englishmen, the archdeacon can't be doing with cushions. This is why he has to act as a cushion himself, when his beloved needs something to prop her feet on while lying on the sofa. Which is what she's doing right now.

'Yes, but surely you're owed a sabbatical,' said Jane.

'Nope,' replied the archdeacon. 'We're entitled to one every ten years. I've only clocked up six.'

'Can't you wangle something? I want to apply for study leave next year.'

'Go ahead.'

'Yes, but I want to spend it in New Zealand. With you. I'll tell the bishop our marriage depends on it. Come along, now. Do it for me. Remember the Penningtons' lovely *Biblical Bonking* book? Quality time. Acts of service.'

The archdeacon sighed. Pity the bishop's wife had given that copy of their co-authored book to Jane, not him. No chance to deflect it. At least Janey had tired of reading him excerpts every bedtime.

'Can I get you a top-up?' he asked.

'Yes.' She handed over her glass. 'And then you can come straight back and carry on the sabbatical conversation.'

'The rules is the rules, I'm afraid. Ten years.'

'Pah. You could at least ask him.'

'Fine. I'll ask him.' Matt hauled himself up off the sofa. 'I wouldn't hold your breath, though.'

He padded through to the kitchen in his Christmas socks and got the last of the Prosecco. He closed the fridge and rested his forehead against it. Oh, Lord. Vexed though the sabbatical question was proving, it was going to look like a cracker joke by this time next week. Which was when he'd probably have to float the suffragan bishop of Barcup possibility . . .

You will infer from this that our good friend Bob Hooty has retired. The big detached Tudorbethan house in Martonbury is vacant. I fear that once again I must trouble the reader with the question of who will be the next bishop. It won't be as convoluted as the appointment of the bishop of Lindchester, I promise, since suffragan bishoprics are not Crown appointments. That said, gone are the days when a diocesan bishop could simply have a conversation in his club with an old chum from theological college, and appoint him. There will be an advert. I believe the archbishop's appointments secretary will have names to commend. Then there will be a shortlist and interviews conducted by a panel. Is the new bishop of Lindchester powerless here? By no means. He will get the person he wants, I dare say. It would be deeply inappropriate of him to take that person to one side and confide his intentions. But once Bob's farewell service was out of the way, it was not out of order for him to enquire, in passing, if he was right in thinking that the archdeacon's paperwork was up to date . . . ?

Bishop Steve has not been idle in our absence. He has made changes. He plans more changes still. One of his earliest moves was to let the lovely PA Penelope go, and appoint an executive assistant. This was a deeply unpopular move on the Close. Even inanimate objects in the bishop's office seemed to cry out at the injustice. There was a stage when the office computer inexplicably autocorrected 'bishop' to 'wanker' whenever the new EA tried to send an email. Goodness. How did *that* happen? The bishop also chose not to appoint a new chaplain, on the grounds that he didn't really need one. This sent ripples of fear throughout the Slope Society nationally. Honestly, if he wasn't such a nice bloke, everyone would hate Bishop Steve.

Of course, there are those who, unmoved by considerations of personal charm, hate him in adherence to long-held principle.

'I hate him, for he is an Evangelical!' declaimed Gene in his Royal Shakespeare Company voice. 'But more for that in low simplicity, he is trying to merge cathedral and diocesan structures like they've done in bloody Liverpool!'

'Yes, darling.' The dean did not bother looking up from her book.

'On the specious grounds that it makes sense and would save money!'

'Yes, darling.'

'What a wanker.' Pause. 'Yes, darling?'

'*No*, darling.'

'Oh.'

Marion is still dean of Lindchester. No change there. She was not the first woman bishop in the Church of England. Nor the second, third, fourth or fifth. Indeed, we are losing track of how many women bishops we now have. Why has she been passed over? I cannot say. Deep in unfathomable mines, the Crown Nominations Commission treasures up its bright designs.

There have been choral changes on the back row of *dec*. We have a new alto lay clerk. He arrived last autumn, accompanied by what the gallant elderly gents in the congregation designated (in the unreconstructed privacy of their hearts) *a jolly attractive oriental dolly bird*. Mr May has somehow managed not to get himself booted out of the choir. He skipped the whole carol concert season re-cuperating from nose surgery, and is off visiting his mother in Argentina at the moment. Actually, I tell a lie, he should be on his way home by now. Tomorrow the loyal Miss Blatherwick will drive to the airport to collect him.

Miss Blatherwick lies awake. Just can't get comfy. Indigestion. Her hand strays to her stomach. She applies her customary self-control and doesn't go looking for lumps. If you look for lumps at 3 a.m., you will certainly find them. She is a sensible woman. If she's no better by Monday, she will make a doctor's appointment.

Downstairs her phone rings where it is charging. A phone call at 3 a.m.! Her heart thumps. Bad news. Or a wrong number. Probably a wrong number. But she gets out of bed anyway, puts on her dressing gown and goes to check.

Voicemail. Unknown number. She listens.

'Miss B? It's Freddie.' She hears wailing in the background. 'Oh God, Miss B, really sorry to do this to you? Probably it's all fine, yeah? Only we're making an emergency landing? So just to say, love you? Please tell my people, if – Oh God. OK. Gotta give this phone back now. So yeah, I'll see you, OK? Love, love, love, love, love.'

Chapter 2

t is the Eleventh Day of Christmas. Eleven pipers piping. Listen. Do you hear them? Actually, there is just the one lone piper in the diocese of Lindchester. He busks to shoppers in Lindford in front of Marks & Spencer, drones a-droning, skirls a-skirling. 'Amazing grace, how sweet the sound.' At intervals his cheeks pop out spherically like a bullfrog's. He nods every time a passer-by chucks a coin, but the piping never stops. Rain drips from the vast lit-up snowflakes suspended over the street. In coffee shops people drink festive lattes laced with gingerbread. Christmas music plays on a loop. The baristas are sick of it, sick of Christmas, wouldn't care if they never heard another Christmas song again, ever. Outside the piper pipes his different tune in the gloom.

Not long now till Epiphany, when we can dismantle it all, get rid of the tree, wonder what to do with all the cards, sling that nub of pudding nobody's going to eat, start the New Year properly.

The Venerable Bea Whitchurch has a knitted nativity set. Walk past number 34 Tennyson Gardens, Martonbury, look down the drive, and you will glimpse the figures kneeling in homage on her sitting–room windowsill. Bea knitted the entire scene herself – years before knitted nativities became a thing – for she is a great knitter. Knitting in meetings, on trains, in front of the telly. She carries her big patchwork bag everywhere, some project or other always on the go.

Perhaps a knitting archdeacon ought to strike dread into the heart? She might not be a cheerful little teapot (short and stout) after all. What if, Madame Defarge-like, she is secretly encoding into that nice snuggly snood the names of clergy lined up for the chop in the new bishop's reign of terror? Measuring out the yarn of incumbency, and snipping it short! O clergy of the Martonbury archdeaconry, beware! Don't get on the wrong side of Bea Whitchurch.

No. It's no good. Even as I wrote that, I could hear Bea hooting with laughter. Bea doesn't really have a wrong side. Obviously, she's capable of being firm when required, and now and then of getting *pretty cross*. But it's becoming clear to me that once again I have failed to present you with an archidiaconal monster. We will be seeing more of Bea later. For now, we will leave her to finish that snood. She is making it for someone who said, 'I love your snood!' Perhaps this is the thing to beware of with our new archdeacon – admiring her handiwork. If you admire it, she is sure to make you one.

Miss Blatherwick is not a great knitter. Miss Blatherwick is a great reader. So, naturally, she has a novel with her now as she sits in the doctor's waiting room. It is *Adam Bede*, which unaccountably she has never before read. But she is not reading it. Instead, she is staring at the wall and thinking about Freddie's message. *Probably it's all fine, yeah?* And of course, it had been. The plane had landed safely. An engine fault, but no disaster. Dear boy. Dearest boy. He was castigating himself now for scaring her. But Miss Blatherwick would rather a false alarm at 3 a.m. every night till kingdom come than imagine him gone. Just . . . gone. Winking out over the Atlantic, with no warning, no proper goodbye.

Well, well. This, too, will probably be fine. And if not, well. She is eighty, is she not? She opens *Adam Bede* to the place she has marked with her bookmark. (Miss Blatherwick does not dog-ear her pages.) It strikes her with sudden clarity that one day she will have read her last book. And if she had enough warning, she might even be *aware* that she has read her last book. She will close the volume, lay it down, and that will be that. A lifetime of reading concluded. And if this appointment today − probably nothing, probably a false alarm − proved to be the beginning of her end, well, she would have the luxury of choosing her last book. And pondering her last words, too. A blessing not to be underestimated. She would have far more leisure than Freddie, gabbling into a borrowed phone on a plane full of wailing people. Even so, she rather doubted she would come up with anything better than he had: love.

We enter the Season of Epiphany. O Epiphany, how your currency has been devalued! The market has been flooded with cheap mini-epiphanies, until the word means little more than 'Omigod! I suddenly saw something in this whole new light?' Miss Blatherwick, had she been sixty years younger, might have described that insight about reading her last book as an epiphany. Who, outside the church, thinks '6 January' when Epiphany is mentioned?

Who thinks of star-led chieftains travelling on imagined camels (a cold coming they have of it) seeking the right thing in the wrong place? 'Where is he that is born King of the Jews?' Who pictures the other mothers coming to their doorways in Bethlehem to watch the commotion? Wealthy foreigners − what can they want here? The strangers depart into their own country another way. What was all that about? The mothers rock their swaddled innocents as night falls in Ramah.

The primates of the Anglican Communion worldwide are travelling now. Lo, from the north they come, from east and west and south! They will gather in Canterbury − for a birth or a death? Will this be the point when one last fatal tap is dealt, and the fragile bowl of the Anglican Communion falls apart along the hairline crack of human sexuality? The right tap, dealt at the wrong time? Light a candle, let your prayers gather there too. 'Dawn on our darkness, and lend us thine aid.'

But our tale is not concerned with primates. Canterbury lies far beyond the borders of Lindchester. We have local fish to fry. So come, rise up (as you are able) and fly with me again. Let us see how the rest of our old friends are faring. It is Saturday. This being

11

the New Year, rather a lot of them are engaged in some form of exercise. Jane has been for a lumber round Lindford arboretum. Freddie heads out, as ever, on his mental long route to Cardingforth and back.

This does not surprise us. But who is that, in £200 running shoes with MetaClutch exoskeleton heel and X-GEL comfort, and top-of-the-range compression gear? He fairly bristles with GPS connectivity, motivational music, heart-rate sensor, and all-round general fitness tracking. That's right. It's our pal Neil Ferguson. We salute him in his New Year efforts to ward off chunkiness. ('Am I looking chunky? Do I look chunky to you? Oh my God – you think I look chunky!') He is taking a little breather now, and sipping his isotonic rooibos, having covered a full kilometre, nearly. Je-sus *Christ*! He checks his gadgets to see if he's dying. In his head he's still that nippy little kid, lethal in the box, demon king of playground fitba. How has this happened to him?

Father Dominic is not running. Not because he doesn't need to lose weight – I'll see your chunky, and raise you mountain ranges of wobbling fattipuffs! – but because he can't run. Well, he *can*, but it frightens people. They start jogging alongside with a defibrillator, just in case. No, Dominic is in his basement cranking away on his cross-trainer where nobody can see him, hoping – like the psalmist's clouds – to drop fatness. Year one of the three-year dieting cycle has commenced.

Dean Marion is not running, either. She is out on her new bike, toiling along a disused railway track a safe distance from Lindchester. Lord, they say you never forget how to cycle! But the first minutes in the saddle after a thirty-year lay-off can be a bit dicey. It is a very nice bike, a Christmas present from her devoted husband. He bought it on condition that he could cycle along behind her, the better to admire her arse. ('If you admire my arse in padded cycling shorts,' pants the dean, 'then you are even sadder than I feared.')

And there goes Father Wendy with Pedro, along the banks of the Linden. Pedro is wearing a new tartan jacket. A Christmas present. I can't make out which tartan from this distance. Hunting Postlethwaite, perhaps. We will just wave as we pass, because I must hurry you to the Close, where something terrifying is happening:

12

Freddie May (back from his run) is odd-jobbing for the vergers' team by chopping up this year's cathedral Christmas tree with a chainsaw.

Argh! I can't look! But wait – Freddie is wearing gauntlets and proper ear and eye protection. He's using his power tool responsibly! Is that a metaphor for his life, I wonder? Perhaps Freddie has steadied down and grown up, in the last year. If so, then we may attribute this to the ennobling and refining force of his *fin'amor*. What acts of chivalry, what ordeals of discipline would Freddie not dare in his quest to win the love of his unattainable mentor? Did he not – at the merest hint of amusement on Dr Jacks's face – shave off the hipster beard he had grown?

Freddie finishes his sawing. Now he's got to take a load of logs over to the ~~wanker's~~ bishop's. Man, he *hates* the guy. But this is like his New Year's resolution? To not hold grudges. It came to him after the whole emergency-landing situation, the need to not waste his entire life hanging onto the bad stuff. It was kind of dumb, anyway, coz Penelope? She was cool with taking early retirement; so why was Freddie all, I will *never* forgive the guy for sacking her?

'What was he grinning at?' asked the bishop's wife.

'I suspect,' said the bishop (grinning himself), 'it was the double entendre.'

'—tendre.' Sonya was one of those very affirming people who likes to join in the end of sentences. 'What double entendre?'

'Um, that would be "wood".'

'Wood?'

'"I've got some wood for you; where do you want it?"'

'—want it. Oh!' Sonya clapped her hand to her mouth. 'Round the back, please! I said that, didn't I?'

The bishop gave a helpless snort. 'Afraid you did, love.'

'No-ooo! Ha ha ha! I couldn't work out what was so funny! Cheeky thing! Well, I suppose he's finally spoken to us. I've been praying for that for months.'

'Mmm,' said the bishop. 'Maybe you should stop praying now.'

'I can't. You know me.'

The bishop gave her a mock stern look. 'Whose job is it to save people?'

'—ple. I know, I know! Saviour complex! Anyway. Zumba! I'll just grab my things, and.' To compensate for finishing the sentences of others, Sonya often left her own incomplete.

'Have fun!' The bishop listened to her crashing around in the cloakroom. There was an *Ow!* and a clatter. (Falling squash racquets?)

'It's huge fun, but I'm rubbish at it!' called Sonya. 'I can't find my. Oh, here they are. Bye!'

There. Our first proper glimpse of the Penningtons. I rather like them. Bishop Steve did not proceed to spend the next half-hour agonizing over Freddie May. In fact, apart from the nuisance of getting the locks changed on the office, Mr May has barely impinged on the bishop's notice at all. Instead, Steve went back to drafting the advert for the suffragan bishop of Barcup job.

And over in Lindford, Matt still hasn't got round to mentioning the subject to Janey.

Chapter 3

Miss Blatherwick lies awake in the night again. Tonight she finds herself pondering the idea of glory. There are choristers singing in the playgrounds of yesteryear:

Glory, glory, hallelujah!
Teacher hit me with a ruler.
Ruler broke in half and we all had a laugh,
And we won't go to school no more!

Yes, that would have been a glorious moment, the rod of the school oppressor snapped. But when had that ever happened? No, there was nothing for it but to endure. To yearn for justice, but to endure.

How the mind wanders. Glory. After decades of sermons, Miss Blatherwick is something of a biblical scholar. Two words for glory: *shekinah* and *kabod*. *Kabod*, if memory serves, means weight. The weight of glory. 'For our light affliction, which is but for a moment' – Miss Blatherwick knows her proof texts – 'worketh for us a far more exceeding and eternal weight of glory.'

Our light affliction. Well, the test results will indicate how light. In emotional ounces and pounds, as it were. And give her a sense of how long the 'moment' might be. Months? Years? Perhaps one ought to view all suffering and challenge – indeed, the whole of one's life – as weight training? She smiles in the dark. Not the absurd body sculpting her dear boy goes in for, but *strength* training, to prepare for the burden of glory, which might otherwise be impossible to bear. Like glorious vestments worked with gold and jewels, so heavy that they made the wearer wade like a dreamer trying to run . . .

She has drifted asleep now. Rain taps at her window. The cathedral clock chimes the night away in quarters. It will pass. It will all pass.

Oh, let it pass! Let this January be over! Dark mornings, dark afternoons. True, the days are drawing out, but in these darkest of weeks the dawn comes a little later each morning. Sunshine lights up the tender red shoots on rose bushes across the diocese. A wren trills the same short phrase over, over. How green the grass is when the sun is so low. The sky of Lindfordshire is marbled with clouds like faded endpapers. On the cathedral flagpole the flag lifts, half unfurling on the slow breeze, then drops again.

It's Monday. Neil is driving to the station. He hears it on the radio. No! NO! He's got to sit on the fecking train to London, trying not to cry all the way to Euston, knowing he's dead, the 'starman', the thin white duke. Oh Jesus, can we not turn this horrible year off and on again?

'Omigod, Bowie! *Bowie*, Jane!'

'I know, sweetums, I know,' says Jane. She's stepped out of a seminar to take the call. 'I actually shed a tear when I heard. It was my Diana moment. Finally! I must be human after all.'

'I'm going to throw a party,' says Dominic. 'This Friday. We can all get pissed and bawl Bowie songs.'

'Count me in.'

'Who even is David Bowie?' asks Leah Rogers.

Oh boo hoo. Someone's died, some old singer from a billion years ago who looks like a weirdo. It's not like he was your best *friend*, Father. It's not like you actually *knew* him. You can't love someone you haven't even ever met. You're like the girls at

school, all literally crying their eyes out about One Direction breaking up. Like who even cares?

Leah slams the car door. At least Mum's back tomorrow.
Everyone expects their *mum* to be embarrassing.

Tuesday. The primates still seethe in the unbearable crucible of
prayer. We wait, fingers in ears, for the explosion. For the mass
walkout by conservative archbishops. If the vessel holds, what will
we find at the end of the process? The famous stone that turneth
all to gold? Some panacea, some alkahest to dissolve all difference,
all hatred and misunderstanding?

'Shame about Bowie,' said Bea to her fellow archdeacon as they
crossed the Close to the palace. 'Part of our youth.'

'Yup,' said Matt. 'Took me by surprise. How much it rocked me.'

They passed the cathedral's west front in silence. They made a
comic pair, the two archdeacons of Lindchester diocese. Man
Mountain and little teapot. There was always much hilarity – meas-
ured in Imperial units of lay-clerk smirks – when the two were
in formal procession together.

'I had the haircut,' said Bea.

'Me too. Wide trousers. The works.'

'Ooh! Lightning make-up?'

Matt could not deny it. Probably still had the photographic
evidence, if he dug around. He rang the palace doorbell.

The door opened. It was Sonya.

'Oh, hi, guys! Come on in. The others are already.'

Bea smiled at the bishop's wife. 'Happy New Year!'

'—Year!' agreed Sonya. 'Hang your things up in the.'

The archdeacons obeyed, not catching one another's eye.

I'll bloody murder you, Bea Whitchurch, thought Matt.

I should explain Matt's last thought, lest the reader fears this tale is
about to take a sudden dark twist. Bea Whitchurch has a naughty eye
for the foibles of others. It did not take long for Bea to spot the
linguistic quirk of the bishop's wife and point it out to her fellow
archdeacon. Matt cannot now un-hear it. Nor can he banish from his

mind Bea's suggestion that if they were cunning, they might be able to lure Sonya into saying a rude word: 'I've been visiting the hospice.'

The two archdeacons, having hung up their. In the. Went through to the large meeting room (—ting room) (*Stop* it, Bea!), where the rest of the senior staff were waiting. In accordance with our custom of not intruding into private meetings to take minutes, we will now leave them to it – pausing only to weave in a tiny narrative loose end. Just before the door closes, we will catch sight of Bea handing over that nice snuggly snood to Marion. If anyone needed a nice snuggly snood right now, it's the dean. The dean will be moved almost to tears. She will put the snood on immediately (conscious of all the folk who needed cherishing with snoods even more than she does).

Our good friend Marion is struggling this January, I fear. She is weighing up whether to put her weight behind the bishop's ideas for a restructure, or if she needs to defend the cathedral's historic independence. At this point, the bishop has merely floated his idea with her. No point taking it to the rest of the senior staff team if she rejects the suggestion out of hand.

A brief word here about the senior staff team. ~~Its main role is to bypass Bishop's Council~~. The composition of these varies from diocese to diocese. Here in Lindchester it is made up of the bishop, the suffragan bishop (situation vacant), the dean, the two (plus two pending) archdeacons, the bishop's EA (as there is no longer a bishop's chaplain) and the diocesan secretary. I commend this body to your prayers. The business they transact behind that closed door will impinge upon our tale. We tiptoe back out now, past the red dining room, observing (like good Anglicans) that we preferred the *old* colour scheme.

'Leah. Psst. Leah,' says Jack in maths. 'Snape's dead!'
  'Duh. I know. Voldemort kills him in *The Deathly Hallows*.'
  'No, the *real* Snape. The *actor* Snape! He died.'
  'Yeah, I *know*.'
  'Liar!'

Leah flips him the finger and bends her head down over her worksheet. *What is the ratio of GREEN cylinders to total cylinders?* Snape is dead? He can't be! How? *What is the ratio of GREEN cylinders* – Who even cares? Leah sweeps her work from the desk and rushes out of class.

The crucible of primates opens. It will be a while before the heat goes out of it and we can see what's left. Gold? Baseness of the worst kind? Guarding the good deposit of tradition? Or legitimizing homophobia? There is no shortage of answers. This is Anglicanism: it depends who you ask. The worksheet wavers through tears. Q. *What is the ratio of TRUTH to total love?* Shall we sweep it aside and rush out? But where would we go?

O Anglican Communion! Best of churches, worst of churches. Church of hope, church of despair. And who – outside your doors, going about their daily business on the streets of Lindfordshire – even cares?

If I could knit you up, like some cosmic knitting archdeacon, I would. But it feels like trying to knit with barbed wire. Barbed wire and human hair.

Father Dominic, shielded to some extent by his low expectations, is nevertheless heartbroken. Again. Again! How long, O Lord? He thinks of the primate of the Episcopal Church, and prays for that grace, that dignity, for himself. To know you are right, yet to bow your head to pain all the same.

The dean stares up at the crucified Christ in the Lady Chapel. She signed that open letter urging the primates to repent of the Church's treatment of LGBTI Christians. It seems to her now that she can hardly bear it. *Cannot* bear it.

The lay clerk of Gayden Parva – more lovely than a summer's day, though less temperate – shares his views about fuckwitted African primates on Facebook.

Archdeacon Matt rubbed his hands over his bald head. Oh Lord. Schism avoided. A week ago, he'd've settled for that. But this was not going to play well in the headlines. The Episcopal Church of America on the naughty step for breaking ranks on the old gay marriage front. Short-term missional and pastoral disaster. But the long game? Hmm. Only time would tell, but it looked to him as though there was now some wiggle room on how we define marriage. Some canny phrasing in that document. He was betting a whole heap of spiritual hard graft – reconciliation, foot washing, tears – went on behind closed doors. Didn't translate well into secular speak, but it would not be wasted.

Jane came in and rubbed his back for him. 'Bummer,' she said. 'Have you remembered Dom's party?'

Dominic's party will be remembered for a long time. Somewhat hazily in some cases, I will admit. Haziness was accelerated by those cases of champagne donated by Neil Ferguson, on top of the supermarket Prosecco laid in by Dominic himself.

I offer the reader some edited highlights.

Neil (in wig, catsuit and platform boots) was heard demanding why that bawheid archdeacon had been invited? Correct him if he was wrong, but this party was a send-off for the 'starman'. Was the archdeacon a Bowie fan? He thought not.

The archdeacon begged to differ. Broke out the old photographic evidence.

Very well. Very well. The archdeacon could stay. Provided he put on the zact same lightning make-up, right now. Eds, where's ma kit? Eds?

Eds was in the kitchen with Freddie May.

Seriously? Yeah, no, thing was, Eds was a sweet guy? He was! Seriously, Eds was the kind of sweet guy guys always go home to, yeah? But Freddie, he was just a bad habit? Like, nobody really wanted him, for keeps? Oh God, sorry, crying now. Lemme make you a cocktail?

Eds' eyes darted round. Save me, someone!

Where, where is the person willing to save poor Ed from a dirty Martini mixed by Freddie May – clad as he is in nothing but tattoos, piercings, and a cheeky pair of gold spandex shorts?

Who else was there? I've lost track. Clergy from the Lindford deanery, naughty graphic designers from London, diocesan staff, old friends, old enemies. Whatever. Let all the people boogie.

'The thing is, Jane. Thing is, the star man has *already* visited us.'

'Yes, darling, he has.'

'Thass the incarnation.'

'You're pished, Dommie.'

'And he BLEW OUR MINDS. Mean it, Jane.'

It is Saturday morning now. Father Wendy plods along beside the Linden with Pedro. Oh Pedro, it's darker than ever, isn't it? It's so hard to believe spring will come. If all you did was watch the dawn, you'd think things were getting worse.

Wendy stops and gazes out across the waterlogged landscape. For a moment, everything seems upside down. The fields look to her like sky covered with a thin film of earth.

Chapter 4

I t is the Week of Prayer for Christian Unity. The Anglican Communion has been spared the awkwardness of entering this in shambles and fragments. Ought we, despite everything, to muster some kind of Hallelujah? (Or – if that smacks of happy-clappiness to you – an Alleluia.) Once again, Anglicans have come to the hard-won conclusion that schism is never the answer. (Unless the question is: what do you call it when there's a split between strongly opposed parties?)

It is not the business of this narrative to tell you what to think. Instead, we swish the biting sword of satire from the morally precarious vantage point of the fence, while in our other hand we seek to hold a torch (like a little candle) as steady as can be. We will point its nosy beam into the lives of our characters, piously humming an old Sunday School favourite: 'You in your small corner, and I in His.'

Blue Monday. 5.30 a.m. The bishop of Lindchester is in his study praying. I realize that I have not yet taken you into Steve's head. Thus far, we have merely hated him from the outside. Here he is, on his knees.

He prays for those who feel hurt and betrayed. He prays for those who are persecuted and shot at, who are flooded or burnt out of their homes. For the hungry and homeless in his own diocese. He prays for friends and family, for his incredible EA (sine qua non), for the clergy and people of the Lindford deanery (whose turn it is in the diocesan cycle of prayer), for cathedral Dean and Chapter, and for lay clerks who excoriate him in ad hominem Facebook attacks. And when he has run out of words, he carries on praying in some private tender scat of the spirit, meaningless, charged with meaning, syllables poured out like pebbles into a stream, intercession too deep for uttering.

It is still dark outside.

Ha, if you'd told Steve at the age of twenty this would be his daily pattern, he'd have laughed. He knows he's a lazy toad by nature. A corner-cutter, a trader on his personal charm. He also knows he's a bear of very little brain. People think he's brighter than he is because he has the gift of the gab. There are bears out there with brains the size of a planet; but Steve (who idled his way through Cambridge and fluked a 2.1) frequently sounds like their equal, because he is not so tongue-tied by nuance.

He has a bookmark in his Bible: 'Be strong and of a good courage; be not afraid, neither be thou dismayed: for the LORD thy God is with thee whithersoever thou goest.'

Ah, he could have skimmed through his life. He could have been one of those maverick, inspirational English masters (O Captain, my captain!) at some public school or other. Generations would have adored floppy-haired Mr Pennington. Sir, with his witty repartee, his dandy clothes. He could have lived in his depth, in the warm shallows, surfing by on the crest of his popularity.

Instead of which, he has to captain this creaky tall ship on a dark and very deep sea. He could have stayed in Aylesbury! If you can't be popular and beloved as a suffragan bishop, then when can you? (He thinks, with the skewing perspective of hindsight.) For him, Aylesbury was like being a curate all over again. Second in command. Sorry, me hearties – I'm just the mate. You'll have to ask the skipper. Have a tot of rum!

Steve has another bookmark; a folded-up page from an old order of service. It is – how lovely, in this Week of Prayer for Christian Unity! – the Methodist Covenant prayer:

Christ has many services to be done:
some are easy, others are difficult;
some bring honour, others bring reproach;
some are suitable to our natural inclinations and
material interests, others are contrary to both . . .

He had thought, when he was first ordained, that he would tough-
en up and outgrow his aversion to conflict. But it seems to him
that all he has acquired over the decades is the knowledge that
everything passes. That, and a sense that the Lord is with him.

If Bishop Steve admitted publicly that his current role is deeply
unsuitable to his natural inclinations, it would sound disingenuous,
of course. Does he not ooze confidence? With his four archdeacons
and his restructures and his growth agenda! Do we not wrinkle
our noses at the whiff of mini-MBA McMellitus management-speak,
the vulgar Evangelical number-crunching Green-itis that lingers
in the room after Slick Steve has left?

Talent pool! When was talent ever a Christian category? Well,
apart from Jesus' parable about the talents, obviously. Which admit-
tedly is how the word entered the English language in the first
place. Yes, yes. *Apart* from that parable – in which those who have
ten are unchristianly *given ten more*, and the poor person with one
talent is punished for not using it! – when was it ever a Christian
category? What is this Evangelical love affair with success? As
though the church were an economy which has to grow year on
year, and increase thirtyfold, sixtyfold, a hundredfold, rather than
being a seed that has to fall into the ground and die? No, we
reserve full shuddering rights when we think of the likes of Steve
Pennington. There goes the C of E. Would we not rather it ceased
to exist, than continued in so uncongenial a form?

Meanwhile, the clergy and people of every Lindchester stripe still
have to crack on with it. They bring good news in word and deed,
in pulpit and out of it, at all times and in all places. They donate
to the foodbank, they volunteer at the foodbank, they are served

by the foodbank. Father Dominic spends many hours in courtrooms, testifying that his Iranian brothers and sisters are genuine converts. The Revd Martin Rogers – the Borough (AND CHURCHES) Liaison Officer – works with homeless shelters, street pastors, respite homes, church ministers, social services, charities, schools. They seek tirelessly to make-do-and-mend Big Society's nets so that nobody slips through. And yet they slip through. Walk through any town in the diocese and you will be asked for change. Spare any change? God bless you. Have a nice day. Spare any change? It is curious, is it not, to be blessed so often by the person in the gutter, who has nothing else to give you?

But whither the diocese of Lindchester? Will Stevangelical prevail? The eagle-eyed among you will have spotted that the post of suffragan bishop of Barcup has now been advertised. You may check out the details in the usual places, and apply, if you feel called. Has Matt got round to broaching this with Jane yet?

Right. About that . . .

'Honey, I'm ho-ome!'

Matt swiftly closed down his CV. Gave her a big smile from behind his study desk. 'How was your day?'

'I bring a bulletin from outside Planet Church.' Jane dumped her satchel and dropped a kiss on the archdeacon's head. 'Nobody gives a stuff about the Episcopal Church gay marriage slap-down! I went in and said, "Torrid week, eh?" and m'colleagues just looked at me. So I said, "the Primates?" And they went, "Oh! Of course! What happened?" These are Radio 4 listeners, and they didn't know! My good friend Spider feared I was breaking some tragic news about mountain gorillas.'

'Mmm.'

'It's just one more instance of our colonial bread coming back to us on the waters.' Jane settled down in his armchair to deliver a seminar. 'Basically, if we hadn't exported our English obsession with criminalizing buggery, we wouldn't have this headache now, would we?'

'Mmm.'

There was a pause. 'I sense you have other more pressing matters.'

'Sorry. Bit distracted.'

'Top secret, eh? That why you hit the boss key when I came in?'

For a second Jane glimpsed the small boy the archdeacon had once been. Caught bang to rights, hand in biscuit barrel.

She laughed her filthy laugh. 'Porn?'

'No!'

'You can watch as much porn as you like, Mr Archdeacon. Provided I get to watch it with you.'

'It's not porn.'

'What is it, then?'

Silence.

'Well, *fine*.' Jane got up and made to flounce out. 'Wait! *Biblical Bonking* says no passive aggression!'

The archdeacon sighed.

'OK, got it.' Jane laid a hand on her heart. 'Matt, I just want you to know, whatever it is, I love you very much, and I promise I won't yell at you.'

The archdeacon nodded. 'All righty.'

'The last bit was a lie,' Jane whispered.

'I realize that,' he whispered back.

We must leave Matt to stew for a bit longer. This is Jane's decision, and who are we to interfere in someone else's marriage? She knows perfectly well what's going on here. Dominic told her the rumours before Christmas and she tootled straight over to Martonbury to cast her eyes over the house. She has already nailed being the world's worst archdeacon's wife, and it would be idle to say Jane is not ambitious.

She opens a nice IPA and snorts. Jane Rossiter, you are a bad person. Get back to the study now, and put the poor man out of his misery! She tilts her head. Yes? Nah. Let the bugger stew.

*

26

If you can remember being at Dominic's party last Friday, then you were not really there.

'Let's have a Rickman night, Eds. Let's watch *Truly, Madly, Deeply*.'

'But we just did.'

'Did not! When?'

'At Dom's. Only you fell asleep on the archdeacon.'

'Did not! Hate that fecker!'

'Uh-huh.' Ed gets out his phone. Checks. 'Looks pretty snuggly to me . . .'

'What! Gimme that.' Neil studies the picture at arm's length because no way is he old enough to need reading glasses. Some vague memory. Someone big and solid holding him. 'Yes, well. And *why* hasn't the recycling been taken out, I'd like to know?'

And so another dark January week draws to a close. Don't despair. Stand in your doorway at six any evening now. Yes. That really is a blackbird singing, juicy and gorgeous as summer berries.

The dean is out cycling again before evensong. They have just reached the halfway point. It's been raining. It will rain again. There are more storms on the way. But today it's mild.

'I'm *completely* knackered.'

'Would you like an energy-packed banana to revive you?' asks Gene.

'Provided that's not a euphemism. Oh!' Marion guffaws. 'What on *earth* is *that*?'

Ah, she's laughing. 'This, deanissima, is a banana guard, a purpose-built protective case for bananas.'

'Good grief! Did you buy it at Ann Summers?'

'Certainly not!' says Gene. 'It's from Lakeland. Sonya-Sonya recommended it. It accommodates every shape and size, and protects against bruising and battering-attering.'

'Stop it!'

'Ladies and gentlemen, the banana guard: a paradigm of inclusive church! Come along now, eat up.'

The dean eats her banana through tears of laughter.

Finally. Gene draws a long breath. The worst is over.

'You know what it's felt like?' she says. 'Like when I was a little girl and my parents fought. Tim and I would sit on the stairs and listen to them screaming and throwing things. We were terrified. Terrified they were going to split up and abandon us.'

Gene knows she was thinking of it. Thinking of leaving. 'Maybe there comes a time when splitting up is kinder all round?' he says.

'No. We can't.' She seizes his arm. 'We *can't* cut one another adrift, we cannot abandon one another! Not now. This world's too dangerous and desperate.' She hauls herself onto her bike. 'Come on, let's get back. Evensong.'

As she cycles, muscles burning, Marion thinks of those cars in Canterbury, lined up and waiting with the press, ready to carry off the conservative primates when they walked out. Only the cars had not been needed. Like the ribbons of the team everyone *knew* would win the cup, they had not been needed.

Oh, please say the evenings are just starting to lighten? begs Marion. Please say the year has turned the corner? She slogs along the disused railway track. Darkness is not the last word. Darkness cannot be the last word.

FEBRUARY

Chapter 5

Britain waits for Stormzilla to cross from America. Here in Lindfordshire the wind rehearses. Vapour trails slide helpless down the sky. Gusts flinch silver across puddles. Listen. An experimental chord in the treetops. A papery percussion of laurel leaves. Somewhere a metal gate gnashes, like the teeth of the iniquitous. Silence. As if between movements. Then *forte!* Leaves fly. Bulb shoots quiver like plucked strings. Up on Cathedral Close the flag is wrapped round its pole, but the free half still flaps bravely.

It is Monday. The bishop's Executive Assistant arrives at the office, driven on the gale like one of the bad nannies in Mary Poppins; rather than descending serenely, the way our lovely Penelope would have done (sugar spoon poised) back in the good old days, before Steve so heartlessly got rid of her. The EA punches in the code on the keypad that replaced the old lock; the one that half of Lindchester had a key for. The code is closely guarded, and changed every three months. Freddie May does not know the code (thinks the EA).

We will slip in behind her before the door closes, and form an opinion. This is Kat. Not Kate. Kat. She is what makes Steve's job viable, and for that, we love her. (Or hate her, depending on what we think of Steve's job.) Steve departed from usual Church practice in making this appointment. Conventional wisdom states that you need to appoint someone who understands the Church, and is a good enough PA. Instead, Steve knew he needed the best person he could possibly poach from the secular world, trusting that he or she would quickly master the Church side of things.

Kat has mastered the Church side of things. I'm sorry to tell you that she finds a lot of it hilarious. How shall we describe Kat? We will wring our hands and fluster about. Well, she's quite tall, a tall handsome young woman, um, with dark hair, dark *curly* hair, brown eyes . . . ? Oh, you know who I mean. We will describe her in every possible way without mentioning it. Because that might be seen as racist, and we're not racist.

Kat is used to this, of course; just as she is used to people asking her where she's from. I'm from Watford, where are you from? No, where's your *family* from? From Watford; where's your family from? No, no, where's your family from *originally*? From London; and where's *your* family from originally? So far, nobody in Lindchester Cathedral has pressed this line of questioning one stage further, and asked which of Kat's parents or grandparents slept with a black person.

Kat shakes her head. Bless them. She makes a mug of tea and settles down to the bishop's emails. Footsteps come crunching across the palace drive. She looks up. Great. The toxic tenor. What does he want?

'Hey . . . I wanna say . . . Kate?'

'Kat. Hi, Freddie. What can I do for you?'

'Ohh, yeah, so I was wondering, is Steve in?'

''Fraid not. He's in London today. House of Bishops. Anything I can help you with?'

There's a lo-o-ong pause. Kat smiles encouragingly, as she pictures tumbleweeds rolling across the vast desert spaces of Freddie's brain. A coyote howls in the distance.

'Um. So can I, like, see him? When he's back? I kinda like . . . just quickly?'

'Let me take a look in his diary for you.' She checks. 'OK, he's got a slot two weeks today at eleven-thirty. Does that work for you?'

'Gah. Yeah, no, yeah, I mean, is that like the earliest? Only, yeah.'

Kat double-checks. 'Yep. 'Fraid so. Want me to book that in for you?'

Freddie tugs his hair. 'Gngnnaah. Hhnnhh. Cool. Yeah. Probably you should do that?'

'OK. All done. Eleven-thirty, Monday eighth of Feb.' She gives him her beamiest smile.

'Cool. Thanks, uh . . .' He grimaces.

'Kat,' she supplies.

'Yeah, Kat.'

Well, well, well, thinks Kat. So we've had a little change of heart, have we? She logs onto Facebook. Sure enough, toxic tenor has deleted his outrageous anti-Steve rant. What prompted that? she wonders. The puzzle detains her for a full three seconds. Kat's priorities are Steve's priorities, and Freddie May is not high on the list.

Perhaps the reader is more curious than the bishop's EA? I will explain. Giles (the precentor) and Timothy (the director of music) – after a brief arm-wrestle over whose responsibility it was – manned up and braced Mr May together. They charged him with removing his frankly actionable Facebook diatribe. Mr May flamboyantly declined. The poor precentor was left with no option but to make a phone call to an old friend.

And so it happened that last Sunday night, while Freddie was sprawled on his bed . . . Hmm. How to phrase this delicately? While Freddie was Enjoying some Me Time, a text arrived. *YOU ARE EMBARRASSING. REMOVE THAT POST, OR FIND ANOTHER MENTOR.* This acted like a bucket of icy water on the soul. Freddie abandoned the matter in hand, and deleted his rant, teeth literally chattering.

Ah, how one deep calleth another! Not just a bucket, a waterfall! Vast Niagaran cataracts of icy dread, each icier than the last. All thy waves and storms are gone over me! Freddie's behind on his rent. He's broke. Everyone's mad at him. Giles, Timothy, Mrs Dean, his mentor. Even Jesus is mad at him! He's hiding from Jesus, coz Jesus is all, Freddie, why are you even doing this, why are you still hating on people? Didn't we talk about this when the plane landed safely?

Plus he hasn't done his tax return yet!

Oh God, oh Jesus! He *knows* this dumb shit is all about desperately wanting Dr Jacks to love him. He tried *so hard* to be a grown-up, and nada. Mentor's not interested. So it's back to fucking stuff up. Even though mentor's *never* gonna play this game; he's never gonna play *any* game. Man, Dr Jacks is like off-the-scale un-manipulatable? So why, *why*'s Freddie still doing it? Here's why: You won't love me, huh? Then watch this – gonna force you to hate me, dude.

Poor Freddie sees all this – and yet he has no power of himself to help himself. We asked, rhetorically, in an earlier chapter: where is the person willing to save Father Ed from Freddie May? We now ask: where is the person willing to save Freddie May from himself? Close at hand. Fear not, gentle Anglican reader (you who have, perhaps, caught yourself in the act of praying for the fictional Mr May). Last September Freddie's gaydar – fritzed to smoking bits by mentor-infatuation – allowed someone to slide under without a blip. I have mentioned this person, but I dare say (like Freddie) you barely noticed. Anyway, this good man waits, still undetected, until Freddie stops crying for the moon and is ready to settle for someone who would only give him the whole earth.

Most of our characters are being obliged to wait for something. That good saint, Miss Blatherwick, is waiting for test results. If she has not heard in six weeks, she may ring the consultant's secretary for an update. From this, she sensibly concludes that it is not urgent, or they would have whisked her in immediately. So she waits.

Leah Rogers must learn to possess her soul in patience too. She has to wait until 1 March to hear which grammar school she will be starting next September. She has already passed her 11 plus (yes, we still have the 11 plus here in the 1950s, just as some of us in the Close still have our milk delivered by actual milkmen), but Leah must wait for Allocation Day. Will she get into her First Choice?

Just between ourselves, she will not. Nobody is allowed to mention this any more, but her *real* First Choice was to be a girl chorister at Lindchester Cathedral. (Huzzah, a Girls' Choir at last!) Only Mum and Dad said no, even with a scholarship they couldn't afford the fees. Yeah, like they couldn't *save up*? Why couldn't they get *proper* jobs like other people's parents? Then we wouldn't be so *poor* all the time. Why did they have to be so *useless*?

(I should just whisper that Mum and Dad were actually protecting Leah here. While Leah is 'Gifted & Talented', she has all the musicality of an eager potato.)

'I spect you only want to be a chorister coz of Freddie May.'

Oops! Jess still had a red slap-mark on her face two hours later.

Anyway, who *wants* to be a chorister? Singing is *lame*. And another thing: no way is Jess going to pass her eleven-plus, coz she's so dumb, so ha ha.

Who else is waiting? Well, the Lindchester members of General Synod wait for the gathering next month, of course. They book London hotels and advance train fares. The diocesan housing officer waits to see how big a headache storm Gertrude will cause him vis-à-vis the vicarages of the diocese. The bishop waits for the dean's decision on rationalizing cathedral and diocesan structures. Father Dominic waits for his bathroom scales to stop being so bloody rude, and acknowledge all his hard work. Jane is still waiting for Matt to fess up about applying for the bishop of Barcup job, because Matt is waiting for the right moment to broach the subject.

And we all wait for spring. It is just getting light at 7.30 a.m. now. In all the parks and gardens of Lindfordshire, the crocuses are up like clusters of pale toadstools. Here and there, a slip of white among the snowdrop spikes. The thrush finalizes his spring repertoire. Collared doves call: Croo *croo* croo. The wild plums blossom. See how long the afternoons are now? Fear not, little flock.

'Good God!' The dean guffaws. 'What on earth is THAT?'

'That, deanissima, is a glow-in-the-dark banana guard.'

Marion laughs so hard the whole bed shakes.

'You never know when you might need to find your banana in the dark,' says Gene.

'I suppose that's a paradigm of the church too?' she manages.

'"Lead, kindly guard",' warbles Gene, in his best Peter Pears voice. '"The night is dark, and I am far from home . . ."'

It is Thursday night. The storm lands. Gene snores through it all. Marion goes to the window and looks out into the whirling dark. Ah, I keep asking to see the distant scene, she thinks. One step is *not* enough for me. I'm hankering for what might have been, too. That bishopric I nearly got. The CNCs that come and go without mandating me. Lead thou me on!

Then, as she watches the churning night, God speaks: 'He who calls you is faithful, and he will do it.' And in that moment she knows she is in the right place. Here. Now. Even though the storm rages. *This* is where she is called to be.

Marion goes back to bed. On her bedside table, the banana guard glows green amid the encircling gloom. Another fit of laughter shakes her.

'The tide's turned, Pedro,' says Father Wendy. 'Yes, I think it really has. The majority are now in favour of equal marriage. If we trust the survey. Do we trust it?'

Pedro offers no opinion. It is Saturday afternoon. The Linden is high. They are dodging hailstorms. Look! Catkins. Knots of rusty old ash keys. Molehills slung out across green field like flicked paint. Father Wendy notes it all as she passes. Moorhens, coots. Black clouds, bright sun. Rainbow!

She is the only one here, now, noticing. Look at your world, look, look at your glorious world. Wendy shines up her soul and reflects it all back.

Chapter 6

O afflicted one, storm-tossed and not comforted! Hot on the heels of Gertrude comes Henry. Lampposts wag and knock, barricades crash over, trampolines take to the air like flying saucers above suburban gardens. In the bare treetops, hear the *frrrrrp!* of shredded carrier bags. Winter will pass. February is a short month, thank God. Those with eyes to see – and who remember to look up – glimpse strange clouds in the cold morning sky, clouds that gleam iridescent as mother-of-pearl. Father Wendy sees them, and stands by the Linden, lost in wonder, love and praise.

Candlemas arrives. Solemn Eucharist in the cathedral. One last curl of Epiphany smoke, and away with the nativity sets. For a moment, we forget ourselves, burst into liturgical glossolalia and remark that Quinquagesima is almost upon us. Let someone interpret: next Sunday is the last one before Lent (which, in common usage, is the relaunch of the New Year diet season).

Spring, yes, real signs of spring now. Jane trudges round Lindford arboretum after nicking off work early. She sees swathes of snowdrops quivering in the wind and her soul leaves the gloomy haunts of sadness. The boughs of mighty limes twist and creak above her. She thinks of those Victorian worthies who planted saplings, knowing they'd never live to see them full grown. Thanks, guys. Thanks for the big trees. The green spaces. For sending it on ahead of you and bequeathing the likes of me a spot of beauty in an ugly town.

But what are we bequeathing to our great-grandchildren? An asset-stripped planet, flooded, burnt and fracked to death. Yeah, sez you, Dr Rossiter – who recycles her cans, then hops on a plane to New Zealand.

She ploughs straight through those ankle-deep puddles that lie across the path. You won't catch Jane mincing round trying not to get her trainers wet. Splosh, splosh, splosh. She gets a perverse hit of nostalgia for the crunching tackle, taste of mud, seeing stars. Happy days.

Then she is overtaken by a young woman who twinkles past in pink running shoes, her long shiny black ponytail bouncing.

Pah. You wouldn't last thirty seconds in a scrum, Missy. Snap you like a Barbie doll, I would.

The snowdrops are out in the palace garden too, but the bishop of Lindchester is not here to admire them. He is away in Cambridge, getting a spot of in-service training with his fellow diocesans. You know the rules: we may not follow him and listen in on their sessions. Those of my readers who prefer not to gaze directly at the practical outworking of the Green report – but rather to view them through the palantíri of social media and the church press – should avert their gaze here. Bishop Steve returns to Lindchester and reports that it was excellent – as indeed did those deans (our lovely Marion included!) who subjected themselves to the ghastliness of a mini-MBA last year, and found it brilliant.

Sorry, I've stopped. Proper High Elvish hand-wringing will now resume: well, of course Stevangelical *would* say that. Is he not a Cantuarian café-church going-for-growth stooge, synchro-swimming in the talent pool with his fellow Greenites to 'Shine, Jesus, Shine'? The age of the true Church of England is passing. The age of the orcs has begun. We shall sail into the Westcott West and fade tastefully away.

Finally, the bathroom scales are Father Dominic's friend! He has lost half a stone since 1 January, by a tried-and-trusted combination of being good, and cranking away on the cross-trainer in what his

38

mother (on a long visit, exploring the possibility of relocating to Lindford) has been instructed *never again* to refer to as his 'glory hole'.

'Why not? That's what it is.'

'Never you mind. We're calling it *the basement.*'

'Well, it's full of clutter whatever you call it.'

'Be that as it may.'

'I'm going to google glory hole. I bet it's one of those euphemisms of yours.'

Spring is in the air. Tomorrow's sermon is written. What better way to celebrate losing your first half-stone – and to escape from your mother reading out eye-watering entries from Urban Dictionary and asking 'if anybody really did that' (*why* had he bought her an iPad for Christmas?) – what better way of celebrating than by going out for a last-Saturday-before-Lent drink with an old friend?

Oh, Dominic! Have thirty years of friendship not taught you that you are on a hiding to nothing trying to celebrate with Jane Rossiter?

'Yeah, right,' said Jane. 'The majority of Anglicans *who never darken the doorway of the church* are now in favour of equal marriage.'

'Look, they self-identify as Anglicans,' said Dominic. 'So why don't you shut up and stop picking holes in something I bet you haven't even read?'

'Personally, I self-identify as a rugby player,' remarked Jane. 'I never play, I'm not a paid-up member, but it's the rugby club I *consciously* never go to, ergo I'm a rugby player. I'm not a gym bunny – although I live quite near the health club, and I never go to that either. Because that's the equivalent of the Wesleyan chapel that self-identifying Methodists don't go to.' She raised her Prosecco. 'But cheers, and hoorah for progress.'

'Oh, fuck off.'

Jane repented. 'For what it's worth, I honestly do think the tide has turned.'

'What you think is worth shit, Jane.'

Jane repented further. 'You're right. I'm sorry. Truly.' Still pouting. 'Plus you're definitely looking trimmer.'

There was a long silence. Oh Lord. Had she ridden him too hard?

Dominic picked up his glass and took a swig of Prosecco. 'Why are you *always* so mean to me?'

'Am I the meanest old woman you ever have seen?'

'Yes, you are. Hit the road' – he leant forward and narrowed his eyes – '*Jackie*.'

'Oh! Low blow!' Dominic was one of the very few people who knew Jane's real name, the one she'd ditched at Oxford, along with the Babycham and stilettos.

'You drove me to it.'

'I know I did. Gary.'

'Ah, ah!' He wagged a finger. 'That's only my middle name. Doesn't count.'

There, they are friends again. I think we can leave them to it now. We will head out of the nice bar they are sitting in, and brave the bacchanalia of a typical Saturday night in Lindford.

It is raining. There goes a pink-sashed hen party. Maid of honour. Mother of the bride. The bride-to-be in her veil and L-plates. They shed pink feathers as they pass. A pink helium balloon is snatched at by the wind: *Here Come The Girls!* They vanish into a club. Music throbs. Bouncers guard entrances where youngsters queue coatless in the cold.

In the upper room of St James's church, Lindford, a group of people pray. Outside the party rages on. Sirens tear past. Shouts. A burst of song. Breaking glass in the alley below. I bet the prayer group sits smug and pious in their cosy room, insulated from all that drunkenness and sin. I bet they are a bunch of hypocrites judging everyone else. The Church is full of them.

The Church that exists in the secular imagination, that is.

These people are genuinely not holier-than-thou. But they may well be kinder. This is the prayer wing of the street pastors. All through this cold night they will receive updates by text message from the foot soldiers out there doing the stuff. Not judging, just doing the stuff. Not using the stuff as a Trojan horse to sneak the gospel into the unsuspecting drunk's citadel, even. Just doing the stuff. Because who else is doing it?

That's what Chloe thinks, anyway. Chloe is a street pastor. We saw her earlier, overtaking Jane in Lindford arboretum. Jane, as we saw, dismissed Chloe as a Barbie doll. That was a shameful piece of objectification rooted in the kind of internalized male gaze issues Dr Rossiter would be the first to interrogate, had she not just been overtaken by someone younger, fitter and slimmer than herself.

Chloe is both tougher and older than she looks. She is thirty-one, a solicitor and a lay member of General Synod. Tonight she is walking round her usual street pastor route, chatting to doormen, to the police, to regulars who recognize her. Basically, she looks out for anyone unable to look out for themselves. The lost ones, the ones who get left behind. Shepherd-less sheep.

She turns into the alley beside St James's. And she finds someone. I know you, she thinks. He is sitting on a step in the back doorway of a club, arms wrapped round his head. Chloe squats beside him. Her blue street pastor's coat rustles.

'Hey. Everything OK?'

Clearly not. Shirt covered in blood. Assaulted? She tries to get him talking, but he's out of it. The cold rain falls. He lurches onto all fours and pukes. Chloe rubs his back.

'Hey. Poor you. It's OK. All done?'

She phones, and another pastor joins her. Together they get him up on his feet and round the corner to the gazebo pitched in front of the church. They sit him down, put a foil survival blanket round him, and get the first aider to check him over. No obvious injuries. They clean him as best they can. Then Chloe sits with him and waits until he's sober enough to be put in a taxi home.

'How's he doing? Have we got his address yet?' murmurs the team leader.

'It's OK,' says Chloe. 'I know where he lives.'

Rain peppers the gazebo. Gusts shake the frame. Frail enough shelter, she thinks. But it's here, and it's still standing.

General Synod meets next week. Hard-core synod types will be eager to know who else from the diocese of Lindchester, besides Chloe, was appointed in the elections last year. You could look it up, of course. Nothing is hidden that shall not be made manifest

41

via the Church of England website. (Unless it is *very* confidential, in which case someone will incontinently widdle it on Twitter because they can't help themselves.)

In the diocese of Lindchester there are three lay members of synod, and three . . . *proctors*?! Well, it says proctors, so I assume that's the correct term for priests when they are incarnate in synodical form. Chloe has already been introduced. She, a pro-LGBTI liberal, is joined by a fierce conservative holding fast to the old school doctrine of Slippery Slope to Abomination (bless him), and a decent conservative of the good egg type. The proctors include our old friend Father Dominic, Virginia (Father Wendy's curate) and Josh Fitzpatrick. All you need to know about Josh is that he will struggle to keep a straight face when synod debates making traditional vestments optional.

Sunday morning dawns. Freddie May is not in church. He has 'food poisoning'. Oh God, oh Jesus, wanna die, please let me die. It's all coming back in jagged fragments. He opens an eye. Sees the blood–soaked T-shirt on the floor.

Ah cock. Cannot *believe* himself, doing blow again so soon after surgery? When's he gonna learn? Ah nuts, and the street pastor? Noooo-oh. Please no. It was her – wossname's, new alto's girlfriend, wasn't it? Naaw, don't let her tell him. Don't let this get back to the precentor. Now the fucking bells are starting. He pulls the pillow over his poor head and cries.

The sun comes out, transfiguring Lindchester into R. S. Thomas's bright field. Turn aside. Turn aside. Light streams through the cathedral's ancient stained glass. Pigeon shadows sail past. Away on the other side of the diocese, the good folk in Josh's café church come up for communion. They pass between data projector and screen, and for a moment, a word rests on them as they wait in the light: *Bread . . . cup . . . glory.*

Chapter 7

The bishop of Lindchester stood in the office on Monday morning. He looked at his watch.

'He's not coming, is he?'

'Looking that way,' said Kat.

'Hmm. Can I ask you to contact him and re-arrange?'

'Sure. You're the boss.'

Over the months, Steve had learnt to interpret that phrase. It meant: *ARE YOU COMPLETELY MAD?* He laughed. 'What, not go the extra mile?'

'You're asking me? Not even an extra *inch*. He's rude, he's tantrumy, he's trained everyone to tiptoe round him. He flat out refused an invitation to take part in the Shared Conversations, and then he vents on Facebook about how you personally betrayed him and denied him a voice. You make time for him today – at his request! – and he doesn't even bother to show up. He needs a good slap.' She started a new email. 'But anyway, let me just quickly contact him to rearrange . . .'

'On reflection, leave it,' said Steve.

'Oh, OK.' She closed the email and gave him her beaming smile. 'If you're sure.'

'I'm bound to run into him on the Close some time.'

'Cool. We'll leave it like that for now, then.' Bet you anything he hides if he sees you coming, thought Kat.

*

Freddie is hiding all right. He's battened down the hatches. Because of (in ascending order on the Beaufort Screaming Habdabs Scale): Miss B, 2 (light breeze of guilt, small wavelets); his landlords; the precentor, 7 (high wind of angst! whole trees in motion!); Her Majesty's Revenue & Customs; culminating in the force 12 hurricane of dread – SEVERE WIDESPREAD DAMAGE! UNSECURED OBJECTS HURLED ABOUT! – that is whipped up by thoughts of his mentor.

It's lunchtime on Monday, and here he is, still curled up under his duvet. He's twenty-five, but he's like a little boy who's run away from home to the bottom of the garden to make everyone sorry – and now he's waiting to be found, only nobody's come looking for him. Maybe nobody cares, maybe nobody's even noticed he's run away? Or maybe they have, only they're bored of his fucking numbnuts soap opera, so they're all, ignore him, man, just leave him out there in the cold. He pulls the duvet over his head.

Uh–oh. Footsteps.

Red alert. Storm Totty approaching. Take action!

Too late. The door bursts open, curtains are ripped back. Duvet yanked off.

'Dude! Totty!' Freddie snatches his pillow to cover himself.

'Up! NOW.' She points to the door. 'Shower, shave, dressed, and downstairs in fifteen minutes. We're going to talk, young man.'

'Fine.' He drags himself up. Godsake.

'Shift!'

'Ow!' He scuttles to the door before she does it again. Du-*ude*! You are *so* inappropriate!

There. Pippa Voysey-Scott, wife of the canon treasurer, is not part of the 'let's tiptoe round Mr Tantrum' brigade.

'What *is* going on with you this year, Freddie Bear? You'd been doing so well! Come on, what's wrong? Out with it.'

Out it all comes.

Diagnosis: You're just having a wobble.

Prescription: Stop being a wally. Get yourself to the clinic. No more drugs. Hand-written apology to everyone you've been rude

44

to. Change those manky sheets and do your laundry. Find an accountant, pull your finger out and look for a job.

And is tomato soup OK for lunch?

Freddie cries into the soup – aw, Heinz Cream of Tomato, just like Mum gave him whenever he'd been poorly! – because he's got what he wanted. Someone cared enough to come looking for him.

'Thanks, Totty.' He wipes his eyes on his sleeve. 'Love you. *Man*. Don't know *why* I'm such an attention whore.'

She rumples his hair. 'Apply brain, Freddie Bear. Work out why. Then maybe you'll be able to move your life on a bit.'

Rain at dusk. Wet roads across the diocese of Lindchester. Wet fields, wet footpaths. Wet roofs, trees, umbrellas, shoes, coats. Misery, misery, woe. Wet sofas abandoned in empty streets. Wet, wet, wet, wet, wet.

Storm Imogen has landed. Oh, this is by far and away the worst yet! cry southern folk in their Londo-centric cocoon. Storms that trash the unimaginable far-flung wastes of The North are not *real* storms. Why, they fit on the screen of our smartphones! But Imogen, now – Imogen has blown actual fences and trees down before our very eyes and caused chaos on Southern Rail.

On Tuesday morning several people on the Close come down to find the apology fairy has called in the night and posted a note through the letterbox. Gene reads over the dean's shoulder.

'He's doubly right, of course. He *is* a complete pain, and you *do* rock, Mrs Dean.'

Marion laughs and shakes her head.

'So, what's in the deanly diary today?' asks Gene.

She runs through her list. 'And the choristers' pancake party tonight,' she concludes. 'Bother. And a group of visiting Methodists on a Quiet Day. I need to think what to say in my welcome.'

'Sisters and brothers,' improvises Gene. 'You are at the cutting edge of decline, and we have much to learn from you.'

'Thanks, darling. I can always count on you.'

She hurries across to the cathedral for Morning Prayer. The wind shivers the crocuses and gives her cloak a theatrical twirl. What she didn't tell Gene is that she has reached a decision. She is going to tell the bishop that she is happy – in principle – to explore the idea of a restructure. The one who has called her *is* faithful, yes; but everything's still a bit raw. Too raw for the salt of Gene's wit. And in any case, Steve is unlikely to want to do much this side of General Synod.

I hope my readers are not alarmed by this tendency among the senior staff to hold out on their spouses. You will remember that Matt has struggled to find the exact moment to mention to Jane that he's applying for the suffragan bishop job. We shall, on eagle's wings upborne, to Lindford ascend, and find out whether they have managed to be candid with one another yet.

The archdeacon tiptoes to the kitchen where Jane is marking student assignments. He hovers in the doorway holding a sheaf of papers. She looks up from her laptop, takes in the situation, and laughs her filthy laugh.

He sighs. 'I know you know.'

'I know you know I know.' She puts out her hand. 'Want me to proofread it before you send it off?'

'Would you?' He passes her his application.

'I wondered when you were going to mention it.'

'I thought about Valentine's Day,' he says. 'Only the deadline's before that, unfortunately. But I've drawn a little heart on it. Look.'

'So you have, you romantic devil!' She starts reading. 'I warn you, I'm in full marking mode. I'm liable to scrawl "support" all over it.'

'Bring it on, Dr R.'

'OK. Just don't send me a pissy email saying you're disappointed with your mark.'

'All righty. Pancakes later?'

'Lovely.' She doesn't look up.

There's a pause. 'Are we OK, Janey?'

She lowers the application. Considers him, head on one side.

'Yeah. We're OK. Another time, why not talk it through with me first? Idiot.'

He sighs again. 'Sorry. Lived on my own for too long. Got a bit too used to keeping my own counsel. I'm working on that.'

'Good.'

'I was . . . trying to pick my moment.' He rubs his face. 'Frankly, you can be scary, Jane. Even for an old ex-copper like me.'

'Yeah. Sorry,' she says. 'I'm working on that, too.'

'Good.'

Pause.

'Well, don't just stand there!' she raps out. 'Make my fecking pancakes!'

He snaps a salute. 'Yes, ma'am!'

The annual game of hunt-the-palm-cross is under way across the diocese, ready for Ash Wednesday. They lurk on noticeboards, on car dashboards, tucked behind mirrors, slipped down the back of desks, used as bookmarks in Bible commentaries. No matter how many you hunt down, doh! there will always be some you miss. In the vergers' vestry in the cathedral Gavin gets out a big brass bowl and tests the blowtorch on a pissy memo from the precentor. The choir rehearse Allegri.

In the vicarage of Lindford parish church a pancake party is in full swing. Father Dominic is in his Our Lady of Guadalupe apron, flipping pancakes, while his mum (who is still visiting) mixes more batter. The sight of someone making pancakes from actual milk, eggs and flour – rather than out of a shake-and-pour bottle – briefly awes everyone in the kitchen. Mrs Todd is an incarnation of pure bake-off!

But then Chloe enters with her new labradoodle and the fickle crowd apostatizes into puppy worship. Even Father Dominic, I'm afraid.

'Oh, look, look, look! Look at *you*! Come to father! What's he called? Cosmo? Cosmo puppy! Oh, *please* say you're bringing him to synod, Chloe?'

Chloe laughs and shakes her head. 'I wish! No, Ambrose is coming over to puppy-sit for a few days.'

'I've got a better plan,' says Dominic. 'Why doesn't Ambrose go to synod as my body double? Nobody will know. Why, we could be identical twins separated at birth!'

'Yeah. And by twenty years!'

'Hush! Identical, just *distributed* differently,' says Dominic. 'He's arranged on a vertical axis, that's all. Eh, Cosmo? Cosmo agrees with father. Yes, yes, yes.'

He hands the writhing pup back and returns to his frying pan.

'Wash your hands!' cries Mrs Todd. 'You'll get puppy slobber in the pancakes.'

'I love your mum,' whispers Chloe.

'Have her,' he whispers back. 'I'll pay you.'

'I heard that, Dominic Todd!'

Ash Wednesday arrives, and now it's Lent. We give stuff up, or take stuff up, according to the prevailing winds of doctrine. Anglicans once again taunt their lapsed Catholic friends by pointing out that Sundays are not part of Lent. What?! Since when? The nuns never told us that! And once again we must all decide at what point we can wipe the ash smudge off our foreheads. Too soon, and it looks as though we are ashamed of our faith. Too late, and we risk the charge of acting like the hypocrites our Lord denounces.

'Remember you are dust, and to dust you shall return.'

Miss Blatherwick wonders, as she stands in the queue waiting to be ashed, whether this will be her last Lent. Whether by next year she will already have appeared at the eternal Eastertide. Perhaps this year will provide that other date, the one waiting to be revealed on the far side of the dash. Barbara Blatherwick, 1935–? Next week she will ring the consultant's secretary. Unless the letter arrives before then, of course. She can picture it lying on the doormat. She will look down, inhabiting that last moment of ignorance, before stooping to find out the results.

*

Envelopes on doormats. The catch in our breath when we glimpse a lover's handwriting. Already these things are acquiring a period feel, like blotting paper or pen wipers.

Freddie May comes down on Sunday morning and finds an official-looking envelope waiting on the mat. Shit. He just *knows* it's a bollocking from someone. Oh God, *now* what's he done wrong? He rips it open as he races, late, to the Song School.

What? The? Actual?

A storm of tiny red hearts swirls round him in the wind.

Chapter 8

Dawn breaks pink over Lindfordshire. Finally, some decent winter weather. Proper hard-core frost, cast forth like morsels – as in the good old Prayer Book days (none of your modern half-arsed Common Worship frost). We were forgetting what winter used to be like. A cold manna lies over everything. Every bramble strand, every blade of grass is feather-edged, all the dead bracken, all the reed heads along the Linden. Every tile on every roof, each single rock in trackside rubble, nothing is spared, nothing neglected.

A big man walks a labradoodle puppy through Lindford arboretum. He enjoys the smush of frozen grass; the tinkly crunch of puddle under boot.

Half-term. Middle-class parents start out with good intentions. They make trips to the library, the museum, the swimming pool, the cathedral. (Is this your first visit? Would your little girl like our animal trail leaflet?) But in the end, one way or another, they crack. They bribe their little ones with Haribo and crassly gendered comics. They stick the kids in the car and visit someone, their sister, old school friend – anyone! The wheels on the bus go round and round, horsey-horsey's feet go clippety-clop. They arrive home and collapse, their parenting bolt shot. It is the witching hour of 'You're Tired' tantrums. And before you know it, the bottle is open and it's self-medicate o'clock.

In some happy cases, Grandma comes and stays for a few days, to allow the frazzled young parents a romantic Valentine's weekend mini-break. Sonya, the bishop's wife (—p's wife) has been off doing just that, down in Reading. She has had a lovely time with little Phoebe, while her son and daughter-in-law went to a luxury spa hotel, no doubt to have a massive row, drink too much, and then accidentally conceive a second Pennington grandchild.

I'm beginning to have a soft spot for Sonya. (Mind you, for which of my characters is that not true, here in the empathy forge of the novel?) She's a valiant soul, juggling supply teaching – nursery and reception, she loves the littlies – alongside being Mrs Bishop. She is a bit lonely in Lindchester. Nobody is mean, but she's not really *necessary* the way she was in Aylesbury. She doesn't even bake, like her predecessor! Poor Sonya feels like a bit of a spare part; especially on Sundays, when she has to choose between trailing around with Steve or finding a church of her own. The problem is, there really aren't any New Wine congregations of the kind she feels at home in. Not near to Lindchester, anyway. And it's a bit of a nonsense driving all the way to Martonbury every week, isn't it? So she ends up worshipping at the cathedral. She's never really got the hang of it – going up to communion the wrong way, or tripping over short genuflectors in the aisle, and generally feeling stupid.

I'm afraid Sonya arrived back late on Tuesday night feeling a bit woeful. Bishop Steve was away at General Synod, of course. The Close was silent. It was choral half-term. Ah, who will be kind to Sonya for me?

Oh no, oh rats, oh *bother*. She'd only forgotten her front door key. Well, never mind, there was a spare one hidden under the . . . Oh rats, oh bother, oh *bum*! She forgot to put it back last time she locked herself out, didn't she? Oh bother, oh bum, oh *piddle*. She looked at her watch. Twenty past midnight. Canon Giles kept a spare key to the palace. She looked across the Close. All the lights were out in the precentor's house. She couldn't go and wake them all up! Again!

She'd have to, though. What was the alternative? Sleep in the car? Maybe she could sleep in the car. But it was flipping freezing. And anyway, what would it look like, the bishop's wife spending the night in her car! Oh, why are you such a twit, Sonya? She tried the palace door on the off-chance Steve hadn't locked it when he left, but of course he had.

By now Sonya had run out of rude words. Apart from one. It waited there behind glass, like those little red hammers for smashing train windows in an emergency. She contemplated it. Yes.

'Bugger!' she shouted (quietly). 'Bugger, bugger, *bugger*!' She sat down on her suitcase. Blinked back the tears. Maybe she could go and find a cheap hotel? But the cathedral porter in his lodge – she'd have to get him to open the big gates again. She'd have to explain, and then the whole world would know she was an idiot.

Footsteps.

She scrambled up. The case tumbled over. Oh, gosh! Hope they didn't hear me swearing. She tried adopting an 'everything's fine, I'm not even slightly locked out' pose.

The footsteps paused. 'Hey, Mrs Pennington?'

'Oh, hi. Is that Freddie?'

'Yeh. Everything OK?'

'Oh, fine, thanks. I was just.'

He came across the drive. 'You locked out?'

'Out,' she agreed. 'Yes. What an idiot, honestly.' She blinked, so that he'd think it was her contact lenses playing up. 'Oh well. S'pose I'll have to go and wake the precentor up and get the spare.'

'Want me to do that?'

She wavered. So tempting. 'Oh, I couldn't possibly.'

'Hey, no worries.'

'OK then. No, wait. Oh!' She thumped her fist into her palm. 'It's just that I did this to them last month, and I don't want them to think—!' He was giving her a funny look now. 'Bother. Contact lenses. Must've got something, a bit of.'

'Listen.' He glanced round and stepped closer as if he was about to tell her a secret. 'So maybe you could've like, left a window open?'

'—open. Well, I doubt it. Steve always checks. He's very.'

'Yeah, no, but maybe I could look? You know, in case? Before we disturb Giles?'

'—Giles. Well . . .'

'Hey, no worries,' he repeated. 'I'm on it.'

He slipped off his coat and tossed it on the step. She watched him vanish round the corner. A clanking. He was never shinning over that big gate, was he? The car was ticking on the drive as it cooled. Sonya rubbed her hands. Her breath smoked. Bright glinty stars above the spire. So flipping cold! Should've brought gloves. She wormed her hands up the opposite sleeves of her coat.

Clang of feet on iron. He must be up on the fire escape. Golly, maybe Steve *had* left a window open! Sonya took a step, and stumbled over her case. For an awful couple of seconds she was hurtling over the drive, fighting to get her hands free to break her fall. Face! Gravel! A & E!

Phew! She winkled her hands back out of her sleeves. Oh my days. Well. *That* could've gone a lot worse! She picked up Freddie's coat and folded it. A parka. Were they still called parkas? It had a big furry-edged hood. She got a whiff of his body spray. Familiar, like those pungent shrubs you smelt in parks.

Suddenly the palace burglar alarm ululated. A moment later, feet came pounding down the stairs. The alarm cut off in mid-wail.

Then the door opened. 'There you go, Mrs P. Attic skylight was kind of open?'

'Wow!' She stared. 'Thanks. You turned the alarm off!'

'Uh, right. So probably you guys should, like, change the code?'

'Of course – you used to live here!'

'Back in the day.' He had his fists in his jeans pockets, arms rigid. He looked down and scuffed up the gravel with his feet. 'So.'

She hadn't just blundered, had she? Had she blundered? There'd been talk, but she didn't *know* anything. 'Well, thanks for rescuing me!'

'Not a problem.'

Sonya held out his coat for him. 'Here you are. Thanks again. You're a total star!'

'Welcome.' He shrugged the coat on. 'Night.'

She watched as he jogged off across the gravel drive.

Gah! Should *not* have done that, numbnuts. Should've walked past, not gone back in there, into his old room, where he and Paul . . .

53

Oh, man. All flooding back now. Should've *known* this was gonna kill. Coz hadn't he loved Paul? But felt kind of betrayed by him as well? Almost hated him for being weak, when he should've been all, no, we can't do this, Freddie, it's not right?

But maybe it *was* right – for Paul to finally embrace the truth about himself? And hey, not like Freddie couldn't've stopped him. Or not come on to him in the first place? Though to be fair, he really *wasn't* coming on to him, more just desperate and needing a hug? Ah, forget it. Crossed wires. Ancient history. We've all moved on since that time.

I suspect this cannot be dismissed as ancient history. However, I acknowledge that right now my readers might be more interested in the envelope full of little red hearts that Freddie received on Valentine's Day. He still has no idea who was responsible. He thinks, maybe Totty? To like cheer him up? Man, he'd love to think it was genuine, that he has a real admirer. In his dreams it's Dr Jacks . . . He pictures his mentor's pained expression, the curled lip.

Nah. In his experience, something that makes you go, aw sweet, that is so thoughtful! Nine times out of ten, it's gonna be a woman. Honestly? He kind of prefers women. I mean, yeah, no, *obviously* he prefers cock, but for company? He's gotta say women. All through school, his closest friends were girls. Oh God, don't say he'll turn out to be one of those gay guys who just gets sick of it all, and ends up marrying a girl and having babies, cos in the end, kindness is what matters, at the end of the day?

He lets himself into the empty house.

Half-term passes. The second Sunday of Lent. The choir are back. An old anthem, but what is this? A new voice?

> Behold, thou hast made my days as it were a span long:
> and mine age is even as nothing in respect of thee;
> and verily, every man living is altogether vanity.

Ears prick up in the cathedral. Orlando Gibbons, of course. The new alto lay clerk? We haven't heard him sing solo before.

Whoa, thinks Freddie. Nice set of pipes, dude. Totally hadn't registered that.

Rain falls, falls across the diocese of Lindchester. It weeps on the homeless, the benefitless, on the weak and helpless. It falls on fractured tree limbs beside train tracks. Trees hacked down for the crime of leaf shedding, for being in the wrong place, for being trees.

How small we are, how fleeting. We are altogether vanity, walking in vain shadow. Ancient trees with your grey piers, your whispering grace-filled aisles – you will outlast us all. The meek shall inherit the earth. I hope your leaves drift in forgiveness over our graves when we are all gone.

Chapter 9

It's time. High time. Miss Blatherwick has already left it one extra week. She rings the consultant's secretary. Engaged. She tries all morning, until she finally gets through. The consultant has been away on holiday. Miss Blatherwick can expect a letter within one to two weeks. If she hears nothing after two weeks, she may ring again.

Being an Englishwoman of a certain generation, Miss Blatherwick thanks the consultant's secretary and rings off, feeling as though she's been pestering. What Miss Blatherwick lacks is a shirty middle-aged son or daughter to hassle the hospital on her behalf. Interestingly, there are no limits to the amount Miss Blatherwick would hassle officialdom on someone else's behalf. She would, for example, doorstep the Almighty Himself in the cause of Freddie May.

Freddie, Freddie, Freddie. Over a year ago, Miss Blatherwick concluded that her constant matroning of her beloved boy was keeping him in Neverland. Furthermore, it was self-serving, arising from her own need to be needed. She renounced all scolding, advising and organizing, and for some months she was rewarded by the sight of him maturing into a responsible young man.

What has gone wrong? Freddie, Freddie, Freddie. Perhaps one ought to— No, now is not the time to go back on her resolve. This wavering is just a symptom of her current predicament. How one clings to one's own frail sense of importance in the face of mortality. Why, she has even caught herself fantasizing about her

56

will! It's all a pitiful attempt to bolster the ego against fears of insignificance. Of course Freddie will cope without her. In the cold light of day one can see that to bequeath him some extravagant sum would be almost as ill-judged as leaving everything to Amadeus, the cathedral cat.

Miss Blatherwick hassles the Almighty in fine Lenten style. Keep my Freddie both outwardly in his body, and inwardly in his soul. Find him a dear someone to be with. Defend him from all adversities which may happen to the body, and from all evil thoughts which may assault and hurt the soul. Keep him. Keep him safe.

As we have already intimated, there is a dear someone. But the dear someone sits twiddling his thumbs in the wings, while that arch-manipulator, Mr Dorian, continues to stride about centre stage of Freddie's heart and raise tempests. Just between ourselves, I suspect Dr Jacks is enjoying his rough magic a little too much to abjure it quite yet. Bad man.

Lindfordshire endures a spot more wrathful nipping cold. Father Wendy walks Pedro (shivering in his tartan coat), and finds herself remembering school milk. Those third of a pint bottles, how on mornings like this they arrived in the classroom frozen. Frozen milk! She can feel those big feathery crystals on her tongue and tickling her throat. Teacher used to put the crate beside the radiator to defrost it. Oh, the horrid sicky taste of warm full fat milk. And waxed paper drinking straws, with their barber's pole stripes of red or blue, that unspiralled when soggy.

'All gone, Pedro,' she sighs. 'All gone. We live in a plastic homogenized world!'

Wendy plods on, pondering whether we are all heading for a plastic homogenized C of E. Was something being lost in all this urgent Renewal and Reform? She knew Guilden Hargreaves had grave concerns. So did the other theological college principals. Yet General Synod had got behind the proposals. Her curate, Virginia, had come back buzzing with enthusiasm. The harvest is white. Wendy can see the pettiness of whinging to the Lord of the Harvest that he's sending the wrong kind of worker into the fields.

'Don't listen to me, Pedro. I'm just being squeamish. Poor Bishop Steve! He's herding a whole bunch of grumpy cats, isn't he?'

Frost skulks in the shadows. A thrush sings, sings a careless rapture. Wendy stops, shields her eyes and squints up at the pussy willow buds. They blaze white like tiny LED bulbs. Magpies cluster in a birch tree. *Chack! Chack!* Their tails lift like latches with each call. Six for gold, seven for a secret, eight, nine, ten!

'What do you suppose ten's for, Pedro? Ten for Brexit, maybe? Oh, what's going to happen to us? Are we really just going to scarper and pull up the drawbridge?'

Little Lindfordshire! The good folk here do not favour the EU. True, I speak in sweeping generalizations. Dr Rossiter would scrawl 'Support!' all over this. But the reader will get a flavour of the debate when I say that Lindcastrians are prone to testiness about imagined EU interference with the Lindfordshire sausage. If leaving the EU is what it takes to regain control of sausage rights, then so be it. Human rights will just have to take their chances.

But enough politics. Father Wendy heads back to her car and sets off to Mums and Tots in Cardingforth. How are our other characters faring? We do not pretend to a godlike omniscience in this narrative. Our eye cannot be on every sparrow. However, I am aware that it is some weeks since we ventured into the wilds of rural Lindfordshire and did a flypast of Gayden Magna vicarage.

It is a sorry fact that the amount of money you spend on your kit is inversely proportional to the amount of time you spend on your sport. Those £200 running shoes and the top-of-the-range compression gear currently languish in the wardrobe.

I knew this would happen, Neil.

To be fair, Eds hasn't said it out loud. But all fine and well for *you*, skinnymalink. Couldn't put on weight if I force-fed you deep-fried Mars bars. Come the famine, you'll be nowhere, pal.

Not that Neil is fat. He's just been *underweight* all his life till now. Och, and running buggers your knees, anyway. Got to think long term and look after your joints. Maybe cycling? Within seconds he's sucked into the world of carbon frames and aerodynamic drag, with auld John Knox nipping his heid about wasting money.

Six grand for a bike?! Aye, but would you just look at it? Neil sees himself scything down country lanes, lean and black and friction-less . . .

Father Ed comes home from visiting and catches Neil shutting his laptop a bit too quickly.

'How was your day, big man? Soooo, I'm just off for a run. I'll cook when I'm back.'

Ed listens to him scurrying up the stairs, and closes his eyes. He has not yet reached the stage of telling himself he's just imagining things. That would mean admitting the possibility there might be something to imagine. The over-explained Wednesday evenings in London. The wide blue 'Would I lie to you?' gaze.

Ah, he's just imagining things.

Archdeacon Bea is not imagining things, however. That is the smell of fresh paint.

'Have you been doing a spot of decorating, Laurie?'

The rector of Risley Hill laughs his easy laugh. 'Well spotted, Bea! Yes, we have. We sprang a bit of a leak in Gertrude. Or was it Henry?' He appeals to the two churchwardens, who make some typically English *ny-ma-ha-mmm* bleats that might be agreement. 'Anyway, as you can see – a quick lick of paint, and good as new!'

He is the kind of man who stands just a touch too close with his sincerity knob dialled right up. The paint fumes are not dis-guising the rat that Bea can smell. She checks through the paper-work. Looks up at the wall.

'Is this where you had problems with damp at the last inspection?'

He tilts his head. Frowns. 'A very good question. Gosh. I wonder?' He looks up at the wall. The churchwardens look up at the wall. They all stand there looking, as if waiting for the fingers of a hand to appear and write *Yes, it bloody is, and you know it.*

'Well,' says Bea. 'I'm going to make a note that this is now urgent, and needs seeing to within eighteen months. How does that sound?'

He nods. 'Grand idea. Great. Super. Thanks, Bea.'

Hmm, thinks Bea, as she drives home. Nothing she could put her finger on. Everything else was in order – registers, insurance, safeguarding, fire extinguishers. Still, something *smelt* wrong with the set-up at Risley Hill. Could it be the rector himself – spiritually a damp wall with a quick lick of paint? Something to double-check with Matt. Bea smiles. And if Matt gets the Barcup job, she can boot Revd Lick O'Paint firmly off her desk onto his.

Yes, Matt is on the shortlist. Bishop Steve has brought Bea into the picture, because he needs ~~a woman~~ a member of the senior staff on the interview panel. The other interviewers are the two chairs of diocesan synod (lay and clergy) and the diocesan secretary. Steve is pleased with the shortlist – four strong candidates. He's also happy that Marion has given her nod of approval to exploring the restructure. Today he is rather a happy bishop.

This does not mean that there are no flies in the episcopal ointment, however. He catches sight of one persistent irritant as he heads home for lunch from a meeting with the diocesan education officer. He's seized by the urge to deal an unambiguous swat.

Freddie sees the bishop coming. He remembers: Nuts! I was meant to go and talk to him. When was that?

'Freddie. A word.'

Too late to duck into Vicars' Court. 'Hey. Listen, really sorry about missing that appointment?' Uh–oh. *Seriously* pissed. 'And the whole Facebook thang?'

'I got your note, thanks. Let's draw a line under it,' says the bishop. 'Now. Talk me through what happened that night. What were you *thinking*?'

Freddie freezes. Fuck, he's heard the gossip. 'Right. Uh, my bad. So I'd been out clubbing? Ah, and probably I'd, yeah, overdone it? A bit?' He winces. 'Ah, a lot?'

'You were *drunk*!' The bishop's hand goes to his heart. 'Freddie, I can't tell you how bad that makes me feel.'

'Look, I'm sorry.' Freddie spreads his hands. 'But the street pastors? They looked after me? Honest to God, it was just that one time?'

Pause.

'Are we talking about the same thing here?' asks the bishop. 'You let Sonya into—'

'Ohh! You mean *that*.' Freddie feels his face burn. 'Nah, I wasn't drunk *then*. I was just—' High. He bites it back in time. La la la.

'Listen, idiot!' Guy looks ready to shake him. 'I took a look at that fire escape. How the hell did you get from *there* onto the roof?'

Freddie throws up his hands. 'Just swang and jumped, I guess?'

'Are you *mad*? If you'd fallen!'

'Nah. Spider monkey genes? Plus a shedload of parkour?'

'I don't care! Don't you ever, ever, EVER do it again.'

'Sure. Hey, hundred per cent, I won't ever.'

He sees the bishop draw breath, then let it out. 'But thank you for rescuing my wife. Another time, confine your gallantry to fetching the spare key from the precentor.'

'Hey. Not a problem.' Freddie backs away and sprints home before the bishop starts asking about the street pastors. Oh boy, that was *death*!

As if a man did flee from a lion, and a bear met him!

There waiting on the drive is a silver Aston Martin DB9.

Chapter 10

Freddie hesitated, and was lost. The driver's door opened. Andrew Jacks got out.

'O mentee mine, where are you roaming?'

Freddie blushed. Dude, do you have to be so *loud*?

'Listen, Dr Jacks, I—'

'O stay and hear, your mentor's coming!'

'Listen—'

'Let me buy you lunch.' He clicked his fingers and pointed. 'Laces.' Freddie bent and tied them. 'That's better. Hand? Thank you. Come along.'

Freddie found himself being walked to the same coffee shop just down the hill from the Close. They passed the new alto (not Angus, but he kept wanting to call him Angus?), who gave them a 'Really?' look.

'Trip no further, pretty sweeting . . .'

What is *with* you today? 'Uh, Dr Jacks, could you maybe stop singing? Only people are staring?'

'Do I strike you as someone who gives a fuck?' He opened the café door. 'After you, sweet-and-twenty-five. Table for two, please. My young colleague here rather enjoys sitting on the deck— Oh. Too cold today? Never mind.'

Freddie snorted.

The barista showed them to a corner table. Suddenly Freddie clicked. This is it: end of mentoring. I'm being dumped.

He groped for the menu. It was twitched from his fingers, same as last time.

'Mr May, I deduce from your recent antics – and a flurry of phone calls from Giles – that you want my attention. *Me voici*. What can I do for you?'

'Oh God! Yeah, no, it's—'

'Eyes. Look into my eyes.'

Freddie made himself lock with The Stare. His heart thumped. 'What do you want from me, Freddie?'

Ah nuts. Don't choke up. 'You gotta *know* what I want?'

'Yes. And *you've* got to know it's impossible. We'll have soup of the day with wholemeal bread, and two mineral waters, thanks,' he said to the barista. 'It's never going to happen, and you know it.'

Freddie made no reply.

'I'm twice your age – ssh! Of course that matters, child. We're different generations. We're not peers. Not in *any* sense of the word are we peers. Ssh. Neither in age nor experience; not socially, academically, sartorially, financially, culturally, grammatically—'

'Jesus! OK. I get it. I'm all-round not good enough for you?'

'*Bravo!*' He leant forward and whispered, 'But then, who is, frankly?'

Unbelievable. Look at him. Total punch face?

'Here's what I think, Mr May. Deep down you know there's no hope, so you're trying to force me to wash my hands of you.'

Once more, Freddie made no reply.

'So that you can add me to the list of father figures who've betrayed your trust. Well, that's not going to happen, either. Can you bear to look at me again?'

Freddie looked.

'We can wind up the mentoring any time you want. But please let's do it like this – after an adult conversation. All right? Not after some spectacular display of fuckwittery on your part, and high dudgeon on mine. Ah, the soup. Thank you,' he said to the barista. 'Let's eat. Ssh. *Benedictus benedicat.*'

Freddie crossed himself, pure reflex. He glared at the food. Man, *hate* lentil soup.

'How now? Moody?'

'Uh, I didn't actually order this? Can I get a panini?'

'Ending?'

'What?'

'Pani*no*. Pani*ni* is plural.'

Freddie reached out and flicked him on the forehead.

Heart-stopping pause.

Then Dr Jacks laughed. 'Exactly. Could you really stand being with someone who spent his whole time paternalistically correcting your grammar, and telling you you're tying your laces wrong? Which, incidentally, you are.'

'Whateva.'

'I watched you do it. Weak form of the shoelace knot. That's why they always come undone. And while trailing laces might be endearing in a six-year-old, I have to confess I find them a little tragic in a grown man.'

Freddie rolled his eyes. He picked up his spoon. Stirred the spicy fucking lentils. Oh, wait. Wait. He put his spoon down. 'I get what you're doing. You're being an asshole to force *me* to end it?'

'Well aimed of such a young one.'

'No. Nooo!'

'Oh, come on, Freddie. Hasn't the mentoring run its course?' He laid a hand on his arm. 'Easy, there. I'm here as long as you need me. But there's a *via media* between lover and mentor, isn't there? Friendship. Have a think and let me know.'

'Wha-a-'?' Freddie stared. 'Sorry, you wanna be . . . friends with me?'

'I wanna be friends with you, dude.'

'Whoa. Ha ha! Seriously?' He broke out the slutty smile. The one he'd never quite dared hit him with before. 'Sweet. So would that be like . . . with benefits?'

'Apart from the immense privilege of being my friend, no.'

'No? G'wan.' He nudged his knee. 'We should totally fuck, babe. I don't mind?'

'You don't *mind*.' Mr Dorian raised an eyebrow. 'Well, that's deeply flattering, of course.'

'Hnn, kinda came out wrong? But seriously, I'd—'

'No.'

''K. But if you change your mind . . . ?'

'You'll be the first to hear. And don't *ever* call me "babe".'

'Cool. Can I call you Andrew?'

'Yes.'

'Awesome, Andrew. Can I call you Andy?'

'Not if you wish to continue singing tenor. Now finish your nice soup, and I'll walk you back.'

After a swift tutorial on the distinction between a Latin cheek-buss (acceptable) and a snog (really not) Dr Jacks parted with his ex-mentee. He then called on his old school chum, the precentor. They enjoyed a leisurely bitch about the choral world, and then he broke the news.

'No! You can't step down!' Giles clutched his wild hair. 'Argh! But you're my Imperius curse! *Now* how am I going to control him?'

'Frankly, my dear . . .' A languid middle finger.

'And also with you. Let me get this right – you and Mr May are "friends" now?'

There was a frigid silence.

'Eek!' Giles made a warding-off cross.

'Yes, friends. I've made a career of behaving disgracefully, but I prefer not to look ridiculous.'

'Ah! Saved by your gargantuan vanity!'

'How well you know me.'

'Oh, but whatever shall I *do*?' Giles cried. 'Ground him? Taser him? Geld him?'

'Why not try a little tenderness?' Andrew rose to leave. 'My love to Ulrika. *Ciao, ciao.*'

From the precentor's house he made his way to the cathedral Lady Chapel and sat for a while. It was dusk, but light still shone faintly through those Burne Jones angels. He could hear the lay clerks behind him in quire, rehearsing for evensong. Suriano? Yes. He hummed the bass line as the *mag* unreeled slowly, sadly.

'Depósuit poténtes de sede: et exaltávit húmiles.'

Candle flames bobbed on the pricket stand. A spotlight shone

65

on the big abstract Annunciation above the altar. It burned and loured. A bright tree against a coming storm, perhaps. A pear tree in blossom – wasn't that what the artist had told him once? He couldn't recall.

The last note of the Amen faded, resolved, yet still yearning. Andrew shook his head. Ah, well. He'd kept the thought of Freddie stashed away for far too long, like that one last unrelinquished bottle of malt. God, what a waste! – but down the sink with it. Even though the label begged *Drink Me, I don't mind.* How very Lenten.

He slipped away before the service, and drove home.

The reader will see that I misjudged Dr Jacks. He has broken his staff and drowned his book after all. I would love to say that naught shall now go ill for Freddie May, but alas! Red-edged letters from HMRC have begun to drop through the letterbox and blight his happiness. He is still behind on his rent. The job hunt? Not going so well. I'm afraid that he is increasingly tempted to slip off to London and – shall we say – monetize his hobby? Just to like make ends meet. Till the gardening work starts coming in again? Nnnn-nah, probably don't do that?

And so February draws to a close. On 1 March Leah Rogers learns that she has got a place at Queen Mary's Girls' Grammar School in Lindford, which she has already learnt to abbreviate to QM. Snow and slush and sunshine greet St David's Day. Refreshment Sunday – the midpoint of Lent – approaches. Rose vestments may be worn by those who enjoy a little harmless liturgical poncing about.

As we glide on our Anglican wings, we note that spring has begun to lay its first watercolour washes across the landscape: brown-purple over the birches, gold across willows, lichen green on bark and wall, and a blue haze of sky over wet wheat fields. There are primroses and coltsfoots along the hedges of Lindfordshire. Up on Lindford Common the gorse is in blossom. Of course it is; for when gorse is out of blossom, then kissing's out of fashion.

*

66

There will be no liturgical poncing in Risley Hill. The fastidious among my readers might be tempted to observe (with a catholic curl of the lip) that there is barely a liturgy at Risley Hill. Let us take a closer look.

The paint has dried on the wall. But the rector stands a little too close to the intern. Not pervily on purpose. He's just a friendly guy. Charismatic with a small and large C! Sometimes that gets misinterpreted, just as people misinterpreted Jesus' relations with women. In Laurie's experience, it's in those seasons of great blessing that the attacks come. Satan fearing his citadels are about to fall. They're experiencing a real outpouring of the Spirit right now. The evil one is going to be seeking to undermine that. Gossip, misunderstanding – Laurie has met with them before.

Three years ago, the really sad business with Becky and her unhappy marriage. There had been real damage to the reputation of the gospel over that, when the archdeacon pulled the plug on the curacy arrangements. A whiff of sulphur about the timing there, just when the Lord was blessing them with so many new believers, and all the staff were over-extended. But God had sovereignly overruled. He'd sent other workers into the vineyard, amen? And he'd graciously shown Laurie the need to put his trust in *Him*, not in men.

Laurie smiles down into his intern's face.

'Super, Sophie. Gingerbread hearts for Mother's Day. Such a *great* idea.'

'Oh, it's not mine. They always have them in Cardingforth, apparently?' Sophie smiles up at the rector. 'The minute I heard, I was, oh, that's so *sweet*? We should *so* do that too?'

'Terrific.' He lets her enthuse about cellophane and ribbon, bathing her in the glow of his approval.

They always have them in Cardingforth! Ah, it is as I predicted. Father Wendy's innovation three years ago has become a sacred tradition. The pedants of the diocese scour the shops for a proper Mothering Sunday card. A thousand times ten thousand daffodils are bunched ready for morning services. Bottles of wine are laid for lightening of Lenten discipline on Sunday. But what is this? Wine in Lindford Vicarage on the Friday before Refreshment Sunday?

*

'It's St Piran's Day,' said Dominic. 'Patron Saint of Cornwall. One doesn't fast on a festival.'

'If you say so, Father,' said Chloe. 'Has your mum gone?'

'Yes, thank God!'

'Oh, I *love* your mum!'

'She calls you "that nice Chinese girl".'

'Ha ha! Close enough. Does she think we should get married? Here. Swap you.' She took the champagne and gave Dominic the puppy. 'Smells good! What are we eating?'

'Homemade Cornish pasties, of course. With my own shortcrust pastry. Don't tell anyone,' he whispered to the puppy, 'but I used *lard*, Cosmo.'

'Gasp! I may make a citizen's arrest.' Chloe poured the champagne. 'How many have you made? Because, can I be a bit cheeky and invite Ambrose? He's a bit gloomy and love-lorn at the moment.'

'Oh, poor lamb. Yes, of course.' Cosmo lapped Dominic's face. 'Can't you buy him a puppy instead?'

'He might be better off,' agreed Chloe.

No kidding, thought Dominic. He'd be better off with a pet velociraptor than with young Mr May.

68

MARCH

Chapter 11

ome! Let us float on high o'er the vales and hills of Lindfordshire. Daffodils dance in graveyard and garden. They stretch in never-ending line along the margins of windowsills and tables, all across the diocese of Lindchester in this week after Mothering Sunday.

Miss Blatherwick's little bouquet stands in a crystal vase. The scent pours into the kitchen as she eats her porridge. *And then my heart with pleasure fills,/And dances with the daffodils!* thinks Miss Blatherwick, for she committed a great deal of poetry to memory in her youth. Her face lights up as she remembers that dear boy running all the way down the nave in his choir robes to hand the flowers over with a kiss.

Joy! Joy of friendship, of daffodils, joy of blackbird song coming in through the window! Joy of spring! Joy of a simple bowl of porridge! Porridge, such a good thing for a person with diverticular disease to eat. Joy of having diverticular disease and nothing worse! Tiresome but manageable, if one is sensible. Fresh fruit and vegetables. Legumes. *Return unto thy rest, O my soul; for the Lord hath dealt bountifully with thee!*

Virginia's daffodils stand on her bedside table. She wakes and smells them. Spring! It's light at 6.30 now. How fast the time has gone. Her curacy is speeding to an end. Ought she to apply for one of the vacancies in the diocese? It feels right to stay. There's all her work with benefits claimants – that's where her heart is. But is now the time to relocate closer to her parents, down in Kent? They are seventy, after all. (Virginia does not move in cathedral circles, or she'd realize that seventy is NO age!)

Guidance is such a complicated thing. If Virginia has discovered anything in recent years, it's that she should give up trying to second-guess the will of God. She'd been *certain* she was called to be a curate at Risley Hill – there had been signs, and confirmation of those signs! – yet here she is in Carding-le-Willow. And it has worked out infinitely better than she'd imagined. She's learnt such a lot from Wendy, although their churchmanship is so different. And now it's nearly over.

Virginia stretches. Sunshine streams in. The angle of the morning light plays tricks with the wall above her. She's noticed this before, like the goblin face she could always see in Grandma's walnut wardrobe. Silly. As though the parish decorators would have daubed something that rude in the curate's house!

Father Dominic has a little bunch of daffs in his study. Chloe Garner gave them to him for mothering the congregation of Lindford parish church so beautifully. Father Dominic gave Chloe a bunch from Cosmo-doodle, which vanished, simply vanished into thin air! Only to reappear in the car on the way to Chloe's parents.

'Great. Thanks, Cosmo.'

Ambrose laughs. She slaps his knee. But at least he's laughing.

'Any developments?'

'Not really. He thinks I'm called Angus.'

'Angus!' she hoots. 'Why?'

'No idea. He only lives on earth part-time.'

'Uh-huh. I noticed that.'

'The rest of the time he's off being Zeus's cupbearer.'

'OK. You've lost me now.'

'Zeus. In charge of the pantheon? With the thunderbolt? Drives an Aston Martin.'

'Oh, *that* Zeus.'

Behind them Cosmo hawks up another daffodil.

'My thoughts exactly,' says Ambrose.

*

The dean gazes out of the drawing-room window. There is a fine array of spring flowers, and one rogue squirrel-planted crocus in the middle of the lawn. A white hive stands among the lavender and rosemary.

'You're worrying about the bees again, aren't you, deanissima?'

She jumps. 'Oh, I didn't hear you coming.'

'Whose job is it to worry about the bees?' asks Gene.

'Yours, darling. Are you worried about them?'

'Certainly not. I have a bee-verger to do that for me.'

'And what does the bee-verger say?'

'The bee-verger says they are all fine,' replies Gene. 'The hive is dry. The roof is sound. The queen is busy laying. The elderly winter bees are tactfully dying off and leaving bequests. The new summer bees will soon be hatching. Swarms will multiply. Everything is progressing nicely, in accordance with the queen's growth strategy. And as ever, the idle male bee is on hand to service her.'

The dean eyes him. 'I believe someone once explained to me what happened to the idle male bee during the mating flight.'

'They're just bees,' says Gene loftily. 'Let's not anthropomorphize them.'

Here, at last, is the first truly spring-like day of the year. All is hazy, as if with holy smoke – smoky sky, smoky white clouds of blossom on the blackthorn. We could almost believe that heaven has leant down and laid its cheek on the landscape. The Linden rushes brown and fast. Great clumps of foam like dead sheep race by, while in the meadows the first lambs gambol, as all good lambs should. Here and there, a turbine twiddles, and a lapwing lollops up into the sky.

How lovely it all is. On days like these, the blurry light seems to grace even the jagged glass that blooms along pub yard walls, like a flamboyant emerald frost. Rococo flourishes of barbed wire scroll out against the sky. *Keep Out.*

In the slick new doorways of Lindford the same message is muttered in anti-homeless studs, like the spikes along every high

73

ledge to keep off the pigeons. It's the students' fault. They encourage them. Coming home late, bleeding hearts melting with too much booze, handing over cash. Mutters in pubs. *Keep Out.* Mutters at the school gate. *Keep Out.* No wonder the NHS is in trouble. Too many people coming over here looking for a cushy life. The country's full, go away. I'm sorry, but there it is. Fact. *Keep Out. Keep Out.*

The council fences off the spaces under bridges and flyovers. Even the kind-hearted mutter. It's sad, but what can you do? There must be hostels and shelters, surely? The government should tackle it. In the meantime, couldn't they sleep somewhere else? I don't know, somewhere out of sight, where we don't have to think about them and feel bad for being fortunate.

Keep Out. Keep Out. Mutters everywhere in Lindfordshire, my Lindfordshire.

Now and then Father Dominic has rough sleepers in his graveyard. So far, it's not a problem. No needles found by Sunday School children, nobody crapping in the church porch, or scaring off the faithful. They just seem to want to be invisible. And safe. Dominic chats to them and does what he can with hot soup and sleeping bags. He offers to find hostel spaces. The Council are in the process of clearing the big camp from Lindford cemetery. O Lord, don't let them all come here instead! He hates himself for even thinking this. For cravenly foreseeing the headlines: *Single vicar in a five-bed vicarage evicts homeless.* He hates the thought of being asked on the Last Day which part of the parable of Dives and Lazarus he'd failed to understand.

More millionaires than ever before! We're turning this whole country into a gated community! he thinks.

> The rich man in his castle,
> The poor man at his gate,
> God made them high and lowly,
> And ordered their estate.

Yes, he can imagine an England where people had no problem with verse three of 'All Things Bright and Beautiful'. And America! Don't get him started on Trump.

*

Similar thoughts exercise the mind of the bishop of Lindchester. Lindfordshire in general espouses the view that the Church should keep out of politics (unless the Church agrees with us, in which case we call it 'traditional values' not politics). Steve is unlikely ever to have a voice in the Lords, owing to the fast-tracking of women bishops (heralded by the glorious headline *Women bishops to leapfrog into the House of Lords*.) But he speaks out locally on matters of justice. The MP for Lindford retaliates by brandishing declining church attendance in the bishop's face. If the bishops would stop meddling in things that don't concern them, if they would only exercise proper spiritual leadership, and teach the people the Ten Commandments, the churches would be full.

Gosh, if *only* we'd thought of that. The honourable gentleman is a genius.

'You're looking a bit miz, darling,' says Sonya. 'Everything OK?'

'I occasionally feel like Sam-I-am,' says Steve. 'They do not like Green church and ham. Here's me, bouncing round the diocese going "Try them! Try them!" People flatly refuse to engage on principle.'

'—ciple.' Sonya sighs. 'Poor you.'

'Would you, could you with a prayer?' improvises the bishop. 'Would you in your underwear?'

She laughs. 'But *some* folk are engaging, surely?'

'Yes, yes. They are. But I'm having a Moses moment: Why did you ever send me to this people?'

'Oh, darling.' She rubs his arm. 'Still, Marion's come on board with the restructure, hasn't she? And there's the interviews next week, remember? You'll soon have another bishop to share the load. I know it's been a bit lonely, but—'

'Would you *stop* mum-splaining!'

'I wasn't! And there's no such thing!'

He raises a finger. 'Hang on.'

'What? You're frowning at me.'

'Got it.' He smiles. 'Could you, dressed as Harry Potter? Would you, poncing in a cotta?'

'—cotta! Ha ha ha! Is that the lacy thing? But think – in the book, thingy gives in and tries green eggs and ham. And he *loves* them!'

'I will hang onto that prophetic word from Dr Seuss.' The bishop gets up from the breakfast table. 'Have a nice day. Got your keys?'

'—keys. Yes, thanks. Wait! OK, yes I have.'

'Good. The fewer lay clerks we have parkouring on the palace roof, the happier I shall be.'

Sonya is correct: the interviews for the bishop of Barcup job are next week. We must suppose that three other shortlisted candidates besides Matt are busily preparing themselves. Since they live outside the borders of the diocese, I cannot be bothered to imagine them for you, frankly. We will concern ourselves with them if they are appointed. Instead, we will lavish all our narrative attention upon our stout hero, the archdeacon of Lindchester. It's Saturday afternoon. We will sneak into the kitchen and eavesdrop.

'Would you like me to give you a mock interview?' asked Jane.

'No fear.'

'Come along, Mister Archdeacon. I want to live in a palace. I want you on top of your game.'

'It's not a palace. Only diocesans have palaces.'

'Well, it's a palace to me. Come along. I can guarantee that after an interview with me, next Wednesday will be a stroll in the park.'

'I bet. But it's really not going to be adversarial, Janey,' said Matt. 'It's more a discernment process.'

This prompted the filthy laugh. 'Well, suit yourself. I tried. Let me know if you change your mind.' She went and got a beer out of the fridge. 'I'll be in the lounge. Watching the England–Wales discernment process.'

Passiontide approaches. Clergy across the diocese emphasize once again that passion does not mean lurve. It is not an envelope of little red hearts swirling in the wind. It does not mean enthusiasm, either. It is not something you put in a personal statement. *I am passionate about hillwalking* (de rigueur for episcopal CVs,

I am reliably informed). Like last week's daffodils – picked, bundled, distributed, displayed, thrown out, composted – passion is passive. It is not doing, it is being done to. Grammar check cannot approve. He was betrayed, he was scourged, he was crucified, he was buried. Consider revising.

Chapter 12

awthorn leaves green the hedges. Sticky buds – tacky as treacle toffee – burst and extend pale fingers in the sunshine. Vapour trails quilt the sky. Hottest February on record, far worse than predicted, even. The headline slips past. But it leaves a splinter of dread for our minds to snag on. A 3 a.m. dread. Have we forgotten something? Missed a deadline, or a sign?

Holy Week is not far off now. Palm fronds are propped in vestry corners; palm crosses bought or made. Donkeys are hired; or hobby horses looked out of the Sunday School dressing-up box. Clergy buy in vast quantities of Fairtrade chocolate eggs. The traditional Passiontide challenge commences, of not scoffing the lot before Easter Sunday.

If you walk round Cathedral Close you will hear the slow mournful ascent of organ tuning. A choral crisis threatens. One of the tenor lay clerks (*can*) has laryngitis. What will become of the Lindchester Mass – with its fiendishly challenging solo parts – on Easter Day?

'Are you mad, Timothy?' asked the precentor's wife. She poured him a glass of Merlot in accordance with the choral myth that red wine is better for the vocal cords. 'He had the whole of Christmas off for his nose surgery. Then what? Straight back to doing drugs.'

'Oh, I *think* that was just a one-off, wasn't it?' pleads the director of music. 'Look, come on, we all *know* Freddie's the only one who can nail the high notes.'

'No. It's agreed: no solos till he cleans up his act,' said Uli.

'Actually, Dr Jacks disagrees,' put in the precentor. 'He thinks it will help Freddie lay an old ghost – of when his voice broke.'

'Ja, right. Dr Jacks – who washed his hands of him!' scoffed Uli.

'Oh, Andrew still has influence as an older, wiser friend,' Giles said. 'Viz Mr May has finally got himself a job.'

'And? Will he *keep* it?' asked Uli. 'He's had jobs before, and blown them.'

There was a pause as they all scanned that last utterance for innuendo.

'We can but hope,' said Giles. 'I think you should give him a chance, Timothy. Do as the great Mr Dorian himself commends – try a little tenderness.'

'Tenderness! Everyone cuts him too much slack, if you ask me,' was his wife's reply. 'He's got to learn. *Das Leben ist kein Ponyhof.*'

Ah, if only life were a pony farm. Better still, a luxury Argentine estancia. Mr May would be in his element there. He could literally be a dude! In the literal sense of literal. But Mr May must make do with a job waiting on tables, alas.

There's a newly opened coffee shop just where the Lower and Upper Towns meet, right by the old stone gateway. Vespas, it's called. The reader can probably picture it: unpretentious, in a locally sourced sourdough, naked-bulby, apple-cratey kind of a way. There are pictures of Vespa scooters on the bare brick walls. The paintwork is grey. Retro coffee cans to hold the cutlery. There's honest white crockery, milk served in dinky little bottles, old school chairs. And a single bloom in an Orangina bottle on every table. Here you may recapture something of that early nineties buzz, when a cappuccino was thrillingly edgy; for this is the home of your cortado, your breve.

Vespas is a hotbed of dapper hirsuteness. Perhaps Freddie might grow his beard back, now he has no mentor to smile derisively? (Coz who gives a shit what *Andy* thinks? *The list of father figures who've betrayed your trust.* The more he thinks about that lamebrain

79

cliché accusation, the more he's, guess what, *babe*, gonna add you to my list of asshole amateur psychologists?) Yes, Freddie is still smarting from that lunchtime recital of Dorian high-handedness. His new boss sports the chops and twirling tache of an Edwardian cad. It was a laidback interview in which they awesomely outduded one another. The waiters at Vespas wear Breton shirts and are called *waitrons*. No, we eschew smirking. Vespas is a force for good in Lindchester: it pays the living wage. This is more than can be said for many a local employer. (Including – tell it not in Gath – the cathedral café and bookshop, though they aim to achieve this by the end of the year.)

If members of the choral foundation were surprised at Freddie's entry into paid employment, Freddie was even more surprised. Honestly? Didn't even know Vespas existed. So he'd been heading downhill to Lindchester station to get the train to London. Only with each step there was this voice going, why are you even doing this, you whore, when you *know* you'll just end up giving the cash to the foodbank? It's not like you'll even *enjoy* it. Plus you'll trash your nose again. Why, why?

Man, what *is* this – like I'm slut-shaming *myself* now? Like I've internalized the haters? He got halfway across the bridge. Nope. No good. Not gonna happen. He turned round and headed back. That's when he saw the advert in the window.

So cool, he's got a job. Only, gah! Now there's this whole bunch of info – National Insurance, tax codes, forms, all this stuff with like *numbers* he can't remember where he put? Probably it's all in his room somewhere, maybe in that old Amazon box where he sticks all the shit he knows he's gotta deal with, but never does? Man, why does sorting one problem *always* just open the door to this whole new avalanche of scary crap? Fucking HMRC coming after him, with their red-letter final demands like some fucking red-eyed psycho, all 'Heeeeere's Johnny!' Oh Jesus. Why's he so dumb? Why hasn't he found an accountant, like Totty said to? Not like he can afford one, but still?

'So, deanissima, who's going to be the next bishop of Barcup?' asks Gene.

'I don't know. I'm not on the interviewing panel,' replies Marion.

'I realize it was never going to be *you*. *You* don't get out of bed for a mere suffragan post! What! Renounce your far-reaching executive powers to become some lickspittle junior bishopette in the thrall of Stevangelical? Is this to be borne?'

'Not helping, darling. Really not helping.'

'Oh.' Pause. 'Well, how about a fortnight's post-Easter break in Havana? Would *that* help?'

'What?' Marion laughs and presses fingertips to temples. 'Havana! That's— well, of *course*, yes, but— Sorry, I can't see beyond Holy Week, Gene.'

'Leave it with me.'

'But I can only manage a week. There's the Deans' Conference, remember.'

'What Deans' Conference? You didn't tell me! Ooh! Is there a spouses' programme? Am I invited? Where is it?'

'Liverpool.'

'Oh, not bloody *Liverpool*!'

'Don't worry. I've already declined on your behalf,' replies Marion. 'On the grounds that you are a total liability.'

'You can't hide me away for ever, deanissima.'

'I can try.'

Term staggers to a close. In Cardingforth Primary the knives are out for the Easter Bonnet parade, an annual tradition in which Mumzillas are pitted against one another under the flimsy pretext of hat decoration. As this is not a church school, the judging will be transparent and fair. First Prize will go to the best bonnet, rather than the bonnet of the poor mite whose parents have just split up.

Pity the poor children whose mums refuse to engage. They will be left to scramble together some amateurish concoction out of paper plates and egg cartons. Leah Rogers despises Easter bonnets. Plus anyway, she's an atheist. She tried making a pagan Ostara bonnet, by attaching Jess's old Barbie with her hair cut off to a sunhat of Mum's, but Ostara kept falling over and then the hat came off. Whatevs. Jess's pink hat with the fwuffy bunny-wunnikins didn't even get runner-up, so good.

Dr Jane Rossiter aches for term to finish. She spends all Wednesday in her office doing wall-to-wall tutorials to damp down deadline panic. Jane is a consummate professional. She marks to the marking criteria posted on the unit Moodle area. She will not penalize those who email her thus: 'hey jane sorry i cant make my tutorial as im a bit under the weather. can I email a draft for feedback thanx in advance.' She is particularly fond of the excuse 'I cant make it because i only just noticed work put me on an early shit', accompanied by the assurance that any advice about how to answer the question 'would be greatly appropriated'. My advice to you, young Flaky, is to buy a Time Turner on Amazon, and make sure you attend your lectures and seminars during the past two terms.

But at least this is keeping her mind off the interview. Sorry, *discernment process*. How is Matt getting on? Jane keeps catching herself nearly praying. His interview is at 2 p.m. A sudden flurry of keen students occupies her till 3.30, by which time it's presumably all over. This now requires the kind of retrospective intercession she remembers from her Christian days, when she'd promised to pray for something, then forgot: *Lord, let it have gone well.* A Time Turner prayer. That said, God – presumed to be outside the constraints of human time – would have no problem granting requests couched in the past tense hortative. Jane is not even clear what she means by hoping it's 'gone well'. That Matt will be appointed? She consults her feelings: pride in her man, and a roughly 2:1 ratio of hilarity to grumpiness at the thought of becoming Mrs Bishop. Then there are Matt's feelings to consider. Which are less ignoble. He just wants to be in the right place, doing the thing he's called to do.

She looks at her watch. The interview panel will be at the fisticuffs stage of discernment by now. Matt should get a call from the bishop this evening some time. There are a few more hours to fill. She sticks a note on her door in case another student rocks up, and goes to get a coffee.

We will maintain our policy of not intruding into bedroom or boardroom. I will just hint that the process of discernment was not entirely straightforward. I hesitate to describe the panel as dysfunctional, but there are historic tensions in the diocese of Lindchester. The decision was not unanimous. But a decision was reached.

Jane was cutting through Lindford arboretum on her way home when the text arrived: *Thunderbirds are go!* She stops. Feels a rush of something. Joy? A collared dove croons. For a second the scene feels shot through with meaning. She texts back: *Well played, Rt Rev Tracy!*

'Hire a donkey. G'wan, do the thing properly. Why don't you hire a real donkey, Eds? I'll pay.'

Father Ed drums his fingers on the Welsh slate worktop. 'Boundaries, Neil? I don't tell you how to do graphic design. You don't tell me how to be a parish priest.'

'Fine. Be like that.' Neil adjusts something or other on his sports gadgetry. Hums lightly. Does a quad stretch.

Oh shit. Ed knows the symptoms. Here it comes.

'Oh, and by the way, I'll be in London this weekend. Mention that, did I?'

'No, Neil. You didn't.'

Neil makes eye contact. Honest as the day is long. 'Aye, well. There's this big project I need to put to bed.'

The phrase twangs as subtly as a Freudian banjo.

'Right.'

'Right. OK. Off for ma run. Gonna shave five seconds off my PB. See you, big man. Mwa mwa.'

No need to hire a donkey, is there? thinks Ed.

Ambrose follows him up the stairs to the lay clerks' vestry after evensong on Palm Sunday. He breathes in Le Male. Ambrose, the invisible alto. If he sang on *can*, not *dec*, would Freddie May actually see him? If he waved, maybe? Probably not.

They're all taking off their cassocks.

'Hey, so I've been meaning to say?'

Ambrose freezes. Me?

Freddie is looking at his phone. Glances up. 'Yeah, nice set of pipes, dude.'

Nigel Bennet, the senior lay clerk, leans round Ambrose and whispers helpfully: 'He's got a nice set of everything.'

Freddie laughs. 'Yeah?'

And now, after months of standing next to each other in quire, Ambrose feels himself coming into focus for the first time. Let all mortal flesh keep silence. Everything hangs in the balance. Yes? No?

'Hnn.' Freddie goes back to his phone.

Ow.

Chapter 13

'Well, let's find a way of making this happen, then,' said the archdeacon to Father Dominic. 'I'll look into funding streams. Heard about the Brownlow Trust? Pot of money from the former theological college. Trustees are a tad tricky – like to play silly buggers with the purse strings. But Bishop Steve's keen to free things up, and use the funds to develop our social justice agenda. Confident you can work with Virginia – if she turns out to be the best candidate?'

'Of course,' said Dominic.

'Nobody's claiming she's a barrel of laughs,' said Matt, getting to his feet. 'But that's something you can help her with. I gather.'

'Mmm.' Curses! Rumours of out-of-hours jollity during General Synod had got back to HQ.

'All righty. I'll run it past Virginia, then, and keep you posted. Bring Martin Rogers into the loop – Borough and Churches Liaison will want some input on the role and job description. But basically, split post: associate vicar here, social welfare officer – or whatever – for the diocese.'

'Sounds fab. But at the risk of putting a spoke in my own wheel, isn't St James's a more obvious choice? Geoff's got so much social justicy stuff happening already. The Food Bank, Debt Advice, Street Pastors—'

'Yep, thought about that. But you've got your Farsi congregation. Anyway, the bishop wants to get behind your work here. Seems to us you're stretched pretty thin, Father.'

'Well, bless you.' Dominic blinked back his tears. 'I've got some stellar lay people, though. Chloe's been a godsend.'

'Chloe?'

'Chloe Garner. General Synod, Human Rights lawyer? You remember the Vietnamese boat people – back in the seventies, when the UK still had a heart? Well, Chloe's mother was one of them.'

'Ah! Got you. Might be good to bring her in on the appointment process.' Matt made a note on his iPad. 'Excellento. I'll be in touch.' They walked to the vicarage door. 'How's Mum?'

'Hale and hearty.' Dominic hesitated. 'We had a trial month. To see if we could stand it, if she ever had to come and live with me.'

'And?'

'Maybe a self-contained granny flat?' said Dominic. 'And a panic room for me? Could the diocese fund that?'

Matt laughed as he wedged his pork pie hat firmly on. 'That's one for the housing officer. Bye for now. Janey sends her love.'

Father Dominic watched the black Mini shoot off down his drive, and vanish with a toot of the horn. Oho! There goes the next bishop of Barcup, or I'll eat my biretta.

That was merely a guess on Father Dominic's part. Jane has not breathed a word. She and Matt are now locked in quarantine, while the formal processes run their course. The new DBS check; the Harley St medical (after which Matt will be admitted into The Fellowship of the Finger, along with all the other senior gentlemen in the C of E). We must all bide our time until the Downing Street announcement.

As he drives, Matt thinks over the logistics of the new social welfare officer post. They need to up their game, no question. Pretty clear which way the winds of austerity are blowing, despite the government's about-face on benefits, after last week's budget debacle. Now is not the time to be poor in the UK, or disabled, or even plain old unfortunate. Obviously, he knew this before getting a lecture from the missis about twat-faced millionaire Tory spunk-nozzles. Still, always good to get a balanced academic perspective on things.

*

Holy Week. Easter comes so early everything's out of gear. Secular cogs whine on ecclesiastical chains. It's nonsense, isn't it? Kids back at school next week, then off again for two weeks – what's that all about? Ridiculous. We should take control, get Easter out of the hands of the Church and fix it, like Spring Bank Holiday. They can still do their Holy Week if they want, like their Whitsun, nobody's stopping them; but at least we can plan stuff properly if Easter Bank Holiday is fixed.

The religious car bonnet is up again, too. The mechanics suck their teeth. Western and Eastern sprockets. Gregorian *and* Julian chains. Bound to get slippage. We *can* sort it, but it'll cost you.

Meanwhile, in every church and chapel people still come. The faithful, the curious, the grieving, the bad, the desperate – they still gather. Stations of the Cross, #PalmsToGo, Experience Easter, Passion Plays, Messy Easter, the triduum. The cruel nails, the crown of thorns.

A cross stands in Lindchester Cathedral, near the baptistery. A rough wooden cross, a barbed-wire crown. All through Tuesday people come and light candles there, as the footage from the Brussels attacks reels out across our screens. At evensong, the procession enters in silence. No glorias this week. From her stall, the dean sees the host of little lights, far off at the west end of the nave. What other prayer can there be, on this day of atrocity?

> Death will come one day to me;
> Jesu, cast me not from thee:
> dying let me still abide
> in thy heart and wounded side.

The last note of the anthem fades. Death will come. It will. Kindly, like a friend. Suddenly, in extreme violence. The flames twinkle, a distant constellation in the black, empty night.

On Maundy Thursday morning, the clergy and lay ministers of the diocese head to the cathedral for the Chrism Mass. Is Thursday really the best day? Might not Monday be more convenient?

'*MONDAY?*' (Enunciated in the manner of Lady Bracknell.) 'The convenience is immaterial!' Happily, this heretical suggestion was headed off months ago by the precentor (clutching his imaginary pearl rosary) the moment it was floated by the bishop. And him a former chorister! I'm very disappointed in you, Pennington Major!

We will not join the crowds for the blessing of the oils. But I will tell you that it's a jolly long service. Especially if you are trying to entertain two small children. And (oh God help us!) number three is on the way. Miriam, the wife of Mr Happy (the canon chancellor), lasted twenty minutes. Chad William wanted to see Bishop Steeeeeve (currently a hero, because he could magically take the end of his thumb off), but little Tabitha kept testing the famous nave echo.

They trawled round the shops to buy an Easter egg for Daddy (*Ssh, it's a secret surprise!*). Chad solemnly offered passers-by his organic mini-rice cakes with the words 'Body of Christ keep you ternal life'. Tabitha screamed and arched in her pushchair. Kind old ladies asked if we're teething? No, we're demon-possessed. Miriam toiled back up the hill to the Close, sick and starving. They sat on the stone bench in the west porch and waited for Daddy, with Chad hammering relentlessly away, 'Why can't I have some Easter egg? Why? Why?' Dimly, Miriam could remember the days when she was glad when they said unto her, let us go into the House of the Lord.

The service was finishing. Tabitha had screamed herself to sleep, thank God. And yes, Chad was eating Daddy's Easter egg. Off and away it sailed, like a helium balloon, the last fuck Miriam gave. She leant her head back. I'm so rubbish. What a dismal grey horrible day. Tears trickled. Snot trickled. Too tired to wipe. The final hymn started: 'Crown him with many crowns.' It was muffled behind the doors, like a heaven she was barred from. One day, maybe a million years from now, she'd get her life back.

There was a mighty clatter of bolts. Miriam hastily wiped her face on her sleeve. The great doors swung open. A blast of music. Out came the cross, the procession, clergy, people.

'Bishop Steeeeve!' shouted Chad. 'Bishop Steeeeeeve!'

Steve turned, saw them there. He reached out to Chad. Picked him up, chocolatey hands and all, and continued on his way laughing.

All hail, Redeemer, hail!
For thou hast died for me;
thy praise shall never, never fail
throughout eternity.

*

It's night. The feet have been washed, mass said, altar stripped.
The people have all gone. Father Ed sits alone in the church of
Gayden Magna by the altar of repose. When the vigil is over, he
must go back to the vicarage. Don't tell me, Neil. Please don't
confess. Not tonight. Though why not tonight? What better night
than this, to admit it is finished?

Ah God, but he doesn't want to know who it is, the one who's
lighting Neil up, making him smile all the time, making him hum
his old Sunday School favourites. Joy! With joy Neil's heart is
ringing, while all the time Ed's heart is breaking.

Is it nothing to you, you ice-cream vans who pass by? The sun
shines this Good Friday. Bright stunt kites swoop, stoop, scoop, up
on the green hill of Lindford Common. The first punts of the
season sally forth on the Linden from Gresham's Boatyard. Yay for
the four-day weekend! Burger fumes from disposable barbecues
rise like fragrant offerings. Lindford arboretum seethes with
rollerblades and Heelys, with scooters, bikes, skateboards and the
occasional exploding hoverboard.

In the afternoon, the Churches Together March of Witness passes
through Lindford Market. Jess Rogers walks with her dad in the
sunshine. She's sad for Jesus. But Leah wouldn't be seen *dead*. March
of WEIRDNESS, more like. Jesus is crucified outside Deben-
hams. Chief priests in borrowed Anglican cassocks wag their heads.
Silence. The centurion proclaims with a Lindcastrian twang that
'Truly, this was the son of God.' Father Dominic leads prayers through
a megaphone. People pause and look. Oh yeah – Good Friday.

The sun goes down. It lays a blinding path across the Linden,
across Martonbury reservoir, across each lake and pond and flooded
field, over every impossible impassable expanse where hope and
heart both fail, a bright highway to the other side.

*

The clocks go forward and Easter comes. Fires blaze in the dark across the diocese of Lindchester. In Cardingforth the vigil happens on Saturday night. After everyone has gone, Father Wendy is left in the church alone, hiding eggs for the hunt tomorrow morning. Not too cunningly – the eggs must be found. She banishes her annual fear that some child is going to discover a lost egg from the 1940s in a cobwebby corner, and eat it. She pops the last egg on a window ledge. There. And now sleep.

Freddie May sleeps at last. His heart is light. He's found an accountant! Handed over that big scary box of crap, all the unopened HMRC envelopes, the pay cheques, the receipts, the whole mess of his life. Leave it with me. I'll work it out. Mates' rates. Pay me when you can. Oh God – Freddie's literally IN LOVE with that guy! Yeah, no, not literally literally, coz – what's her name? Hot Chinese girlfriend, street pastor? – but yeah. He'd only been standing right next to him for like months in quire, without knowing the guy was his literal saviour? Total legend. And tomorrow he's gonna nail that solo. Face down the bad memories. Yeah. All good. Because Easter?

The cathedral sleeps. The new Paschal candle lies on the vestry table. Easter lilies wait in the dark, legions of pale angelic trumpets. Up in the bell tower the mufflers are off. The air is crammed with pent-up Alleluias. And outside, in some garden, the first blackbird whistles.
Surrexit!

Father Ed gets back from the dawn vigil to smell bacon cooking.

'Made you breakfast, big man. Happy Easter. Buck's Fizz? Thought I'd, ah, come to church with you later. If that's OK.'

He sees Neil's hands are shaking as he holds the bottle. His heart goes out to him. 'Darling. Just tell me. It's OK.' And it will be. At the last.

'Aw shit. Can't hide anything from you.' Neil peels the foil, untwists the wire. 'What gave it away?'

Ed is shaking too. 'Those Wednesdays in London. Last weekend.'

'Aye, well. Well. Here goes. Coz he's, ah, been wanting me to tell you.'

With the world's worst timing, the cork flies.

'Look, I admit it,' says Neil. 'I did an Alpha course.'

Chapter 14

Of course, Neil rapped on Ed's skull for suspecting him of straying again. But what of that? 'To God be the glory, great things he hath done!' Neil sings in the kitchen, he sings in the shower, he sings in bed. 'The vilest offender who truly believes!' And Ed laughs. He can't stop laughing at the big fat Easter joke that has been sprung on him.

'Oh, and apparently, no swearies if you're a Christian! Know that, did you?'

'No,' said Ed. 'I have to confess, I had no fucking idea.'

'That's what I told 'em. I said, how come the priests *I* know are all potty-mouths, eh?'

'They mean you can't swear if you're an Evangelical,' said Ed. 'Out of interest, what's their teaching on homosexuality?'

'Och.' Neil waved a hand. 'It's batshit. Doesn't add up.'

'Did you by any chance tell them so?'

'Heh heh heh. We went the full fifteen rounds on that one. Well, you're wrong there, pal, I said. I hear *you* saying that, Dan – that's his name, Dan – I hear *you* saying that; I don't hear *Jesus* saying that. The Bible says? I'll give *you* Bible says! Look at you wearing your daft wee hipster hat (no offence) in church. And what about women speaking up and teaching and *usurping authority* in church, eh? Got a problem with that? No. So don't Bible *me*, pal, I was in the Boys' Brigade – I've got Bible coming out of my ass. Aye, and another thing – *you* don't believe it either, Dan, not deep down, I said. You know it's homophobic, and you *know* that's not right, coz basically, you're on the side of life. And they are, Eds. That's the weird thing, the thing I don't get: they honestly are. You can *feel* the love coming off them. But they keep banging on, Yeah, but the Bible says?' He shrugged. 'That's what I mean. Doesn't add up.'

'So you're not repenting of your disordered gay lifestyle?'

'Disordered gay lifestyle?! The only disordered thing round here is *you*. I've told you how to stack the dishwasher properly, and look! What's this? Eh? Which way up do the forks go?' Neil wagged a finger.

'How was "the Holy Spirit weekend"?'

'Unfeckin*believable*. Woo hoo! You won't believe this, but I actually got slain! You know – keeled over backwards, like they do? They have people there to catch you. Seriously, by close of play, I was *off my face* on Jesus. Will you stop laughing!'

'Sorry, can't help it. This is why I thought you were in love with someone.'

'I am! ". . . sweeter and sweeter as the days go by . . .",' sang Neil. 'Remember back in the nineties, rolling on pure E?'

'No, Neil. Actually, I don't.'

'Well, like that, only better. Everything's . . . shiny. You, this kitchen . . .' He paused.

'That *might* be another thing Evangelical Christians aren't meant to say,' said Ed.

'Aye, I was just wondering that.'

Everything is shiny for my lovely Ambrose too. I realize I haven't described the invisible alto properly yet. I gave the reader a glimpse of a big man walking a labradoodle, but this will no longer suffice.

So – big in what way? Brick outhouse big, like archdeacon Matt? I think not. If Ambrose is brick built, it is in the manner of one of those 1960s Roman Catholic church bell towers; the kind that on closer inspection turn out to be fire stations. He is tall and a bit lanky, without being skinny. Rangy. Rangy is the word. He has big hands and feet. And you know what they say about men with big hands and feet? Exactly. They are useful in goal. And in goal is where we will find him this Easter Monday. Before we head off to the match, let me just swiftly add – to preclude the possibility of your picturing some Nordic Eric Northman-type blond giant – he has dark hair and eyes. Nice enough looking, but not drop-dead gorgeous (or trust me, there's no way he would have waited invisibly on *dec* for so long).

It is the annual fiercely contested Easter Monday match on the Chorister School playing field. Headmaster's Eleven vs Choir Dads. The headmaster's team includes an assortment of colleagues' sons back from uni, lay clerks and choral scholars, and (brilliantly!) Kat, the bishop's EA. The Choir Dads are a bunch of sporty middle-aged blokes whose dodgy knees and waning talent are offset by cynical violence.

Storm Katie batters the south of England, but the sun shines here in Lindchester. The big trees creak, some daffodils are felled, but that's the sum of it. Chaffinches sing in dancing hedges. The grass has been mown, the white lines are fresh on football pitch and running track. (Did you feel the little spurt of adrenalin there, at the thought of school athletics?) The after-match tea is already laid out in the school hall under cling film. There has been a pleasing amount of competitive baking; though some lead-swingers have bought *supermarket cakes*. Ah, we still miss Susanna! The new Mrs Bishop has done her best. Look, there is a plate of Sonya's signature chocolate ~~concrete~~ oatcake.

Kick-off approaches. Studded feet clatter round the Close towards the pitch. Smell of mud and trampled grass. There goes the whistle. Shouts from players, encouragement from the crowd. A pigeon rises – *clap-clap-clap* . . . soar . . . Up on the spire the weathercock swings, watching the tiny players with a golden eye.

I will not bore you with a detailed match report. Final score: Headmaster's Eleven 7–2 Dads. 'Man' of the match (eye roll) was Kat, who scored four of her team's seven. Freddie May scored two; the other was an own goal. Ambrose made several good saves. He might have saved the two he let in, were it not for a tender-hearted streak that did not enjoy seeing any team comprehensively tonked. Well, that and a brief lack of focus after some shirt-off celebrations at the other end of the pitch.

Yes, Ambrose's world is shiny. Here's why: he has just looked for the second time directly into Freddie's face. Normally he only sees him in his right-hand peripheral vision as they stand on *dec* (apart from during the psalmody – if the altos aren't singing – when he gets to sit and contemplate Mr May's hinder parts and delight in his legs).

The first full-frontal episode resulted in Ambrose carting a box of paperwork home on Easter Day. The second went like this: the match was over and they were all heading back to the school for tea. Freddie overtook him, with Kat riding on his back, both belting out 'We Are The Champions'. Then he wheeled round and doubled back to Ambrose.

'Hey, well played, Angus.'

'Ambrose.'

'Gah! *Ambrose!*' He gave him an arm squeeze. 'Sorry, I – Whoa! Nice guns, man.'

'Thanks.'

'Welcome.'

And that was it.

'He's into you,' sang Kat in his ear.

'Nu-uh.'

'Yuh-uh.'

'Naw, dude, he's my *accountant*?'

'Your accountant's into you.'

'Stop that! Look, he's got this hot girlfriend? Telling you.'

'Yeah, and I'm telling you.' She dug her heels in. 'Hi-yo Silver away! I want my tea.'

The bishop and his wife watched them go.

'Look! Well, praise the Lord!' said Sonya. 'I'm so glad we came to watch. Aren't you?'

'No. *Not* my favourite way of spending a Bank Holiday.'

'—liday. I know, love. But it's important for Close relationships, isn't it? Socially, I mean. The Easter match is really—' said Sonya. 'Did you know Kat could play like that?'

'Of course I did,' said the bishop. 'That's why I appointed her.'

'—ted her. Really?'

'Yes. There was very little between her and the second choice. So in the end it came down to me wanting an EA who could snaffle up those opportunities in the box, and tuck away a tidy goal or two in the crucial Easter Monday fixture.'

'Oh shut up, grumpy!'

It is a scrappy off again, on again week. There is no joined-up thinking across Lindfordshire about school holidays. One might have hoped for joined-up thinking in schools, of all places. A nice flowing Marion Richardson line of thought, with no fancy loops. Instead, we get this ransom note mishmash: some schools open, others are closed. It's a childcare nightmare.

Where is everyone? The dean has gone away. Not to Havana – no, Havana requires more than the inside of a week, Gene conceded that. Seville? Ooh, what about Capri? What would give his deanissima most pleasure?

'To be honest, Gene, what I'd like most in the world is just to slump in some cottage somewhere.'

She slept in the car on the way to Shropshire. As she drifted off, she thought of the little lights still flickering in the dark cave of the cathedral, winking out one by one under the foot of the cross. Atrocities in Turkey. Brussels. And now Lahore. That park at Easter, all sunshine and family picnics, games of football. No warning. Who knows how it will be? An airport queue, an underground platform, a lorry crossing the central reservation, cancer, a ruptured artery . . . Every light winking out. Every single light. The terrible pathos of the human condition! How brightly we shine, and then we wink out.

But what would it be like, she wondered, to wait all night *inside* the cathedral for the Easter vigil? To hear the great door opening, to see the Paschal light coming, one tiny flame coming towards you through the dark? Coming to wake you. 'Little girl, get up.' A tear slid down her cheek. She blotted it before Gene saw. Hush. He is risen. Don't cry.

> My flesh in hope shall rest,
> and for a season slumber,
> till trump from east to west
> shall wake the dead in number.

*

96

Father Dominic has nipped off on a cheeky break to Gran Canaria. It will not be a highbrow affair, this holiday. He will take a pile of prize-winning novels he's been meaning to read for yonks, and he won't open a single one. The archdeacon of Lindchester is doing Low Sunday for him – ooh, just think! If he has Virginia as an associate vicar next year, arranging cover will suddenly get a whole lot easier. Goody-good!

Virginia's heart flutters a little every time she thinks about her conversation with Matt. Is this a sign? Guidance? To be the diocesan social welfare officer! Does it have her name on, as the archdeacon seemed to think? Obviously, they will have to wait and see if the funding is there. Then there will be proper process to follow. Virginia would no more try to circumvent proper process than she would fiddle her tax return!

TAX RETURN! Gah! Except, now he's got an accountant, he doesn't feel so angsty. Oh man, the thought that HMRC are gonna send their scary shit to Ambrose, and he's gonna talk to them? Aw, that's only like the most romantic thing anyone has done for him ever? Freddie caught that one before it escaped out of his head for once. Mostly there's this random cog in his brain that slips, and oops! too late, another dumb sentence falls out? Man, he hates when that happens? Coz he kinda wants Ambrose to not think he's a total airhead. I mean, yeah, no, lost cause. No kidding, the guy has all the evidence, the big old box of Freddie May's fuckwittery and failure.

The list of father figures who have betrayed your trust. Na-a-aw, don't do this to me, don't make me look at this. Just get out of my head, *Andy.* I'm so not that walking cliché with unresolved father issues?

One by one the lights wink out. One day we are going to have to go in there and face it. The box of failures, the cupboard under the stairs, the glory hole.

APRIL

Chapter 15

Whan that Aprille with his shoures soote,
The droghte of March hath perced to the roote . . .

The drought of March? You're having a laugh, Geoffrey! But sweet April showers bless Lindfordshire all the same, breathing life into the tender crops. The small birds make melody. Folks long to go on pilgrimage. Off to foreign lands they fly, lamenting the price hike in the school holidays. If they are clergy families, they bundle into the car and head for the holiday cottage borrowed from wealthier relatives and friends, in Devon, or Norfolk, or Northumberland. Stephen Fry's voice booms out *Harry Potter*. The clergy person at the wheel thinks *I could have been a banker, an entrepreneur, I could have made serious money*.

And just as they did in Chaucer's day, folks go on pilgrimage to cathedrals. Here in Lindchester, they climb the pilgrim path that snakes round the mount, up to the ancient shrine of St William. They walk in the footsteps of generations of the devout, the halt and the lame, the angst-ridden wealthy. What are they seeking? Answers? A blessing? Or just a spot of culture and a way of entertaining the kids in the holidays? They stop, as their forebears did, for refreshment in one of the hostelries along the road. Vespas, perhaps, where they might encounter a modern incarnation of Chaucer's squire, as fresh as is the month of May, singing and dancing as he waits tables. There are some video clips doing the rounds on social media, of him belting out 'O sole mio' in his stripy Breton top, like a gondolier. He's becoming a bit of a local celebrity: the singing waitron of Lindchester.

Down by Gresham's Boats all the weeping willows sport mops of lime-green hair. Long lappets of weed wave in the Linden. The pussy willows have turned duckling-coloured. The dog's mercury is out; and look – primrose clumps and celandines among last year's fallen oak leaves. Ah, those ancient oaks! They might have been cut from eighteenth-century paintings and pasted there, they are so English, so quintessentially English.

> They swear they'll invade us, these terrible foes;
> They frighten women, children, and beaus,
> But should their flat bottoms in darkness get o'er,
> Still Britons they'll find to receive them on shore.

Was there ever a more Heart of Oak region than Lindfordshire? Landlocked, an island within an island, with the islanders' deep instinct (like the polite natives of the *Punch* cartoon) to 'eave 'arf a brick at strangers bogusly coming over here, taking our jobs, scrounging our benefits, draining our NHS. We're full, geddit? England is full. I'm not racist but. #Brexit? Bring it on. 'Heart of Oak!' Tis to glory we steer. Britannia triumphant!'

Kat, the bishop's EA, generally finds herself in the 'Not you, love' category, broadmindedly exempted from the 'Go Home' remarks. Yeah, thanks for that, guys. We will join her now in the bishop's office, as she tractors through the bishop's emails so that he won't come home from holiday to an inbox of 300. There's a knock on the door.

'Hey! Come in, sweet cheeks.'

'Hey. Brought you a Billy cake* from work.'

'Nom nom! Put the kettle on.'

Freddie obeys, then comes and straddles the spare office chair and rests his chin on the back and gazes at Kat.

'What?'

'So you were right? Turns out he's into me?'

---

* A kind of marzipan, sultana and cherry Eccles cake, baked in honour of William of Lindchester to a genuine medieval recipe dating back to around 2014.

'Told you.'

'Yeh. *Man*. Did I read that one wrong. Seriously thought he was straight?'

'Straight? Ha ha ha! You need to book that gaydar in for an MOT!'

'Yeah, yeah.' Freddie lets his arms dangle. He swivels the chair. Sighs.

'And?' prompts Kat. 'So are you guys dating now, or what?'

'Dating!'

'Well, are you? Do you like him?'

'Yeah, no, I *like* him, but.' He thinks for a bit. 'I dunno.'

Kat rolls her eyes. 'It's complicated?'

Freddie fires an imaginary gun at her. 'You got it.'

'Tell you what. You make the tea, and we'll see if we can uncomplicate it.'

Well, I place quite a bit of confidence in Kat's ability to sort Freddie's head out for him. While she endeavours to do this, we will rewind and find out how Ambrose finally declared himself. Heavens, I have made my poor reader endure enough less absorbing scenes of a hard-core Anglican nature – why should we skip over this happy moment?

Freddie whistled as he walked back up the hill from Vespas. Life was looking good. Sun: shining. Work: good. Finances: good. (Well, getting better.) Voice: good. Still on a high after acing his solo part in the Lindchester setting on Easter Day?

Except: total downer. The old bastard himself had been there to hear it. Laird. Sir Gregory Laird. Afterwards, he'd been all, and here's my lovely protégé. Ruffled Freddie's hair! Actually did that? Can you *believe* that guy?

Yeah, Mr Laird, like you didn't piss on my dreams back when I was fifteen doing my first recital. *You'll probably only ever be average. Nice tenor sound, but average. That* was a special moment. And now I'm all of a sudden your blue-eyed boy, your wossname, Pygmalion? Guess you've forgotten how you blanked me when my voice broke? Like I could help it! Like I went, wahey, let's do the voice change right now, and balls up this mega-important première and make Laird look like a dick in front of the entire whole choral world! And fourteen years on you're telling everyone, here's my protégé, here's this amazing talent I nurtured. I always knew he'd go far, this one.

Fuckwad.

And I just stood there, like I was agreeing? Yep. Just sucked it up. Inside I was, have you *any idea* what you did to me? I'm not your fucking protégé, asshole. You fucking ruined my life! But no, I'm six again, just standing there wanting Mr Laird to love me. Love me, pay me some attention. Dude, I would've done anything for you to just love me!

Freddie felt it again as he walked. Gripping his throat, a hand choking off his voice, still not letting him say those things. Gah.

But Miss B, though? Hero! *Shame on you, Gregory Laird.*

Whoa.

Silence? I mean, Total. Fucking. Silence. Then Laird did his embarrassing Shakespeare bow: 'What, my dear Lady Disdain! Are you yet living?' Turned his back on her and was all, moving on, how are the plans for girl choristers shaping up, Giles?

Freddie carried on up the hill. Kind of took the edge off his success, whenever he remembered Laird. But the solo. Yeah. That was the business. In his mind, he was seeing the condors, the way they waited, high on the Andes, waited for the sun to come up and the air to warm, and then they just stepped off and rode the thermals. Yeah. Like that?

'Hi, Freddie.'

'Dude, Ambrose! Hey. Didn't hear you coming? Just finished work. You?'

'Yes.'

'Here.' He dug in his pocket for his wallet, peeled off some notes. 'Ta dah! First instalment for you.'

'Cheers. That's kind.'

'Hey. *De nada*, my friend. Thanks for rescuing me?'

They walked for a moment in silence.

'Know what I'm thinking?' began Freddie.

'We should get married and buy a puppy?' suggested Ambrose.

'What? Naw. I was—*What?*' He stopped and stared up. Ambrose smiled. 'I—What breed?'

'Labradoodle?'

'No way! Golden retriever. Anyway, *what?* That's not what I was thinking!'

'OK. What were you thinking?'

'I—Aw. Now you made me forget.'

'You have that effect on me, too, to be fair.'

Uh-oh. Freddie tugged his hair. 'Um. You're not . . . uh, coming onto me, here?'

'A little bit,' admitted Ambrose. 'Maybe. Is that a problem?'

Freddie began walking again. Eesh. Awkward. 'Listen, don't want to get all judge-y, but you know? Only I kind of have this rule – don't go with people who are in a relationship?'

'That's a good rule.'

'Soooo . . .'

Ambrose waited.

Shit, what was her name? Hot Chinese babe? Miraculously, it came to him: 'Chloe?'

'My cousin? What about her?'

'Your cousin!' Oh God. Wait. Oh. OHHHH! 'Did you send me a—Was that you, with the little red hearts?'

'That was me.'

'Oh, *man.*' His face blazed. 'Now I feel dumb. Coz I thought— Gah.' Shit, shit, *shit.*

They passed under the big archway and onto the Close.

'You thought she was my girlfriend?' Ambrose laughed. 'What do you think now?'

'Oh God, I—Listen, you're a nice guy and all, but I'm just not . . . feeling it? Sorry. Only I'm kind of coming out of a, a thing, not a relationship, but. There's this guy – and my head's still all . . . Make sense? Shit. I mean, obviously, I'd do you. One hundred per cent. If that's . . . ?'

Ambrose shook his head. 'Thanks, but that doesn't really work for me.'

'Cool. No worries. So all I'm saying is, right now's not a good time for me?'

'OK.' Ambrose smiled again. 'So, hang fire on buying that labra-doodle, then?'

'Yeah. No, *retriever*! But yeah. Sorry?'

'Not a problem, Freddie. See you around.'

'Bye.' Freddie watched him disappear into Vicars' Court. Face palm. *Obviously, I'd do you?* Classy.

Ambrose saw the panic in Freddie's eyes and knew to back off and wait a bit. But he was smiling as he let himself into his little house. He might be reading too much into what Freddie had blurted back there, but it sounded as though the Mighty Dorian had stopped playing dog in the manger at last.

The local train chuntered from Lindford to Martonbury. Jane was checking how long it was going to take her to get to work, once— Ahem-ahem, my lips are sealed. The daffodils were past their best now on the embankments. Who had planted them? she wondered. Maybe they had simply been tossed away over garden fences as rubbish? It was a windy day. Young trees wagged like metronomes. The train stopped in Barcup. Another time she'd get off here and have a nosy round, see if she could track down the Anglo-Saxon shrine site. Shame the house wasn't here. Too pricy, probably.

Off they went again. Next stop Martonbury, where this train terminates. Jane alighted onto the platform, taking all her luggage and belongings with her. Well, there was no denying it: the old town centre of Martonbury was easy on the eye. The brickwork of the Georgian houses was velveted by the weather to a pale terracotta. Jane glimpsed forsythia and magnolia in walled gardens, and caught the tom-catty pong of flowering currant. There was a dinky little butter market in the cobbled square, two real ale pubs, an award-winning family butcher, and a posh cheese shop. She could quite see herself tying a Chanel headscarf under her chin and sallying forth. In gloves. With a basket over her arm. 'I'll have a pound of scrag end of neck for the bishop's broth, my good man. And a bit of skirt.'

She passed a dress shop – aha! This was the place for her from now on. The mannequins in the window were wearing what Jane's mum had always described as 'nice frocks'. I bet they still stock Doreen bras, and petticoats. And bed jackets, probably. Quilted bed jackets.

The shops petered out as she headed off up Barcup Lane. Of course, the palace (as she persisted in calling it) was not that lovely Queen Anne mansion there, set back from the road behind wrought-iron gates and smothered in wisteria. Oh well. Before long, the Georgian mansions gave way to Victorian terraces, and then she was in Tudorbethan territory. There it was, in all its half-timbered glory. Ha ha ha! Pampas grass! Maybe she could host a diocesan swingers' party as her first act of hospitality?

My readers will see that Gene will shortly need to look to his laurels, if he wishes to retain his title as most disgraceful clergy spouse in the diocese of Lindchester.

Chapter 16

re you sitting comfortably? Skim ahead, if you have a low boredom threshold, for I am about to induct you into the mysteries of The Four Instruments of Communion. It is possible that this phrase conjures up church organs and guitars for many of my readers. Perhaps staunch eight o'clockers might picture the psaltery and harp instead, and cymbals both loud and high-sounding, as duly listed in Psalm 150 (in the 'if it was good enough for St Paul, it's good enough for me' version of the Bible).

But no, this is not what is meant at all. The Four Instruments of Communion are as follows: the Archbishop of Canterbury, the Lambeth Conference, the Primates Meeting and the Anglican Consultative Council. My readers are probably already acquainted with the first three of these (however distantly); but the joyous music of the fourth instrument may not have sounded in your ears yet. I will spare you the bother of googling it, or of prevaricating Englishly (i.e. frowning and saying 'That sounds familiar . . .' until the information is furnished; whereupon we pretend we knew all along).

'The role of the Anglican Consultative Council (ACC) is to facilitate the co-operative work of the churches of the Anglican Communion, exchange information between the provinces and churches, and help to co-ordinate common action.' Its composition is no mystery, for it is our good pleasure to wash all Anglican laundry transparently and in public. This is our best and costliest gift to our ecumenical partners – to draw the fire of the media, so that everyone else may launder with some degree of privacy. I mention the ACC, not because I am about to play you a sonata on this august instrument – indeed I cannot: they have been meeting in Lusaka, where we may not follow – but more to alert you all to the full range of musical possibilities within Anglicanism. Contrary to the impression given by this narrative, the average Anglican is not a testy university-educated white Englishman. She is an African woman in her thirties living in sub-Saharan Africa on less than four dollars a day. How easy it is, in little Lindfordshire, to lose sight of the fact that we play upon the kora, the kalimba and the drums as gloriously as we do upon the Father Willis.

Bishop Steve has been following the ACC meeting with much anxious loving care, braced for another dishing-up of the sex marriage brouhaha. He gradually unclenches. Trust in the Lord and do good, he reminds himself. If you sit a bunch of Anglicans down together, they generally find it hard to hate one another. It's always simpler to demonize at a distance, or in the abstract. He's guilty enough of that himself. Pennington, the porcupine, quivering his quills of self-justification when under attack, instead of listening, and seeking to understand. And allowing certain lay clerks (bless them) to emerge from screaming stereotype into brothers in Christ, for example.

Our good friend the archdeacon of Lindchester has also been keeping tabs of the ACC, of course. And apart from the odd rumour – fake letters and umbrage – he is reassured by what he sees.

It's 10 p.m. This, I understand, is when you should contact your archdeacon, because that's when he or she will be at their desk and your email is most likely to get immediate attention. At other times, your plea will be deep-sixed under 300 competing demands. Right now, though, Matt is in the middle of a DM exchange with his fellow archdeacon. He doesn't tweet, he just lurks on Twitter in a monitoring capacity, checking the clergy aren't making nobs of themselves on social media. Bea tweets cheerily about church things and knitting, adhering to your mum's golden rule: If you can't say anything nice, don't say anything at all.

But all bets are off when it comes to direct messages.

BEA	Parish review at Our Lady and St Michael's tomorrow.
MATT	Our Lady and Mike the Spike. Enjoy!
BEA	WT Flip is a maniple?
MATT	Part of a motorbike engine?
BEA	HA HA HA HA! Seriously tho?
MATT	Hang on . . . 'a subdivision of a Roman legion, containing either 120 or 60 men.'
BEA	Ooh. Will line them up and inspect them closely.

Lord, have mercy. But the advert has now gone out for two more archdeacons in the diocese of Lindchester. If you know what a maniple is, do apply. Then at least someone might be able to brandish it valiantly on the diocesan shore, against the incoming tide of the ~~talent pool~~ Strategic Leadership Development Programme Learning Community.

But enough! Away with sin and sorrow. Grab your wings and join me. We will revel in Lindfordshire in the spring. All the old brown bramble tangles are tasselled with green. Daffodils wither to crepe paper and cherries blossom instead. Water spangles in tractor ruts. It's all shining, everything is shining – the broken glass underfoot, the tossed plastic bottles and bags, the scrap metal in the yards, every windscreen. Even things you didn't know could shine are shining today: the yellow handrails at the station, the black railings of the arboretum, shrink-wrapped bales in fields, each twig, each metal roof. Every ivy leaf reflects the sky.

Jane is trapped in a departmental meeting, answering emails while the head of department talks about UCAS tariffs. A BBC alert flips onto her iPad. No! She glances up, and sees the same shock bloom on colleagues' faces all around the stuffy room: *Not Victoria Wood.*

2016 is dismantling our youth, thinks Jane, as she jogs round the arboretum the next day. And now Prince! Dear God. Death is taking down the posters from our teen walls one by one. Rolling them up. 'Golden lads and girls all must,/As chimney sweepers, come to dust.'

And yet the sun still shines. The Queen turns ninety. A full peal is rung in Lindchester Cathedral. May is out along the hedgerows already. Pedro has cast his tartan clout. Today he is walking beside the Linden with Virginia. Father Wendy has gone on a mercy dash to look after the grandchildren, because her son is working abroad and her daughter-in-law is poorly. Virginia is chirpy. She's mentally pulling together her personal statement, ready for the Social Justice Officer post to be advertised. She sees that it's a lovely day, but the detail escapes her.

The detail, ah! God is in the detail, in the quirks, in the qualia, down the cracks, in the corners. Notice it all; let nothing be lost. Count your blessings, Virginia! Name them one by one, the way Father Wendy does:

Dandelions sprouting along wall tops among the jagged glass.
Tart pink of flowering currant.
A buzzard, patient on a post.

All the dog-walkers of Lindfordshire are out today. Two men stroll with a labradoodle beside the river. Don't panic: the puppy has been borrowed, not bought. They are just going for a walk. They are not getting married.

'Why've we stopped?'
'It's a kissing gate.'
'Ha ha ha, sure it is.'
'Seriously. I'm a country boy.'
'Dude, you're full of shit. But whatev—? Uh. Hnn. Cool.'
Well, *that* went well. Why not just headbutt the guy? Moving on.
The metal gate clangs behind them. They walk in silence. Ah, c'mon! There's birds, there's sunshine, ducklings. Life's good, no? Be happy! Why can't he be happy?
'Gimme the lead? My turn.'

111

'OK.' Ambrose hands it over. 'Don't let him go, though.'

'Aw, why not? He'll come back, won't you, guy?' Cosmo tugs.

'No. Chloe tried it last week, and it took her the best part of three hours to catch him. He thinks it's all a game. Heel, Cosmo!'

'Puppies just wanna have fun, I guess.' Cosmo tugs, like '*heel*' is for sissies?

'Maybe. But puppies need boundaries to feel safe.'

Silence. 'Uh, did shit just get metaphorical there?'

'I don't know. Did it?'

'Coz if it *did*, you should probably know, this here is one baaad dog? He'll give you the runaround? Y'know? Steal your shit, fuck with your head, hump your friends? You're totally gonna end up hating him.'

'You think?'

'Dude, I *know*.'

Ambrose smiles. 'Oh. OK.'

'OK. So. Cool.' Cosmo tugs on the lead till he half-chokes, going after something in the grass. The sun breaks up on the water like flashbulbs going off. Man, this is so weirdly hurty? Why does it *hurt*? I can't do this. Can't we just fuck, get it over with? I don't know how to like . . . *be* with him?

'Don't worry, Freddie. He'll run out of tricks before I run out of patience.'

'You're a patient guy, huh?'

'Trust me, I'm an ox. Damn! Sorry, did he just eat something? Here, boy. Cosmo, drop it. Come on, spit it out.'

Freddie watches as Ambrose kneels and prises a manky tennis ball out of the dog's jaws. Cosmo laps his face. Ambrose laughs and rumples his ears, his fur. 'Good boy. Yeah. Good boy.'

Oh *man*, now I'm filling up? 'Probably he doesn't deserve you?'

Ambrose stands. He shies the ball across the river into the rushes. Then he smiles at Freddie again. 'Well, it's not about deserving, is it?'

#Shakespeare400. Across the diocese of Lindchester we go bard mad with fun activities (free to download!) and quizzes in every school. Friday is non-uniform day! Yay! Well, provided you bring in a pound for the school fund and dress up as a Shakespeare character.

Leah Rogers went as Sir Toby Belch, and got sent to the head's office for belching in literacy, which was blatantly not fair. All the boys were burping too, it's just that Leah was WAY better than the boys; she could say, 'To be or not to be' in one single belch and the furthest they could get was 'To be or'. Plus in her humble opinion it *was* both big and funny.

The celebrations in the cathedral on Saturday afternoon did not showcase any virtuoso belching displays; although I feel sure the choristers would have acquitted themselves well had they been called upon. Nor did Freddie May appear as Bottom. (Don't ask.) The Mighty Dorian (as a favour to his old friend, the precentor) delivered a brilliant public lecture on Shakespeare's sonnets in the afternoon, much as he used to when he was an English don (only without stumbling drunk off the podium and passing out, still quoting).

The concert in the evening featured all the pieces you would expect, and the party afterwards at the precentor's went on long into the night. Miss Blatherwick heard them still going strong at 2 a.m. She'd not been sleeping too well again recently. Her window was open. She was an old-school believer in fresh air. Honkytonk piano riffs tinkled across the Close. Rowdy singing. Not a song she was familiar with.

An owl called. 'The staring owl . . . Tu-whit, tu-who – a merry note . . .'

The dean heard the song too, and she recognized it from her granny's chapel.

> Count your many blessings, name them one by one,
> And it will surprise you what the Lord has done.

Count them, name them. The calling owl, the chiming bell, the piano riff, the ACC, good friends, all songs and sonnets and labradoodles. All the blessings of this life. 'Golden lads and girls all must,/ As chimney sweepers, come to dust.'

It's not about deserving. It never is.

Chapter 17

'Fire and hail; snow and vapour; stormy wind fulfilling his word!'

The showers sweet sputter into spite. They usher April out again, clattering on roofs and patios across Lindfordshire. Snow! Snow in April, for heaven's sake! It powders the green baize of the landscape like tailor's chalk, outlining lost earthworks for the circling buzzards to see. Even when the sun blazes again, drifts linger on the high tops in the rock clefts, among sheep and gorse. Turbine blades flash like Saxon swords on a distant hill, and crows creak homeward to roost as the sun goes down in fire.

The first fledglings are in the undergrowth now. Miss Blatherwick steps into her garden and claps at the nest-raiding magpies, favouring the humble worm-eaters above species that dine on baby blackbirds. It is sentimental nonsense, she knows; but there one is. She presses her hand to her left side. Perhaps another paracetamol. Plenty of fluid. Tiresome, this diverticulitis. But it's not the end of the world. She needn't pester her GP with it.

It's not the end of the world, Leah. Why did grown-ups *always* say that? I'm not STUPID. I KNOW it's not the end of the world. But it WAS my best pencil, and Jack BLATANTLY snapped it in half!

Leah storms off. Jess dawdles behind, singing and skipping and literally talking to snails and garden gnomes like she's got special needs. Leah is sposed to walk her home. Well, Jess should —king well keep up then! (Leah's eyes dart from side to side, in case God hears the F-word. Then she remembers she's an atheist.) Jess should keep up, if she doesn't want to get snatched by a —king stranger and murdered—

She freezes.

The whistle-pitch scream comes again.

Oh God, oh Jesus! Leah belts back the way she came. Let it be OK, don't let anything— She hurtles into the alley. There's Jess. Alone.

'What? What happened?'

'It was a bee!'

Leah grabs Jess and shakes her. 'Idiot! You stupid, *stupid* IDIOT!'

'It flew at my face!' Jess tugs away. 'It was going to sting me. Like the killer bees you told me about!'

'That's in South America, you moron!' Leah scrubs her eyes with her sweatshirt sleeve. 'Why do you have to be so dumb all the time?'

Jess touches her arm. 'Don't cry, Leah.'

'I'm not crying.' A sob blurts out. 'I thought—' Leah stamps her foot. Why did her voice have to go all stupid? 'I thought a *paedo* was snatching you!' she squeaks.

Jess's eyes go wide. She looks round to check. There are no paedos in the alley. 'It was just a bee.'

'I was going to kill him. I mean it. I know how to kill people,' says Leah. She sniffs. 'Maybe you should learn.'

'But you said I'm not allowed to do karate.'

'Well, you could learn a different martial art. One more suited to your physical physique.'

They start walking, side by side. Everything's gone weird and super-real. The wooden fence knocking in the wind. Her trainers hitting the tarmac. The dog poo smell. A blackbird runs on the path ahead. Leah's fingers are cold. They've gone tingly.

'You mean like kickboxing?' suggests Jess.

'Well, maybe. But your legs are a bit short. You've got to think about your strike range.' She feels her little sister's hand sneak into

115

her own. 'Not to be rude, Jess, but the other thing is, you aren't actually very aggressive, are you? You need to tap into your inner aggression. I won't be here for you next year when I start at QM, remember?'

'OK. I'll *try* to be more aggressive.'

'Hey, there's this Brazilian martial art that's based on dancing, though! You'd be good at that.'

'Dancing! Cool!'

'Yeah. It's called caipirinha.'

'Yay! I'm good at dancing. Can we ask Mum? Coz I bet I could do . . . What's it called again?'

'Um, caipirinha? Or something. But girls can do *anything*, Jess. You need to remember that.'

'OK.' Jess does a little skip. 'So does it go like this?' She does a twirl and a kick.

'Yes. That's amazing, Jess.' Obviously it isn't; it's crap. But it's a scientific fact you should never demotivate younger children. If you're an older sibling, you have to be a positive role model literally *all the time*.

Talking of role models. Let us don our time-travelling wings and swoop back to the previous Saturday, and the party that kept the poor dean awake and counting her blessings.

You will have noted that Andrew Jacks – ex-mentor of the lovely Freddie May – was once more on the Close. Perhaps you've even seen that YouTube clip from that occasion? Just google: 'The Gentlemen of Lindchester Cathedral Choir sing "Jambalaya".' It features Dr Andrew 'Andy' Jacks tap-dancing.

'You're not going to share that anywhere on the internet, are you, Mr May?'

'Nu-uh, not me. Nope. I absolutely one hundred per cent am not gonna do that.'

'You little shit.' Andrew laughed. 'Well? How's it all going, friend? Come. Sit and talk to me. I hear good things about your perform-ance on Easter Day.'

They sat on the third step of the precentor's grand staircase and Freddie poured out his heart. So yeah, that bastard Laird? His job

116

at Vespas? Oh, and he'd finally *finally* got an accountant, and . . . um, so yeah?'

'Interesting! Do I note a certain bashfulness here? Enlighten me: has accountancy become a euphemism since my philandering days?'

Freddie squirmed. 'Naw! Guy did my tax return, is all.'

Andrew leant close. 'Don't look, but is that tall dark brooding alto over there your *accountant*? The one who is currently amusing himself by visualizing the earth dropping from the sexton's spade onto my poor coffin?'

'Wha'?' Freddie craned round. 'No, yeah, no, I mean, yeah, that's uh, Ambrose. So we're like – we're friends, OK? He's a sweet guy? I mean, he sings on *dec*, obviously?'

Andrew nodded. 'Oh, obviously.'

'Gah!' Freddie wrapped his arms round his head.

Andrew laughed. 'Would you like the benefit of my advice?'

Freddie bumped his head against his shoulder. 'Dunno. Yeah. Kinda?'

'Very well. Once upon a time, when I was a couple of years older than you are now, there was a very lovely man in my life.' He broke off.

The whole party slowed down round Freddie. Noise, slow. Pulse slow in his ears: doom, doom, doom. He watched the bubbles rise in his cava. Little beads of gold. Up . . . and gone. Up . . . and gone.

'What happened?'

'He died.'

Freddie put his hand on Andrew's knee. 'That sucks.'

'Indeed it does. And while I don't regret getting my heart broken . . .'

Freddie saw him tilt his head, like he was checking this?

'Anyway, I do regret the time I wasted not believing my good fortune.'

'Hnn. Can totally relate to *that*,' said Freddie.

'I suspected you would.'

'So that's your advice, yeah? Like, *carpe diem*?'

'God, no!' A fey shudder. 'How hackneyed. I just wanted to mention this: please entertain the possibility that despite your

117

manifold sins and wickedness, someone might find you altogether lovely.' He patted Freddie's knee and got to his feet. 'That's my advice. *Ciao, bello.* The Lord grant you a quiet night and a perfect end. All yours, Lanky,' he said to Ambrose as he wafted past.

A quiet night and a perfect end. That would be nice. When did Jane last get a full night's sleep? Not since she climbed aboard the menopause cakewalk. Still, she uses the time profitably when she wakes with a hot flush in the wee small hours of Saturday. First, she lies there trouble-shooting imaginary work scenarios that will never happen. Then she broods over past conversations with colleagues. These night-time sessions provide a welcome opportunity to hone and edit her ripostes to levels of unanswerable brilliance, in a way that's simply not possible under the ad hoc arrangements of real life. This done, she moves on to the Four Last Things. Matt snores beside her. Perhaps she should suffocate him with a pillow? On the whole, no – sheer short-termism. Because who would bring her a cup of tea in the morning?

Heaven, hell, death and judgement. Of these four, the only one she believes in is death. And yet, does she *really* believe in it? Even though parents and grandparents, great-aunts, even school friends and colleagues, have died – doesn't it still seem ludicrous? As if they might reappear one ordinary day and laugh at you for falling for it.

Yes. Despite all the evidence, there's a defiant streak in Jane that won't accept that it has to be this way; that our lights will just dwindle out, or get snuffed, and that will be that. Rage, rage, and so on. She is not one of those who will go gentle into any kind of night, good or bad. It makes her want to fold her arms the way she did as a small girl, when grown-ups hilariously claimed to have pinched her nose off. 'Look! Here's your nose, Jackie!' 'That's your thumb.' 'No, it's your nose! I've got Jackie's nose!' Did they think she was thick, or something?

She can see that this stubbornness might map rather well onto a belief in the resurrection, of death being swallowed up in victory and so forth. The trumpet shall sound, and the dead shall be raised incorruptible. But she doesn't believe in the resurrection of the dead, either.

Nor does she believe in heaven and hell as eternal destinies. As the man said, hell is other people. (Or more specifically – judging by what she's seen of Matt's job – hell is other people's parishioners.) That said, heaven is also other people. Probably. If human love is the greatest good we can know.

Her poor heart races round the globe to Danny. There is still a baby-shaped gap in her embrace that nothing else will ever fill, even though Danny is a great six-foot-four lump of a twenty-two-year-old now. But he might be back next month. Maybe in time to see his step-dad made bishop . . .

But judgement, now. Judgement. What do you think of *that*, Dr Rossiter? If you don't believe in heaven or hell, why are you so exercised at 3 a.m. by the image of two cosmic turnstiles, labelled *Sheep* and *Goats*, that will admit you to one or other of those destinations?

Part of the human condition? Probably. Only a psychopath could come through life unscathed by guilt. Even if we're basically decent, there's the constant wear and tear on our compassion every time we fail to relieve the suffering of others – it takes its toll.

Sheep?

Goat?

What will the verdict be? It's probably the Hillsborough inquest that's fuelling this. Justice and vindication after twenty-seven years. Crowds of thirty thousand on the streets of Liverpool for that Magnificat moment. And now Orgreave? Another toxic vat of corruption and cover-up ripe for opening. Ah, *here's* the tender spot. Goat! Class traitor! She'd wasted the early eighties plunged into the radicalism of the Christian, not the Students' Union. Yeah, that'll be what prompted that Susanna Henderson moment – baking flapjacks and taking them to the striking junior doctors outside Lindford General Hospital. Because it's the same fucking battle. Pissing on the truth, pissing on the poor. The same wankers who'd burnt their fifty-pound notes in front of beggars, and sneered at the eighteen-year-old Jackie Rossiter, were now dismantling the NHS. Literally the same ones.

If she had her time over, Jackie – with her short A's and her perm, her Isle of Wight holidays, her Campari – Jackie would stomp the shit out of them in her proudly deployed white stilettos. Why had she gone native? *Tried* to go native – of course it hadn't really taken. You can take the girl out of Blackgang Chine . . .

If she could go back and rescue those shoes . . . *You'll need a couple of smart frocks and some high heels, Jackie.* Oxford made me ashamed of where I come from. Ashamed of my people. Oxford called me chippy whenever I committed the cardinal sin of taking things too seriously.

It'll be getting light soon. The blackbirds of Lindford whistle. The archdeacon of Lindchester snores. Jane gets up and makes herself a cup of tea. She opens the back door and steps out onto the cold patio. My shoes, where are my poor old rejected shoes? Maybe Judgement Day is a lost property box. Where everything is restored?

MAY

Chapter 18

Woe unto you who have booked a round of golf, bought disposable barbecues, or planned a picnic. Woe to the jolly little stalls erected on Cathedral Close for the May Market. Woe to the medieval frolics in the grounds of Lindford castle. Woe to all townie pub ramblers in the wrong footwear and non-waterproof coats.

Yes, woe to the whole pack of them; for see how rain ascends like wrathful smoke from the fields! O world turned upside down – rain rising, not falling? Lord save us all. Motorways smoulder. Plashing wildfire devours our landscape. Some wag looks through a window and says, 'Well, I don't know about you, but I wouldn't mind a spot of global warming!' Jousting is cancelled for health and safety reasons. In every parish church in Lindfordshire, the marble knights turn on their tombs at this pouncet-box milksoppery.

Look, Lord, in mercy upon Lindfordshire this Rogationtide! 'Although we for our iniquities have worthily deserved a plague of rain and waters . . .' To prayer! For who knoweth if he will return and repent, and leave a blessing behind him?

The sun comes out in glory in the afternoon. Not because it *must*, or because (with silky flouncing hair) we're worth it, but because it simply does. Because it may. And with one heart, the grateful people of Lindfordshire say: 'Typical! Why couldn't it have been like this this morning?' They all of them walk past the blessing without noticing it.

Well, perhaps not all of them. Our lovely Father Wendy notices, as she plodges through the mud with Pedro, along the banks of the Linden. She notices the rape fields mustering their yellow fire. She sees how the mayflowers crowd the hedges and how the ancient pear trees are clotted with creamy blossom. She catches the scent of crab apple and cow parsley and sees bluebells in the mushed-down rust of dead bracken.

And because there is nobody about, she sings: '"Hail the day that sees him rise!" Nearly Ascension Day, Pedro.'

But Pedro is intent on the moorhen dabbing along the path ahead. Wendy pauses to watch how the water is combed as it rushes white over a little weir. Graffiti blights the lovely old brickwork of a humpback bridge: 'Happiness is a journey not a destination,' it chides. She walks on, but now she notices the litter-clogged trees, abandoned sofas and highchairs, compacted car cubes stacked in the scrapyard.

She reaches down to stroke the greyhound's silky ears. 'Oh dear. What will become of us all, Pedro? Why do we ruin everything?' She steers her thoughts back to Ascension Day, and her sermon. The homecoming. The hero returns. She pictures an open-topped bus in Leicester. The crowds filling the streets as the victorious team comes home. Our champion has conquered. Rejoice! Everything is new! Don't stand bereft in the stadium, staring at the empty pitch.

Miss Blatherwick is another noticer. In the evening she takes her customary constitutional round the Close, down the steep steps, along the river, then back up the pilgrim path again, and home.

Spring is too far on. This is not good. It is a symptom of a global disease. How long will we tell ourselves there's nothing to worry about? As she climbs carefully down the precipitous steps she hears a snatch of music from above. Someone rehearsing in the Song School. Alto voice. She knows the tune. Ah yes, Herbert. Vaughan Williams setting. She delves into her inner anthology for the poem.

Sweet spring, full of sweet dayes and roses,
A box where sweets compacted lie;
My musick shows ye have your closes,
And all must die.

Yes, all must die. All, all. The sycamores on the Linden's banks tower like lime-green thunderclouds, bright, ominous. But there's her old friend the blackbird, still singing away. He, or his descendants, will be on the same tree, still singing, after she's breathed her last. And the bluebells will come up again and again, every sweet spring, among the stitchwort and ramsons. And all manner of thing shall be well. Brace up, Barbara.

She forges on – passing unkissed through the kissing gate – in her Burberry mac (a shrewd investment in the 1950s and still going strong), and her trusty galoshes. Suddenly she realizes: she has bought her last clothes. These will see her out.

This is not true for my other characters. Some buy clothes on whim (O reason not the need!), others out of necessity. The archdeacons of the diocese of Lindchester are messaging one another again on this very subject, even as I write.

BEA   Could knit you a mitre if you like.
MATT   Ta. But the missus is all over it.

Jane is indeed all over the task of kitting out her man in proper episcopal glory. The announcement will be next week, and at some point after that Matt will be consecrated in York Minster – Lindchester being in the Northern Province – and then installed in Lindchester Cathedral. (*I WAS GLA-A-A-A-AD!*) I have not fixed the dates yet, but of this we may be certain: he will need 'Episcopal Wear'. I'm a bit disappointed that Matt is such a low-maintenance bloke, really. He's inclined to treat his new kit like a uniform, old ex-copper that he is. He has no instinct for sartorial anguish. Neil, now! Neil would bring the proper levels of stress to shirt choice. But Matt's rubbish. Have you got it in my size? In purple? How much? Sorted.

Dr Rossiter has been forced to step into the breach.

'God, I *lurve* vestments porn!' says Jane. 'Fifty Shades of Purple! OK. I've decided: I'm going to buy you a zucchetto.'

The archdeacon eyes her. 'Is that a make of Italian scooter?'

'No, you ineffable proddywoddy! A zucchetto,' she consults the webpage again, 'as any fule kno, is an eight-segment cap lined with chamois and finished with a looped cord. *A looped cord* – think of that! Made from – fan me someone! – made from *our red purple imitation ribbed silk.*'

'That's for poofs.'

'I'm telling on you! I'm reporting you to Stonewall. And the Vatican.' Jane continues browsing. 'I want to buy you something for your special day. Something you'll really like.'

'Buy yourself a sexy dress, then,' says Matt. 'I'm using J and M Sewing, same as always.'

'Suit yourself. Wait! Would you like a Canterbury cap?'

'No.'

'Sure? It's made from a high-quality red purple velveteen . . .'

'No.'

'G'wan, g'wan. It's constructed to fold flat when not in use.'

'Stop Wippelling me!'

'Ha ha ha! You love it, you old pervert.'

Matt doesn't exactly love it. But he's aware that his new job is going to tread repeatedly on Janey's sore toe. From now on, the whole church world is going to call her Mrs Tyler. She's obviously made the decision to be amused by it all. Rather than, a) never showing her face at anything churchy, or b) kicking people in the slats when they say: 'Oh, you're the bishop's wife, aren't you?' And for this he is grateful enough to put up with any amount of private piss-taking.

Polling cards wait on hall tables, or propped on mantelpieces, or pinned to noticeboards. Super Ascension Thursday dawns. Local council elections, Police and Crime Commissioner elections, and in some places – though not Lindchester – voting for a new mayor. And everywhere, God has gone up with a merry noise, though few these days hear the trumpets.

Today, some Lindfordshire voters find their pencils hovering as they stand in the secrecy of the plywood booth. It's safe. It'll be CON HOLD. They wrestle with a temptation to drop an adulterous X in some other box. Just to register a certain discontent with the way things are going down in London town. True, we've got to crack down on immigration. But voting against taking 3,000 unaccompanied children? That's not right, is it?

What a nation of piss-taking nose-thumbers we are! Voting in a Muslim mayor, dubbing our ships Boaty McBoatface. Best of countries, worst of countries. Serious only about never taking stuff seriously. God forbid we should be caught out in earnestness.

The gentlemen of the choir gather ready for solemn Eucharist for Ascension Day. The canons arrive, Mr Happy cutting it fine as usual. The dean lays down her burden and takes her customary deep breath. Calm, calm.

The precentor looks at his watch. 'Where's Tarty McTartface?'

'Gone for a wee,' says Nigel, the senior lay clerk. He turns to Ambrose. 'What is it, Mr Hardman? Did you just sigh?'

'I wish you guys wouldn't all call him that,' says Ambrose. 'Everyone does it.'

An *Oooh!* ripples round the choir.

'I *think* you'll find Mr May self-identifies as a tart,' says Nigel.

'So? That still doesn't make it OK,' says Ambrose.

The senior lay clerk inclines his head. The word *prig* hovers, all unspoken. 'It's meant affectionately. We've all known Freddie since he was . . .'

'A tartlet?' suggests Giles. He intercepts a flash from the dean's eye. 'Sorry.'

'Ambrose is right,' she says.

Everyone looks away. Up at the ceiling. Down at their black shoes. Smirks are repressed. Madam Dean has spoken.

'So can we agree that the names stop, please?' says Marion.

There's no time to process this: the spurts of resentment and hilarity, the prickles of self-justification. Footsteps. Freddie flies in, tugging his surplice over his head.

'What?' he whispers to Ambrose. 'What just happened?'

'Ssh!' says Giles. He presses the button and away out of sight up in the organ loft, the organist winds up her improvisation.

Silence. The *ting!* of a tuning fork. The antiphon begins.

'Men of Galilee, why gaze in wonder at the heavens?'

*

127

'Mr Bennet has a point, though, deanissima,' says Gene. 'Freddie eagerly embraces his tarthood.'

They are standing in the deanery garden with a glass of Krug each. The deanery bees ply their fumbling trade in the apple blossom.

'Well, he shouldn't,' says Marion. 'It's limiting. Nobody takes him seriously. I feel sad I hadn't spotted the dynamic until Ambrose pointed it out.'

'He doesn't *want* to be taken seriously. People have conveniently low expectations of vacuous little tarts,' says Gene. 'But as always, you are right, O Queen. From henceforth I will slut you no sluts.'

'Thank you.'

They take a silent turn about the lawn. A blackbird trolls the opposition from the top of the deanery roof.

'Are Mr May and Mr Hardman an item these days?'

'I'm not sure that's any of our business,' says Marion.

'Of course it isn't. But that doesn't mean we don't want to know.'

The gentlemen of the choir could have answered Gene's question with a resounding *No*. They were all privy to the 'Don't slut-shame me, asshole' tirade that broke over Ambrose's head in the vestry afterwards.

'Ah! A classic of the genre!' said Nigel, as the door slammed. 'Are you all right there, Mr Hardman?'

'I'm fine.'

Freddie is not fine. He is out running. Pounding out the miles until it hurts.

Entertain the possibility . . .

Entertain the possibility . . .

But he can't. He knows what's gonna happen: he's gonna trash the whole thing before it's even started. Coz that's the only thing he knows how to do?

Chapter 19

The glorious weekend weather lasts; though the air sweats with pent-up rain. People dither between sunglasses and umbrella as they set off in the morning. Cherry blossom is on the turn, like tissues dunked in latte. Cloudbursts. Sunshine. Sodden lilac droops over fences. The horse chestnut candles are out. It's fan yourself with the pew sheet, shorts-under-cassock weather.

And, like a thunderstorm that fails to clear the air, Tartgate lingers. The Song School twangles with rumour. Freddie and Ambrose stand side by side in quire, sealed in separate dimensions of the multiverse. The more sensitive choristers register all this on their 'scary-grown-up-fight' barometers, and they struggle to concentrate. Poor old Timothy very nearly loses his rag. The precentor very nearly phones Mr Dorian. Everyone agrees: this is ridiculous. But everyone is rather hoping someone else will deal with it.

In the end, it is Ambrose who takes matters in hand.

Freddie heads home after evensong on Tuesday. Hating this, *hating*— Whoa! He whips round. There's Ambrose behind him, totally blank and all, *What?*

'Dude. Not cool.'

'Sorry?'

'You grabbed my ass!'

'When?'

'Just now!' For a wild second Freddie doubts himself, the guy's so totally, I did not do that? They stare at each other. 'You so did!'

Then Ambrose grins. 'Oh, all right then.'

'Ex*cuse* me? Unbeliev— Oh, wait.' Freddie puts his fists on his hips. 'Yeah, I see where you're going with this – like, I'm a tart, I should totally be up for it?' Freddie catches sight of Nigel and a bunch of the other guys, making for the King's Head. They're all looking this way. He drops his voice. 'Dude, you do *not* get to do that, 'K?'

'OK,' whispers Ambrose.

'Plus you don't get to call the guys out on what they call me?'

'OK.'

'And most of all, you *don't* get to tell me how to act, yeah? Ever. I mean that? You do *not* get to change me!'

'OK.'

The guy's still smiling! 'Stop fucking *agreeing* with me!'

'No.'

Freddie flings his hands up. *Man*, this is like trying to keep hold of a frog? The conversation keeps jumping away from him? Problem is, it's starting to get funny, and it's not funny. He heads down the steps. 'OK. So's you know. But yeah, listen,' he mutters, 'sorry I lost it.'

'Well, sorry I upset you. I don't want to change you, Freddie.'

'Yeah, yeah.'

They stop again. He's *still* smiling down into Freddie's face, like this moment, this literal moment, is everything. And Freddie panics and wants to shake him. No! You got it all wrong, man. Coz I *should* change?

'You're fine how you are,' Ambrose says.

Freddie shakes his head.

'Really?' says Ambrose. 'Because from where I'm standing – dayum!'

'Uh, o-ka-a-ay.' He tries to laugh. Man, you're only *blushing*? What are you – twelve? 'I guess.'

Off they go again. Slowly, so they won't overtake his landlord, walking ahead of them there. Freddie looks down at his Converse. Laces trailing on the cobbles again. *A little tragic in a grown man.*

'Does this bug you?' he asks Ambrose. 'The shoelace thing?'

'Not even slightly.'

Freddie sees the canon treasurer going into the house. Hears the door slam, rattle of letterbox. 'Hnn. So apparently, I use the weak form of the shoelace knot?'

'The what? Says who?'

'*Andy*. Says I'm tragic.'

'Andy's a tool,' says Ambrose. 'Who's Andy?'

'Dude. Only Andrew Jacks?'

'Oh. Him.'

'Not a fanboy, huh?'

Ambrose snorts. 'Sorry. I know he's your mentor.'

'Was. We like, wound that up?'

'Ah!'

'Yeah. So now we're "friends". Coz apparently, I'm not good enough to ever be more than that?' They reach the drive. 'Wa-a-ay too dumb, too young, too ungrammatical? Oh, plus my dress sense?'

'There you go.' Ambrose shrugs. 'He's a tool.'

'Yeah, no, no, but you gotta say, he's a class act?'

'OK. So maybe he's a Philippe Starck power tool.'

'Ha ha ha! *So* gonna tell him that!'

They stop outside the house. Wahey! Awkward goodbye klaxon!

All around the Close Freddie can hear singing. Like, bird arias? On the rooftops. In the trees. And here's this actual golden laburnum, dripping down golden flowers over their heads, and maybe it's gonna rain, and maybe not?

'So, uh, Totty's expecting me for dinner? Catch you later?'

'See you, Freddie.'

Freddie lets himself in. He runs up the stairs, heart hammering as if this is a karate contest about to happen. He pauses on the landing and looks across the Close. Aw. There he goes. Freddie rests his forehead on the pane and laughs. Philippe Starck power tool! Guy totally kills me? Plus he's got that big-but-gentle vibe going on? I mean, not normally my thang, obviously – coz hey, why fall for sweet guys, when there's emotionally unavailable bastards out there happy to fuck with your head? *But*?

131

And now, randomly he's remembering his frog, Trevor, his pet, back in the day? How you had to hold him, gently, under the armpits. You had to not squeeze him, but still hold him firmly, so he didn't keep jumping out of your hand?

Ambrose passes the broderers' room. Freddie sees him run his hand along the lavender hedge in front of the canon chancellor's house.

Not thought about it for like *ever*, but weirdly, Freddie can almost feel that frog? His skin? How his little heart pulsed under your fingertips? How you *could* crush him, but you never would? Man, loved that little dude so *much*. But then he died? And Dad was all, well, you didn't look after it properly, son. I warned you. You didn't clean the tank, did you, like I told you? No point crying like a girl. It was your responsibility. No, you're not getting a puppy now. You can't be trusted.

Freddie stays watching till Ambrose has vanished through the archway into Vicars' Court. And he's crying like a girl *again*. Yeah, thanks for that, Dad. You were all, prove to me you can be trusted, son, then we'll talk. I was *seven years old*! And you totally stood by and let it happen, let that frog die, just to teach me I can't be trusted? Guess I got *that* lesson down, didn't I?

The birds sing. The golden blossom hangs. Freddie leans his forehead on the glass and weeps. And somewhere else entirely in the diocese of Lindchester there are canal boats gliding at field height through corduroy ridge and furrow meadows. There are little tributary rivers – the Marton, Whistle Brook, the Carding – winding through fields fuzzed with rushes. Somewhere there's a pair of peacock butterflies flirting round the gorse. There are crows following the harrowing tractor, and a bank of cowslips.

And maybe it's going to rain, and maybe not.

On Thursday morning, a sporty black Mini pulls up in a car park in Martonbury. Hold onto your zucchettos, everyone! True to my prediction, Downing Street has just issued the following:

132

The Queen has approved the nomination of the Venerable Matthew Tyler as Suffragan Bishop of Barcup.

The bishop-designate arrives at the Martonbury foodbank, to help serve guests. He goes on to visit St Eadburh's School in Barcup, to dedicate the new Mindfulness Garden and Labyrinth. His wife is not present. She has a full-time job. She attended the welcome meal the night before, and that is quite enough stuffed-shirtery for anyone.

If you check the diocesan website, you'll see that the Bishop of Lindchester, the Rt Revd Steve Pennington, is delighted that Matt has been appointed. He states how much the diocese will benefit from Matt's many gifts as a pastor and strategist.

STRATEGIST!

Cue sinister chords on the Father Willis! Let all who have hands commence to wring them liberally.

We do not favour this love affair with strategy. We have serious reservations about the way things are going in the diocese of Lindchester. It is symptomatic of the entire Church of England – Lindchester as microcosm, if you will.

For who would have dreamt when Dr 'Safe-pair-of-hands' Palgrove was appointed as archbishop of Canterbury, that he would suddenly display such urgency for renewal and reform? Was he not put in as a nightwatchman? He has no business trying to reverse-sweep sixes all over the ground. He and Rupert of York (may he give battle in vain!) seem hell-bent on bypassing existing synodical structures (worrying precedent!) to push through their top–down agenda. Top–down! Since when was salvation top–down? And when did our Lord ever have a strategic plan for evangelization, pray? Well, apart from when he appointed the seventy, and sent them out in pairs ahead of him to all the places he was planning to visit, and gave them detailed instructions about what to say and do. *Apart* from that, when did he?

And now look at Lindchester! The rot set in with Paul Henderson. Until Paul Henderson, Lindchester had always been a gentle middle-of-the-road catholic sort of a diocese. And after him came Slick Steve – who has gone and appointed a suffragan in his own image!

At least when Bob Hooty was in post there was *someone* to put the other point of view, to be a voice crying out in the wilderness that this is all too hasty. But now who's left on the senior staff to sound a note of caution about the course we are on? To complain that it's all too theology- and consultation-light, and too management jargon-heavy? Who will speak up and say that the soul of Anglicanism is in peril, that we are selling our birthright for a mess of business pottage?

Ah, how different things might have been, had Guilden Hargreaves been appointed to the See of Lindchester instead of Stevangelical. *He* would have valued vocation above recruitment. *He* wouldn't have imported non-biblical categories like 'discipleship' into our discourse, over and above traditional scriptural terms like 'inclusive church'. Guilden would have been a shepherd to the diocese, not a CEO! True, he might not have been able to augment 'serious reservations' with 'practical solutions'; but to lament and to act are such divergent charisms, it is wrong to expect any single personal statement to combine them.

#ThyKingdomCome The 'great wave of prayer' for Evangelism During Pentecost ripples through the still waters of the Lindchester diocese. There are some who greet the invitation to pray with joy. Others have a bit of work to do. They may not care for the stable, but in the end, they find a way of backing the prayer pony. If you follow the hashtag, you will get a flavour of what's going on across the diocese.

Lindchester Cathedral is not hosting a Beacon Event, but there is a Lord's Prayer trail which you may explore. In Lindford parish church, Father Dominic and his congregation have been using the Novena booklet (with a Farsi translation) and lashings of incense. It is discovered by accident that labradoodles will eat Prinknash charcoal if it's left lying about the vestry. Father Wendy and her curate Virginia organize a prayer walk around Cardingforth and Carding-le-Willow. In Risley Hill they host a big bless-up and invite the Holy Spirit along. The worship band sings how grade is our guard. Josh, the pioneer minister on the Hollyfield estate in

134

Martonbury, baptizes a family of five in a birthing pool; and someone pinches the collection money.

*

On Pentecost Sunday morning in Lindchester Cathedral, the choir sings Elgar's 'The Spirit of the Lord', of course.

'He hath sent me to heal the broken-hearted, to preach deliverance to the captives and recovery of sight to the blind . . .'

The people come up for communion. Light streams through stained glass and spills in rainbows on them as they pass. 'So the LORD God will cause righteousness and praise to spring forth before all the nations.'

And all over Lindfordshire, the petals drift from apple trees. Gently. Very gently.

Chapter 20

When upon life's billows you are tempest-tossed,
When you are discouraged, thinking all is lost . . .

ather Ed is in his study trying to say his morning office.
It's like having a Sankey and Moody jukebox in the
kitchen! He reminds himself that Neil will be heading
for the station shortly.

'Count your many blessings, name them one by one!'
Ed should count his blessings, of course. They are manifold.
Creation, preservation, all the blessings of this life . . .

'And it will surprise you what the Lord has done!'

*. . . but above all for thine inestimable love in the redemption of the
world . . .*

'Are you ever burdened with a load of care?' Neil sticks his head
round the study door. Booted and suited for London. Ed gets a
waft of bespoke aftershave.

'Frequently,' replies Ed. 'Are you off?'

'In a minute.' Neil comes and sits in the other tatty Dralon
armchair. His gaze scorches over the naff coffee table between
them, with its box of pastoral tissues and bowl of pebbles from a
Northumbrian beach. Ed's study is the one remaining pocket of
resistance to Neil's aesthetic reign.

'Listen, I've been thinking, big man.'

'OK. What is it?'

'I've been thinking I should maybe find another church to go to.'

Silence.

'Because I'm driving you mad. Ah ah ah. Don't argue. You know me – I can't not interfere and tell you how to do your job. But the thing is, I need to be involved in a church that's actually *doing* something.' Neil pauses. 'No offence.'

'Oh, none taken.'

'Och, you know what I mean, Eds.'

'Yes. You mean I should run an Alpha course.'

'Well, you should. But we'll not argue,' says Neil. 'So anyway, I'm asking for a recommendation. Where will I find the right kind of church for me?'

'Hmm.' Ed strokes his chin. 'Which of my colleagues has pissed me off recently?' He ducks out of the way of the cushion. 'OK, if you want a lively charismatic church, there's Risley Hill. Brr!' Ed shivers. 'Or St Mary's, Martonbury. Oh, and St Mary's have got a church plant, if you want something a bit more edgy.'

'Ooh! We like edgy.'

'We're talking "pioneer ministry" here. This is the Wild West of Fresh Expressions. I hear they all wear WWJD Stetsons instead of vestments.'

Neil looks sternly at him. 'These are your brothers in Christ, Eds. What?'

'Nothing. I'll find you the details.'

'Cheers.' Neil leans forward and rummages in the pebble bowl, as though they're Quality Streets and he's after the golden penny. 'Ah, one more thing: what's a reader?'

Ed considers, and rejects, a comment about vocations for frustrated women of a certain age. 'Well, it's a non-ordained ministry. There's a two-year reader training course, and then the bishop licenses them to preach and lead services. Why?'

Neil tosses the pebble back and gets to his feet. 'No reason.'

They hold one another's eye. 'OK,' says Ed.

'OK. Well, I'm away.' Neil blows him a kiss and leaves.

The front door closes, and the Porsche roars off. Ed is safe to laugh out loud. Oh Lord! He shakes his head. Neil, a *reader*? Yes, it *does* surprise him what the Lord has done, frankly. And unless he's mistaken, the Lord has barely started.

Ed returns to Morning Prayer. But something niggles at him. Like unwashed hands, or a half-done chore. He pauses. It's bloody Alpha, isn't it? It's not that he thinks Neil is right – he's not – but Ed struggles to articulate why he is wrong in any way that doesn't sound like Neil's snootiness about Dralon armchairs. Which is ridiculous. Ed objects to Alpha on theological grounds, not because it's naff. Although it is, of course.

A church that actually does *something.*

It's not about *doing*, it's about *being!* Ed wants to shout. He leans forward and picks up the pebble Neil has just tossed back. It's round and flat, like the golden penny. A perfect ducks-and-drakes stone. How long does it take to wear a pebble away to a grain of sand? he wonders. Centuries? Millennia? This pebble might have lain on the beach when the old Northumbrian saints walked there. And now, here it is, in the hand of Ed Bailey, clerk in Holy Orders in twenty-first-century England.

He tries to imagine them – Aidan, Cuthbert, Chad. Missionaries to the pagan Anglo-Saxon tribes. All at once, the saints leave their illuminated pages and become real men who skimmed stones on real beaches. And he glimpses something like a family tree, a thread of light zipping back through the centuries linking him to them, and beyond them, through the Fathers, to the apostles – and Christ himself. It's true, he thinks. I literally have a spiritual ancestry. Why has he never thought this before?

The Anglican family tree has many branches. Do we trace our recent lineage back to the Oxford Movement, to Lightfoot House liberalism, or to Holy Trinity Brompton? Or, giving our leather-bound Bibles a reformed and manly thump (underpinning the faithful proclamation of God's word, and not forgetting the unique value of women's ministry) do we trace ourselves directly to the one mediator between God and men, the man Christ Jesus?

Why does it matter, even? We are all still Anglicans, aren't we?

Indeed we are. But like a bereaved family at the graveside fighting over Grandma's rabbit fur coat, we sometimes lose perspective.

But let us draw back from the big questions. Our brief is to describe one small middle-England diocese. Is it true to say that with Captain Stevangelical at the helm, and Matt the First Mate on the deck, the good ship Lindchester has well and truly left the haven of Lothlórien and set her course for Nafftown? Next week sees the interviews for the two new archdeacons. It will not have escaped your notice that the archdeaconry of Lindchester will shortly become vacant, too. Once all four posts are filled, the bishop will buy a white Persian cat to stroke, and embark on the next stage of his bid for world domination.

Ah, Susanna Henderson, how we will miss you and your stain-removing prowess! I fear there will be blood on the oatmeal palace carpets before the year is out. Because play it whichever way you choose (and believe me, the bishop has played it every possible way as he lies awake at night), the restructure means people will be managed out of posts they have held comfortably for years.

But that lies in the future. For now, May dawdles across an un-suspecting landscape. Unmown rugby pitches are golden with buttercups. The first fiddle tops of new bracken uncurl, fuzzy with bristles like coiled caterpillars. It rains. Oh, the crowding-in grey and green of a wet English May, when puddles look trout-ringed, and roads are ghost-ribboned with tyre marks. Breathe in. What is that smell? Cow parsley and rowan blossom in the rain, nothing more. But to anyone who has ever sat an exam in England, this is the fetid stench of revision and dread.

Well, well, well. Here we are at last. Jane hangs her coat and bag on the stair-post acorn. Silence. Her morning was silent too. Exam invigilation. She looks round. Oak panelled hallway, woodblock floor. She opens a door with a big clacky wooden latch. The lounge. Stone fireplace. Cream walls. Beige carpet. Dents from furniture feet.

Jane goes all round the downstairs. She has no instinct for this, not a Pinterest bone in her body. She isn't making notes for the decorator. Why bother? Magnolia throughout. She'll tell everyone it's Farrow & Ball Georgian Putty. She can live without those sunflower kitchen tiles; but other than that, she has no views at all.

She goes upstairs, clacks more latches and sticks her head into the empty rooms. Six bedrooms. Two bathrooms. Jane is meant to be choosing a study. Matt has a big downstairs study with separate access from outside, plus loo and mini-kitchen, so Jane won't have to negotiate boundaries, or lock horns with his PA over kettle access.

The choice of study is this: front-facing, so she can see who's coming and going; or rear-facing, with a view over the garden. She goes into one of the back bedrooms and looks out. Nice big lawn. Perfect for holding disgraceful champagne-and-shagging garden parties and scandalizing the neighbours.

She flicks a dead bluebottle along the sill. Dammit. This is meant to be fun. It *has* to be fun. Or she's going to end up killing people.

I would love to steer Jane in Gene's direction, so that he can mentor her in her new role. Sadly, nobody else has thought of this. Bishop Steve has wondered whether Sonya might offer moral support? Matt headed this idea off. Ideally, the two bishops should swap houses. Sonya would be near to the kind of church she prefers. And Jane would enjoy the high-camp soap opera which is the Close.

Talking of which, how is Freddie doing? It's Thursday afternoon. He finishes work at Vespas and heads up the hill. He's halfway home when the heavens open. He has no coat, so he shelters in a doorway. Choice: late for rehearsal, or get soaked.

But wait, here comes a man with a big golf umbrella!

It should be Ambrose. That would be perfect. But it's not Ambrose. It's Bishop Steve. Too late to pretend he's not seen Freddie. After a tiny hesitation, he gestures.

'Nah,' says Freddie. 'I'm good.'

'Don't be daft.'

So Freddie ducks under the umbrella. Or kind of half under? Coz personal space? The rain drums down like on a tent. They set off like a bad three-legged race. Well, this isn't at all awkward. Freddie does what he always does – blurts out a bunch of random crap?

'Oh God, that plane going down?'

'I know. Desperately sad,' says the bishop.

'Can't get it out of my head? Like, they would've been still strapped in their seats?'

140

'Probably, yes.'

'And they'd be all, oh my God, I'm gonna die, I'm gonna die? And they'd be in the brace position, with the plane falling, knowing they were all gonna die? Then BOOM!'

'Er. Yes.'

Ah nuts, he's coming across like some kinky disaster junkie, or something? 'I'm only saying, coz that happened to me, when I was coming back from Argentina last time? Only not the actually dying, obviously?' Stop now. Just stop.

'That must've been completely terrifying, Freddie.'

The rain drums. It comes rushing down the cobbles like this is a river they're wading up?

'Yeah, only weirdly? No. It was like . . . In my head, even when everyone was screaming, right at the end, I was all, it's OK, it's OK. Gonna hit the ground running. And he'll be running to get me? Like when you're small, and you're scared, and then you see your dad running to get you? Anyways, so we landed. Everything was fine?' He laughs. Or tries to. 'Yeah.'

'I'm glad.'

They walk in silence till they get to the arch. Gah. Maybe next time, talk about the cricket, yeah?

The rain's eased off but it's still tapping and dripping off the trees all around.

'So yeah, thanks for the——' He gestures at the umbrella. 'Catch you later?'

The bishop watches him sprint off towards the Song School. He thinks of that plane falling off the radar. And of every sparrow. Every life. And the father always running towards us.

Chapter 21

Freddie did not realize, but that awkward conversation under the umbrella almost broke the bishop's heart. Steve was in the Upper Sixth when he lost his father to a sudden massive brain haemorrhage. The last time he saw him was school sports day, 1978. A perfect June afternoon, white lines on fresh-mown grass, swallows flying high, wild roses in every hedge. The bishop remembers it, these days, in slow motion. Second lap of the 800 metres. Kicking off the final bend. The home straight. He passes Johnson and Backhouse. Draws level with Foley. Foley fights back for fifteen metres. But Pennington's got the finish. It's his race. He pulls away. And there's Dad waiting at the finish as he'd promised, cheering, as Steve crosses the line. YES! The roar of the crowd in his ears, lungs bursting, heart bursting, legs giving way. He could see Dad's lips moving: *Well done!* But when he tried to find him afterwards in the throng, he'd vanished. The car was discovered hours later, of course; upside down in a field, still seventeen miles from the school.

Freddie's plane anecdote made it into the bishop's Trinity Sunday sermon. The Father, always running to meet us in the Son, by the Spirit. Elsewhere in the diocese of Lindchester preachers variously used bananas (three sections in one peel); apples (skin=Father, flesh=Son, pips=Holy Spirit); and a triangle of hares with communal ears.

In Father Wendy's Messy Church they coloured in Celtic Trinity patterns and made salt dough Trinity pretzels. Neil, beginning his tour of lively churches, disgraced himself at Risley Hill when he caught sight of the children's cut-out 'Trinity cross' craft activity. (Seriously, HOW could nobody have seen that it looked like a bunch of penises?)

Likewise, the canon precentor – having outsourced the proof-reading of the service booklet to some bungling amateur (mentioning no names, but watch my eyes, Mr Bennet) – lost it while singing 'God in three parsons, blessed Trinity'. Philip, the canon treasurer, was on chorister duty. He used the tried and tested water-steam-ice illustration, and the canon chancellor anathematized him as a modalist.

Our good friend Father Dominic – after reassuring the former Muslims in his flock that the Trinity is not a denial of monotheism – went round to Chloe's to lunch and enjoyed Trinity Sundaes (three flavours of ice cream in one glass). Ambrose was also there.

'Where is he?' asked Chloe, as she poured the Prosecco.

'Not coming.' Ambrose began feeding Cosmo. 'You sure, buddy? Well, OK then. Can you believe he likes wasabi peas?'

'Did you even ask him? Oh, *Ambrose*. Freddie May,' she explained to Dominic. 'He was meant to be coming, but hopeless here's wimped out again.'

'No, I'm just taking it nice and steady, playing the long game,' said Ambrose. 'Sit! Wait . . . Good boy! I'm still wooing him.'

'*Wooing* him?' Chloe hooted. 'What *is* this – the eighteenth century? Whoever says wooing?'

Dominic tried a handful of wasabi peas, and bit back a scream.

'I say wooing. It's a good word.' Ambrose held out another nut. 'Wait . . . Good *boy*!'

'Isn't it a work of supererogation, though?' asked Dominic, eyes watering. 'Like wooing a free buffet.'

Silence. Ambrose carried on feeding the puppy.

Oops. Dominic and Chloe exchanged looks. Oh, come *on*, does he seriously not know what Freddie May's like? Maybe he thinks he can change him. Oh Lord! Good luck with that. But no, who's to say – maybe Freddie *can* change? We can all change. Maybe Dominic Todd should change, and stop being so catty.

'Well, all power to your wooing elbow!' he said, raising his glass.

'"Woo woo ch'boogie!"' sang Chloe.

'Thanks, guys,' said Ambrose. 'And now let's talk about something else.'

So they talked instead about #Brexit, about the Church of Scotland allowing gay ministers to marry, and whether vanilla ice cream was wrongly stigmatized as unadventurous and dull, whereas in fact it was subtly gorgeous and could only be appreciated by a refined palate.

Then they moved on to the newly created Diocesan Social Welfare Officer post. True to his word, Matt had brought Chloe into the frame. She had helped shape the job specification and the wording of the advert (which you may see in the church press and on the diocesan website). The bishop had shaken the Brownlow Trust by the throat until the trustees coughed up the funds. So it looked very much as though Dominic was going to have a clergy colleague at Lindford parish church. Possibly Virginia, possibly not. But either way, goody-good.

But there are other appointments to be made in the diocese of Lindchester first. On Thursday – once Steve has had time to turn round after the meeting of the House of Bishops in York – interviews will take place for the newly created archdeacon posts. The interview panel will be able to make two very good appointments from a strong field. More I cannot say. Please imagine that the successful candidates are much-loved clergy from elsewhere, and will need time to break the news to their current congregations. Meanwhile, if you like, you can exercise yourself with the question: 'And how much are four archdeacons going to cost the diocese, I should like to know?' or lament that there was no proper consultation (which is the Anglican way of complaining that nobody asked you).

It's Friday morning. Bishop Steve is praying, processing yesterday's interviews, committing it to the Lord. He knows he is not a patient man by nature. An 800-metre specialist, not a marathon runner. 'Stephen would do well if he bothered to apply himself' – to quote pretty much every school report he ever got. It's true: he's always been a dilettante blessed with flashes of effortless brilliance.

But love – there is no end to love. Enduring all things, believing all things, hoping all things. He has come to see that the Spirit is gently implacable, like a heavenly mason at work on his pet project. Hasn't he felt it, year on year? The fashioning hand at work, chipping away at his impatience with sustained effort, and replacing it with something more durable. Until he's become a grafter, of all things. Steve Pennington, a grafter!

This is probably his last job, isn't it? There will be no parachuting out of Lindchester to go and be brilliant elsewhere, if he gets sick of fishing all night and catching nothing. He looks at the bookmark in his Bible, as he does every morning: 'Be strong and of a good courage . . .'

The fish are there! But the poor old C of E is toiling through the dark hours, despairing, mending the nets, toiling again, despairing again. Has the word now finally come? 'Put out into the deep water, and let down your nets for a catch.' Deep water – that's where we are all heading, whether we admit it or not. But the catch – the word seesaws between meanings – what's the catch, the miraculous catch?

I am not God. The miracle is not my responsibility, Steve reminds himself. My job is to remain at my post and be faithful. And to overhaul the nets of the diocese – however unpopular that makes me.

It is still green and grey in Lindfordshire, as May drifts to an end. Swallows dip low over cow-squittered meadows. But the rain holds off. Good gracious – fair weather for the Bank Holiday? Unheard of. At last, Ambrose's patience is rewarded. Saturday 8 p.m. His phone buzzes and his heart does a reverse two-and-a-half somersault pike off the high board.

FREDDIE	Yo! You hungry? Pizza overload here. Wanna get involved?
AMBROSE	Maybe. What kind?
FREDDIE	Meat feast.
AMBROSE	Would I like to get involved in your meat feast? Hell yeah.
FREDDIE	LOL. You're dirty ;-)

Guy totally cracks him up. Freddie can never one hundred per cent tell when he's kidding? So yeah, they finish the pizza between them, but then suddenly it's, now what? Hnn. Hadn't thought this one through. Coz maybe Ambrose wasn't kidding, maybe it's about to get awkward?

Freddie starts tugging his hair. They're still at the table, with beers and all the pizza boxes.

'Uh, so listen, Brose – you're . . . still into me? A bit?'

'No.'

Whoa. OK. Read that one wrong.

'I'm into you a lot.'

'Tsh.' Freddie swats him. 'Seriously, no, listen: you do get that I mainly prefer older guys?'

'Oh good. Because I'm thirty-two.'

'Yeah, no, I mean like *a lot* older? Like forties, fifties?'

'OK.'

Man. He does this the whole time? Goes OK, like he's agreeing – only is he? Or is he all, I hear you, dude, but you're wrong?

'Cool. And just so's we're clear, you do get that I'm not vanilla? And I mean, *really* not?'

Ambrose laughs. 'Yes, Freddie. Receiving that loud and clear.'

'OK then. Cool.'

It goes quiet. Guy's smiling at him. Cathedral clock chimes. All the blackbirds singing. Gah! Get me outta this, somebody?

'Would you like to see some close-up magic?' asks Ambrose.

'Whoa!' Freddie sits right up. 'You can do close-up magic? Awesome!'

'Sure. Got a pack of cards?'

Freddie races off, opens random drawers in the dining room. Where does Totty keep them? OK, here they are.

'Man, gotta tell you, I get crazy excited for this stuff? Like it's real magic? Literally?'

Ambrose moves the empty boxes aside, shuffles the deck. Fans the cards. 'Pick one.'

Freddie picks one.

'Look at it.'

Freddie looks at it.

146

'Tell me what it is.'

'Seriously?'

'Seriously.'

'OK. Two of hearts?'

'Ah! Two hearts beating as one. Good. Put it back, anywhere.' Freddie slips the card back. Ambrose shuffles again. 'Now, I'm going to find your card.'

Freddie guffaws. 'Are you for real?'

'Watch.' Very slowly, Ambrose starts dealing the cards out onto the kitchen table. He keeps glancing up at Freddie, like he's checking, is this your card? And Freddie cannot stop laughing. He's literally shaking, crying with laughter? And the whole time, here's Ambrose, super serious, slowly turning the cards over?

He stops. 'Is this your card?'

'Nope.'

'Yes, it is.'

'Is not! That's the ace of diamonds.'

'Yeah. That's your card.'

'Bullshit! Told you, two of hearts. Yeah, it is – and you literally went *two hearts beating as one*!'

'When?'

'Just now!' For one second, Freddie wavers, the guy looks so blank. 'You so did!'

'Really?' He's frowning at the card. 'I thought I said I'll buy you a diamond solitaire.'

'You are so full of shit!' Freddie wipes his eyes. His stomach hurts. 'So where's my card, huh?'

Ambrose sits back. Scratches his jaw. 'Hmm. Maybe you should check your back pocket?'

'No way! No fucking way! This is awesome!' Freddie checks both pockets. 'Nada.'

'Oh.'

Freddie starts laughing again. 'Dude, admit it – you can't do magic at all, can you?'

'I can,' he says. 'I'm doing it.'

Silence. And there's a blackbird still singing? 'Aw, are you getting metaphorical with me again?'

147

He leans forward and whispers. 'Why don't you check in your wallet?'

'Whoa!' Freddie stares at the wallet, lying there on the table from where he paid the Deliveroo guy. 'Get the fuck out of here! Awe-SOME!' So he checks? Nothing. Tosses the wallet back down. '*Man*. Can't believe I just did that.'

'Not there? Weird. Look in the fridge.'

'No fair, dude! Teasing me? Told you I'd believe anything, I'm that crazy for magic.'

Ambrose puts the cards back in the box. He's smiling. 'Then I'll practise a bit more.'

'Yeah right, magic man.'

The minute Ambrose went, Freddie checked in the fridge. How dumb was that? Then he checked the cards, and – well, duh – the two of hearts was there in the deck. But later, when he was getting undressed, he was still kind of half-expecting the card would drop from his shirt, or turn up under his pillow?

Something wakes him in the night. He lies there, listening to the owls, the clock? And he's all, know something – I'm happy? That is so weird, it's like my actual heart is smiling? He drifts back to sleep.

On the other side of the Close, blocked by the cathedral, the blue light of an ambulance flickers.

Flickers.

Flickers.

JUNE

Chapter 22

reddie was one of the last to hear. It was choral half-term, so for once he'd been able to say yes to working a Sunday at Vespas. Traded it for getting Bank Holiday Monday off? All day long he waited tables, and man, he must've got through his entire repertoire of Italian songs, like three or four times? Shedload of tips. Get in!

His heart was still smiling as his shift ended. And he was thinking, tomorrow afternoon, if Brose wasn't already doing something, they could maybe hook up? Not one hundred per cent sure where he was going with this; but hey, the guy made him laugh? Good thing, no? Tomorrow morning was for Miss B's garden, of course. And this time he was *so* not going to let her pay him? Man, it felt good to just help her out for nothing, and not be desperate for the cash? Aw. Love ya, Miss B.

Such were Freddie's happy thoughts, as he jogged back up the hill on Sunday evening. I wish we could spare him. He had inevitably missed all the shocked exchanges that ricocheted round the Close. *Collapsed. Taken away by ambulance.* Of course, there were intercessions at the 10.30 Eucharist and at evensong. Candles were lit and tears shed at the shrine of William of Lindchester. And now there was the helpless waiting.

The canon treasurer and his wife were oblivious. They'd whizzed off on Saturday to their place in Norfolk. Pippa was not going to be there to break the news gently to Freddie. People assumed he already knew; indeed they rather hoped – when he arrived back from work – that he might have an update. This was what ran through the mind of the senior lay clerk, when he passed Freddie under the big archway onto the Close.

'Freddie. How are you coping? Any news?'

'Hnn?' Guy was all, I'm so sorry for your loss? 'What? Dude, you're kinda freaking me out here?'

'Oh no!' Nigel laid a hand on Freddie's arm. 'You haven't heard?'

'Heard what?' He felt his pulse kick into overdrive. 'What's happened?'

'Sweetie, it's Ambrose. I am really sorry.'

'Oh, Jesus. What happened?'

'I'm sorry, we all thought you knew. He's in hospital.'

Freddie could hear Nigel talking. *Stroke. Middle of the night. Ambulance. Intensive care.* It was all echo-y, like in a movie, when something super bad's happening? But I saw him only last night! He was fine! Freddie heard his own voice going, 'Oh my God. He's gonna be OK?'

Running tests. His cousin's with him. Waiting to hear more.

'Oh my God. I don't believe this?'

He felt Nigel grip his arm. 'Are you all right, sweetie? Listen, Alan and I are in tonight. Come to us. I'm just off to buy wine. Yes? Freddie?'

'Yeah, no, yeah.' He blotted his eyes. 'Thanks, but Imma go to Miss B?'

'Of course. Would you like me to walk over with you? No? Well, you take care, Freddie. Really sorry to break it to you like that. Ring me if we can do anything. Promise?'

'Sure. Thanks, man.'

Nigel watched him go. Damn damn *damn.* You cack-handed *idiot*, Bennet, assuming he knew. Would Freddie be all right? Should he follow and make sure? No. Miss Blatherwick was a safe pair of hands. She'd look after him.

But Nigel had forgotten that Miss Blatherwick was away for the Bank Holiday weekend, visiting her friend Christine down in Barchester. Freddie had forgotten this, too. It came back to him just as he reached out to press her bell. No-o-o-o! You knew this, numbnuts. This was why you were gonna do her garden tomorrow morning – surprise her when she got back?

He sat on her doorstep and wept. Shit. *Shit!* All he could think of was Ambrose? Only last night! Laughing at me, all 'Then I'll practise a bit more.' What if he never got the chance? What if that was *it*? Oh God, let him be OK, let him be OK? Jesus, he can't *die*! But what if he does?

The blackbirds were all still whistling, like nothing had happened? This can't be real. What am I gonna do now? Oh Miss B, why aren't you here?

Then he was remembering Andrew that time? Saying, *I do regret the time I wasted not believing my good fortune.* I can't ring him. Can't.

He rang him.

'Mr May. How lovely.'

'Dude, is this a good time? Only I didn't know who else to call? Oh God.'

'What's wrong?'

Freddie spilled it all out.

'You poor darling,' said Andrew. 'Now listen carefully. As is your wont, you're busy catastrophizing. You haven't established the facts yet. Ssh. No – listen to me, please – no, those aren't *facts*, Freddie. Those are the whispers going round the Close echo chamber. You need to ring the hospital—'

'Dude, I can't! I just can't? They won't talk to me, plus I don't know what ward, or—'

'Stop. You're panicking, sweetheart. I'll ring for you. What's his surname?'

'Uh, Hardman?'

'Ah! Always good to find, as Mae West so sapiently remarked. Which hospital?'

'Lindford General? But no way will they tell you. Dude, it's not like you're his next of kin, or anything. Why—'

'Oh, I'm very persuasive. I'll ring you back. In the meantime, I want you to go and find Mr Bennet and take him up on his kind offer. Hush, manchild; do as you're told.'

'Oh God, Andrew – what if he dies?'

'What if he doesn't?' Silence. 'Why not focus your thoughts

153

there instead? I'll ring you back. So, to recap: what are you going to do next?'

'Uh, find Nigel and Alan, I guess?'

'Good. And what am I going to do?'

'Ring the hospital?'

'I am. Then I will ring you with some proper information, and we can take it from there. *Ciao, bello.*'

It is June now. The wind strokes a hand over the silky barley fields. Bracken fronds have unfurled into ostrich plumes. The early hay has been mown. Nettles fire off puffs of pollen in the sunshine. The elderflower is out. It smells the way wren song sounds – sharp, clear. Essence of a June day. Bottle it, save it, hoard it while you can.

In the south people turn their heating on and moan. Rain lashes Europe. Paris floods. But here in the Midlands the warm weather holds. Tar bubbles on country lanes and the careless get sunburnt. There are elms in leaf, dropping their hoppy seedpods on woodland paths. They are the offspring of giants felled in the seventies, suckers from long-gone stumps, but they too will succumb to disease before they reach maturity.

So May has gone. We may never live to see another.

But I am sporting with your patience, dear reader. Like Freddie, you are anxious to know the facts of poor Ambrose's condition. You have already discerned, I'm sure, that this is no *Game of Thrones* narrative. We do not repeatedly lure the reader into caring about someone, just in time to see them killed off. Occasionally we hurl characters off rooftops, but there is something there to break their fall.

This is unrealistic, of course. In the real world, nobody is safe. Bad things happen to good people. In the real world, the Divine Author does not intervene and put stuff right, even when to do so is clearly a no-brainer. Escapist Anglican nonsense? Perhaps. But like travellers on a train who see the sun bouncing off puddles and distant windscreens, readers may get a glancing reflection of some bright truth from the lies that fiction tells.

*

Freddie passed under the lime trees on his way to Vicars' Court. The blackbirds whistled heartlessly. Someone was barbecuing. Life went on, the way life does.

Suddenly he remembered the hymn he sang at Bishop Paul's farewell service: 'It is well with my soul.' Back then, he'd googled it and discovered the heartbreak that lay behind the words. And he'd known he could never do that, never say it was well with his soul, when blatantly, it wasn't? But now, as he walked, something crept up on him. Like an arm round his shoulders? Like when the plane was going down – *Brace! Brace! Brace!* – but a voice in him was going, *It's OK. I've got you.* And weirdly? He kinda knew this would be OK too, whatever happened. Somehow Ambrose was safe? 'Even so, it is well with my soul.'

When his phone rang, he was almost calm. And yes, Ambrose was safe. Not a stroke. He'd suffered a sudden attack of labyrinthitis – infection of the inner ear – that had knocked him flat as a drunken sailor in a force ten gale. He was likely to be kept in for several days, and was currently on a drip to prevent dehydration, and off his face on benzodiazepine. Freddie could visit – though he mustn't expect to get much sense out of him.

'Whoa, persuasive or what? How come they told you all that?'

'A mystery! Perhaps they thought I was the bishop of Lindchester?' said Andrew.

'You *lied*? Dude!'

'Merely a precaution. I feared my own name might not prove a ticket to Mr Hardman's good will. Imagine that.' He sighed. 'Still, as I suspected, he was happy for the ward clerk to update the bishop.'

The bishop of Lindchester, little knowing that his name had been taken in vain, is having a moan to his EA during their diary session (shoehorned into Tuesday morning, because of the Bank Holiday).

'Well, judging by the number of delegations and handbaggings and angry emails I've had,' he says, 'I am simultaneously taking the diocese down an evangelical route, *and* a worryingly liberal one.'

'Must mean you're getting it about right, then,' says Kat. 'Looking ahead—'

'To what can I compare this diocese?' Steve flings his arms wide. 'We played Hillsongs to you, and you did not dance! We held a Service of Benediction, and you did not genuflect!'

Kat stares at him steadily. 'Right. So looking ahead. Next week, couple of things. Shared conversation guys and synod reps, meeting at the palace. I've got it down for a finger buffet. Do you want me to book the caterers?'

'No, no. I think Sonya's happy to do that.'

'Really?' Kat makes a note. 'OK. You're the boss.'

The bishop swallows the implied insult to his wife's culinary skills. Or is it thoughtfulness, relieving her load? He chooses to believe the latter. 'Actually, you know what – book the caterers. Then Sonya can go to Zumba after all.'

'Sure?' Bright smile. 'OK.'

Half-term comes to an end. Holidaymakers inch home along motorways towards Lindfordshire behind self-aggrandizing caravans. The Excite-Me Buccaneer Pro-Glide Plus. The Mutual-Climax Marauder. The 4x4s head up the pilgrim way and deliver choristers back to the school. Virginia proofreads her application for the post of Diocesan Social Welfare Officer one last time, then hits send.

Miss Blatherwick takes her cup of peppermint tea (soothing for the digestion) into her little garden, to enjoy the nice tidy beds and pray for Freddie and Ambrose. Oh, if only she'd been here! But no, Freddie was fine. He doesn't need matroning.

Ambrose is discharged from hospital to his cousin's house. Apparently, Freddie had visited, but Ambrose must have been well out of it. He's lost weight, feels horrible. He's still cornering on two wheels. But he lasts the journey and makes it up the stairs to Chloe's spare room without vomming.

Swirly-whirly-whirly.

It will pass. He's an ox. Tells himself it's a hammock, lazy day, drifting. He remembers the nurse saying, 'Is this your playing card? It was under the pillow.' He smiles. He'd known without looking: two of hearts.

Chapter 23

I n? Out? The EU referendum hokey-cokey is hotting up in Lindfordshire. The bishop of Lindchester – without, of course, telling people how to vote – urges everyone to take this seriously, inform themselves, make prayerful decisions and exercise their democratic duty. It has to be said that the posters in windows and on wayside hoardings across the diocese mostly have a #Brexity flavour. The joint debating society of Queen Mary's Girls' and Queen Mary's Boys' Grammar Schools in Lindford proposes that 'This House believes Britain is better out than in the EU' – and the sons and daughters of Lindcastrian yeomen carry the motion.

On Wednesday evening, Lindchester Cathedral hosts a referendum debate, with an august panel, including the local MP (leave) and Lindford University's vice chancellor (remain). The dean (remain, but scrupulously neutral throughout proceedings) will be chairing the discussion. Serious-minded people from all over the region will attend. Dr Jane Rossiter – will she be there?

What? You think Jane is going to waste an hour and a half of her life listening to doom-mongering Murdoctrinated members of the public, while they spout – under the guise of asking a question – a bunch of 'facts' about immigration, or quote some fictitious percentage of the EU budget squandered on admin; and otherwise spill great vats of toxic slurry dredged up from the collective unconscious of England, my England?

She would rather snort wasabi. On the grounds that even if her brain exploded out through her ears, at least it would be over quickly.

Hell, she would *even* rather sit through a three-hour pre-board meeting in an un-air-conditioned room, listening to colleagues arguing about marks and in-year reassessment. Indeed, this is exactly what she has just been doing. But she must *still* drive up to the Close rather than go home for a shower and a beer, because Matt's Mini is in for a service, and the man needs a lift home. This does *not* mean – however much Mister Archdeacon has hinted that she might like to join him for the debate – that Jane is going to subject herself to the xenophobic rhetoric of a bunch of rubicund spunk-trumpets. No siree, Bob. She's going to park at William House, then go to the King's Head for an IPA, to underline her stance against the invidious mission creep of Matt's vocation.

She gets out and slams the car door. Her clothes are sticking to her. She blots her face on her sleeve. Ah, she can already taste the hops, is mentally pressing the beer glass to her cheek and sighing in bliss! Blood pressure is returning to normal. But as she leaves the car park there's a lean, sinuous figure loitering in her path. Someone she's meant to recognize, judging by his demeanour.

'My *very* dear Mrs Bishop-to-be of Barcup!' He holds out a fey hand. 'And how are we this evening?'

Jane eyes his hand but doesn't take it. 'We are in an advanced state of murderous ill-humour,' she says. 'And you are. . . ? I want to say Dick.'

'Gene.'

She considers this. 'Nope. Still want to say Dick.'

He laughs. 'I love you already! I'm Mr Dean, clergy spouse and fellow-sufferer. Are you off to join the Lumpenproletariat in the cathedral—'

Jane snorts.

'—or can I tempt you to a drink in the deanery garden?'

'Now we're talking. Got any beer in your fridge?'

'Certainly not.' He gives a dainty shiver. 'But I *do* have a rather special 2011 Nuits Saint Georges Clos de L'Arlot already chilled.'

'Oh, go on then,' says Jane. 'I've got drunk on worse.'

It is now less than six weeks till Matt is consecrated. I suddenly feel a lot better about Jane becoming a bishop's wife.

Come, I must trouble you to fly with me once more. If you wish, you may leave red, white and blue vapour trails across the grey sky for the official celebration of Her Majesty's ninetieth birthday. Listen! That is the sound of Walton's 'Crown Imperial' being coaxed from all organs great and small. Red, white and blue flowers grace the pedestals of both town and country churches. Parry rehearsals waft from the cathedral Song School. With the *Vivats*! Ooh, the *Vivats*! Red, white and blue bunting – finally dried out from the 2012 washout of the diamond jubilee – decks streets and church- yards and vicarage gardens. Gazebos sprout up, ready for parties. People consult their weather apps. In? Out?

Wheat stands thick and motionless in campion-trimmed fields. Ah, there is so much that's soft and gentle this June, this warm and hazy June. The bowing grass feathers, the haze of Queen Anne's lace, the floating willow fluff, the felted moss carpets creeping over stones and paths.

Father Wendy notices all this as she walks through waist-high weeds along the riverbank. Beloved, let us love, she thinks. Let us be soft, let us be kind, forgiving, being forgiven. Let forgiveness creep like moss over all our hard rocky places.

Lest you think that Father Wendy does nothing but walk her three-legged dog along the Linden for a living, we will join her in her study, where she has just concluded Virginia's ministerial development review thingy. Her very last one! Goodness, where have those three years gone?

'May I say something, Wendy?' asks Virginia.

'Of course.' Eek! Like all good-hearted folk, Wendy automatically assumes that the *something* will be something unpleasant. Virginia is quite a long way into her speech before Wendy grasps that she's being unreservedly thanked for all she has done in her role as training incumbent.

'And you've taught me not to take myself too seriously,' says Virginia very, very seriously. 'I've become much less black and white

159

in my thinking as well. Wendy, I never told you this, but when things fell through at Risley Hill, I was bitterly disappointed.'

'Well, of course you were,' says Wendy.

'I'm afraid I was ungracious to you.'

'Well.' Wendy scans for a way of contradicting this truthfully, and settles for a forgiving pastoral silence instead.

'If I'd gone to Risley Hill, I'm pretty sure I wouldn't have changed and grown like this, or got involved in social justice issues,' states Virginia. 'I doubt very much if I'd've stood for General Synod, either. What I'm really saying is, even if I don't get the job next week, I'm confident this is the kind of ministry I'm called to. So I just want to thank you for . . . everything.'

'Oh! Bless you, that's very kind. I'm not sure what I've *done*, exactly. But thank you.'

'You've modelled another way of being church,' says Virginia. 'And although I don't share all your views on scripture and marriage and so on, I do respect your position. And I can accept that there's a . . . breadth.' Virginia conveys this breadth with a preacherly gesture. It is roughly eighteen inches wide.

'Yes, a breadth,' agrees Wendy. 'I've always loved that John Robinson quote, myself: "The Lord hath more truth and light yet to break forth out of his holy word".'

'Of course.' Provided it's the right kind of light and truth, Virginia appears to be thinking.

'Well, I'll be praying for you on Tuesday. What time's the interview?'

'I'm on at eleven.'

After Virginia has left, Wendy turns and nearly says, Oh, Lulu! But Lulu has been gone a long time. Now there is Pedro. So she talks to Pedro instead.

'Oh, Pedro. I was a very poor second best for Virginia, wasn't I? But it seems to have worked out all right.'

A quotation comes to her. Tolkien. She's wrestled with it over the years. 'Things might have been different, but they could not have been better.' 'Is that true, Pedro?'

Would this be what she really thought, at the very last, when she looked back on it all? That despite the deaths, the grief and woe, it could not have been better?

Personally, I'm fairly clear things would not have been better for Virginia at Risley Hill. All is not well in that church. Archdeacon Bea was a bit perturbed by her visitation, you will remember. She had a word with her colleague, Matt, and got the history. She now knows about the rector's close friendship with another man's wife a few years back. Just a friendship. A miscommunication. A nothing. But a nothing which nonetheless spelt the end of Becky and Martin Rogers' marriage.

We have noted Laurie, the rector, standing a little too close to his intern, and bathing her in his sincere approval. What's his game? Does he have one? Is this the tip of an iceberg, or is it just a little free-floating chunk of ice? It's probably nothing at all. Another nothing.

But I'm glad Virginia ended up as Father Wendy's curate.

Sonya got home from Zumba on Thursday to find the bishop loading the dishwasher.

'How did it go?'

'It went.'

'—went. Oh dear! Was it awful?'

'Pretty awful. I could cheerfully strangle m'friend Roland. He won't *listen*. And with the best will in the world, nobody can have a shared conversation with a foghorn.'

'—horn. What did he say?'

'Abomination!' Steve scraped the remains of the caterers' finger buffet into the bin. 'The myth of the fixed gay identity!'

'—titty. Yes, but don't we think it's a myth, too? I thought we did.'

Steve slammed the dishwasher shut. All the wine glasses jangled. 'How was Zumba?'

'Oh, fine. Did that nice guy from the choir come? You know, thingy? The one who's been so? Him?'

'Ambrose? No. He's still signed off. But his cousin Chloe was there.' Steve frowned.

'What?'

'Nothing. Look, sorry, love, I'm going for a stroll, to clear my head. Sorry to be such a grump.'

Steve had learnt over the years that you could outwalk your irritations, the way you could outwalk a cloud of midges. He headed down the steep steps off the Close, then out along the Linden. For the first half-mile, they were still whining round his head. Argh! How he hated the scheming and conniving, the manipulative rhetoric on both sides of the debate! The threats and bullying, online and off. Roland! Oh, I would not be – not quite – so sure as you! Even if you are right. Oh, poor old Sonya – he'd nearly bitten her head off back then.

I'm going to run away and teach English on some remote Pacific island! I hate you all! And you hate me back! I *know* you call me second-choice Steve! I know you'd prefer that hand-wringing fop from Barchester Theological College!

Oops, here came the most terrifying of the cathedral dames. He smiled and murmured a greeting as they passed one another. Please say he hadn't been ranting out loud. He carried on striding. The midges were falling behind now. He found space for that little puzzle from earlier: Chloe thanking him for ringing the hospital to ask after Ambrose. He'd slipped into autopilot, winging it. Clearly, she was touched by his pastoral concern, so it seemed best to take the credit with a self-deprecating smile. Mystery, though. Maybe he had a doppelgänger. Good. The doppelgänger could run the diocese while Steve drank rum punch on his island.

Steve had not been ranting out loud, but he had looked sufficiently mithered to earn himself a place on Miss Blatherwick's prayer list. By the time he reached the footbridge, his soul had returned to its rest. He caught a glimpse of himself as a gnat whining in God's ear, and laughed. Lord, how small we all are.

Chapter 24

illow fluff hangs in the air. Moss creeps over stony paths. But where is the softness now? Here, here in our flesh. How small we are. Why do we have no tough hide, no plated shell? Why have we evolved as if for trust?

Those were Father Wendy's thoughts, as she walked along the Linden on Monday morning, thinking about the gay nightclub massacre in Orlando. She remembered – of course she did – her daughter, Laura, on that zebra crossing all those years ago. How absurdly easy we are to kill. Look at this poor skin of ours! We have no defences, none, against hatred and knives and bullets, against hurtling mangling metal.

'Things might have been different, but they could not have been better.' Can she say that? No! How could things *not* have been better? If the driver had not been distracted; the assault rifle not bought, not made, not invented. Oh, to wind back, and make this not happen. Make it never, ever happen.

Mary, mother of us! All Wendy can think of is blood. Spilled. Tipped over. Wasted. There is nowhere to take her pain, except to the cross. She can do nothing but weep there, in that terrible place where there was no defence against hatred, nails and spear, or the sword that pierces the heart.

Across the world candle flames burn. Rainbow flags flutter at half-mast.

'Well, it looks as though muggins here is the lightning conductor again,' said the bishop. 'At least he said it to my face this time. I suppose that's progress.'

Kat had her *If you say so* expression on. 'I'm guessing you've not checked Twitter, then.'

'Argh!' The bishop flung his hands up. 'Do I want to?'

'You don't. Out of interest, why didn't you tell him you're going to the vigil?' she asked. 'He'll think you changed your mind because of him.'

'Then let him think that. Kat, he's hurting.'

'We're all hurting,' she said. 'But he's bang out of order, barging through here like that and screaming at you.'

'Yes, well. Setting aside his manner, what do you think about what he says?'

There was a long silence. Steve waited. 'OK,' said Kat. 'Here's what I think. Freddie says he's being "erased"? Maybe he should try being a gay black woman.'

There was another silence.

'That's a fair point,' said the bishop.

'He didn't even acknowledge my existence just now. I mean, we're not playing Top Trumps here, but you know?'

'Yes,' said Steve. 'I'm glad we aren't, because I'd probably lose.'

Kat half-laughed. 'You'd *so* lose, Steve. At least you realize that. But Freddie?' She shook her head. 'Don't get me wrong. I care about him. But there's not much room in Freddie May's head for anyone except Freddie May.'

The bishop's crime had been to ask for prayers for the victims of Orlando without mentioning the LGBTI community. He then responded – aghast at himself – with another blunder: that of *presuming* to pray for the LGBTI community, while opposing equal marriage. It looked as though the only mistake he had managed to avoid was that of remaining silent.

He took a coffee back into his office to calm down, whereupon he foolishly ignored his EA's advice. Ah yes. How charming. @FreddieMayTenor, deploying the LoveWins hashtag like an incendiary device. Boom. How do you like them apples, homophobe? Maybe when he was as old as Methuselah Steve would just shrug this kind of thing off. 'Jesu, lover of my soul, let me to thy bosom fly.'

Once he was composed, he went back out to face the coming week, and to check that Kat was doing all right. Did she want to take the day off?

No, she was fine, but thanks for the thought. They went through the diary. Interviews tomorrow for the social welfare officer; ordination of priests on Saturday; meeting with the dean, Matt and Helene from HR on the restructure; announcement of the two new archdeacon appointments the following week. Hah, a chance to be hated by the arch conservatives instead, unless he was very much mistaken. 'Cover my defenceless head with the shadow of thy wing.'

Jane was supposed to spend Monday in a day-long faculty training session. Before she met Matt, she would have had no qualms about throwing a sickie; but the man had such a sweet dogged diligence to him, dammit, that she was shamed into professionalism. So here she was in Sweet FA Lecture Room 2. And she didn't even have the heart to play bullshit bingo with her poet friend, Spider. The full house – synergy, light touch, deep dive, digging down, solutions-focused, moving forward – slipped by unticked.

At lunchtime, she escaped to the park to eat her Sainsbury's meal deal. She glanced up at the sign by the gate as she entered. There was the familiar blue logo with its ring of yellow stars. Lindford arboretum, regenerated by those bastards in the EU, pumping their bastard millions into the run-down provinces. Did Jane trust the Brexiteers to look after anything outside London and the home counties? Did she bog roll.

She found a bench facing the lake. Sometimes there were kingfishers, would you believe it. Here, in the centre of Lindford. She got her phone out to check the news. Jesus. Really? Scoring political points off Orlando? What's *wrong* with you people? Oh, what are we doing here, Matt? Let's run away to New Zealand. Let's be *migrants*, and abandon this toxic fractured me-first other-hating country.

165

I miss my baby boy, she realized. Be safe, Danny. She should have known not to read those desperate text messages from the nightclub. *Mommy I love you. They shooting.* Damn. *Damn* this toxic fractured me-first other-hating race we belong to. Let's hold a referendum on humanity: better in, or out?

Jane stared across the lake. And there went the kingfisher, low, fast, piping as it went. She caught a bright patch of light flickering on the water. A ring of stars. Ah bollocks. Migraine.

Nothing else for it. She got up and headed home to sleep it off, handing her lunch to the homeless guy on the next bench. Before long, all words would turn to scribble. Tears began to leak out. Let them. Handy pressure valve. So what was this all about then? It was usually some massive iceberg she'd failed to spot. Ah yes. She'd leave if it wasn't for Matt, be long gone to New Zealand by now. Turquoise sea. Kingfisher sea. Halcyon days down under. But Matt still believed. Believed there was an anti-venom. Believed the cross made a difference. He voted Remain.

By now her head was a shaken tin of spangling brangling metal triangles. She blotted the tears with a sleeve. There was no leaving. There was no believing, either. Just a desperate grab for the coat-tails of Matt's faith.

People gathered. In Florida, in Soho, in Sydney. They packed the streets. They linked arms. They sang. Humanity: best of races, worst of races. In the cathedral, Dean Marion led the vigil for Orlando. She spoke of the prophet Elisha. 'Open our eyes, Lord. Let us see that those who are with us are more than those who are with them.'

The bishop was at the Lindford vigil, in St James's in the heart of the clubbing district, where the street pastors scoop up the helpless and lost. Many of our friends were there. On the church floor, a circle of tea lights twinkled like stars. Geoff, the vicar, led the prayers. Then a man began to sing in the silence. An old revivalist hymn. 'Jesus paid it all. All to him I owe.'

'Och, would you believe, nobody knew it!' lamented Neil. 'Do you know it? Why not? I thought they'd all join in!'

'Well, I'm sure you sang beautifully, darling,' said Ed.

'Right. So there was me, like a big jessie, voice cracking. Come on, guys, little help here?' Neil shook his head. 'I thought ma wee friend from the choir might bail me out, but no. Sat there on the floor all wrapped up in his rainbow flag. Och, don't look at me like that, we all know he's a drama queen – there were people looking out for him.'

'Good.'

'Then *finally* someone joins in – thank you, bishop! He was there, the bishop. Me and Dom and a bunch of others took him for a drink afterwards. In the Lion.'

'No! You're kidding me.'

'Why not?' demanded Neil. 'He havered, but I said Ah ah. What would Jesus do, bishop? I *think* you'll find he'd go and drink with the sinners, am I right? So we'll have no arguing, if you please.'

Ed laughed. There were no immovable objects in the path of Neil's irresistible force. Well, that would give the diocesan comms officer an exciting hour or two, if the story got into social media. A bishop walks into a gay bar . . . He couldn't wait to hear Dom's version.

Neil was half-right. There were people looking out for Freddie. But he fended them off. #LoveWins, right? Then how come he was eaten alive by hate? That hymn totally killed him. 'Jesus paid it all.' That's the one that swung it, back in juvie, in chapel – converted him? 'Sin had left a crimson stain, He washed it white as snow.' And then the plane landing safely? Ah cock, he was *so* not gonna be like this ever again? But this morning? Yep, there he is, screaming at Paul? (Face palm: *Steve.*) Sure, he can say sorry, and Steve'll be all, I forgive you, let's draw a line under it – AGAIN. Freddie has zero credibility here. Talking the talk, all, ooh, #LoveWins, when honestly? He's just as big of a hater himself.

And Chloe and Ambrose, they're all, come back with us for a bit? But he can't face it. Man, they are both so sweet, and the vibe tonight is all so 'What unites us is stronger than what divides us'? He knows he'll only spoil it. Catch you later, guys.

167

And the world goes on. Virginia goes for her interview, and gets the job. Last year's deacons pack their bags and go on their ordination retreat. Hedges are thick with honeysuckle. Thunder mumbles off stage. Flash floods drown the golf courses of Lindfordshire, turning lanes into rivers and dips into fords. The sun comes out, and for a moment the grass heads are made of light, though no one sees it.

On Thursday Father Wendy drives to the crematorium for a funeral. She passes the landfill and thinks of buried sin. Turfed over, watered. A green hill far away.

She hears the news on the radio as she drives home. Jo Cox, MP. Murdered in her Leeds constituency.

Scrap your sermons. Start anew. Write something like this: We must throw away our divisions, our hatred, our greed. We must bury them all, turf them over, water them with tears, if we are ever to inhabit – leave or remain – a green and pleasant England.

Father Dominic is trying to write his sermon. But he can't concentrate. He's remembering school, and how much he hated it. Todd, you big fag, lend us your English essay. *Slaughterhouse 5*. Suddenly he recalls the passage about reverse time. The un-bombing of Dresden. Planes flying backwards, dousing the fires, sucking the bombs back up. The women in the factories dismantling them, the specialists burying the components. Hiding them. Where they will never be found. 'So they would never hurt anyone ever again.' That was the quote.

He thinks of Pulse nightclub. The bullets sucked back into the rifle. The wounds closing. The dead getting back up. The events in Birstall reversing themselves, Jo Cox alive again. And not just that – all the bullets, all the hate in all the world, in all of human history, all sucked back out, undone, dismantled, buried. And no more hurting and destroying in all God's holy mountain.

Chapter 25

The summer solstice dawns. The longest day of the year, we tell one another, northern-centrically. Longest of days, shortest of days. It all depends on your point of view. Everything depends on your point of view, because the British people are sick of experts. What's important is *your* truth. Postmodernism has gone to seed, bolted like old rhubarb. Rhubarb, rhubarb, rhubarb. Words can mean whatever you want them to mean, facts are anything you conveniently invent – and there's glory for you. Glory, glory, hallelujah, in the Humpty-Dumpty EU referendum debate. Why, it is purely my whimsy that today our planet's rotational axis is most inclined towards the sun, and that it is therefore the summer solstice in the northern hemisphere. You believe whatever you like.

Petrol rainbows smear on roads and run down the gutters. The sun comes out again. Mackerel sky, mackerel sky over the diocese of Lindchester. Not long wet, not long dry.

It's Jane's birthday. Fifty-five today. She should really get up, but she's still wrung out after last week's triple migraine extravaganza. Like a hangover with none of the fun beforehand. There's a breakfast tray on the bedside table, a red rose in a vase, empty cafetière, croissant shrapnel. She stretches. A bumblebee shadow floats on the muslin curtain. Old *bombus*, droning like a Lancaster bomber.

This is it. This week. In, or out? She ponders the curious suspended state on *this* side of any liminal event. Losing your virginity, for example. Nothing you read, or imagine, or hear, can convey the experience in advance. There is no shortcut. You have to go through that door yourself, in order to look back and ask if that was it.

Or getting your degree results. Hah, not quite such a public ordeal these days, is it? Jane can vividly remember that walk across Oxford to check the board at the Examination Schools; the weird timelessness when the results were already decided, but she didn't yet know. A day much like this, gravid with rain and eschatological menace.

Or getting married. That before/after divide. The bride in the porch. The groom waiting. (Not that it had been like that for Jane.) Wait, what about giving birth? – good one! She recalls her surprise at seeing the cot wheeled into the delivery room. That was when she grasped it was *really* going to happen. This bump would be a baby in the cot. Hell, our foremothers made their wills before their confinement. Yes, it would soon be over; the babe would be out. Maybe you'd both be alive, and maybe not.

Yeah – death. No shortcuts and evasions there. We all have to go through that door by ourselves, and face the results of the ultimate referendum: sheep/goat? Not that she believed in all that. But, oh, Shakespeare was right. Conscience makes cowards of us all, as we contemplate that undiscover'd country . . .

What undiscovered Britain lies on the other side of the vote? Life is comprised of moments like these, she thinks. When it all hangs in the balance, could still go either way – until it goes one way. The box is opened and the cat is dead. She thinks of all the players of history, whose life's narrative looks so fixed now – it was like this for them, too. All those votes and arguments; the battles, plots, negotiations, all the human schemes that *could* have gone either way. They would have felt contingent upon so many variables at the time, only to be reduced to plonking determinism in the student exam scripts she'd just been marking. She imagines GCSE history questions decades from now: *What were the causes of Britain's vote to leave the EU in 2016?* Or: *What were the reasons why Britain voted to remain in the EU in 2016?*

But this pregnant pause, this holding of the breath, will be forgotten and swallowed up in what happens next. In, out. Win, lose. Yes, no.

Such are Jane's musings on her fifty-fifth birthday on Midsummer morning. Tuesday, Wednesday, Thursday still lie ahead. A little plane toodles above the Lindfordshire landscape trailing a *Vote Leave* banner. A few valiant souls – including Ambrose (now more or less recovered) and Chloe – campaign door to door for Remain. Chloe is called a chink, and told to go back where she came from.

In Lindford General there are births and deaths. Elsewhere committees action things, or not. People shop and book their holidays. They renew their passports. They pay rent, or mortgages. They claim their benefits, or beg. They go to work, they look for work. They splash out, they eke out.

The clock ticks. The unimaginable approaches. On Thursday morning myriad little plywood portals will open up to the undiscover'd post-referendum country, from whose bourn no traveller returns. We must all walk into the booth alone and make our cross. There will be no time-travelling Doctor to report back from 2020 with reassurances or warnings.

You, dear reader, have the advantage over my characters. You could be the Doctor. You could seize them by the lapels and remonstrate. You could open champagne and pour them a congratulatory glass. Depending on your point of view – and assuming any of this were real. But we will linger here a bit in the limbo of ignorance, where my people are still processing other matters.

There is sport! The European Championship is unfolding. English cricket and rugby are prospering. We may barely spare them a nod, overshadowed as they are by the Referendum. The ordinations in Lindchester diocese straddle the great divide. Priests last Sunday, deacons this. The two new archdeacons will be unveiled on Friday. If Bishop Steve truly were the cat-stroking Bond villain some take him to be, this would be an excellent week to bury the news that he has appointed a gay woman to the post of archdeacon of Lindford. But he really isn't that clever. He wasn't even clever enough to spot *quite* how his WWJD drink in a gay bar was going to play among his more conservative clergy. He has morphed into a curious hybrid: the homophobic gay Mafioso.

Ah, if only all this had happened hereafter, there might have been time for many words on these matters. But events have overtaken us, dear reader. Your author is not omniscient. Nor am I omnipresent. We cannot be everywhere all at once. We must choose.

We will fix upon Tuesday, after evensong. Poor Freddie had not yet found a way out of the corner he'd hated himself into. 'Love your neighbour as yourself' does not play so well, if you are locked in self-loathing.

'How are you doing?' asked Ambrose. 'I was worried about you after the vigil.'

And there it was. *Worried about you*. In his experience that was code for: Look everyone, Freddie's gonna do something irresponsible and dumb again. Cue the judging.

'I'm good,' he said. 'Hooked up with a couple of guys, went back to their place?'

'Did that work out for you?' Ambrose asked.

They were standing under the big lime trees on the Close. Swifts and swallows flittered low over the grass.

'Excuse me? This is none of your business. Seriously.'

'OK.'

'No, not OK.' Freddie got right up in his face. 'Don't do that *OK* thing, when you're totally disagreeing with me? So I went back to their place, and yeah, we got fucked off our faces, had ourselves a threesome, and know what? It was good, it was fine. Is that *OK* with you?'

'If you're happy, yes.'

'Yeah, I'm happy.' He stepped back. 'And I don't owe you anything. Not a thing. Just so's we're clear?'

Ambrose raised a hand, like you do in class, when you're not sure the teacher's gonna like it. 'Actually, you still owe me another fifty quid. For doing your tax?'

'Shit.' Freddie's face burned. 'Totally forgot about that. Oh man, really sorry.' He checked his wallet. Shit. Must've spent it. 'Uh, listen, lemme go to the cashpoint?'

'No rush.'

'No, no, no. I'm on it.'

'Well, why don't I walk down with you,' Ambrose suggested, 'and we can stop off at the King's Head on the way back, and I can buy you a drink. Maybe?'

Gah. 'Cool. Only I'm buying?'

'OK.'

They didn't talk as they headed off the Close and down the hill. Shit, shit, *shit*. Freddie could hear him humming; sweet, up in his head voice. Ah, here I am giving him seven kinds of grief, but he just carries on being a sweet dude? It *should* make Freddie wanna play nice, but no. He was all, I'm *so* gonna make you cry! Like they were fucking choristers for God's sake, and this was Chinese burns? Man, why couldn't he just grow up?

They reached the cashpoint. He got seventy out, peeled off fifty. For one second he thought Ambrose was going to refuse it. Felt his temper flare BOOM, but no, Ambrose took the money, and left Freddie scrambling to deactivate his rage.

'So yeah, cheers for doing my tax?' he mumbled. 'Appreciate it. And uh, sorry for being a total bellend. I'm just—'

'I love you.'

Freddie stared. 'Dude! You can't say that!'

'Say what?'

'I love you?'

'I love you too.'

'No— Gah!' Freddie covered his face and laughed. 'Man, you're so . . . This is like talking to a frog.'

'A frog!'

They started walking back up the hill to the King's Arms.

Oh. My. ACTUAL GOD? 'Yeah, so I had a pet frog, back in the day? Trevor? Totally loved that little dude, I'd be maybe six, seven, chorister, anyway, so yeah, I'd be holding him and he'd be trying to jump away, so I'd have to keep like . . . and when I'm talking to you, the conversation, y'know, jumps and I can't keep a hold of . . . stuff.' He snatched a breath. 'Is all I'm saying.'

They'd reached the pub doorway.

'Maybe you should kiss me,' said Ambrose, 'and see if I turn into a prince?'

'Yeah, funny guy.' Man, what's *with* you? You'd give him a blowie in a heartbeat, and you're too shy to kiss him? He leant up quickly. Planted one on his lips. 'There you go.'

Pause.

'Did it work?' Ambrose asked. 'Try again.'

'Ha ha ha.' Freddie opened the door. 'You coming, or what?'

Ambrose ducked under the low beam. 'Maybe it takes a while,' he said. 'Maybe you'll just wake up one morning and find it's happened?'

On Thursday we signed off our choice with an X, never believing it would really happen. On Friday morning, we woke and found it had. And that nobody had a Plan B. What have we done? What have we done? Did we really mean it? Can't we wind back? Think again? Uncross the X?

Dean Marion woke in the night to hear rain. The cathedral clock chimed three. Gene was standing at the window looking out at the first grey light of dawn.

'Is everything all right?' she whispered.

He was silent a long time.

Oh no, she thought. She heard him sigh.

'No. I'm afraid everything's fucked, deanissima,' he said. 'And yet at the same time, everything's all right. If you think you know how the story ends.'

The sun comes up over this green and pleasant diocese. Hay lies in sodden windrows. A slit of sky runs along a water channel through a field, as though the world might split in half. The wind stirs shoals of silver-backed leaves on the trees, and a magpie flies up, wings a blur of light. The bowing grass heads are all light. The river running is light, the church spires rearing, the sheep grazing, the cars driving: they are all light. The children playing, people walking, working, shopping, begging: light. All we see is light; not the things, but the light bouncing off them. Nothing but light.

And this is the judgement, that the light has come into the world. This is how it ends. Nothing but the light, streaming back at us from future glory. No words or truths or facts of ours can comprehend it. And yet it is always breaking into our darkness through that tiny pinhole where the two lines intersect. On a green hill far away, where a cross marks the spot.

Chapter 26

An umbrella lies smushed flat on the pavement like a broken daddy-long-legs. We will limp past it into the Luscombe Centre in Lindchester's Lower Town. Perhaps you had forgotten this place existed? It is on the opposite side of the River Linden, a stone's throw from Vespas – if you have a good throwing arm, or a medieval trebuchet – hidden, as they say, in plain sight.

Would you like a tattoo? Would you like to place a bet on the European Championship? Who are all these people? Why are they dressed like that? Why are they so fat? Why are they in mobility scooters – wouldn't they be healthier if they walked? Why are those children not in school? Who wants curry and chips in a tray, with gravy? Who on earth buys their bras from a charity shop? What *is* this place? Why is everything so ugly and depressing and made of concrete?

From down here in this invisible town, you can look up at the golden weathercock, riding high on the cathedral spire, remote, in another golden world. A world peopled with gentrifiers, hipsters, opera buffs, entrepreneurs, experts and professionals, all chattering as they buy their cortados and pastel macaroons, assuaged by the knowledge that wealth trickles down. Given the chance, would you vote the way they told you? Or would you give them two fingers, and think *diddums* when their golden playground got trashed?

*

Miss Blatherwick looked out of her kitchen window on Monday morning. Oh my goodness, whatever had happened? She put on her mac and hurried out. The wind roared all around the Close like an autumn gale. Oh no – her poor apple tree had toppled over! It was a heritage variety, a rare Lindchester pippin. The trunk had not snapped, nor had the roots been torn up, but the tree lay aslant across her lawn. Help!

There were little apples on every branch. It would have been a good harvest. That's what had caused it. It was top-heavy. And all this rain must have weakened the soil. The soil Freddie had cleared so zealously of overgrown shrubs and brambles – maybe they'd been keeping the tree anchored?

Miss Blatherwick stood and stared. Rain freckled her glasses. Could it be saved? Pruned and propped back up, tethered to something? Everything felt like a metaphor to her right now. Oh dear.

She blew her nose and went back inside to ring a tree surgeon.

'Well, *this* is fun!' said Gene on Monday evening. 'It reminds me of that thrilling childhood moment when someone hits a cricket ball through the classroom window. Everyone stands there paralysed. Except this time it's not the classroom, it's the window of the National Rare Glass Museum. Oopsy-daisy, Maisie!'

'Thanks, darling,' said the dean.

'Everyone rounds on Blokey McJokeface Johnson. "Look what you've done now, Blokey!" So he scarpers – and who can blame him, frankly?' Gene warmed to his metaphor. 'Hark, the distant crash and tinkle of priceless artefacts! Quick! Someone fetch a grown-up! Wait – there *are* no grown-ups. *We* are the grown-ups! Nobody has a plan, nobody has a clue! Well played, Britain!' He clapped. 'Turn up late to the party, behave boorishly, leave early. And God help the rest of us.'

'Amen,' said the dean. 'Lovely sermon, vicar. Now could you please stop.'

He scraped a foppish bow. 'I am yours to command, deanissima. Shall we – in a valedictory spirit – open a bottle of something European, and watch England get knocked out of the European Championship?'

The dean laughed. 'I *think* I'd back us to beat Iceland, darling.'
Oh dear.

Yes, Miss Blatherwick is right: everything feels like a metaphor at
the moment. The tumbrel rumble of thunder, the battling of sun
and cloud, the rainbow of hope arching over everything. Referendum
fallout continues to rain down on the whole of the diocese of
Lindchester and beyond. What am I saying? Of course beyond! It is
not all about us, for heaven's sake. Poor Freddie was bluntly reminded of that by Ambrose. Perhaps you have wondered about Ambrose,
and his saintly forbearance. He is an ox, as we know. But even an
ox may be goaded beyond endurance.

We will wind back, briefly, and join them after evensong on that
Friday, in the lay clerks' vestry, as they took off their cassocks.

'Hey. You doing OK, Brose?'

'Not really.'

'Wanna go out for a drink?'

'No, thanks.'

'Cool.' Freddie dropped his voice, came close. 'Want company?
I mean, we could chill at yours, maybe?'

'*No*. Thanks.'

Freddie flinched away. 'Dude, are you . . . mad at me?'

Ambrose stared at him in disbelief. 'Look. I woke up this morning
to find £120 billion's been wiped off the FTSE 100 overnight.'

'Sure, but—'

'We've screwed the economy. We've shafted the Scots, and torn
up the Good Friday agreement. We've destabilized the whole
European political landscape. We've trashed the future for the next
generation, and legitimized intolerance and racism. This is a nightmare of global proportions. And you're seriously stressing about
whether I'm mad at you? What the hell, Freddie?'

There was total silence as Ambrose hung up his cassock and left.
Every eye was tactfully averted. Then one by one, small conversations broke out. Football. Someone's car had a flat tyre. Our old
standby, the weather. Everyone longed to crack a joke to diffuse
the tension, but what could they say?

The whole nation longs to crack a joke. We cannot bear too much earnestness. We watch one another, take the emotional temperature, try to come to a consensus: too soon to take the piss out of ourselves? Still too soon. And there's a sick lurking fear that pisstaking may be partly to blame for this mess. We eye our family and friends, sound them out before we rant or gloat. Because who knows how they voted? Who knows why? What swayed them to put their X here, not there? There's poison in the water supply. Fault lines run through everything and the trolls are out from under the bridge.

In far-off London town Parliament is in disarray, as though someone is rampaging round a bridge party with a leaf blower. Careers whirl away in a flurry of resignations. The stunned days go by. Your author stands like Count Bezukhov on the battlefield in his glasses, asking in sweet bewilderment, 'What happened?' What has become of my gentle comedy of Anglican manners? Let us pick our way through the smoking rubble of questions as best we can.

What have we done? (Can it be undone? A second referendum? A loophole? Do enough people have cold feet?) Is that a march of protest, or a tantrum? Was it a fair democratic process, or a pack of lies? A triumph, or a disaster? Best of times, worst of times? It still all depends on your point of view.

And so June skulks away out of the back door when nobody is looking. July the first dawns. All across Britain silent soldiers appear in First World War uniforms. 'We're here because we're here,' they sing. Because one hundred years ago, day dawned on the Somme and by sunset 19,240 were dead. For our tomorrow, they gave their today.

In our today, there are people going to work. There are children skipping in playgrounds. There are horses grazing in fields. These things are still going on. There are vicars taking services. There's a woman selling the *Big Issue* by the station, and a piper piping outside Marks & Spencer. There are fast trains whizzing to London. There are foodbanks and nightclubs. There is a black woman from Watford being told to go home. There is a man out running, running till it hurts, running to see if he can escape himself, running

179

like a hamster in a ball, trapped in the tiny curved-in-on-itself world of his own ego.

And there is a woman with a three-legged dog, praying for the man, as she walks down by the riverside. Praying for this poor world, riven by hatred, riven by love. "'Gonna lay down my sword and shield,'" she sings. "'I ain't gonna study war no more.'"

Jane saw the soldiers in Lindford as she walked to work. She's been thinking, everything's fucked. Why am I still here? Why the fuck am I not already packing my bags for New Zealand? For God's sake, Matt. Why are we here?

And there were the soldiers, like an answer: 'We're here because we're here, because we're here, because we're here.' Because I voted Remain, thought Jane. Because I'm British. Because this is my home. Because I'm still fucking *here*. I just am.

Freddie cannot escape from his own head. Even if he reaches out, says sorry, it's still gonna be about him, him being needy, all, please make me feel better about me?

He gets out of the shower, pulls on some sweats. Goes and stands on the landing looking out across the Close towards Vicars' Court. So he woke up one morning and realized, yeah, it's happened. Frog's turned into a prince – but he left it too late. Didn't believe it in time. He's been writing a text in his head for days. (*Dude, I get that this isn't about me, it's a global disaster, but I was only trying to . . .*) Just can't sign it off. He's not even seen Ambrose all week. There's someone depping for him – what's that about? Is it really the labyrinthitis again, like Nigel says? (*Dude, heard you're ill. Sorry if I . . .*)

Ah, why am I even here? Everything's shit, everything's trashed. The whole country's fucked. Overnight, everyone hating on everyone else?

But just as he thinks this, he sees the bishop go past. And boom, Jesus is in his head: *So what will you do, my friend? About the hating?* Suddenly he's crying. And now here comes that hymn again, the one Neil sang? 'Jesus paid it all. All to him I owe.'

180

*

It's the bishop's day off. A long overdue evening in with Sonya. The doorbell goes. Hoorah, there's the Deliveroo guy, early!

'I'll get it.' He opens the door.

Oh bollocks.

'Hey, Paul. STEVE! So yeah, I'm totally gonna make an appointment with Kat? But that won't be for like weeks, and I just wanna say it quickly now to your face, coz I like said all the other stuff to your face? Uh, basically, sorry? I was out of order. We disagree, but I don't wanna be hating any more? Ah shit. Sorry.'

Steve's heart goes out to him in spite of everything. 'That's OK, Freddie. I'm sorry I hurt you.'

'Thanks, man.' He wipes his eyes on his sleeve. 'Won't happen again. I know I can't expect you to like, go on forgiving me—?'

'Yes, you can,' interrupts Steve. 'Or I'll have to stop being a bishop.'

'Ha ha, I guess.'

They stand a moment, irresolute.

Saved by Deliveroo! 'Well, here's our meal. Thanks for coming, Freddie.'

'No worries.' A moment's hesitation. 'Catch you later.'

Freddie wanders across the Close to the old battlements. He *so* needed a hug back there? Yeah, right – hugging bishops? How'd that go for you last time, huh? He looks down. There's the Linden. He can hear it rushing, but he can't see it through the leaves. Ah, just do it. Text him. Put yourself on the line. He gets out his phone. His whole body is shaking like crazy.

Missing you, sweet guy.

Send?

Delete?

The Linden rushes by, out of sight. How did this happen? Why are we here? I don't know. But here we all are. Down by the riverside, right by the edge, ready to cross. Lay it down, lay it all down. Sword, shield, the whole lot. Let's not carry it any longer. Let's not study war. Let's lay down our hate. Lay down our fears.

181

Then lay down our love. Put it all on the line. We can't do much, but we can forgive each other.

JULY

Chapter 27

The dean woke. No, no, no. Not good. Yet good to wake from, and realize it was a dream. She lay in the grey light. No dawn chorus. One by one, the songsters had left off. A clattering chatter of magpies in the tree outside the window, that was all. And Gene's steady breathing beside her.

She allowed her mind to go back and turn the dream over, as if flipping something dead with a stick. A large mother rat with a dead baby rat clutched in its paws, and a trail of tangled misshapen aborted foetuses dragging after it, still attached. The creature was dying. In her dream, she knew she ought to put it out of its misery. But she couldn't, just couldn't do it. Even in her dream, she didn't like herself for this cowardice. The rat was squeaking softly in distress. She knelt and stroked it, and wept for it.

Yes, good to wake from *that* particular offering of the subconscious. Marion slipped out of bed and went downstairs to make herself a cup of tea. While the kettle boiled she looked out across the garden towards the hive in the gathering light. Are you all right, bees? It's not you I'm fretting about, is it?

Ah. It came to her: an anniversary, of sorts. So many years had now passed, she had to stop and calculate. Seventeen years. She could revisit the episode these days and feel sad. Just sad. As if she were watching some other poor woman, haemorrhaging on the floor of the department store loo, looking at the red emergency cord, knotted up out of reach. She could kneel beside her and stroke her, and weep for the lost only begotten.

'Everything all right, deanissima?'

'Oh! I didn't hear you coming!' She leant her head on his shoulder. 'Bad dream, that's all.'

He held her, and they looked out across garden at the little white hive among the lavender. Were they all still asleep? Oh, the mystery of bees! Their frightening cycle of birth, death and rebirth. 'The work of bees, and of your servants' hands.' Mother bees, mother bees. She was back in the Easter Vigil, with the precentor warbling the words of the *Exultet*.

> O Truly blessed night,
> when things of heaven are wed to those of earth,
> and divine to the human.

'It will be all right,' she said to Gene. Even though it's still dark now, she thought.

'Oh yes, it will,' he agreed. 'In the end.'

In the end, yes. But what comfort is that now, when it is still night?

Since the Referendum results Father Wendy has gone back and re-read that Tolkien story. 'Things might have been different, but they could not have been better.' She can see now. This kind of comfort can only blossom between two old enemies whose sin has been purged away and who can finally say, 'We have lived and worked together now.' It must never be offered from a position of privilege and security to a brother or sister who is still suffering, thinks Wendy. Bless them all, those well-meaning folk who had tried to explain Laura's death to her with talk of God's timing, or tapestry seen from the other side in glory.

She watches the willow fluff take its complex routes along the unseen paths of the wind. The way the vote breaks down along class lines has given Wendy pause. Here in her little rural pocket of England, she'd sensed which way the wind was blowing. But that the same current was passing unseen through so many communities! She stops and looks out across the ripening wheat towards the concrete skirts of the cooling towers rising vast, silent on the horizon.

'What if this is judgement?' she says to Pedro. 'What if we have sinned? What if Brexit is Magnificat?'

I sense your impatience, reader. Enough theologizing! Did Freddie send that text? He did. We will loop back to where we left him on the battlements, and find out what happened next.

Gah! Had it sent? He double-checked. What if Brose was still mad at him? What if—

But Freddie had barely got the wind in his what-if sails of catastrophe when the answer came.

Look round.

What the? Freddie turned. And there was Ambrose. They proper did the whole running into one another's arms laughing thing? Here it was, the hug he'd been aching for?

'You're here! Why— Were you—? Oh God!'

'I was coming to find you, yes,' said Ambrose. He wrapped his arms tighter. 'I saw you at the bishop's.'

'That. Yeah, I was like, saying sorry? Coz . . .' He saw from Ambrose's face he know coz why. Duh, this was the Close. Everyone knew everything. (Plus the Twitter rants, obviously.) 'He's kind of an OK guy and I don't want to hate him, so.'

'I like him,' said Ambrose. 'You know he actually rang the ward, when I was in hospital? Just to find out how I was doing?'

'He did?' La la la. 'Awesome.'

'What?'

'Nothing. So, you're recovered again?'

'Pretty much, thanks.'

'You're not . . . Are we cool?'

'I hope so. Sorry I was a shit. Can we forget it?'

''K.'

Freddie heard the swifts round the cathedral, *shwee, shwee, shwee.* Clock chimed three-quarters. So the hug was still going on, and in a moment it was gonna get awkward, only not yet? Freddie breathed in. Ah! The actual air was sweet? Bees in the lime blossom – he could hear them, G, G sharp? – all off their bee faces with the sweetness?

Now would be a good time to say it. About the frog prince? G'wan, say it. Felt himself starting to tremble.

'Uh, so, wanna go to your place? Or?'

Ambrose smiled. 'I want to do a lot of things, Freddie.'

'Good to know.' He dialled the slutaciousness up a notch. 'Like what?'

'Things you've never done before.'

'Well, good luck with that one.' A-a-and dial it back down. Please don't be getting all judge-y on me? 'Give it your best shot, dude.'

'OK.' He thought a bit. 'I'm going to make you . . .' He put his lips to Freddie's ear.

'Ooh. You got me. What's that?'

He whispered it again.

'Nope. French? I got the mouth part.'

'Um, maybe google it?' suggested Ambrose.

'Aw, too shy? That's so sweet!' Freddie got out his phone. 'How'd you spell it?'

Ambrose told him.

'*Croquembouche*? Ha ha ha! I don't think so, dude. "A French dessert consisting of choux pastry balls"?'

'That's the one!' he said. '*Croquembouche*. I'm going to make it for your birthday.'

By now Freddie was literally *crying*? 'Can you even cook *anything*? Dude, look at this bad boy – this isn't just a cake, this is like a cake *Dracula castle*! And you're seriously gonna make me one?'

'Sure.'

'You are *so* full of shit.' Freddie wiped his eyes. 'Na ah, this is your close-up magic again. *Croquembouche*! No way.'

'Well, I bet I can learn.'

'Dude, stop with the frog thing? Seriously, now.' Freddie shook him. 'So's we're clear, I'm talking about sex, OK?'

'Oh! Right.' Ambrose frowned. 'Something you've never done before . . .'

'Why does it have to be something—'

'Because I want to be your first.'

188

'Are you for real?' He was! Ah, come *on*. What happened to, *I don't want to change you, Freddie*? 'Look. Unless you've got some kind of magic re-virginating machine, it's not gonna happen.'

'Yeah, but can I still try, though?'

Ah, fuck this. Why had he thought this could ever work? 'Hey. Knock yourself out.'

'OK. Sort of by word association – from *croquembouche*, I mean.' Ambrose cleared his throat. 'Have you ever been French kissed?'

'*What?*' Freddie stared. 'French—? What is *with* you? Yeah, guess what, I have – and then some! Only like a bazillion times, with maybe a bazillion different guys?'

'Yes, but was that ever with a guy who was ridiculously in love with you?'

Silence. The swifts calling.

'Naw. See, now look, you've made me cry— Whoa, um, OK . . .'

Yeah, that would be a first. Never felt like this before. Oh, man. What if? What if everything could be a first from now on; what if everything could be new?

Bees. Bees. Bees. In the lime blossom all round. Humming in G. And inside of him, humming, and his heart buckling under the weight of all this sweetness?

What if? What if what's done could be undone? The unkind word unspoken, the box unticked, the bullet sucked out, the car bomb unexploded? Rewind, rewind – the war undeclared, Iraq un-invaded, Saddam untoppled, the cities un-razed to the ground? The twin towers rising, hurling the planes back out. How far back must we go to untangle it all? All the way back, until the apple is unpicked and we walk with God in the garden in the cool of the evening, naked and unashamed?

Miss Blatherwick carries a bucket of water out into her garden and pours it round the roots of her apple tree. My poor Lindchester pippin, she thinks. Much diminished, but standing up again. The water pools in the trough dug by the tree surgeon. Will it survive its trauma? She watches as the water sinks into the earth and vanishes. Then she

189

looks up at the pruned branches. The leaves hang limp. Will it recover? She carries the bucket back and refills it at her sink.

My poor country, she thinks. Things torn up by the roots, toppled, broken. Goodness knows what will happen to the Labour Party she has voted for all her life. Conservatives in disarray. The pound plummeting. It will take years for this to play out. She knows she won't live to see the outcome. What can she do?

She heaves the bucket out of the sink and lugs it to the tree. What can one do but pour out one's hope and prayers like water?

Across the land suitcases are packed, and people travel to York for General Synod. Marion is no longer a member. She stood down, worn out, after the women bishops vote was finally carried. We, too, must pour out our hopes and prayers from a distance, as the #SharedConversations about human sexuality enter their synodical stage.

It is Sunday evening in the deanery garden. The sun is out, briefly.

'Is there hope for the C of E, deanissima?' Gene serves strawberries and champagne to celebrate Wimbledon (and her escape from synod). 'What do you think will happen?'

'I don't know,' she says. 'It will probably be like it was with women bishops. You think you've arrived at a costly agreement, then people go back to their separate bunkers and get talked into changing their minds.'

'And yet here we are, with lady bishops.'

'Here we are, indeed.' She eats a strawberry. It is a perfect English strawberry, like the strawberries of childhood. 'I hope folk manage to listen. I always think of Cromwell's words to the Church of Scotland: "I beseech you, in the bowels of Christ, think it possible that you might be mistaken."'

'Why, yes – before going on to stomp the bejasus shit out of them in the Battle of Dunbar.'

'Oh shut up,' says the dean.

Gene inclines his head. 'But it is a happy sentiment, nonetheless. Ah, there go our lovebirds!'

They both wave to Freddie and Ambrose as they pass the deanery gates hand in hand.

'How long do you give it before Mr May self-destructs and wrecks it all?' whispers Gene. 'Six months? Three?'

She shakes her head and closes her eyes. The air is full of humming. The bees, her bees. For now they are lost in sweetness.

Ah, Freddie! He is overcome by sweetness, lost, all undone by love. It is always love that undoes us, undoes it all, unravels our snarled-up knot of hate and fear, all the way back to its source.

Chapter 28

Everything's shit. Everything's changing. Why can't everything stay like it was?

Leah is hiding in her secret den. Even the secret den isn't going to be here much longer, because the plot at the back of theirs has been sold, and soon some moron builder will build a stupid house on it.

It's raining. When she was young she used to pretend she was a mouse or a hamster, hiding in a tin can. Now she's eleven she pretends it's bullets ricocheting and she's an orphan in a war zone. But now everything's shit, that's not a good game. Actual scary things could happen, they literally could. In England! All the grown-ups are scared, and moaning, *What's happening? Honestly, you can't even go for a wee without something else happening!*

It's history. Happening IRL, not in a *Horrible History* book. It's all the fault of Brexit, which wasn't supposed to happen, according to the grown-ups. So why did you LET it happen, IDIOTS? But whenever Leah tries to ask what's going to happen now, they immediately go, *Oh, it'll be fine. Don't worry.* If it's going to be fine, why don't you all SHUT (THE F) UP about how shit and scary everything is? If only Jane hadn't moved away, Leah could've gone to ask her.

Plus her lame parents won't buy her a proper phone! Not even for a 'leaving Junior School and going to Big School' present. So Leah is having to pretend she couldn't care less about Pokémon GO.

She hugs her skinny arms round herself. The rain eases. Drops ping on the roof from the trees. She can smell the plant-y smell coming in, from the smushed-down weeds. Raindrops drip, like white flashes, in the open doorway.

If only she could be Arya in *Game of Thrones*. Not like a regular girl. A girl who can look after herself, who can swordfight and have her own sword, Needle.

Oh, why couldn't she have stayed ten? Ten is the best age for a girl, ever. You can do everything the boys can do when you were ten – *and* be better, ha ha! But now! At break Leah seriously heard one of the lame pink girls go, all super-excited, 'I literally can't wait till I'm like a C cup!' Like that would be awesome. Yeah, well, she doesn't do karate, none of them do, they don't ever get hit in the chest – which literally KILLS. Leah can tell you what would be awesome – if she was growing *knives* out of her chest instead, like Boadicea had sticking out of her chariot wheels. *Magic* knives, so when the boys nudge and stare they'll get their stupid eyes gouged out.

She hates boys *so much*. Thank GOD QM is girls-only. Maybe she's a lesbian? Except she hates girls too, frankly, especially Kerryn Barrymore. So probably she's just a misanthropist who hates everybody.

Nearly everybody. Ssh.

Here in the secret den she can get the thought out and look at it, like something really expensive she's shoplifted and can never show anyone, ever. She shuts her eyes and hugs herself tighter.

"'Pōkarekare ana . . .'" She can hear him. The whole cathedral was packed with Lindfordshire schools for the Leavers' service and everyone was hyper. *He* was there with a microphone, leading the singing. Everyone knew the song from Sing Up! All the girls were squealing, 'OMG!'

No way would he notice her, no way— Her heart bumped, he was coming over, smiling!

'Hey, Leah. How's the karate? Fourth kyu? Way to go! High five? Yeah! You rock.' Ha ha ha! Kerryn Barrymore's face!

"'Ka mate ahau i te aroha e.'" I could die of love for you.

193

The soft rain tingles on the roof and her fingers tingle, and everything is bulging out or pressing in till she wants to groan, like something big might happen (why, why won't something happen?), only she can't tell what.

What would Jane say, I wonder, if poor Leah went to her for comfort? Perhaps it's as well that Jane has moved away from Cardingforth, because I'm afraid it would only be Hopkins's carrion comfort, despair, on offer right now.

Monday, late afternoon. She was out running in Lindford arboretum. Holiday in Wales weather, like jogging through a cloud. The puddles under the lime trees brimmed with violent green.

Jane was still surprised at the depth of her Brexit grief, and at a loss to understand it. Presumably she was trudging through the various predictable stages: denial, anger, bargaining, depression. Yep, depression. Stuck there, for now. Acceptance was still some way off.

And there was guilt in the mix somewhere. Snarled up in her roots, probably (argh, the white stilettos Mum spent too much on, mouldering in some landfill). Her Marxist forebears – miners, shipbuilders, self-taught WEA members – what would they make of all this malarkey? What would they make of *her*? First of her family to go to university – Oxford scholarship, no less! Not bad, our Jackie, not bad at all. Her people had been proud of her, and she'd come away with a degree in how to be ashamed of her background. Who had she been trying to pass muster with? The very dickheads who were now trashing the country – the way they trashed restaurants back when they were students.

Thank God term was over, anyway. The history department had become a perfect political microcosm, with micro-factions trolling one another on social media. Tomorrow they were all going to rock up to the cathedral for the Faculty of Farts and Inhumanities graduations, don their robes, and sit together on the platform smiling like saltwater crocodiles.

Jane plodged on through the puddles. A century from now would 'Labour' have the same fusty ring as 'Whig'? Don't say this was the end of broad church Labour – or the end of Labour, full stop.

Hah! General Synod was happening, wasn't it? For once, the press wouldn't be rolling its eyes at the in-fighting, and predicting a split. In fact, the good old C of E with its 'shared conversations' was looking like a grown-up outfit for once. Modelling a different way of handling conflict, was Matt's view.

Yes, it was a consolation, of sorts, for someone who was about to become Mrs Bishop. Next week at York . . . Argh! Maybe she should buy herself a new pair of white stilettos, and wear them with pride?

The days roll by, all unconcerned. Herds of cumulonimbus graze across the Lindfordshire sky. There is willow herb and convolvulus; and in the evening honeysuckle pours out its scent for night-time moths. Along trampled mud paths, patient cows come home to be milked.

Are things steadying down a little? Can we unclench yet? We are a nation stuck at the airport with all flights cancelled. Surely *someone* will arrange something? We can't stay here for ever. The new Prime Minister – will she sort it out? But oh, what if in five years' time, we look back on *this* as a golden era? Lord, have mercy. April Fool-type appointments must be believed in. 'You couldn't make it up' has become the new normal.

Miss Blatherwick waters her wounded apple tree. The end of the choral year approaches. The gorse is in blossom, and kissing's *very* much in fashion. Yeah, no, only, kissing's fine and all, but du-u-u-ude? Around five minutes from eye contact to kit off, is more what Freddie's used to? A *week*, and still no action? Really? God, don't say he's just not into me?

On Tuesday morning, Freddie decides to swing by the bishop's office, catch a word with Kat. Quick update, tell her how things stand with Ambrose? (How do things stand, exactly?)

'Hey, girl. How's things?'

'Hello, Freddie.' Doesn't look round from her computer. 'What can I do for you?'

195

He pauses in mid-action, reaching for a chair. O-ka-a-ay. He's in the doghouse, why? Gah. Last time, storming past her and busting in on Steve? He slaps his forehead.

'Ah, nuts. So Imma go out, and come back in – this time with flowers, maybe . . . ?'

'You do that.'

Still typing. Jeez. Checks his boys, yep, both still there. ''K. Laters.'

Five minutes, and he's back with a bunch of sweet peas from the treasurer's garden? Kat looks at them for maybe thirty seconds.

'OK,' she says. 'Get a vase.'

He obeys. Fills it at the tap, sticks the sweet peas in, comes and puts them on her desk.

'So I'm a tool,' he says.

'You certainly are.'

'Sorry.'

She stops typing, spins her chair round. 'Sit.'

He sits. 'Are you gonna lecture me? Naw! Babe. C'mon, Kat, I'm sorry. Can't we just—'

'You can hear me out, or you can leave. Up to you.'

He slouches down. 'Fine.'

She leans forward. 'Here's what I said to Steve at the time: you think you're being erased? You should try being a gay black woman.'

Freddie blinks. 'Right.'

'See?' Kat laughs. 'I told you to get that gaydar in for an MOT.'

'What? Yeah, but no, it's a *guy* thing, not—'

'Why's it a *guy* thing?' she demands. 'Don't gay women count?'

'Yeah, no, but, but, listen, all I'm saying is, gaydar's guys checking out guys. Course gay women count!'

'Nope. You don't really see me at all,' she says. 'You only see women when you want something from them. Diagnosis: sexist oinker.'

'Oh!' Freddie gapes. 'That is *so* not true!'

She raises her hands. 'I'm done.'

'Man. You are so mean to me.' He juts his lip.

'Plus you're manipulative,' she says. 'But anyway, what can I do for you?'

196

'Nothing. Just checking in to see how you're doing.' He gets to his feet. 'Gotta run. Late for work?'

She rolls her eyes as his footsteps crunch away on the drive. Idiot manchild. She leans forward and breathes in the sweet pea scent. Ah! Grandma's garden. For a second she sees Gran, arms folded, shaking her head. *Ah ah, shame on you.* Kat sighs. Damn, she *was* mean to him. Jealous, probably. Because where is she going to find a keeper like Ambrose?

Synod ends, and the reps from Lindchester wend their way home. Virginia finds herself uncharacteristically weepy. It was all so draining. And then there's the stress of a house move looming. Is it wrong of her to think that if she weren't a single woman, the diocese would have sorted her housing out by now?

Dominic emerged from the Shared Conversation in far better spirits than he'd expected. Present mood: cautious optimism? Of a restrained 'let's not hurry' Anglican kind, of course. Like a mighty glacier moves the Church of England. It was not wall-to-wall homophobia. There were a whole bunch of good-hearted people whose heads hadn't caught up with their hearts yet, poor darlings.

Good disagreement. Lordy, it wasn't cheap, was it? LoveWins was not cheap. He thought about that extraordinary Muslim man who had hugged a suicide bomber and saved dozens of lives. There it was – the best of humanity and the worst of humanity, locked in an embrace at the moment of death. Would he, Dominic Todd, ever be capable of love like that? A love that doesn't try to save itself, but seeks to absorb violence and hatred in its own flesh, no matter what the cost.

Across the diocese of Lindchester people wake to the horror of Nice. Father Wendy and her husband turn off the news. They drive to Laura's grave a hundred miles away, and weep with their arms round one another. Two kilometres of carnage. All those lives ploughed under and smashed. These poor shell-less bodies of ours, evolved as if for trust. Where does it end? What hope is there for us?

*

Sunday comes round again, the final day of the choral year. The dean feels tears on her face as she administers the wine. 'The blood of Christ.' She makes her way along the communion rail, following the president. The body, the blood. The body, the blood. For a second the roof vaults are reflected in the wine as she holds out the chalice to the woman kneeling in front of her.

Behind her in the quire a solo voice begins to sing the anthem. 'Erbarme dich, mein Gott, um meiner Zähren willen!' Have mercy, my God, for the sake of my tears. Marion thinks of the emergency cord, hanging all the way down to the floor, plumbing the depths, to where humanity lies helpless, drowning in blood.

Chapter 29

The French flag hangs at half-mast up on Cathedral Close. Everything is numb. This week schools will break up, Parliament will go on recess. We limp on, as though the end is in sight and it might all be over soon, the awfulness. We need a break, space to process it. Don't let anything else bad happen; no more coups, no more massacres, please. Don't let Trump win.

Is it partly our fault? Absurd. And yet it feels as though our Brexit butterfly wings have caused hurricanes. What have we done?

In the midst of this numbscape, the big day arrived. A welcome break from removal firm boxes and trips to the town dump, if nothing else.

Jane did not buy white stilettos for the occasion. But she did buy a pair of ridiculous white platforms in which to strut her stuff as Mrs Newly Consecrated Bishop. She teamed them with a knock-out tight dress and a sardonic expression. Her fashion sense had been forged in the furnace of the 1980s. Thus her dress was black (in a heatwave, huzzah!), her handbag white, her sunnies white-rimmed and her chunky plastic jewellery black and white. If you cannot be matchy-matchy as Mrs Bishop, Jane would like to know when you can.

It is not possible, dear reader, for me to smuggle you into Bishopsthorpe to see how Jane conducted herself during that over-night stay with Rupert of York. Nor can we mingle with the glad crowds in the Minster on Tuesday, getting there early to bag a good place in the unreserved seats in order to see our right trusty and well-beloved hero consecrated in his *blue-purple* (shudder!) episcopal shirt.

Matt was one of two ordained that day. The other candidate was a woman. The order of service did not contain a rubric *If there is to be a spontaneous protest, it may happen here* – though it might as well have done. This is the C of E, after all, where dissent can be liturgized into harmless eccentricity. (*The congregation rolls its eyes while the protest takes place. In the event of the protest continuing, the dean may instruct the organist to weaponize the organ.*)

Protests notwithstanding, it all went off smoothly. Nobody passed out with heatstroke under a welter of vestments. Certainly it went better in real life than it had done in Jane's dream the week before, in which she was late for the service because she'd been slum-mocking about in her trackies reading a novel. The new outfit was nowhere to be found. Shit, bollocks! She was hurtling through a maze of corridors – jerry-built by her subconscious out of her comprehensive school and the Fergus Abernathy building – unable to find the Minster.

No, the reality was a relief. Matt's father was beside her, still calling her by her predecessor's name. Happily, 'Jen' was close enough for her to pretend she hadn't noticed. She might have enjoyed the service more if Danny had been there. But Jane had to concede that skiing in The Remarkables during your half-year break probably had more allure for a twenty-two-year-old. He'd be back for Christmas. Besides, she had her lovely surrogate son on her other side. At one point, she was about to nudge Freddie and whisper: 'Hey, I get to boff a bishop now. Never done that before!' when a memory obtruded. Oops. Well held, Jane.

Once the post-service milling about, photos, and lunch were over, the new bishop of Barcup and his wife headed back to Lindford in the black Mini that coordinated so pleasingly with Jane's outfit. Matt was driving. Jane fell asleep for Prosecco-related reasons. We can join them as they cross the border of the diocese of Lindchester again.

*

200

'Huhhh. Bleah. Was I snoring?' Jane smacked her lips and sat up. 'Why've we stopped?' They were parked by a barley field in the middle of nowhere. Her head ached.

'Sorry, can you fire up the satnav?' said Matt.

'We're lost! Mister I-know-the-way! Ha ha!' Jane opened the glove compartment. 'What's this?' She pulled out a flat box. 'No! What—?'

'Open it.'

'Oh, Matt.' Ah, that knife-edge, where an upsurge of love wrestled with *Fucking hell, what if I hate it?* She planted a kiss on his cheek, and opened the box. It contained a chunky silver-and-sea-glass choker.

'Are those happy tears?' asked Matt.

'They are!' wailed Jane. 'It's gorgeous! Oh, Matt.' She kissed him again.

'Phew. Well, I thought since I was getting new bling, you should as well,' said Matt. 'And I know that if you got your druthers, you'd be heading off down under.'

'Rubbish.'

He gave her what Jane's mum always described as an old-fashioned look. 'I'm an ex-copper, Jane. If you google "lecturer posts in New Zealand", I can put two and two together.'

Jane closed the box. 'Please tell me you weren't checking my browsing history.'

'I don't take this for granted, Jane – that you're going to trail around after me and my job.'

'Don't fucking try to fob me off!' Sixth months of pent-up row bulged like a monsoon cloud. 'Yes or no. Were you checking?'

'Not really. I—'

'Not really? What's *that* supposed to mean? Oh, I'll just *half*-check—'

'Look, will you shut up and let me explain?' he snapped. 'Your laptop was on, I saw the open tab, that's all.'

'Why were you nosing around looking at my laptop in the first place?'

He tipped his head back, closed his eyes.

'And don't fucking sigh at me, Mister!'

'Janey, can we please not fight?'

'Let's not spoil your "big day", you mean?'

He made no reply.

She glared out of the window. A pair of white butterflies spiralled above the hedge. Argh. Now I feel like a cow. You made me feel like a cow, you pig.

'Sorry. I need some fresh air.' She stuck the jewellery box on the shelf, got out of the car and stumbled off in her ridiculous platforms towards a gate.

Silence. She leant on the top rail and hated herself. Too darn hot. The barley stood motionless. She could hear it ticking in the sun. There was a dark stand of trees and a farm in the distance. Everything was waiting. The whole landscape, pausing between acts. Term had ended on a cosmic scale. And now Big School loomed. Out there. On the other side of summer. But now, now we wait. Tick, tick, tick.

Matt got out of the car too, came and leant beside her. The sight of the purple sleeve jolted her afresh. Oh God, what have we gone and done?

'I'm sorry,' she said. 'It's all been a bit mad.' He opened his mouth. 'Don't you *dare* say Brexit and mansplain everything.'

He slipped an arm round her.

She leant her head against his big shoulder. The white butterflies spiralled past them. Sometimes she could almost feel his faith, like a powerful engine idling, and then it was possible to believe it might still all be OK in the end.

'God, I wish we didn't have to go home to box hell.'

'That's good.' He smiled. 'Because I've booked us into a nice B & B for the night, in that farm there.'

'What?' Jane laughed. 'You old rascal! But I should warn you, I've run out of knickers.'

I will not trouble you with the bishop of Barcup's reply, reader.

Over in Martonbury the empty 'palace' waits in all its fresh magnolia splendour for Matt and Jane to move in. Bea, the archdeacon of Martonbury, has tootled round with her hoe, to keep the weeds down in the flowerbeds. The garden has fallen off somewhat from the glory years when Janet Hooty reigned. But we cannot keep harking back and moaning. That is to say, we shouldn't, but we always do. It's in our Anglican DNA, born as we were amid divorce and dissolution.

Talking of which, how is everything over at Risley Hill, where the vicar stands too close to his intern? We have often wondered – with Archdeacon Bea – what is going on there, in that apparently lively and growing church. Please don't say it's that tired cliché, the adulterous vicar.

And now someone else is wondering, as he plods round his 5K running route in his £200 running shoes and top-of-the-range compression gear, cutting corners, stopping for a breather, and still kidding himself he ran the full 5K non-stop. (There are parts of 5K his nature waiting to be fully redeemed.)

Neil finds himself in a bit of a quandary. If he's going to test out his vocation to be a reader, he can't skip from church to church. He'll need the backing of his vicar before selection. He told Neil that, the bishop, in the bar that time. So Neil's tried to get stuck in at Risley Hill. Joined a home group, and volunteered for the welcome team, the coffee rota, Alpha, prayer ministry, you name it. No dice. Because apparently he's a young Christian, and needs to be nurtured before taking on a role. He's trying really hard not to hear the subtext. But nope, it's there. Gay, out, and in a relationship? Don't bother volunteering, sunshine.

He slows to a walk. Steep hill. Stitch. Dying.

Truth is, he doesn't fit in. Especially home group. He's reined in the auld potty mouth, but *KINELL!* The day after, he wanted everyone to pray about the Brexit train wreck, but would you believe, a couple of them start spouting a bunch of batshit cray cray stuff about the EU building being the Tower of Babel – hello? And the vicar's wife! Seriously, has *nobody noticed* she's a lush? With her wee bottle of 'water', and her 'post-viral vertigo'! As if Neil doesn't have enough fall-down drunks in the family not to spot the signs at forty paces. It's like he's banging on their window, waving his arms, *Hoose on fire!* and they're staring out like *he's* the crazy one.

Och. Time to find a new church, eh? What d'ya think? I'm in your hands, pal. He jogs the last quarter mile downhill to the vicarage. "'A little talk with Jesus makes it right, all right!'"

The holiday season starts. Bishop Steve and Sonya set off for France-France, hooray! and spend seven hours in stationary traffic on the road to Dover. Crowds hunt wild Pokémon up on the Close, which is either great fun, or a bloody nuisance, depending on who you ask. Two men with a borrowed labradoodle walk hand in hand, taking it steady, seeing how it goes. Amadeus, the cathedral cat, pours himself down off the deanery wall like a jug of tabby cream. He slinks across the precentor's yard and springs up onto the kitchen windowsill. He stares in, tail tip twitching, at the Chorister School hamster in his cage.

The heatwave mutters off into the distance trailing thunderclouds. The church hall in Cardingforth is transformed into Noah's Ark ready for next week's holiday club. Martin, the Borough (and Churches) Liaison Officer works with schools and foodbanks to set up out-of-term children's lunch clubs. He is joined by the new diocesan Social Welfare Officer, Virginia, who will be licensed in the cathedral, come autumn.

What a lot of licensing and whatnot is lined up for the autumn! Virginia, two new archdeacons and a suffragan bishop. The precentor will have his work cut out with the choreography. Doubtless, there will be requests for modern worship songs, which he must compel the lay clerks to sing. They will react like Regency dandies being required to sully their eyes with a farrier's bill. But for now, there will be a lull.

Lord, let there be a lull, prays the dean. The French flag still flutters at half-mast, and now they need a German flag. Munich is on lockdown. Eighty dead in Kabul – an Afghan flag too? She suddenly sees the Close thick with flags, an Olympic Parade of Mourning. Too much, too fast. She wants to turn her face away. Ah well, in two weeks Gene is whisking her off to a mystery destination. Perhaps he's right, she just needs a holiday.

Has it always been like this? Rio is less than a fortnight away. Four years since the London Olympics. She's probably kidding herself, but she looks back on that opening ceremony as though it happened in a different country, and in a long-gone kinder age.

Chapter 30

The Lord told Noah to build him an arky-arky!
Build it out of gopher barky-barky!
Children of the Lord!

I t's the first week of the long holidays, and parents in the Cardingforth area are grateful once again to Father Wendy for taking the kids off their hands every morning this week, for a quid a pop.

Leah Rogers flatly refuses to go. It's lame and babyish, plus she has to practise her katas for the grading next Sunday, and she's NOT GOING. YOU CAN'T MAKE ME! In the end she agrees (for £5 extra pocket money) to take Jess and collect her at the end of each morning so that Mummy can have a lie-in. Please, Leah, Mummy's really tired right now.

Mummy's in bed when Leah comes back from dropping Jess off. She's still in bed when they come in at lunchtime. Jess looks at Leah with scared eyes.

'It's fine,' says Leah. 'She's just tired. I'll make us cheese toasties.'

The cheese has gone mouldy, but Leah cuts the mouldy bits off. 'It's just penicillin,' she tells Jess. 'It's good for you. It's been scientifically proven.'

'Then why are you cutting it off?' asks Jess, scared again.

'Duh. So we don't accidentally overdose.'

You have to act responsible when you're an older sibling. You can never let yourself be scared too.

Father Dominic is not an older sibling, he's an only child. How he'd longed for a little brother or sister as a boy, so he could escape from all the babying and be treated like a grown-up. And now – apparently – some feckless Angel of the Intercessions has stumbled upon that childhood prayer at the back of a filing cabinet and belatedly granted a spoof version.

A frenzy of bleeps breaks into his Morning Office. Oh Lord, *now* what's she doing? He belts from study to kitchen.

'Mother, I can smell burning!'

'It's all right. I've beaten the flames out.'

He stares at the charred Renfold Parish Church centenary tea towel in the sink. 'Well, at least the smoke alarm is working.' He opens a window.

'The end was dangling over the hob,' she says. 'I'll buy you a new one.'

'Didn't you smell it?'

'You know I've got no sense of smell,' she says. 'I'm as— What's the word for it? Anyway, I'm as thingummy-bob as a post.'

'Or a bat,' says Dominic. 'You're definitely as mad as one.'

'I'll give you mad, sonny Jim! And besides, it's mad as a hatter. Oh, yes, they were all mad in the Luton hat factories. It was the mercury fumes.' She prods the tea towel with the washing-up brush. 'So the moral of *that* tale is never play with mercury.'

'I never do.'

'Good. Pass me my crutch, would you, love? Thanks. I'm going to take the bionic hip for a shower.'

'Do you need a hand with the stairs?'

'Oh, I'll give a yodel if I get into difficulties.' She clomps towards the hall. 'Good leg down, bad leg up.'

'*No*, mother. We've been through this. *Bad* leg down, *good* leg up.'

'No, it's not.'

'Yes, it is. It *is*. Fine. You go ahead and try.'

'Ow!' She laughs. 'Well, it's good leg *something*. I was nearly right. Oopsy, I need a winch. A winch, a winch, a winch.'

'Come along, I'll give you a bunk up.' He puts an arm round her waist. 'I've got you. A winch for a wench. Up we go.'

'As soon as I'm off these crutches, I'll be out of your hair,' she says. 'Four to six weeks, they say. You'll still get your holiday. *And* it'll be cheaper once the schools go back.'

'Don't fret.'

'You can tell that chappie from the diocese you won't be needing a downstairs shower.'

'As it happens, I'd quite like one. For guests.'

'I'm not moving in with you, Dominic.'

'Too bloody right you're not!'

But we both know you are, he thinks.

Father Wendy locks up the church hall in Cardingforth after the second day of the holiday club. 'Everything was fine and dandy-dandy! Children of the Lord.'

Is everything fine and dandy-dandy with Becky Rogers? wonders Father Wendy. *Leah's collecting me, coz Mummy's too tired to get out of bed.* That doesn't sound good. She'll call round later in the week and check.

She turns on the radio and sits down to a very late lunch – oof! And there's the news. An eighty-four-year-old French priest, murdered as he celebrates the Mass. Oh, world! You horrible, horrible world. I have nothing left to give for you, no more prayers, no more tears. But tears trickle down her cheeks all the same. In the patch of sunshine on the kitchen floor lies the ghost of an old dog who would have cried with her. Oh, Lulu. Wendy wipes her eyes.

Wendy remembers her gran, explaining why she'd given up midwifery and gone in for teaching. *It was all the blood. I couldn't be doing with it.* I can't be doing with all the blood, either. Oh dear, oh dear. I can't stop crying.

The sun goes down over the diocese of Lindchester. '"Keep watch, dear Lord, with those who wake, or watch, or weep tonight,"' prays Miss Blatherwick. (Is there no comfortable position?) Who else is

208

awake? Leah is awake. (What if Mummy's got mental health issues? What if she has a breakdown?) Marion is awake. (Should they put together a bid to the government scheme to fund extra security for big services?) Matt is awake. (Everything shipshape for the move? Janey coping?) Dominic is awake. (Get over yourself and agree to move in, you mad old hatter. We'll jog along somehow.) Virginia is awake. (What if the house the diocese has found her is ghastly?) Ambrose is awake. (Freddie, Freddie, Freddie. Should he float the possibility of a holiday together? A weekend? Still too soon?) Neil is awake. No, I tell a lie: Neil's asleep, but not before giving Ed a dose of insomnia with his panicking. (Aye, but what if some nutso comes at you with a machete, out in the sticks? You and three auld ladies! You're a sitting duck!)

The Gayden Magna church clock chimes tinnily in the distance. Half past two. I hope he wasn't too scared at the last, thinks Ed. You can't have dreamt, at eighty-four, that a martyr's crown had been laid by for you. Bless you, bless you, standing by your altar, faithfully serving to the last. I hope you weren't too frightened, my brother. I hope you could already feel those kind hands pulling you through from the other side, delivering you safe and sound. Rest in peace, rise in glory.

Neil snores. No, I'm not getting a stab-proof vest, you twit. Imagine standing at the altar dressed like that! No, we just have to trust.

The last days of July pass. It's Saturday. Swallows gather in twos and threes to natter on telegraph wires. An old woman waters a withered tree. A tabby cat spots an open window, and tenses to spring. The Chorister School hamster stirs in his sawdust nest and dreams his hamster dreams. Brides wake. Grooms wake. And life goes on, as in the days of Noah.

We just have to trust. But what if you know you can't be trusted? What if you know you'll just trash it all? Better get it over with, no? End it now. Maybe that way, it won't hurt so much? Yeah, only problem is, how can you end a thing that's not even a thing yet?

So they're back in the King's Head? Sitting opposite each other, coz that's what Brose likes? Antidote to all those months on *dec*, apparently? There's eighties music playing, like all his dad's favourites, he kinda half-knows them?

OK. Cards on table time. OK?

'So, Brose. Where's this going? Our, uh, what's it even called, this relationship? thing? we've got? I get that we're "taking it steady", but I just need to know, is that like synonymous to "*going* steady"? Coz yeah, I'm a bit all, left wondering?' He sucks in air. Man, really shit breath control, there? Clears his throat. 'I mean, what am I s'posed to say, when people ask, is all? Like, what do you think of me as?'

'A tart. Definitely. What?' Ambrose does his innocent face. 'That's what you said.'

Freddie knuckles Brose's arm. 'C'mon, dude, I'm serious – what *are* we?'

'Oh.' He sits there, like it's a long division sum he's trying to work out in his head?

'I mean, maybe we're just buddies?' Freddie prompts him. 'Coz it's not like we're actual *lovers*, is it?'

'You're saying we don't love each other?'

'Aw, c'mon.' Drops his voice. 'We don't fuck each other, is what I mean.'

'Oh. Right.' He goes back to the mental maths.

'So?' Freddie draws little circles on the back of Ambrose's hand. 'Kinda wondering if you have *any* plans in that direction? Ever? You know?'

'Oh, I have plans.'

Ba-doom. World-tilt there. 'And? Gonna share them?'

Guy just smiles. 'Maybe.'

'Oh man. This better not be your *croquembouche* shit again.'

'What?' His face falls. 'You don't like *croquembouche*?'

'Hello? I've still never had any?' Freddie skims a beermat at him. 'You were all, I'm gonna make you *croquembouche*—'

'I said for your *birthday*,' he protests. 'That's not till the end of August!'

'Just can't wait for that, babe – to see what bullshit excuse you come up with.'

'To be fair, I've actually been concentrating more on my magic.'

'AGH!' Freddie slumps forward and thunks his head on the table. He despairs. Literally? He sits back up. 'Look, admit you can't do magic, either.'

'Got a pack of cards?'

'Oh sure, coz I always bring cards to the pub.' Eye roll.

Brose leans forward, whispers. 'Check your back pocket.'

'Nu-uh.' Freddie folds his arms. 'Nope. Not falling for that again.'

'OK.'

They wait. Staring match. Barman walks through, collects some empties. The song's still playing. Yeah, be good to be indestructible, to never get hurt. Ah, nuts. Freddie's gonna crack, he knows it. Can't help himself. With a big sigh he checks – whoa!

'No fucking way!' He only pulls out a deck of cards! 'What the? You! Ha ha! When did you do that?'

Ambrose shrugs, like, Weird! He can't explain it. Then he takes the cards out of the box, shuffles them sloppily overhand, like maybe a six-year-old would? Aw bless. He hands them to Freddie. 'OK. Check they're just normal cards.'

Freddie flips through. 'Look fine to me.'

'Is the two of hearts in there?'

Freddie finds it. 'Yeah.'

'OK. Put it back. Now shuffle them for me.'

'See, this here's how you shuffle.' Freddie does the whole riffle-and-cascade thang. Hands them over.

'Maybe I should try that,' says Brose. 'Damn! Sorry.'

Freddie's crying with laughter, I mean *crying*? He gathers up the scooted cards from all around the whole table. 'Dude, you suck, you proper suck at this? Admit it, you have no clue— Whoa!'

'What?' He sits there acting blank, with a card stuck on his forehead.

Freddie guffaws. 'Is that meant to be the two of hearts there?'

'Yes. It isn't?'

'Sorry to break it to you.' Freddie plucks the card off and shows it to him. 'The Joker – oh, wait.'

The guy's only laughing at him? *Gold!*

'Have you been playing with me this whole time?' asks Freddie.

211

'Possibly. A tiny bit.'

'Naw!' He wraps his arms round his head. I am so dumb. *Man.* 'No fair!'

Ambrose puts the cards back in the box. Smiles into Freddie's eyes. 'So. My plans. Want to come away with me next weekend? Maybe?'

'Dude, I can't.' Shit, shit, shit. 'I'm working.'

'Can't you rearrange your shifts?'

'I can't. Babe, it won't work. I'm – gah! OK. Maybe. Yes.' He grips his hair. 'No. Yes. But I'll let you down. So's you know. Don't trust me, you hear?'

'Well, I'll let you down too,' he says. 'That's normal. It's what people do. And then we forgive each other.'

AUGUST

Chapter 31

August. Every year we have such high hopes of you as we run on empty through July, telling ourselves how blissful it will be to have nothing to do. No pressure, no deadlines, no task but to relax and enjoy ourselves.

The countryside is lulled to drowsiness. Thistledown floats. Hoverflies ply the ragwort. Bees ply the honeysuckle. Cafés ply their trade in historic Lindchester as punts ply the Linden. Season of booze and mellow stonedness in the parks and gardens of Lindfordshire.

But Leah is not happy this August. Even getting her third kyu was Meh, not YAY! Karate brown belt was meant to be cool. It was cool. So how come Leah just felt bad? She'd walked two miles to the club and back by herself on Sunday for the grading, coz Mummy was still 'too tired' to drive her. She'd taken the grading fee out of Mum's purse, like Mum said to. But then there was no more money for food, so on Monday afternoon Mum said to take her card and get some more out. She told Leah the PIN number. 'Get out fifty pounds, Leah, and buy some picnic treats. You and Jess can have a picnic in the garden.' And Jess was all, 'Yay! Can we get Haribo?' And Mum went, 'Get what you like.'

Jess had gone to bed now. Leah was out on the flat roof. There were some birds crashing about in the big tree. Then it went quiet. A feather floated down. The ice cream van went past towards where the comp was. (BIG SCHOOL – no, don't think about it.)

Why, *why* had she done it? She only looked coz Mum would never let her see the bank balance. BIG mistake. For a second she thought it was all OK, they still had thousands of pounds. Only then she saw the minus sign. Oh God! She'd glanced across at where Jess was spinning round the lamppost. Her hands went all shaky. *No money!* Yet money came out, fresh, like it had just been printed.

But everything had been ruined. Obviously, she couldn't explain to Jess how come after all they weren't buying all the treats in the world, and Jess went all why-why whiny and Leah yelled at her. 'Because *not*, OK????' in the aisle in Spar, and people stared. Then she had to pretend she had a headache, so Jess wouldn't be frightened. They went home and Jess put up her princess castle play tent and made Leah a special bed to lie on coz of her headache, and then Leah pretended to feel better again. But even the Coke and Tunnock's teacakes tasted crap.

Supposedly, they were going on holiday next week. Mum was going to find a really good last-minute deal. Leah picked at the warm scabby roof. It was like lumpy sandpaper. She wasn't meant to climb out of her bedroom window like this, but who even cared? It wasn't like Mum was going to tell her off, was it? Coz Leah would just say, fine, then I'm telling Dad you're just lying in bed all day and not looking after us properly.

Leah could do anything right now. *Anything at all.* Mum would have to let her, or she'd tell Dad. It was like a dream come true.

Except there was no money.

What if they couldn't go on holiday? What if they couldn't afford her QM uniform, and train season ticket? What if she had to go to Cardingforth Comp, with the big scary kids after all? NO! Stop thinking about it!

Oh, maybe she should tell Dad anyway? Even if it *was* 'a total betrayal'. Except Dad was away in France. And maybe Mum would be well again tomorrow, like she promised. Leah lay down flat on the warm roof and shut her eyes. *Freddie May. Freddie May.* Her heart twisted all up on itself, like an animal in a tight burrow trying to turn round. A long way off she heard a train, *unkerty-tunk, unkerty-tunk, unkerty-tunk.* Everything sucked. What if nothing was

216

real? She rubbed her wrists on the sandpapery roof. Hard. *I hate my horrible life.*

On the other side of Cardingforth, Father Wendy's husband Doug was hitching up the caravan and checking the tyre pressure with his little gadget thingy. He liked setting off in the evening and driving at night to avoid the holiday traffic. Wendy was just composing her out-of-office message when she remembered: I never did pop round to check on Becky Rogers! Botheration. Scoot round now? No, Doug would get cross. Wendy dithered, then made a quick call. No answer. She left Becky a message, hoping all was well. She'd text Madge, and ask her to look in on them. You are not indispensable, Wendy Styles, she told herself. And you and Doug desperately need a holiday.

Dean Marion, also desperately in need of a holiday, has been whisked away by her devoted husband on a luxury cruise in the Land of the Midnight Sun. She had once mentioned in passing that this phrase had enchanted her as a good middle-class girl reading her copy of *Look and Learn* (and falling in love with the emperor's grandson from *The Trigan Empire*). Marion has to be very careful what she mentions in passing. I do hope Gene is not going to surprise her in the cabin in a Janno outfit.

Jane has also had a surprise sprung on her by her devoted husband. It is Wednesday, the day of their house move, and she is enjoying a luxury spa day. She sweats in the sauna in her clapped-out old black swimsuit, accessorized with the same sardonic expression she wore for Matt's consecration. Spa day. Fer feck's sake. She's guessing that her predecessor considered this kind of carry-on a high treat.

Still, it beats unpacking boxes, so bless Matt for trying.

The door of the sauna opens and two more women come in. They all say 'Hi', then Jane shuts her eyes again. Damn. Since hitching her wagon to Matt's, the number of people she's meant to recognize has quadrupled. But after that first flinch, they are pretending not to know her either. My, this is relaxing. Jane sticks it out for another couple of minutes, then goes for a swim.

217

She floats starfish-wise. *These* are the good old days. Hindsight will prove it. The present always feels like a disaster. She tries to let it all drift away. Brexit. Labour Party meltdown. The joke/threat that is Trump. Climate change. The move. The whole Mrs Bishop kit and caboodle— Uh-oh. I know who that was, thinks Jane. Helene from HR, and her partner. But that's OK. Because I didn't see them.

'Who was that?'

'Matt's wife.'

'Damn. Did she recognize us?'

'What if she did?'

'Oh, I know, but I was hoping we wouldn't run into anyone. I don't want Steve getting any more green ink letters over my appointment.'

'The bishop's a big boy. He can cope. Kay, everyone's entitled to a private life.'

'I know. Sorry.'

Of course everyone is entitled to a private life! But that doesn't mean people won't talk about you. Even Evangelicals – to whom gossip is anathema – will talk about you, under a veneer of prayerful concern. In choral circles, however, we are less squeamish. *Quod erat demonstrandum.*

On Wednesday evening, the Music Department convenes at the precentor's house to transact some choral business. Let us sneak in and eavesdrop, as they discuss the Lindchester Cathedral Community Choir concert this autumn (Haydn's *Creation*) in a – let us boldly coin a neologism – conbibulous manner.

'*Ja*, but too bad,' says Ulrika. 'We've booked James Lovatt now. Freddie can sodding well sing in the chorus with everyone else – like he's paid to do, you know? *Gott*, he's such a bloody divo.'

'Tut tut!' chides the senior lay clerk. 'After he sang the Lindchester setting so brilliantly at Easter!'

'He's a lazy bum,' says Ulrika. 'Nigel, trust me, he turns up at his singing lessons with me, and just sight-reads!'

'Because he's bored, darling,' says Giles. 'He needs a challenge.'

'He can't just swan in and cherry-pick the solo parts. He has to *earn* it,' says his wife. 'Oh, look. Is Laurence asleep?'

'Wha'? Still here.' The organist lurches upright in his corner. He does his trademark wasp-swatting-at-a-picnic wave, before subsiding back into the chair depths like a sea anemone closing.

'Bless him,' says Giles.

'Maybe Ambrose will be a steadying influence?' suggests Timothy.

'Plus he can explain, if a mean person uses a big word,' says Iona, the sub-organist.

There is a choral 'Ooh!' at this.

'Freddie's not as thick as he acts,' says Timothy.

'No, that's just a decoy,' agrees Iona. 'He's actually even thicker. It won't last. He'll drive Lanky mad.'

'God! Don't say that!' says Nigel. 'We don't want another back row break-up on our hands.'

'Oh, for God's sake, can we shut up about Freddie bloody May?' Ulrika gets up. 'I'll fetch another bottle. *Scheisse!*' She stumbles over a pouffe.

'Steady, old girl!'

When she's safely out of the room, the precentor whispers, '*Entre nous*, effortless virtuosity is an affront to her Lutheran work ethic.'

'No offence to Mrs Littlechild, but Freddie needs another voice coach, Giles,' says Timothy.

'No funding,' Giles replies. 'Unless Dame Barbara pops off and leaves us a bequest . . .'

They cry out against the idea of Miss Blatherwick's demise.

There is a crash and a volley of German from the kitchen.

Giles leaps up and bounces off the doorway in his haste. He takes it in: open window, upset cage with its door wagging. 'Oh bollocks!'

'He's got Boris!' wails Ulrika. 'That cat is a wanker!'

Oh dear. We will tiptoe away, as the Music Department of Lindchester Cathedral hunts (with ill-suppressed maudlin mirth) for the missing Chorister School hamster.

On Friday, a select group gathers at Father Dominic's for a themed evening of pre-Olympic caipirinhas, made by everyone's favourite cocktail waiter. Dominic can't go away while his mum is still recovering from her op, but he can still have fun. (She can go to bed and take her hearing aid out.)

Yes, home or away, let August be the month of fun. Sadly, August is only fun if you have money – as Becky Rogers knows, curled under her duvet. As parents who rely on school breakfast clubs know. As the homeless, evicted from Lindford cemetery, know. As the trafficked workers in nail bars and carwashes know, painting the nails and valeting the cars of the holidaymakers heading off on their well-earned break. As indeed we all know, deep down, when we wake at 3 a.m. with a jolt of dread from dreams of burning ships, and lie wondering if we have forgotten something.

Freddie wakes before dawn on Saturday as though someone has wrenched the covers off. Like it's the police? Fuck. He knows it's his fault. But what has he done this time? Where even is he? It comes back. He's still at Dom's? Man. OK. Scanning, scanning. Nope. Nothing. He's done nothing wrong. Technically, he's done nothing wrong.

He lies back down. So, Brose is calling for him at ten, and then they'll set off for the weekend. Cool. Bag packed, work shifts covered, all waxed and good to go. Weekend in the country, getting it on at last with the sweetest guy on God's earth – what's not to like?

Oh Jesus. You *had* to do it, didn't you? You *had* to find a way of complicating it. Yeah, no, it's just a favour to a friend, no? Keeping him company for a week on his cousin's yacht, all expenses paid? Can I interest you in that proposition at all, Mr May?

Your lovely company, Mr May, to keep me off the booze. No other services required. Yes?

Hell, yes.

I mean, he wasn't gonna say no to Andrew Jacks, was he?

Probably better not mention it to Brose, though?

220

Chapter 32

The kind hands waiting to nurse us through. Yes, that is the hope. Good Lord, deliver us. Land us safe on Canaan's shore. In the midst of life, we are in death. We are all going to die. Dress it up how you will, we are all going to die. Which do you prefer — the impossibility of faith, or the impossibility of no faith? Why is there something, rather than nothing? Because there just is — get over your anthropocentric self? Is that intellectually satisfying? Either way, it's all too big.

Some such thoughts passed through the mind of Dr Rossiter at 3 a.m., as she lay in her new bedroom in a miasma of fresh emulsion, listening to an unfamiliar set of night noises, and the rather more familiar sound of Matt snoring. The empty paint cans were lined up by the back door, near the wheelie bins. *Durable Matt.* Yep, that was her man. Durable Matt, with crisis-resistant faith. The house had been pretty much straight when she tootled back, pedicured and hot-stone massaged, from her spa day. Before long, they were going off on a well-earned holiday. Portugal. It would all be fine. Let's pretend that none of the crap is happening.

This strategy is the one we have tacitly decided to adopt as a nation. Operation Head-in-Sand. Referendum? La la la. If we do nothing, maybe it will all go away. Let's quietly forget it all, never actually get round to Article 50. Because it looks like all we're going to get is a more rubbish version of what we already had until 23 June — with another recession thrown in for good measure. We won't get to pull up the drawbridge and be a Norway-type Great-again-Britain, all pudding and no greens.

Anyhow, it's still the holidays. Olympics, yay! Rowing and cycling golds! Go Team GB! We'll worry about it all later.

It is an attitude that scandalizes Ulrika. What a nation of piss-takers, you know? This is how fascism begins. *Ach Gott, ach Gott!* The window left open, the big fat fascist wanker cat getting in and killing the poor little hamster while she was boozing in the next room with the piss-taking English!

Poor Uli has taken Boris's death hard. The following day she made a sad trip to Pets at Home in Lindford, and bought a new Boris and put him in the spring-cleaned cage.

'There,' said her piss-taking husband. 'Nobody need ever know, darling.'

But all Uli can think of is the littlest choristers, and how trauma-tized they will be if they find out – and of course they will find out! This is the bloody sodding Close, *ja*? And somehow, she finds her heart is breaking for her own little boys, for the redundant roof box and roof bars gathering dust in the garage, the family summer holidays that have slipped away never to return. Empty nest! How did it come round so fast, when all the time she was tearing her hair out over those lazy bums not doing their homework and chores? Ach, why was she always telling them to grow up?

Meanwhile, in the neighbouring house, little Chad William, the chancellor's son and heir, trots in to Mummy (vastly pregnant on the sofa and feebly watching *Peppa Pig* with Tabitha because she is a bad mother; she is not making salt dough or going to the library for a Family Fun Day).

Chad says, 'Mumma, I saw a wat.'

'A what?'

'A wat. It came out of my bedwoom floor.'

'A rat! It was probably just a mouse, sweetie. How big was it?'

'Huge and big and giant.'

Miriam lets her head slump back against the sofa. Oh, bloody hell. Mice she can ignore. Rats must be dealt with. She heaves herself up and goes to phone the cathedral office.

It's Monday morning, and a doorbell rings on Sunningdale Drive. Upstairs, under her covers, Becky Rogers weeps. On the doorstep Madge, retired nurse and Father Wendy's right-hand woman in Cardingforth parish, waits. Madge looks at the overgrown lawn. Hmm. She peers through the window. Evidence of girls: a play den made out of blankets. Comics, crisp packets. She presses the bell again. No answer. She texts Father Wendy to let her know. She'll call again this afternoon.

Where are the Rogers girls? the reader asks. They are off on an adventure, yay! They are going exploring on the train! They have a picnic in their backpacks. Jess has her pink Barbie backpack, Leah has her black-and-white karate bag. It is SO exciting! They are taking the train to Lindford, and then another train to Martonbury! TWO TRAINS! They are going to visit their old friend Jane, who has moved house, and lives in Martonbury, and they are taking her some biscuits and a card to say welcome to your new house!

Dear Jesus and God, please, please, *please* let Jane be in and let her be able to help us. Don't let them put Mum in the loony bin, and don't let it be my fault, I will do anything you ask, I promise I will never not believe in you again, I'm sorry for everything, only let it be all right, Amen.

Let it be all right, let it be all right. Some version of this has been prayed down the ages by people of faith, and by people whose faith is known to God alone (the squeamish Anglican way of saying non-Christian). Hands still grope in prayer's direction. The words *Oh God* still tumble from unbelieving lips. *Let it be all right.*

You can bet Freddie May has been praying it.

Ambrose stopped the car.

'Little walk?'

'You betcha.' Bit of outdoors action? Get in.

They headed down a narrow path. Birds. Butterflies. Sky kinda cloudy, but sun on their backs? His heart was going crazy. Should be total heaven? But now, not so much. Tried to blank the whole Andrew thang from his mind, but nu-uh.

They stopped and Freddie aimed for flippant? 'This another of your kissing gates?'

'No. It's a spanking stile.'

'Course it is. Coz you grew up in the country, right?' He vaulted over.

'Seriously,' said Ambrose. 'Old country custom. When the plough-boys were coming home, if they caught a milkmaid climbing over a stile, they were allowed to spank them.'

'Bull. Shit.'

'You don't believe me?'

'Nope.'

'Oh. OK.' He climbed over and they carried on walking. Little path went between hedges. Hoverflies hanging in the air, then zipping away.

'I'd totally let you, though?' Freddie cut him a sideways look. 'Yessir, any time.'

Brose leant in and whispered, 'I'd figured that out, thanks.'

'Ha ha ha! That obvious, huh?'

'Out of interest, how far would you trust me?'

'The whole nine yards, babe.' They stopped. There was a gate, and cows standing by a tree, lit up by the sun. Freddie fired up some weapons-grade slutaciousness. 'Try me.'

'OK. How about you tell me what you're feeling so guilty about?'

'Huh?'

'So it's not hanging over us all weekend. Maybe?'

Freddie laughed. 'I'm not feeling guilty! Why would I be feeling guilty?' Shit shit shit. 'Ask me something else?' He set off again, swishing the weeds with his hand.

'Wait.' Ambrose caught his arm. 'Can I confess something?'

Freddie's heart skipped into crazy double-time again. 'Sure.'

'I came out of uni with no debt. Basically, through gambling. Professional poker.'

'Seriously? No way! You're a professional gambler?' Freddie wavered. 'Wait. Is this another of your wind-ups?'

'No,' said Ambrose. 'But you can't be sure, can you?' He took Freddie's hand and pressed it to his chest, like maybe Freddie would feel his heart beating there, and believe in him?

'Nope. No idea. You got me.'

'That's my point, Freddie. I'm good at bluffing and misdirection. At lying, basically. And you aren't.' He kind of smiled, but sadly. 'You're *really* not. So please don't pretend nothing's going on, OK?'

'Gah!' Freddie bumped his head on Ambrose's shoulder. 'OK, fine. So there's this friend, we go way back? Known him half my life, since school? And he was, uh, wanting me to go on holiday with him, end of the month? And I kinda said I would?' He shrugged. 'Yeah, so not that big of a deal. I'm just sweating the small stuff, like the arrangements?'

Ambrose smoothed Freddie's hair back, and kissed his forehead. 'OK.'

Tell him, you dick. He knows you're lying. 'Nnngah. It's Andrew? Sorry!'

'What?' Ambrose flushed. 'That cunt!'

'Wow.' Freddie stepped back. 'Wow. Stay classy, Brose.'

'OK, fine. I apologize to vaginas everywhere.' He stood there, like eyes wide, breathing hard through his nose? 'Ah, I *hate* that guy. The way he talks, the way he acts. Andrew Jacks? Really?'

'Sorry sorry sorry.'

'Yes, and I'm sorry for the C-bomb, there. I never say that. But come *on*. What the hell, Freddie?'

'Look, listen. It's a schmucky thing to do, I get that? Dude, I *told* you not to trust me?' Freddie felt himself filling up. But then he could hear Kat: *Plus you're manipulative.* He sniffed the tears back. 'So.'

'So,' repeated Ambrose. 'What now?'

'I don't know? Probably, this is the part where I get dumped?' he whispered.

'Wrong. This is the part where we do some serious talking. Agh!' Ambrose snapped a hand through the tall grass. 'Why would you do this? Freddie, please understand I'm *demented* with jealousy here. It's like he's deliberately flaunting his power over you. You did tell him about us? Oh my God, you didn't!'

'Sorry. I kinda— So he was all, I just want your company? He's scared he'll fall off the wagon, if— Normally he goes with his painter friend, only this year she's—? It's not anything. I mean, he

225

totally emphasized, "no other services required"?' Freddie rubbed his eyes. 'Listen, I'm sorry. Don't be jealous. You want me to bail? I'll ring him. Yeah? Yeah. Probably I should do that?'

'I'm not going to tell you what to do.'

'*Shit*. Now I've ruined everything, haven't I?'

'Well, you've given us some work to do, that's for sure,' said Ambrose. He began walking back to the car.

Freddie choked on a sob, felt like his throat had literally broken? He stumbled after him. 'Brose, I'm so sorry. Are we going back to Lindchester?'

'What? No!' He turned. 'Of course not. This is just a fight, not game over.'

'I hate this. I can't do this stuff!'

'Sure you can.' Freddie saw him relenting. 'We fight, then we talk, then we find a way of making up. That's how it works.'

'Yeah, but it won't work. Dude, I'm telling you – I can't be trusted.'

'Says who?' asked Ambrose. 'You keep repeating that. Who says you can't be trusted?'

And right then – with like seriously spooky timing? – his phone began to play: *I'm Alright*.

'Do you need to get that?' asked Ambrose.

'Nah.' Couldn't his dad, just for once, let it be? He'll leave a message.'

He left a message: *Ring me, son*. He left several messages. Freddie ignored them all. In the end, in desperation, Mr May senior called the only other number he had: Miss Blatherwick's. He remembered how the famous Miss B had always looked out for his feckless heart-breaking waster of a son through his schooldays, and after. She could pass the message on. Break it to him gently.

Chapter 33

There was the doorbell. Janey must have forgotten her key. Hullo. Matt could see two small figures through the dimpled glass. Local kids? He opened the door. Oh, crap.

'Morning, girls.' He scanned beyond them for Mum or Dad. 'Lovely to see you. What can I do for you today?'

The older one, Leah, was looking daggers at him. Sudden flashback to that safeguarding malarkey with tartypants a couple of summers back.

'We've come to see Jane,' she said.

'We've brought some biscuits and a card,' added the younger one, beaming up at him under a wonky mum-cut fringe. Little sweetheart.

'To say welcome to your new home,' explained Leah.

There was a pause. Does not compute, does not compute.

'That's very kind of you,' said Matt. 'Janey's out right now—'

Whoops! The old pastoral antennae gave an almighty wag. He clocked a look of despair on the older girl's face.

'—but she'll be back any minute. From her run. So if you're happy to hang on . . .' His mind zipped through the possibilities. No way was he going to invite them in, given Leah's history of porky-pies in the safeguarding department. Nor could he turn them away. Something was clearly amiss. Awkward kid, but Janey had managed some kind of rapport with her, back when she'd lived on Sunningdale Drive too.

'I know. Why don't we potter along and find a café and get us some breakfast? I'll text Jane, and she can join us there. All righty?'

The older one stood biting her lip. Tears brimming.

'We've actually *had* our breakfast, I'm afraid,' said Jess.

'Second breakfast, then?'

'Like hobbits! Yay!'

'Bingo!' said Matt. 'Like hobbits.'

But Leah nudged her.

'What? Why can't we?' demanded Jess.

'*Because*, OK?' hissed big sister. 'We should go.'

Yikes. How the hell to hang on to them till Jane rocked up, without it sounding like enticement? Couldn't start tempting them with sticky buns and pop, could he? 'Look, the thing is, I promised Jane I'd treat her to a slap-up breakfast,' improvised Matt. 'Why not join us? She'd love that. You can give her the card.'

'Yay!' said Jess. 'Can we have hot chocolate with marshmallows?'

Leah yanked her arm and muttered something.

'Why not? I like hot chocolate!' whined Jess.

A whispered exchange Matt couldn't hear. They were going to bolt. Come home, Jane! 'Breakfast's on us, of course. Jane's treat.'

'Fine,' snapped Leah.

So *that* was it. Poor kid was worried about money. What the hell was going on back at home? 'Okey-dokey,' he said. 'I need to get some shoes on, and text Janey. Want to explore the garden while you wait? Peachy. Won't be a tick.'

He shut the door, already speed-dialling the diocesan HR and safeguarding lady. Needed Helene to file a case note PDQ. Lordy, what a world they lived in, where you couldn't scoop up two desperate kids and give them a hug!

A-a-and breathe. Jane got the desperate message from Matt, and rose to the occasion magnificently. She rather liked Leah, having been a cross-grained little besom herself at that age, raging at her assigned gender role and hating the adult world on principle.

We may leave the Rogers family safely in the bosom of the diocese of Lindchester now. Phone calls were made to Becky's GP

228

and parents, and to Martin in France, who cut his holiday short and sped home to his girlies. The girlies had a lovely night camping out at Jane's and Matt's (all duly logged by Helene) in sleeping bags (YAY!) while they waited for Dad to come home. After that, the bishop of Barcup and his wife were able to shoot off to Portugal to recover. Phew.

All shall be well, and all shall be well, and all manner of thing shall be well. This is not to say that everything shall be peachy on every given occasion. Did you tick the *I Agree* box without reading the terms and conditions? I never promised you a rose garden, reader. Or if I did, it was not a rose garden with the thorns edited out. Indeed, where would we be without thorns to prove that the grace of God is sufficient for us? I hesitate to suggest that there will be a reward in heaven for those who torment the flesh of others in order that grace may abound. But if there were such a reward, then the vicar of Risley Hill would be laying up treasure for himself, all right.

The archdeacon of Martonbury was drafted in to help support the Rogers family at this difficult time. Matt couldn't help thinking a woman's touch might be required, a spot of the old listening and hand-holding. Rather than the bloody irritating problem-solving mansplaining approach he himself went in for (according to the missus).

So Bea did some hand-holding. Becky felt able to pour out her heart, as she had in the past to Father Wendy. What had triggered this crisis? Perhaps it was the hideousness of the school holidays, that sudden lack of structure that had been holding each wretched day in some sort of shape? But I think it was hope that did for Becky. Misery we can wade through. It is hope that poleaxes us. Hope came in the form of a phone call, a suggested getting together to catch up, an offer of fellowship in Christ (nothing more, of course), and the chance to pray together.

Becky should have told Laurie to take a hike. Had she learnt nothing three years ago? Yes, yes, but she was lonely. She went back in, telling herself it was just friendship, that she wasn't hoping for more. Friendship was what she needed, anyway. But I'll tell you something – the vicar of Risley Hill wanted more. Not hanky-panky, it may surprise you to learn. Too obvious, in a tabloidy vicar-rhymes-with-knicker kind of way. We will not bother with that weary trope. What Laurie wanted was adoration. Adoration was what fuelled the hungry engine of his ego. He even wheeled out the old classic 'My Wife Doesn't Understand Me'. As the reader knows, this is generally a synonym for – how to phrase this for a god-fearing audience? – grazing your goats on Mount Gilead among the lilies. Be that as it may, this is not what Laurie meant. His complaint was really, 'My wife doesn't believe my hype any more.'

After a couple of meetings, and heart-to-hearts, it dawned on Becky that she wasn't just lonely, she was ravenous. Lead me to Mount Gilead! Bring me your lilies! I will graze the heck out of them! She wanted this man as much as ever. *More* than ever. They both knew Julie was an alcoholic – though only Becky was pre-pared to name it. They both knew she was never going to change, and that he should leave her for Becky! He had suffered enough. Surely! In desperation she tried to force his hand: her, or me. And for the second time, Laurie withdrew, and stopped answering her texts.

This was the tale that Becky sobbed out to Bea. It was not quite the tale that Laurie told later in the week – sincerity dial cranked right up to Tony Blair levels – when the archdeacon of Martonbury scheduled a conversation.

Look, yes, it was a pastoral misjudgement on his part to respond to Becky's request to meet. Yes, Bea, he ought to have remembered that poor Becky was a needy lady, with a lot of issues. Look, Bea, as far as he recalled, it had all been at *her* instigation. And he believed that their God was a God of abundant grace, who might still bring his healing touch into that situation. But sadly, it was not to be. Or not yet. He had gently retreated as soon as it became clear things were still tricky. He was praying for the Holy Spirit to invade Becky's life, and make her truly the woman God in his wisdom planned for her to be, and—

'So you'd be quite confident your text messages back you up here, Laurie?' Bea cut in. 'If it came to that.'

She watched to see if the dreaded phrase *Clergy Discipline Measure* would flash through his mind. If it did, it went too fast for her to see.

'Of course.' Laurie spread his hands. 'If I still have them on my phone.'

'Not to worry,' replied Bea. 'Becky's probably still got them on hers. How's Julie?'

'Look, Bea, as you probably know, Julie has her struggles. But God's working through that situation, and bringing a blessing to our family.'

'Am I right in thinking she has an alcohol problem?'

'No, not any more, praise God. She just suffers from low mood, sometimes. But she's a brave lady, and I really honour the way she deals with that.'

Hmm. 'Well, you know there's support available, Laurie.'

'Of course, Bea. The diocese has been a real blessing to us over the years.'

He was repelling her at every turn with his light-sabre of sincerity. The smell of rat rose heavenward like a burnt offering. A little chat with the bishop elect of Barcup was in order. When he got back from his break in Portugal.

Talking of rats, I know the reader has been on tenterhooks about the rodent infestation in the house of the canon chancellor. Fear not! The pest control people have been in and put down those special plastic box traps that conceal all evidence of rodent slaughter, and can be passed off as tiny rat caravans to small children. Before long the house will be pest-free again.

Next door, in the precentor's house, Boris II is guarded from cat-attacks 24/7.

Forget the rats, you say? What about poor Freddie?

He thinks now, that he will look back on that break with Ambrose as a perfect golden time, like the last week of the summer holidays; or the end of childhood, almost, before you find out the bad stuff? Everything, all the bazillion things he'd done with a bazillion guys – every single thing was like a first again? And then,

231

all the regular things of just being with someone? Cooking. Singing. Watching the Olympics in bed. Laughing till he seriously thought he'd tear his intercostals? And out on the heath, you could hear broom pods splitting in the sun, like twigs snapping? Drone and buzz of insects. And this stillness over everything. Smell of hot bracken – that was always gonna break his heart for ever afterwards, make him think of that time?

Right after that massive fight, they went for a pub lunch. That's when Brose said, 'Freddie, I'm going to need you to make a decision.'

And him panicking. 'Dude, I choose you! It's you I wanna be with, not him? Half the time I like almost *hate* him? But you, you make me smile – in my actual heart, like all the time, the entire whole time, it's you?'

Turns out Brose meant, kayaking or horse riding? Doh. But hey, he'd managed to say it finally?

But then the fight over money? Dude, I can't let you buy me stuff. And he was all, so who's paying for the week on the cousin's yacht? You let Jacks comp you a holiday, but I can't buy you lunch? Gah. Then he was, would you buy me stuff, if you had money?

'Babe, I'd buy you everything.'

'Like what?'

'Uh. Like, maybe an owl?'

Brose laughed. 'You'd buy me an owl?'

'Yeah, a Scops owl? Tiny, and super cute, you know? Like a tennis ball, only with feathers? Then I'd buy you a peach tree. 'Cept you haven't got a garden?'

'I've got a garden. I've got a house in Lindford.'

'No way! I did not know that. Plus I'll buy you yellow socks. With black stripes. Like a bee? And a hot-air balloon.'

'To match the socks?'

'Whoa, like a giant bee? Awesome!'

Random stuff – it keeps floating through his mind as he packs his bag. He gets the suit out of the wardrobe, the 'I'm a loser' suit, the 'I'm the bishop's chauffeur' suit, the 'standing in the dock getting sent to juvie' suit.

The funeral suit.

Ah, shit. His entire whole family gathered. This was going to be like a knife slicing him open, top to toe, and everything was gonna come sprawling out.

SEPTEMBER

Chapter 34

Mist lies across the diocese of Lindchester. Archipelagos of trees float in a white ocean. Cows break the surface like pods of sea mammals. We wait. For term to begin. For the new session of Parliament. For autumn. For a fresh start, for forgiveness, a clean page in a new exercise book and a sharp HB pencil.

But not quite yet.

How are our friends faring in this misty limbo? Has Sonya been busy bottling the produce of the palace garden? Alas, no. The larder shelves stand empty of Kilner jars. But she has done her best, poor thing, floundering in her predecessor's shadow. She has gathered plums and windfall apples and put them in boxes by the gate with a sign: 'Help Yourself!'

August edges to an end. House martins gather like crotchets along telegraph wires. The dean and the bishop have both returned from holiday and braved their work inbox. The bishop finds that his invaluable EA has already been in like a bomb disposal expert and made things safe for him. The dean – less fortunate in her PA – wades through 300 new emails. NOOO! A bit of medieval masonry has fallen in the south aisle. Argh! Nets have gone up as a precaution. Marion mops her brow, and ploughs on with her task. There. The inbox has been faced down. Nobody has died. Gene opens a Dom Pérignon 2006 to mark the fact that one tiny bit of sandstone narrowly missing a verger does not *actually* constitute every dean's nightmare: CATASTROPHIC FAILURE

OF THE FABRIC (which is more your 'spire crashing through roof' scenario).

Miss Blatherwick waters her poor Lindchester pippin. The last few apples have all puckered up to the size of walnuts. But there is still sap in the twigs. It will take years to recover, her metaphor tree, but recover it will. Or so one trusts, knowing one might not be around to see. She carries the empty bucket back to the house to refill it. Then she pauses, bent at the sink to catch her breath. No. One bucket would have to do. Goodness, what a nuisance this condition is. So draining. The sleeplessness, the appetite loss.

She lowers herself into a chair. Her mind wanders to her dear boy. She'd offered to drive him to his grandfather's funeral, of course, but part of her had been relieved when he said no. Let him be all right. Miss Blatherwick has very little time for Mr May senior, frankly; though one tries to forgive (as one hopes to be forgiven).

We last saw Freddie disconsolately pondering the hated suit, and dreading the nightmare family reunion that lay ahead. Brose was going to run him to the station the following morning. The only silver lining was getting out of that week on the yacht without pissing Andrew off. Hey, you can't argue with a funeral? Except he *had* to go and blurt it all out anyway, how he should never have accepted in the first place, because Ambrose? And then Andrew was really sweet about it, like bless you, you could have brought him along too?

He tossed the suit on the bed and sat down. Looked round at Ground Zero. Gah! Totty had told Mrs Thing months back not to clean his room till he tidied it. *Man*, it was rank in here. He should get onto it. Mugs, skanky running kit, junk food cartons. What are you – fourteen? What if Brose ever wants to stay over? Get *onto* it, yeah?

But he just sat there.

Silver lining? Not so much. Right now, given the choice? he'd be on that yacht. Yeah, he would. He'd be off his face, getting it on with some older guy, like a total cheating whore, fighting with Andrew, blocking it all out, coz *anything* would be easier to deal with than his family. Older half-brothers still calling him Polly, his dad insisting he sang 'O for the wings', and not listening, not *getting* that it was a treble part, even if it was Granddad's favourite. Like *hello*? Have we forgotten the history here? The tiny matter of the camming thang and getting kicked out of school? Not to mention the whole escort era, the— ah, let's not even go there? But according to you, Dad, I'm meant to stand there and sing, like I'm still Gramps's little angel chorister, who didn't get cut out of the will and told never to show his face again?

Ah, cock. Freddie knew how it was going to go down. He was going to flake. Brose would drop him at the station, and Freddie would get on the London train instead, disappear on a three-day crash-and-burn. And everyone would be gathered at the crem, all, where's Freddie? I thought Freddie was coming? And then the coffin would arrive, and his dad would shrug and they'd start without him. Same old. I gave you a chance, son, and you blew it. You'll never change.

Yeah. That was totally how it would go down.

Freddie was wrong about this. He went to the funeral, in a new suit (an early birthday present from guess who), acquitted himself honourably, and sang that treble aria in his man voice — even though it was all wrong — like an angel. Let us speed back on the time-travelling wings of fiction and find out why.

The reader may picture Freddie's panic when he heard Brose's footsteps coming up the stairs. No-o-o-o! Not good, not good! He tried to keep him out, but nu-uh. Guy was an ox. Just picked him up, carried him into the middle of the mess and stood him there. Had himself a good long look round?

'Impressive. Five months' work, Totty says.'

'Ah, Jesus, Brose! Don't do this. I'm dying here?'

But he just laughed. 'You still think there's something I can find out that will stop me loving you? Go and grab the hoover and some bin liners and let's get this sucker sorted.'

And afterwards, when finally it was turned round — clean sheets, windows open, carpet vacuumed, smell of polish in the air — they sat together on the edge of the bed. Freddie leant his head on his shoulder. And Brose was all, 'See? I'm still here, Freddie. Still love you. So now let's talk about me coming with you to the funeral.' And Freddie was,

'No way! Dude, you think *this* was a mess, you ain't seen nothing.'

But he was all, 'Bring it.'

BACK TO SCHOOL! Hush, hush, whisper it not!

Leah has been taken by Dad – at last! – to the official school outfitters of QM. This historic emporium is called – completely brilliantly – Thrashers. The official bottle-green blazer with the red Tudor rose on the pocket has been purchased, along with the official black trousers (Leah would rather gouge her eyes out than wear a skirt). She has the pale green shirts (which *must* be tucked in); and the green striped tie, which Dad has taught her how to tie properly.

The train season ticket has not been bought. For now, the Rogers girls are living with Dad in Lindford. Leah will be able to walk to school. Dad will drive Jess to Cardingforth in the morning, and then Madge will drive her to Lindford at home time. Mum is staying with Grandma and Granddad until she feels better again.

Everything will be OK. Leah rubs her hand over her head, and feels the thrill of her new short crop. Boy hair, she has boy hair now, like Arya pretending to be a boy to save her life! She listens to the strange night noises of Lindford, and tells herself: It's all OK. *You've coped really well, Leah. I'm really proud of you. You don't need to worry any more. You're only eleven. You don't have to be responsible for everything.* That's what Dad said. She hugs his praise to her chest like the blanky she doesn't have any more, because she's too old to need it.

Nothing to worry about.

Apart from Big School . . .

No, no! She feels like she's bracing her entire self against a door. But the door is slowly opening all the same. The minutes are ticking down. Tomorrow is the last day of August. Then it's September. There's nothing she can do to stop it. The only good thing left is the party tomorrow. Secret surprise. *His* birthday. Ssh . . .

It went off like a dream. Totty kept Freddie busy with some invented garden chores until the appointed hour, then sent him across to the precentor's, carrying a box of windfall apples. That's when the fuckers all burst out, *Surprise!*

Aw! You guys! All the back row, whole music department – he gazed round, mouth open – clergy Chapter, Janey and Matt, Dom, Marty and the girls, Miss B, Kat, Ed and Neil. Chloe hanging onto Cosmo's collar. The staff from Vespas, laughing at him. You knew, all day you knew, you bastards!

Literally everyone was here? And Ambrose, standing there with his big smile. You did this? Naw. You actually did this all for me? And here I am, still in my waiting tables gear, holding a dumb box of apples? He turned round to find somewhere to put it, and—

'Whoa! What the actual fuck is THAT?' Uli was bringing in like a yard-high Christmas tree cake tower, with sparklers fizzing out the number twenty-six?

'It's your *croquembouche*,' said Ambrose. 'I was up all night baking it.'

'Bull. Shit. That's off the internet.'

'Oh, OK, then. Ha-a-appy birthday to you . . .'

And everyone joined in. Like maybe they like, *liked* him? even though most of the time he was a pain in the ass, and right now he could only stand there crying, still holding the box of apples like a total idiot?

And so August ends. A last handful of days before the House returns and the political music must be faced. (What have we done, what have we done?) The northern hemisphere tilts into autumn. Is this the tipping point, these last few days of perfect balance, of calm, before everything changes?

'What on earth is fig urine?'

'What on earth is *what*?' asks Father Dominic.

'Fig urine,' says Mrs Todd. She is still living at the vicarage. The summer is over, and Father Dominic has not yet been saved. 'Oh, I see! It's figurine! The hyphen was in a funny place.'

'Thank God for that.' He fans himself. 'I thought you were on Urban Dictionary again.'

'That! I don't believe a word of it. It's just dirty schoolboys making stuff up.' She jabs the screen with her finger as if squashing ants. (Why, *why* had he thought an iPad was a good idea?) 'What do you make of this gay bishop coming out business?'

Nice segue, mother. 'I'm rather longing for the day when people are just people, and this kind of thing isn't news.'

'If only people would mind their own beeswax and not get their knickers in a wotsit, a thing, a twist. That's my considered opinion.' She deals a few more ant-killing jabs. 'It was "a major error" to appoint him, it says here in this article.'

Dominic glances. 'Oh, Gafcon. They probably mean, why didn't we hear about it in time to head it off? Poor darlings, they can't keep their face pressed to every window.'

Silence falls in the kitchen. Mrs Todd pursues a private line of thought.

Oh Lord. Here we go again.

'That tall boy is very nice.'

'It's actually a dresser, but thanks.'

'No, you daft ninnyhammer. That tall young man. You know. Accountant. Thingummy's cousin.'

'Ah! Ambrose, you mean.' He shakes his head. 'He's got someone already.'

'Oh. Anyway, as soon as this hip is better, I'll be out of your hair. You can have your life back.'

You *are* my life now, you silly old bat. He leans over and kisses her cheek.

'What's that for, all of a sudden?' she demands.

'Nothing.' He gets to his feet. 'I'm off to take this wedding. Try not to set fire to anything while I'm out.'

'Pish and tosh.'

Father Dominic walks down the vicarage path in the sunshine. September at last! One of his favourite months of all. Goody-good. And the last wedding of summer. A pigeon croons in the sycamore tree by his gate.

Is this the tipping point? he wonders. When the House of Bishops meets later this month, will there be a change of heart about marriage? Does he dare let himself hope?

Chapter 35

*T*his time tomorrow, I'll be looking back on it. Leah invented that mantra on the two-mile walk to her last karate grading. Mantras were Zen. Plus they gave you a sense of calm and perspective. *This time tomorrow . . .*

The kitchen clock ticked. Five past six. She was sitting alone at the table, already showered and in her uniform. That weird new clothes smell was coming off her shirt. Her new schoolbag was in the hall, with her new pencil case in, full of new pencils and the embarrassing novelty fast food rubbers from Jess, which she *had* to take with her, or Jess would be hurt.

She stared into her bowl. Chocolate cereal was meant to be a special treat. Dad didn't approve of Nestlé. It looked like rabbit droppings. The milk had gone all brown. She stirred it round and round and felt sick.

This time tomorrow. This time . . . It wasn't working. Focus, you idiot! Get in your fighting zone. Visualize a calm place. *This time tomorrow, I'll be looking back on the first day of QM.* See? You can do it. And this time next year, it would just be, huh, whatever, same old. Because then she'd be going into Year 8, and a whole nother bunch of new girls would be starting. Probably they'd be feeling sick too, and thinking, Maybe if I actually threw up, I wouldn't have to go? Except you'd still have to go the next day, and then your first day would be everyone else's day two, so you'd be like the *only* new girl. You'd be totally on your own. Everyone else would be a day ahead of you, knowing stuff, and you'd look stupid and keep having to ask about everything.

Oh God, what if she got lost and couldn't find the right classroom? What if she cried, like a total stupid cry-baby? Except it had been scientifically proven that crying was not a sign of weakness. Freddie had cried at his party. You actually had to be pretty cool and OK with yourself to cry in public.

(Please don't let me cry.)

Dad was coming! Quickly, she rubbed her eyes and made herself spoon up some rabbit poo and swallow it. For a second she nearly sicked it straight back up, but no, it slithered down, all bobbly and slimy.

'How are you doing, darling?'

She twitched a shoulder and scowled. *Don't* let him start his lame vicar-y stuff about Jeeee-sus being with her, like she was a Junior School assembly he was taking, or something.

Tick-tick-tick. Ten past six. Oh, let it be over!

'You're a lot braver than I was at your age,' he said. 'I was nearly sick every day for the first term.'

'Huh.'

'All right if I take a photo of you in your new uniform and haircut before you set off?'

'What? I'm not *that* lame, Dad.'

'I know. But it's for your mum. So she doesn't miss out.'

'FINE.'

8.20 a.m. Chloe was just finishing her run-before-work. Her pink trainers crunched through the fallen beechmast. What a lovely day! She saw them in their new uniforms as she left the arboretum. QM Girls, QM Boys, Lindford Comp kids, all creeping like snails unwillingly to school. Aw, bless! The littlies looked more like tortoises than snails, with their humungous backpacks, and their little necks too skinny for their collars. Ha ha! Flashback to herself in plaits and braces and geeky glasses. Oh, hadn't she been a perfect little sitting-on-the-front-row-and-shooting-her-hand-up homework lover? A half-pint ethnic Hermione Granger!

Cosmo lolloped along beside her on his lead. He didn't really get the running thing, daft beast. Every intoxicating new smell and he *had* to screech to a halt to explore it – Ow! nearly dislocating her arm and jerking her flat. Wow! Who knew how intoxicating the urban environment could be? For a dog, that is. There were plenty of signs of human intoxication – yeuch! – still lying about from the weekend. This was her street pastor pitch. She'd just done the new rota. They were stretched a bit thin at the moment. Could do with a few more recruits. Maybe she should— Ow!

'Cosmo! *Stop!* Here, boy.' He bounded back. 'Look, we need to decide a lamppost policy. We both have to go round the same way, OK? Good boy.'

Cosmo wagged and squirmed in delight. Treat? Treat? Cosmo came back! Where's his treat?

8.45 a.m. The registration bell would be ringing. Martin could almost hear it echoing in his soul. His heart thumped on Leah's behalf as he studied the picture on his phone. Look at her! Standing tall and white-faced in the hallway, scowling. His brave girl! He fired off some desperate arrow prayers: Lord, let her have a better time of it than I did. Let her fit in, somehow. Let them not bully her.

The photo wavered a moment. Then Martin blinked. What was he thinking? Nobody in their right mind was going to pick on Leah Rogers, even if she flatly refused ever to fit in. Was she a changeling, this fierce martial daughter of his? Oh, but let it be all right. Let her have a good day, be with her, let her not be lonely, let her find some kindred spirit!

He blew his nose. Now he ought to send the picture to her mother. Although—

Send it. She was *not* a bad mother. He was *not* going to punish her by seizing this chance of getting custody. He did not need to do that. His first priority was the girls and their long-term well-being, which would *not* be best served by their parents fighting over them in court. He made himself take a mental step back. The events of the summer were unfortunate. It was unfortunate that the girls' mother was suffering from depression and had not sought help. It was unfortunate that he had been unaware of the situation, and that the girls had suffered as a consequence. But he would not apportion blame, either to himself, or the girls' mother. Although—

Leah, first day at QM. Hope all is well with you. M.

Send.

Personally, I would quite like to apportion a bit of blame. So would the Venerable Bea Whitchurch. We would both like the rector of Risley Hill to take the rap for the havoc he selfishly caused. Bea has done what she can, but all her offers of pastoral support have been rebuffed. She can only watch and pray – and prepare a thorough briefing for the new bishop of Barcup, to land on his desk the minute he is officially installed.

It will be a busy season of installations this coming term in Lindchester Cathedral. Installations and Collations (the proper term for the plumbing-in of new archdeacons). The precentor cracks his knuckles, and readies himself for the exquisite anguish of fine-tuning the liturgy. Out come the well-worn copies of 'I Was Glad'. Laurence, the organist, dusts off his favourite thunderous French volleys (which to the untutored ear sound like a dyspraxic ogre trampling up and down the manuals). Iona, the sub-organist, day-dreams an improvisation that almost, but not quite, seems to include phrases from 'Send in the Clowns'.

A whole new set of music folders have now been bought for the Lindchester Girls' Choir. For political choral reasons that are entirely beyond me, the girls may not yet be called 'choristers', nor may they wear cassocks and ruffs. But it is a step in the right direction. We look forward to their first appearance at evensong after half-term. The precentor has asked the canon chancellor to identify suitable readings for the occasion (and no, the passage about Lot's daughters is *not* suitable, thank you, Father).

'It was fine.'

That, as every parent knows, is all that any self-respecting child is allowed to divulge about their day at school. Martin Rogers had cleared his diary in order to be in, so that Leah wouldn't be coming home to an empty house. As every parent knows, only one

246

permitted question remained. Into this frail vessel Martin poured all his parental angst:

'So what did you have for lunch?'

'Food.'

In another clergy household altogether, the same question was posed.

'Chips and veggie burger, and salad, and then— Oh, I meant to say, I met this really cool girl? She does karate, so we all call her karate girl? She has her hair cut really short, and I *mean* short? Can I get mine— Yeah, sorry, and then there was three choices of pudding or yogurt, oh, or fruit? We tried to go up twice only they caught us, you have to scan your— Science is going to be awesome, this other girl, Rachel, says her older brother at QM Boys says that if you, like, stockpile chemicals each week and hide them in this hole in the bench, then later in term you can actually get this really MASSIVE explosion going, and the teacher goes ape, and you can be all, innocent face, I have no idea what just happened? We are *so* going to do that, her name's Leah, and ha ha ha, you won't believe this? Go on, guess! Never mind, you'll never guess, only her dad's a vicar too? I mean, how awesome is that?'

'Sounds fabiola, darling,' said Kay Redfern, the archdeacon elect of Lindford. But her eyes met Helene's and they both had the same thought. *Leah Rogers? Uh-oh.*

Uh-oh is exactly what the bishop of Lindchester thought on Thursday morning, when Kat reminded him about his next engagement. He'd been rather hoping Freddie wouldn't get round to booking an appointment. Oh well.

'Freddie. Good to see you. Have a seat.'

Kat slipped back out, leaving the door ajar, as per Steve's instructions.

'Uh, yeah, so, just wanted to like give you my thoughts, like, formally, to your face, if that makes sense, like, ahead of your thang?'

Pause. 'My thang?'

'Uh, House of Bishops?'

'Ah!' Steve smiled encouragingly. 'Fire away.'

'Cool. OK.' Freddie studied his shoelaces. 'So.'

Steve waited.

'Yeah, listen, do you believe gay sex is sinful?' he asked.

'Well, I bet *some* of it is,' said Steve.

Freddie snorted. 'Yeah, no, stop making me laugh, I'm serious here. I bet some straight sex is sinful.'

'Me too.'

'Right. Just not like, major league sinful?'

'Look, Freddie.' He sighed. 'As you probably know, I still believe – looking at the general drift of the Scriptures – that there's something about the union of a man and a woman that's normative.' Freddie was staring at his laces again. 'Part of God's original plan in creation. Even setting aside procreation, there's a complementarity—'

'Yeah, no, no. A of all, it's not all about difference, coz otherwise, why not the animals, yeah? They're even more like, "complementary" to Adam. And B of all, if we're on creation, think about it, what about, it's not good for man to be alone? But you're all, Freddie, I'm sorry, but actually you *do* have to be alone, you can never be with someone, coz that's not part of God's original plan?'

'I'm—'

'Yeah, you are, dude. It's like you're saying, so, you're left-handed? Cool, that's not a sin. God still loves you, but you can't ever use your left hand. You don't *have* to use your right hand, but left hand? Nu-uh.' He stood up abruptly. 'Forget it. Who am I kidding? Not like I'm gonna change your mind, Paul.'

'Steve,' said Steve.

He flushed. 'Steve. Catch you later.'

'Can I pray before you go, Freddie?'

But he was off.

The bishop stood a long time in his office, looking out across the drive, feeling like a total and utter failure. A verse floated into his head: *Let God be true, but every man a liar.* It was breaking his heart but he could not, could not abandon the position he still believed was the truth.

He watched the crocodile of choristers coming back from their morning rehearsal. Remembered his own first day at a different cathedral school. Shorts. Knee socks. Yellow chorister cap. Homesick and weepy. But it passed. It all passes.

Will we ever be out the other side looking back on this debate? This time next month, next year, in five years, in ten years?

Chapter 36

Mist lies across the diocese of Lindchester again. Spire top, rooftop, treetop, hilltop – all are rubbed out. Then the sun burns and the landscape smokes like the aftermath of some disaster, the way it did in harvest days of yore when they still burnt the stubble.

Jane stared out of her new bedroom window on Monday morning. Pah! The mist did not fool her. Another miserable hot day lay in store. She could feel it, like a pending migraine. It's autumn, for God's sake! Season of boots – boots, I tell you! She pulled on her jeggings and BOOTS, but wisely went down the upper-body layering route, so that she didn't end up ripping off her jumper and sitting in the departmental strategy day in her bra.

But I'm right, and you're wrong, weather. She jabbed a finger. Let's not forget that.

Sadly, Matt was not there for her to shout at cathartically on some trumped-up pretext. He was off on his very first College of Bishops jolly, where they would be locking mitres over 'Issues in Human Sexuality'. And for the very first time, any episcopal imbecility that ensued was going to impinge directly on Dr Jane Rossiter. Huzzah. She was very much looking forward to being put in the invidious position of needing to smack the chops of anyone who disparaged Anglican bishops, while inwardly admitting they had a point.

Still, it was all rather lovely. Later, as Jane stood on the quiet platform at Martonbury station, she was forced to concede that it *was* gorgeous. The stillness, the hedges glowing with hips and haws. A feeling surprised her: joy. As palpable as an old friend sneaking up on her and bursting out. She narrowed her eyes. That bastard was praying for her down in Oxford, wasn't he?

We can neither prove nor disprove Jane's theory for, as you know, we may not join the College of Bishops as they gather to deliberate. But we may, in a heartfelt Anglican manner, pray for their discussions, speculate, and pour anticipatory scorn on anything they might come up with. We have done our bit. According to temperament, we have campaigned, tweeted, blogged, manoeuvred, kept well out of it, shrugged, or wept tears of despair. It is now out of our hands, and in the bishops'. Or God's (though not all Anglicans can say that without needing to get their toes surgically uncurled afterwards).

Tears of despair were certainly what Freddie shed after his aborted talk with Steve. Ambrose asked how it went.

'Babe, no offence, but I really don't wanna talk about it? Coz yeah, total crash and burn? Had all this stuff planned, but every word, and I can literally hear myself sounding dumber than a big dumb thing? So I panic? And I'm, I *have* to get out of here? Nice one, Freddie. Coz now Steve's all, what can you do? You just can't reason with them! Ah, Brose, I seriously do not know why I'm even trying to convince him? Not like he's gonna make all the difference, you know? Yeah, like there's not shedloads of other conservative dickwads ready to screw us over yet again? But it's like, I *have* to change Paul's mind? Man.'

'Paul?'

'Gah! Steve. I keep randomly doing that?'

Ambrose had an idea it was not so very random. But he held his peace.

At the very hour when Jane was ambushed by joy, Giles, the precentor, was on the platform at Lindford station, waiting for the train to London. There was to be a gathering of precentors to give thought to That Which Must Not Be Named, but may only be alluded to *sotto voce* as The Unhappy Event.

Alas, reader, it cannot be denied that the Event will come. Not soon, we pray. May it be happily and gloriously deferred for many more years. That said, it cannot be allowed to catch the cathedrals of our land unawares like a thief in the night. Thus it is not unreasonable to speculate that every precentor already has a secret file hidden under a secret code word on his or her hard drive against that day.

We will wave Giles off, and spare a thought for him and his fellow black-clad clerical colleagues sweltering in the armpitty embrace of London with the hot breath of the Tube all close up and personal. Here in the temperate zone of the Midlands, we fare slightly better, though we are menaced by thunderstorms. On Tuesday, an ominous light charges the air at dusk, as though a red filter has been slapped on the cosmos. Leah Rogers tackles her first lot of maths homework at the kitchen table, and the room fills with threat. Dominic's mum calls him to the window to look at his doolally geraniums, and tells him 'The End Is Nigh.' Up on the Close the cathedral radiates pink light. Miss Blatherwick stops to get her breath, and gazes in wonder. Goodness. The entire red/orange spectrum burns like a *trompe l'oeil:* cherry leaf on the lawn, all the cotoneasters and nasturtiums, her little car.

Yes, across Lindfordshire every red secret is briefly laid bare by this unseen nutter at the colour dial. Poor Neil, out running along narrow lanes between berry-studded hedgerows, suffers a non-specific attack of John Knoxitis, and has to sing as he runs. Aye, he's a bad man, but 'Jesus paid it all'. All. All. All. No condemnation, you hear me? 'I'll wash my garments white in the blood of Calvary's lamb.'

Lord have mercy! But then the sun sets. Phew. As you were, Lindcastrians.

'But why, Mummy?' asks young Chad William, the chancellor's son, on Wednesday morning. He is wearing his little pale blue St William's school sweatshirt for the first time. 'Why didn't Mrs Wathbone need me?'

BECAUSE MUMMY IS A CRAP MOTHER, OK? 'Because Mummy made a mistake, darling,' says Miriam. 'Mrs Rathbone needs you to start nursery tomorrow.'

Bloody staggered starts. Though staggering is appropriate. Staggering is the word right now. Staggering back up the mount, pushing the pushchair, sweat pouring off her in this heat. *Are you still here? Haven't you had that baby yet?* Why yes, I had the baby last week! I just stuffed this giant fitness ball up my dress because being pregnant IS SO MUCH FUN!

The hospital bag is packed and waiting in the hall. Sonya is standing by to look after Chad and Tabitha, when the time comes. Ah, God! Miriam has been pregnant for ever, and it's *still* a week till the due date. And then they'll probably let her go another fortnight, unless these bloody Braxton Hicks turn into the real thing. Three weeks!

'But *why* doesn't Mrs Wathbone need me till tomorrow?'

'Darling, I've explained. Mrs Rathbone doesn't want everyone starting nursery all at once.'

'But why—'

'Chad, *please* stop asking. I just made a mistake, OK?' She stops walking and gets her breath.

'Jinky! Jinky! Jinky!' shouts Tabitha, jerking in her pushchair.

Great. She's come out without the drinky beaker.

Why? Why? Why? Jinky jinky jinky!

Poor Miriam slumps over the pushchair handle in despair and looks down at the pavement. Why don't we all lie down on the pavement and howl in misery? That seems like a sensible plan.

She raises her head. Café. Just opening. Thank you, Jesus! They can probably kill thirty minutes of this godawful day in here. She wrestles the pushchair through the door.

If Miriam is hoping for a nice anonymous space in which to hone her submission for the Bad Mother Award, she will be disappointed. The café is Vespas. And there he is, the crazy dumb blond who keeps nearly getting kicked out of the choir. The one there was all the rumours about. Mercifully there are no other customers yet.

'Hey, guys! Table for three? Let me grab you a high chair and some menus. Hey, Chad, how's it going? Dude, cool sweatshirt!'

253

'Mrs Wathbone didn't need me today coz Mummy made a mistake.'

'JINKY JINKY JINKY!'

It happens while Miriam is bending over the pushchair to unbuckle Tabitha. That little pop, like treading on a grape.

Her eyes widen. Whoosh. No, no, no. She looks up at Freddie. *His* eyes widen. 'Uh, ambulance?'

She grips the pushchair handle and nods.

'No worries. I'm on it.'

As it happened, Freddie barely had time to cross the café and flip the sign to 'Closed'. Hence the headlines: *Woman gives birth in restaurant in less than five minutes.* Perhaps you saw the iconic photo: that little scrap swaddled in a Breton shirt, in his mum's arms.

Up on the Close, by the chancellor's front door, the hospital bag still waits, packed and ready.

Well, well, well. Freddie May: lay clerk, accidental midwife and total flipping hero. I for one was not expecting *that*. Like Freddie (whose legs went the minute the ambulance arrived and the paramedics took over) I need a little lie-down. Mother and baby both doing well, you will be relieved to hear. Noah Frederick Lawson, 9lb 7oz. And lest you are worried about Chad and Tabitha: 'Fweddie gave us cookies to eat while Mummy was having Noah, and I did a dwawing of a giant twactor. Look!'

You only get a finite number of heartbeats. It came to Freddie that night, as he lay in Brose's arms, head on his chest. He listened to the steady *doomf, doomf, doomf.* You only get so many heartbeats? The tiny little dude, slippery in his hands? Stroking his knobbly little back, and Miriam wailing, 'Oh my God, oh my God, is he alive? Is he alive?' And Freddie all, Babe, he's yelling, sure he's alive. Wrapping him up and giving him to her?

Ah, he could still feel the little heart fluttering away against his palm? And now Brose's heart, *doomf, doomf*, and his own pulse in his fingertips, in his throat, his ears? The miracle of it? And suddenly he was shaking again, delayed shock probably, and he was all, oh, Jesus, he so needed to be a dad? To hold his own child like that? But how would that ever happen?

The arms round him tightened, gathering him in close. Hushing him. It's OK, Freddie, I've got you. Ssh. It's all OK.

Our stout hero the bishop of Barcup is home from his first episcopal gathering.

'So,' says Jane. 'More delays.'

'Well, the slower we go, the more we take with us.'

'Talk about the mills of God!' snorts Jane. 'You've appointed "a reflection group" to assist with "the process of discernment"?'

'Yup.'

'And this group contains no LGBTI people?'

'Nope.'

'But several known conservatives?'

'Yup.'

'Jesus. What hope is there?' She raises her hand. 'Rhetorical. I know you brim with hope. From your big bald bonce down to your Doc Martens.'

He smiles. 'Well. At any rate, let's wait to see what they come up with before we despair.'

'And in the meantime,' says Jane, 'there's always beer.'

It is harvest weekend. Strange and florid squashes line church window ledges. There are dahlias and apples, and the traditional cauliflowers fluffy. Come, ye thankful people, come. Come to the cathedral (where the flower guild have excelled themselves) for the long-promised Installation and Collation of the new archdeacons.

It is Saturday afternoon. We will rise to the ancient vaults on our eagle wings and look down. There is Matt in the congregation in mufti and awkward liturgical limbo (former archdeacon, but not yet installed as bishop). Here come the clergy of the diocese. All the tribes have come up: high, low, charismatic, liberal. Let us wave to Father Ed, to Wendy and Virginia, to Martin and to our dear friend Father Dominic. And here are the cathedral clergy. Behold, how good and pleasant it is.

Everything is done reverently and in order. The choir is Glad. No lay clerk smirks in the worship songs. Kay Redfern and Alan Bowes add Venerable to their names. About time too! There is applause. Bishop Steve preaches. We stand to sing. 'All my hope on God is founded.'

But we only have a finite number of heartbeats.

Dominic feels it kick off. Wild frenzied galloping. He stays calm. Makes his way out along the row, finds a steward. Says: 'Heart.'

Then he is lying down. Heart racing faster, faster. Could this be it? What, *now*, Lord?

'Me through change and chance he guideth.'

A white face swims over him. Ed.

'Only good and only true.'

Ed squeezes his hand. 'God unknown, he alone.' Whispers his name. 'Dommie. Dominic.'

'Calls my heart to be his own.'

Chapter 37

Sometimes the end bursts into the middle, catching us out while we are still in the thick of it. The bookmark halfway through the novel. Bills unpaid, dirty fridge, browsing history not deleted. And all those things we were going to say. I'm sorry. I love you. Writers plan, then we must stay close to our characters and follow the line of words to see where it goes. But no matter where the line takes us, the novel will eventually close. There will be a last word, and that will be that. *The End.*

But not today. It is not the end for Father Dominic. This makes me happy, because for a moment I genuinely thought he was a goner. The line of words does not go via that route. He did not die at the back of Lindchester Cathedral, after all. No, he merely made a complete tit of himself.

'Well, I wouldn't put it like that,' said the GP on Monday morning.

Dominic had not met her before. She was about twelve.

'From what you've described, it sounds like SVT,' she went on. 'Supraventricular tachycardia.'

'Blimey.'

'So basically, that just means an abnormally fast heart rate? It's not life-threatening, but it's pretty scary while it's happening.' She was enunciating clearly and giving him the encouraging smile he reserved for old biddies. Sauce!

'I see.'

'Then it sounds as though you had a panic attack on top of it. People often feel as if they're dying during a panic attack.' Another biddy-soothing smile.

'OK.'

'So I'm going to refer you to a cardiologist for an ECG. They probably won't find anything, unless you have another episode of SVT while they're actually doing the ECG. Let's quickly take your blood pressure, OK?'

Don't you mean my BP? Dominic bared his mighty arm.

'Do you smoke? No? Excellent. Weekly alcohol intake?'

'Oh, let's see.' What were the current guidelines? And more urgently, what preposterous claim had he made last time? 'Obviously, it varies.'

'Ballpark?' She applied the cuff. It was one of those automatic machines.

'Ooh, say, fourteen units? Give or take.'

The cuff gripped his arm like a policeman apprehending a criminal. Argh, I confess! Then it eased off.

'Hmm.' She studied the monitor. 'That's a bit high. We'll take it again in a moment. Could you just hop on the scales for me?'

Of course it's bloody high! thought Dominic, as he bent to unlace his shoes. I've just been lying to you about my alcohol intake.

'Are you under a lot of stress at the moment?'

He opened his mouth to deny it. That's when the tears surged. Mum. Dear old mum. What on earth was he going to do about her?

As he walked home across Lindford, everything looked so very dear and lovely that it hurt. Michaelmas daisies. Winking knees through busted jeans. Of course – Freshers' Week. He kept getting a mawkish urge to sing the hymns of childhood. What was that Primary School hymnbook? *With Cheerful Voice*. Wavy green and blue lines on the cover.

> Fair are the flowers,
> Fairer still the sons of men
> In all the freshness of youth arrayed!

He battled his way through the leafleteers outside the Fergus Abernathy building. Pizza and paintballing. 'Yet is their beauty fading and fleeting.' He wanted to scoop them all up. Come to Father! Take care of yourselves, my darlings. Be kind. Don't get hurt, don't waste a single minute of your precious lives.

He blotted his eyes and walked on. Oh, pull yourself together, Todd. What a dreadful time to be reaching adulthood, though. Austerity and inequality, hatchet job on the welfare state, Brexit fallout, Labour tearing itself to ribbons. And Donald Trump! Lord, were they *seriously* going to elect him? Dominic pictured that iconic Thatcher and Reagan *Gone with the Wind* poster. Are we really careering back there again?

He was approaching the vicarage. Quick, happy face for mother. His father had been carried off by a heart attack when Dominic was nine, and it wouldn't do to make her fret. Dominic's own heart was currently behaving itself, but golly heck, that tachycardia scared him! It was as though his old Honda had been fitted with a jet engine.

He turned into his drive. The first leaves were sidling down from the branches. All this fading and fleeting beauty. 'My Jesus, thine will never fade.' Oh, my Jesus. Oh, holy Mary, Mother of God, pray for us sinners, now and in the hour of our death.

'Honey, I'm ho-ome!' he called as he opened the door. 'Nothing to worr—' Oh my God! 'Mother, I can smell gas!' He belted into the kitchen.

Mrs Todd looked up from her Sudoku. 'Oh, have I left it on again?'

Dominic lunged at the hob and turned off the hissing ring, then opened all the windows. 'You're a complete liability!'

'Still, not to worry,' she said. 'It's not the kind that poisons you. It just blows you up.'

'Oh, well, that's *fine* then. *Except it blows half the street up, too.*'

'Pooh, fusspot. What did the doctor say?'

He told her. 'So everything's fine. Apart from the palaver of getting a twenty-four-hour blood pressure monitor fitted. White coat hypertension, indeed! I'm not scared of *you*, Dr Missy! You're younger than my second-best biretta! I didn't actually *say* that,' he added.

'Really? I always say things like that.'

'I know you do, dear.'

'But they aren't worried about you? Jolly good.' She picked up her biro and set to work briskly on the grid. He saw her sneakily wipe her eyes. 'I'm just putting any old number in,' she explained. 'I hate Sudokus, but they're meant to ward off dementia. Did you know you can get human ashes put into fireworks?'

'Honestly, mother. Even after I'm dead you're determined to blow me up!'

'I was thinking of me. I'd quite like to go out with a whizz-bang.'

'Not a chance,' said Dominic. 'I'm having you made into a nice pair of diamond cufflinks.'

They fell silent.

'What a funny old life,' she said at last. 'Still, I'm glad we've got a bit longer.'

'Me too. Sorry I gave you a scare like that.' He squeezed her hand. 'Come on. Give over, you old trout. Why not move in properly? It'd be a load off my mind.'

'I'll trout you, sonny Jim.'

'Is that a yes?'

Mrs Todd blew her nose. 'I don't know. Oh, go on then. Yes.'

'Calloo-callay! O frabjous day!' Dominic danced a little jig.

'Go on with you, you daft ha'porth. I'll put the kettle on.'

Mrs Todd was not alone in being glad to have Dominic around a bit longer.

'I *so* wished you were there, darling,' said Father Ed. 'With your Boys' Brigade CPR training. I thought poor old Dommie was going to die, and all because I was sent to Scouts. Anyway, he's fine, thank God.'

'So basically, the wee jessie had a panic attack?' said Neil.

'Hmm.' Ed stroked his chin. 'I wonder if there's a module on "Bedside Manner" in the reader training course?'

Neil treated him to the wide blue stare. 'Who said anything about reader training?'

Ed waited to be asked why the recycling had not been taken out. But instead, Neil began fidgeting with his new Fitbit.

'Och, fine, so you know about that, then. Problem now is, there's no way himself is going to recommend me,' he said. 'Him, Laurie. The rector. Not since I braced him about his wife being an alkie.'

Ed's eyes popped. 'Wow. Um. I didn't . . . Was that your place to—?'

'Aye, but that's the thing, big man,' Neil burst out. 'It's *nobody*'s place. Nobody's saying anything, and that poor lassie needs help, you know? Oh, I was tactful. I didn't just wade in. But no. Apparently, we all have to pretend everything's fine, because God's healed Julie of her alcohol dependency, praise him. *And* I haven't done my five thousand steps today,' he added. 'I'll maybe go for a quick run, clear ma head.'

'That's a bit worrying about Julie, Neil. You might want to have a chat with Archdeacon Bea,' said Ed.

'Don't look at me, pal. I'm not dobbing him in.'

'OK.' Ed raised his hands. 'But look, don't you think it might be time to find another church? I know Josh is desperate for help over in Martonbury. And there's the street pastors. You might like that.' Ed stopped. Damn. He was sounding like his mum suggesting good books to take on holiday. 'Sorry. I'll butt out. Tell you what, let's call round on Dom with a bottle of fizz later. Make a fuss of him.'

'Fine, but we're taking Bolly. I'm not drinking his crappy Prosecco, you hear?'

It was a nice little gathering, though a *leetle* more sedate than it might have been, had Dominic's new colleague Virginia not joined them. Virginia's licensing as the diocesan officer for social justice (and associate vicar of Lindford parish church) will be this Sunday. She has moved into her new house, rented by the diocese from none other than our lovely friend Ambrose. (He'd been letting it since he'd moved to Vicars' Court, and was glad not to have student tenants again.) The following Saturday will be the installation of the Rt Revd Matt Tyler as bishop of Barcup, after which we can slump back and fan ourselves with a Book of Common Prayer (or perhaps an iPad with the Daily Prayer app open) and recover.

Father Dominic's survival is not our only cause of rejoicing. Up on the Close, the metaphorical bunting is out for little Noah Frederick too. The individual who made an off-colour joke (something about it being a dramatic first encounter for Mr May) got vaporized by a flash from the dean's eyes.

'Not funny, Gene. Look, we all need to start taking Freddie much more seriously,' said Marion. 'I think he responds well to being given responsibility. He's proving time and again he can be trusted, if we are only prepared to give him a chance.'

'I repent in dust and ashes, deanissima. Though *personally*, I fear Mr May is on countdown to self-destruct. All this worryingly grown-up behaviour . . . But no matter. More wine?'

But the dean waved away the vintage Pomerol. There was much on her mind. She had begun sounding out the members of Chapter about the restructure, ahead of the crucial meeting. After that, the game would be afoot. Would folk grasp the bishop's vision? Or would some need to be eased into early retirement? Oh Lord, was it going to be a bloodbath of employment tribunals and recrimination?

The Lawsons are prepared to give Freddie a chance. They have asked him to be Noah's godfather. Of course they have! Freddie's heart just melts with love for that little dude? Does he wanna be godfather? Hell, yeah!

Except now – as he and Brose walk Cosmo along the riverbank – he's projecting into a catastrophic future, where he gets back in with the wrong crowd? Then it's the whole stealing and drugs thang again, which lands him in prison? – I mean, what kind of a godfather is *that* for a little dude?

'Or alternatively, maybe none of that will happen?' suggests Ambrose. 'Maybe you'll have a brilliant singing career instead, get married to some guy who adores you, and live happily ever after?'

'Whoa. Dude.' Freddie stops short. Blinks. 'You're thinking . . . Did I just hear the M-word there?'

'Freddie, it's a bit soon to be talking about marriage,' says Ambrose, all pretend stern. 'We can't even agree what breed of dog we want.'

'*You* brought it up, not me! Ah, *man*!' He swats him. 'I don't know why I even bother talking to you.'

They walk on under a horse chestnut tree. Freddie kicks the broken conker cases. Cosmo is going wild for some smell. Then Ambrose bends and unclips the lead.

'Wait up! Is that OK?' asks Freddie.

'Yep. Chloe's been training him.'

They watch Cosmo tear off along the path.

'That dog is mental,' says Freddie. 'No way is he coming back, my friend. Nu-uh. Gonna be here for hours.'

'Watch this.' Ambrose whistles.

Nothing.

'AHA HA HA! Told you!'

But then, no way! No fucking way, he's only coming running? Crashes through the weeds, screeches to a halt, tail wagging. Starts leaping up at Brose?

'Good boy!' Ambrose gives him something from his pocket. He clips the lead back on.

'Well, whaddya know?' marvels Freddie.

Ambrose cuts him a side look. 'He comes back because he knows he'll always get a treat from Daddy.'

'That so?' Freddie rattles his tongue stud round his teeth. 'Then Daddy needs to keep them treats coming. Is my thought.'

Stillness. The dog pants. Another conker patters down through the leaves.

'I'm on it, Freddie.' But like Gene, Ambrose knows the count-down clock is ticking.

OCTOBER

Chapter 38

September dawdles to a golden end. How mellow it all is. In the parks of Lindfordshire (though no longer on the palace roof) we still catch whiffs of that elusive pungent shrub the bishop's wife has never quite identified. But the summer holidays have been packed away now. Ah well.

Michaelmastide! What if, right there, palm against our palm as we lean on a window, there were angels looking in? Would they sense our yearning? Our whispered *Let it be all right*. Would they pity us, trapped here, still not knowing how the story ends?

In Lindchester Cathedral, the chapel of St Michael is crammed with angels. There are Burne-Jones musicians, pale hands on harp and hautboy. There's that macho bronze Michael, for those who prefer their angels ripped and looking as though they can kick satanic butt. The flower guild have placed a brass vase of Michaelmas daisies at his feet. High above in the gloom hang cobwebby standards from battles of long ago. Ghost flags of ghostly battalions. The sunbeams pass through them.

An angel of another stamp sits quietly. A guardian angel, I think we must call her. It is Miss Blatherwick.

Lights flicker on the pricket stand. Above, hangs a new acquisition, a painting of Michael standing not on Satan, but on a human body. His left hand grips what looks like a bloody newborn. The interpretation (for which we may thank the canon chancellor) refers us to the tradition in which Michael conveys the souls of the dead to judgement. 'The body represents a human being at the time of death. The "baby" represents the soul of the deceased. Artist: M. Johns, 2015. (Egg tempura, gold and silver leaf on wood.)'

Miss Blatherwick is not sure she cares for this gory modern icon. One prefers to picture the hour of death as a peaceful slipping from one room to the next. One rather hopes not to be clenched in a giant fist and delivered up to judgement, like a joint of meat deposited on the butcher's scales. But perhaps this is simply to speak from a position of luxury. In poverty, or battle zones – in Aleppo (Lord have mercy!) – could *any* poor soul expect to depart in peace? In fact, who can say with confidence how the end will feel, even if one is fortunate enough to 'cease upon the midnight with no pain'; wafted to heaven on a Finzi Amen, as it were?

Would one not *still* be afraid?

Miss Blatherwick gets up from her seat, winces and then crosses to light a candle. She murmurs a prayer for her dear Freddie. (Let him not give way to his fears and spoil everything!) She remembers all those for whom this day will be their last. She prays for those being bombed in Syria. For those (scandalously!) starving in modern Britain. For the Labour Party, who must now put aside division, and all pull together. For the Church. For America. And for all sorts and conditions of men.

Let it be all right.

Let it be all right.

She sets off for home, to see if she can manage some porridge now. My word, what a picky eater she is becoming. She has no patience with herself.

Dean Marion, too, has said prayers for the Labour Party. Let us knuckle down, stop fighting, and become an effective opposition. Oh, please let Labour not become The Unelectable leading The Irreconcilable Tribes into the political wilderness for forty years (*thanks*, Gene). She prays for Chapter as well. For unity. They meet next week to discuss the proposed restructure. She fears they may lose a lay member over this.

Our good friend Father Wendy also shoots up a quick prayer for Labour. Then she dons her Marigolds and sets to work on the house in Sunningdale Drive.

Madge is here, too, polishing the inside of the French windows with old newspaper and vinegar. I don't believe anyone has ever done that, in all the time that Becky has lived here with her girls. The plan (knitted up by Archdeacon Bea) is that Becky will come back next week to meet with Martin, and discuss The Way Forward. They all agree it will be much nicer for Becky to come home to a clean, tidy house, ready for a fresh start.

Wendy sets about the fridge, throwing out the liquefied salad (oh, yuck!) and cleaning vegetable slime from the drawer.

'Know what I honestly think?' says Madge. She is kneeling on the worktop, shining up the back windows now. Her reflection hovers angelically on the other side, above the patio. 'I think the girls are better off with their dad in Lindford.'

'Oh, but they'll want their mum.'

'Leah seems settled. I for one wouldn't want to jeopardize *that*.'

Ah. They both know what an unsettled Leah looks like. 'What about Jess? Is it fair to unsettle her? She still has two more years at Cardingforth Primary,' Wendy points out.

'Maybe she can live with Mum, and Leah with Dad?' Madge starts humming. It's a song she's learnt from Jess, who never stops singing and chattering on those drives home from school. A Maori lovesong. That Freddie May (is it bad that Madge *still* laughs whenever she thinks of his rude mural in the curate's bedroom?) had been in and led a singing session, apparently. Now half the school wants to be a chorister.

'They should think about getting her into the cathedral girls' choir,' she says, pursuing her line of thought out loud. 'She sings like a little angel.'

'Oh dear!' Wendy laughs. '*That* won't go down well with Leah! Becky told me she set her heart on it. But she's like me, poor thing. Tone deaf.'

'Huh. We all tiptoe round that girl. It's all right for her: she's bright. Oof!' Madge clambers down from the worktop. 'With the best will in the world, Jess won't be passing her eleven-plus. She'll end up at Cardingforth Comp.'

'All mine went to the local comp,' says Wendy. 'I'm not a big fan of grammar schools.'

'Nor me, to be honest,' says Madge. 'I failed my eleven-plus. Still feel like a thicko sometimes.'

'Exactly! That's what it did to people. I passed, actually,' admits Wendy. 'But my best friend Linda failed. I can still picture us, that September. We stood at different bus stops on opposite sides of the road, pretending we couldn't see each other. We never really spoke again.'

They look at one another, in their Marigolds. And they laugh.

'What price your fancy education now, posh girl?' asks Madge.

We have eavesdropped to some purpose. Leah is settled. She really is. Martin gets texts at home time: *Going to Lyds*. His father's heart rejoices that his lovely difficult girl has found a friend at last, in the daughter of the new archdeacon of Lindford. The two of them take Kay's dog for a walk round the arboretum, and gather conkers.

I should probably mention that Kay sometimes gets a text at exactly the same moment: *Going to Leahs*. In fairness, they eventually go where they claim they have been. It is considerate of them to spare their parents the worry in the interim.

And Freddie May has been given a Choral Outreach role. Goodness!

The director of music was hugely impressed back in July, when Freddie stepped up at no notice and wove musical magic at the Primary Schools Leavers' Service in the cathedral. It was clear Mr May had been hiding his teaching charisma under a bushel, and could communicate in coherent sentences when he chose. They had been under-utilizing his talents. Timothy has set about rectifying that.

Needless to say, Mrs Precentor does not approve. But Mrs Precentor has no *official* role in the governance of the music department. All she can do is rant at the precentor in private. And rant she does: *Um Gottes Willen!* Timothy is rewarding bad behaviour! Freddie is still skiving off rehearsals and being a dick about Haydn's *Creation*! Oh, poor Princess Frederica can't bear to sing with the Community Choir, because Roger's sharp and hurts his precious ears! Fine, let Timothy go ahead and make him a choral animateur – it will end in tears.

The dean, however, looks kindly on the director of music's decision. As we know, she believes that Freddie can be trusted. I wish I could say that Freddie believes it. And that Miss Blatherwick's prayer will be answered. And that it won't end in tears.

'They only blooming nicked my cocktail ciggies!' says Kay to Helene. 'Little monkeys! They smoked them up a tree and made themselves puke. Karate girl swore her to secrecy, but Lyds always tells me everything.'

'Karate girl!' Helene folds her arms. 'That kid is a minx and a little fibber.'

'Should I tell her dad? Bugger, this is a bit awkward. He's technically on my patch, isn't he?'

'But you're not his line manager,' Helene replies. 'That's Geoff Morley at St James's.'

'Wow. You're scary. I don't know how you remember all that.'

'It's my job to remember.'

'But should I bring it up with Martin, though?'

Helene shrugs. 'Up to you.'

'Well. Anyway, they probably won't do it again if it made them sick.'

Hmm, thinks Helene. If that's all they do, we'll have got off lightly.

October dawns. Today is Matt's installation, at last.

It is raining. This is a bummer, as Jane has decided to wear her black velvet opera coat, which has not had an outing since her wedding day. She teams it with a 1940s-style wide-legged black jumpsuit, her silver-and-sea-glass choker, and her trademark sardonic expression.

She sits at the front next to Matt's dad again, who calls her Jen.

The cathedral is full. The front five rows are reserved for family and friends. Good God! It must be like drowning. Everyone Matt has ever known will pass before his eyes as he ponces down the aisle. Jane turns and scans the throng. There are his sisters and his cousins and his aunts – the whole cathedral shebang always reminds her of Gilbert and Sullivan. Former parishioners from all over. She clocks a line of hardened middle-aged reprobates who can only possibly be coppers. A lanky ginger one winks. She quells him with her Grande Dame eyebrow raise, and turns back to face the front.

Damn. This is why the sardonic expression must be deployed: Jane cannot let herself ponder why she is alone today. Where is the Rossiter tribe? Where is Danny? Heck, where are her friends? She should have invited Spider. Dommie is robed up and in the procession (with his smelling salts and brown paper bag, she devoutly trusts). Her surrogate son is on choir duty. She is sitting next to a kindly old boy who can't even get her name right.

But she is not letting herself think of that. Today is not about Jane Rossiter. It is about her big bald bloke, who she loves more than— Dammit! Sardonic expression!

Once again, Lindchester Cathedral was full of our friends. It went off rather well, with all the bells, whistles, trumpet stops, crooks, mitres, words of welcome from ecumenical partners, handshakes from the chain gang, bunfight afterwards – everything, in short, that such an occasion requires.

We were not obliged to sing Slane in 4/4 (*Deo gratias*). There was no worship band (shudder), and the lay clerks sang the Modern Version (sneer) of 'The Lord's my shepherd' with reasonable grace. I will just dob in the precentor, by telling you he illegally emended *that* line in the hymn 'In Christ alone'.

So we now have a properly installed bishop of Barcup. He will be referred to as 'the bishop of Barcup' until such time as his new sobriquet is ratified.

Before we take our leave, let us hover tenderly above the throng. See how these Anglicans love one another. They greet one another with a holy kiss, gossip, mingle, reminisce and try to eat chicken satay from sharp sticks without stabbing their uvula. A select group will head out to Matt and Jane's house afterwards to party properly.

Two eleven-year-old girls slip away from adult supervision and meet behind a pillar.

'So did you tell her?' mutters one.

'Yeah. Don't be mad. Sorry.'

'What did she say?'

'Served us right we puked.'

'But did you tell her about—?'

'God, no!'

Their eyes dart left and right. Nobody's heard them. Nobody need ever know.

'Good. See you at school then,' says Leah.

Chapter 39

There is a real nip in the air now. October! Where has the
year gone? And golly, what a year!

Sonya-Sonya is plumping cushions in the palace
ready for the (expanded) Senior Staff meeting. Three
archdeacons and the new bishop of Barcup for the
first time, although it's just Matt, of course.

She nips back to the kitchen and arranges some chocolate oat-
cakes on a plate. (Bea and Matt will get the giggles later, as they
watch their colleagues' first encounter with Sonya's amalgam-
trashing signature recipe.)

The bishop leans against the Aga with his coffee.

'We never guessed back in January what lay in store, did we?'
says Sonya.

'Right then!' He drains his mug, mind on the agenda. They are
having one of those companionable marital conversations, chunt-
ering along on parallel lines without ever intersecting.

'Little did we know what a huge watershed the EU referendum
would be!'

'Once more unto the breach, dear friends!'

'—friends. Have fun.'

'You too.'

What Steve doesn't realize, and will probably never know, is that
whenever Sonya hears the word 'watershed' she half-pictures a
stone shack with a slate roof on the side of a mountain. In Wales,
perhaps. Bike shed, coal shed, watershed. She has never stopped to

ask herself what goes on inside. Pumping of some kind? But she knows how to use the word correctly, so I think she will get to the end of her life with that building still intact, rain dripping from its eaves and sheep wandering by among the gorse.

Oh Lord! Everything's changing. Lindford vicarage is in chaos. A bunch of cowboys employed by the diocese are here to install a downstairs bathroom. Dominic's dining room will become his mother's bedroom. Who needs a dining room? He always entertains in the kitchen. The kitchen is the beating heart of a house, after all. A whole raft of decisions now looms about Mother's bungalow and effects. But there's no rush. Calm, calm.

Next week he's having his ECG, and getting that wretched twenty-four-hour blood pressure monitor fitted. Why on earth is he dreading it? Because he feels guilty, that's why. As though his poor health is his own fault, and the tests are going to lay bare the weak foolish workings of his heart for the whole world to see. Still, on the plus side, some things are changing for the good. He has a colleague to share the load now. The bane of his life – rotas – are no longer his concern. Virginia has revealed herself as Queen of Spreadsheets. Goody-good.

St Francis Day is upon us, when vicars everywhere consider holding a pet service. It will be like God's holy mountain! Ferrets will lie down with rabbits, Jack Russells with rats. What could possibly go wrong?

Talking of animals, Cosmo is in disgrace. Or, put more properly, Chloe is in disgrace for not controlling her rapey dog. It turns out that the promise of treats is sufficient to override every temptation, apart from the scent of a lady dog in heat.

'He's not rapey. He's a dog,' said Ambrose. It was Wednesday evening. 'He's a good dog. Aren't you, buddy? Yeah. Good boy.'

Cosmo sat up at this. Good boy? Good boy? Treat?

'I know, but I was *mortified*!' lamented Chloe. 'Just when I'd trained him to come back!'

'Look, the other owner has to take some responsibility, too, no? Was she off the lead?'

'She was actually tied to a fence.'

'What, and they'd just *left* her?'

'It was two girls, playing. They were up a tree. I gave them my card and told them to get their parents to ring me. But I haven't heard back.'

Ambrose shrugged. 'Then maybe everything's fine?'

'Fingers crossed. Probably he's still too young to make puppies. Oh God!' Chloe laughed. 'It went on FOR EVER! I kept trying to make polite conversation. So, how's school? – la la la, this isn't *at all* awkward – do you girls have any hobbies? Then one of them was promptly sick in a bush. I know! Maybe she was grossed out.'

'By animals being animals? Oh, c'mon.'

'Well, I don't know. We didn't all grow up on a farm, tractor boy.' She gathered her papers. 'So, that's the update. If some irate dog-owner handbags you, that's probably what it's all about. Thanks for walking him, Brose. Is Freddie—'

'He's busy.'

Chloe hesitated. 'OK. Byesy-bye.' She headed out to her street pastors' meeting, where they were training up some newbies. Damn. That Freddie May. Don't let Brose get hurt. Please.

So that is Leah and Lydia's dark secret. They had been strictly warned to keep Dora (the Explorer) away from other dogs. They had failed in their duty of care by climbing a tree to smoke the archdeacon's cocktail ciggies.

Still, they got away with it. Nobody need ever know!

Oh, the changes and chances of this fleeting world. Chapter has given a green light to the restructure. It is ever our high principle not to linger in boardrooms, dear reader. Be thankful. I have spared you much tediousness. You may protest that I have also barred you from many an interesting committee meeting. But if you are the sort of person who finds committee meetings interesting, I dare say you are a deanery synod rep or something, and get quite enough fun already. Chapter's approval was never really in any doubt. Deans do not proceed with this kind of thing unless they are pretty sure they won't be hung out to dry. But – as Marion feared – there has been a resignation.

Gene rose to the occasion with a bottle of Taittinger Comtes de Champagne 2005, not because they were celebrating (they were not), but in accordance with his motto that there is no situation in life that cannot be improved by a bottle of champagne.

Marion barely had the heart for it. The resignation was not a grand storming out. That might have been easier to endure. No, they were losing a real saint, a former university VC who had served on Chapter faithfully for fifteen years, but who felt out of step in the current climate. He sensed it was time to stand aside to make room for new blood. He hoped Marion wouldn't interpret his retirement as a criticism of her leadership. He continued to have every faith in her.

'So! The game's afoot!' Gene raises his glass. 'To you, deanissima! What happens next? A category five shitstorm makes landfall in the Close?'

This earns him her most reproachful stare. 'Gene, you have remembered how many people have died in Haiti this week, haven't you?'

He smites his breast.

After a moment she answers. 'Well, what happens next is that those people whose jobs are at risk will be informed. Then there's a period of consultation.'

He is too chastened to riff on the theme of 'consultations'.

'I expect we'll be making any announcements in the New Year,' she continues.

This time he can't resist: 'Because shafting people in the week before Christmas would be a PR disaster. Even though shafting them in January is probably worse.'

She does not dignify this truth with a reply.

There is a culture shift in C of E all right. We respond to it like a bunch of lay vicars choral being forced to sing Graham Kendrick. Or (cast your minds back) like Oxbridge dons in the eighties, having their first brush with the Research Selectivity Exercise.

Let us pause to recall the unregulated golden age. Those gracious Georgian rectories, the parson on his horse, the palaces with their deer parks, the canonical houses on the Close with their well-stocked wine cellars and staff laying fires of a morning. Queen Anne's bounty bankrolling us all.

Ichabod! Was it for this that we trained? How can we sing the Lord's song in a strange land? God forbid that The Regulators turn our churches into cookie stamp McMellitus franchises, banging on about Jesus, as if Jesus was the answer to the world's problems. No, let us hang up our harps on the willows along the Cam and the Isis, and sit down and weep as bankruptcy swallows us all.

'Name and shame businesses employing "too many" foreign workers! Arseholes.' It was Friday afternoon and Jane was in full flight. 'What next? Businesses employing too many women? Yeah, let's make sure women aren't taking the men's jobs! And while we're at it, why don't we make the queers all wear a little badge? Oh, I know –a pink triangle! A Britain of opportunity and fairness! A level playing field. Yeah – *that we own.* We *own* the level playing field, and if you can't afford the rent, ooh sorry.'

Spider flattened himself against Jane's office wall and blew his cigarette smoke out of the crack in her window. 'You're preaching to the choir here, Jane.'

'Can I just point out that that's an atheist's idiom?' said Jane. 'Aficionados know the choir spends the sermon Whatsapping each other to say what a bell-end the preacher is.'

Spider did his wheezy smoker's laugh. 'Respect for your insider knowledge there.'

Jane had not finished. 'It happened so fast! We woke up one June morning, and everything had changed. Now we, the "liberal elite", are strangers and pilgrims in this post-truth country. Here we have no abiding city, my friend.'

'Good. Good. I'm liking your biblical imagery here,' said Spider. 'And at the edge of our dreams comes the crunch of jackboot on broken glass.'

'Oh, you old poet you!' said Jane. 'But yes,'

They stood looking down over the town of Lindford. Mosley's blackshirts had marched here, back in the day. Could it really happen again? Spider ground out his cigarette on the window frame and flicked the butt out through the crack.

'Maybe it won't get that bad?' he said.

'Yeah. Maybe it will just be rubbish, not the end of the world?' said Jane. 'Like now, only more hate-filled and rubbish. For us, anyway.'

'Yeah, for us. But for those at the bottom of the pile . . . ' He shook his head. 'So keep the red flag flying, and all power to Corbyn's elbow, comrade.'

'Amen,' said Jane. But she simply did not see it happening. Which left what? Dear God, the C of E playing opposition for the next decade?

The house on Sunningdale Drive still waits, spick and span. Wendy pops back to whisk away the 'Welcome Home!' flowers and cake. The fridge hums. It's home time. She can hear the comp kids as they shout and shamble past.

Becky must hate this house, Wendy realizes. What happy memories can it possibly hold for her? Maybe she can't face coming back, and that's why she bottled out of the meeting with Martin? Not bottled out – rescheduled. Surely Becky must see that every week that passes will cement the girls' new regime with Dad a little more firmly? Is that what she wants? Wendy closes the front door on the quiet house.

Over in the far-flung corner of the diocese of Lindchester, Father Ed waits up to hear how Neil got on. It is Saturday night. Or rather, early Sunday morning.

'Heh heh, poacher turned gamekeeper, that's me, Eds!' He fills the world's most expensive kettle. 'I'm telling you – the world of clubbing looks a wee bit different when you're on the outside looking in. And not melted off your face,' he adds.

'Was it what you were expecting?'

'Pretty much, aye. Keeping an eye out for the ones who need it. Chatting to the door staff. Praying.'

'So you enjoyed it?'

'Yep.'

'Good.'

But something has just tilted. Neil buries himself in his phone. Ed waits. The stealth kettle silently boils the water on a higher astral plane.

'Fine then.' Neil skids his phone onto the worktop. 'I spotted ma wee friend. Coming out of Casa, off his tits, with some guy. He sees Chloe and me and it's all, hey, no worries, guys, bae's cool with it. Well, we all know *that*'s a lie. But what can I say – without sounding like the world's biggest holier-than-thou hypocrite?'

Ed hugs him. 'Listen. That's all forgotten, Neil.'

'We both know it's not, big man.'

'Well, forgiven, then.'

'Aye. I don't always feel it, though.'

'I know. But it's always true.'

The kettle clicks off, but they continue to stand there in one another's arms.

Chapter 40

"B e our strength in hours of weakness.'"
Father Dominic is still singing his Primary
School hymns on Tuesday as he sets off for
Morning Prayer. He says the office in church with
Virginia these days, rather than in his study, where
Mother might burst in at any moment to deliver a triumphant
noun-free non sequitur: 'I always *said* thingummy was a wotsit!'

"'In our wanderings be our guide.'"

Bleep! Trrrrrrrrump! Donald the blood pressure monitor starts up
his crazy attention-seeking self-inflation again. Argh! *Beep-beep-beep!*
Not now, Donald! I can't stand stiff-armed like a zombie in full
view like this! The next instalment of diocesan cowboys (painters
and decorators) watch him as they drink coffee in their van. He
carries on walking. *Bleep! Trrrrrrrrump! Beep-beep-beep!* Oh, stop it!
The wretched thing's going to carry on trying until it gets a reading,
isn't it? He gives in and stands still at the end of the drive.

How lovely life is this crispy autumn morning. He is a bit spaced-out
through lack of sleep – the monitor has checked his blood pressure every hour during the night. A robin whistles. The air is alive
with insects. They drift and float in the sunshine like lit-up snowflakes. Everything is beautiful in the light, he thinks. Even the nasty
biters, bless them. And will you just look at his lovely sycamore tree? It's
on fire! Oh, he's a happy bunny in spite of it all. Because of it all?

> Through endeavour, failure, danger,
> Father, be thou at our side.

281

Bleep! Donald deflates. Dominic notes down what he was doing ('Standing') and sets off again. He almost wants to skip. He's like a man who has found treasure buried not in a stranger's field, but right here, here in his own garden, where it's been all along.

Dominic is not the only person in the diocese of Lindchester suffering from sleep deprivation. Our good friend Miss Blatherwick, unable to get comfortable, recites the prayer of St Augustine as the cathedral clock chimes the hours away. "'Keep watch, dear Lord, with those who work, or watch, or weep this night.'" Sometimes she hears nocturnal organ practice, sometimes just the wind and the owls. On the other side of the Close the canon chancellor paces with little Noah Frederick draped over his shoulder like a bar tender's cloth. Hush. Hush. Don't cry, little one.

Hard times. Hard Brexit. Hard hearts in far-off Westminster. No cash for the NHS. There it goes, the bus-side promise of 350 million crocks of gold a week. Off and away it floats, to land somewhere over the rainbow, among figmental white cliffs, where there are no blacks, no dogs, no Irish. Farewell, tenderness. Farewell, Scotland – and who can blame you?

Christmas appears in department stores and supermarket aisles. Strapped-for-cash parents lie awake and wonder how they'll afford the kiddies' presents this year. The pound falls. The hungry poor lie awake and wonder what the hell they'll do if food prices go through the roof. The hungry rich lie awake and wonder how much longer they can hack this new diet, maybe they should nip downstairs for an organic oatcake?

In graveyards and doorways the homeless wrap themselves in discarded duvets (cheaper to buy a new one than get them dry-cleaned, frankly) and try to sleep. There is a padlock on Luscombe Gardens to keep them out. The more determined kept climbing over the railings, so all the bushes have been cut back to make the place less attractive to rough sleepers. It's sad, but at the end of the day this *is* where children play, the children of hipster homeowners. We really can't have needles and bottles and weirdos in the communal garden, here in this gentrified pocket of Lindchester's Lower Town. Back in the day, this is where the cholera-infested slums were cleared and good housing put up for the malnourished leather workers. A statue of Josephine Luscombe, campaigner, stands in the locked garden among the scalped shrubs.

We lie awake in the night, listening. Can you hear it? There's a train coming. Bound for glory. Mind the gap. Mind the ever-widening gap. And in the daytime, cloud columns rise from the cooling towers in Cardingforth, like smoke from distant cities put to the torch. Horses swish their tails in paddocks, beside electrical substations all humming and mysterious. DANGER OF DEATH KEEP OUT. New houses are going up on the outskirts of Lindford, like a promise of good things to come. But who will be able to afford them?

Hush! Enough of all this liberal elitist bremoaning! Life goes on. It's not *all* bad, is it? Look at the lovely weather we are having, all sun and rain and double rainbows. A wealth of fungi burgeons across the diocese of Lindchester – flamboyant, comic, delicate. It's everywhere once you start noticing. Let us pause to relish those Regency racehorse-type names – the Blusher, Queen Bolete, the Deceiver. But we are English. We divide the fungal world crudely in two: mushrooms and toxic toadstools. Sometimes we kick them as we pass. No real reason. Just the casual joy of smashing up stuff we have no use for.

But hush. Hush. Don't cry. It's not all bad.

Somewhere, out on a disused railway track a woman slogs along on her bike and clears her head of this world's woes. A man cycles along behind, custodian of the banana guard, ready to succour her if she faints and grows weary.

Somewhere, two vicars get the giggles right before a funeral, when a blood pressure monitor bleeps, and they cannot, very nearly cannot stop laughing in time.

A woman opens a scary official envelope to find she has been granted leave to remain in the UK.

A man opens another envelope and finds a cheque for the foodbank.

A teenage boy gives up his seat on the train.

A retired midwife drives a little girl home from school, and they sing in the car. "'This train is bound for glory, this train.'"

And up on Lindford Common, where the gorse is blooming – and gorse is always blooming somewhere – two men walk a labradoodle as the sun comes and goes between the clouds.

'Leah?' whispers Jess. She stands like a little ghost beside her sister's bed.

'What?'

'I wish Mummy was here.'

'Yeah, but we're seeing her tomorrow after school, remember? After her and Dad have had their "meeting"?'

'Yes, but I want her to come back *for real*.'

'She will. Granny says she's improving all the time.' *Oh God, don't let her get well.* Leah deletes this wish from her mind. But another one flashes up: *Don't let her come back and wreck everything.*

'Leah?'

'What?'

'I don't really want to go back to our house. Do you?'

Leah is silent. She must be responsible and say the right thing. She must not scare Jess by yelling, *Duh, no! I hate that house! I'd rather kill myself!*

'We'll have to wait and see, Jess.' That's what grown-ups say. *We'll see.* Which means No. No, you can't have what you want, you can't do what you want.

'Can I get into your bed, Leah?'

Leah hesitates. It's not Jess's fault she sometimes still has accidents, even though she's nearly nine. 'Um. For a bit, maybe.'

'Yay!' Jess climbs under the duvet.

They lie there. A car goes past. Light wipes round the ceiling from the crack in the curtains. It goes quiet.

'Leah?'

'What?'

'Do you think if we ask her, she'd come and live here instead?'

Awkward. 'Um, technically her and Dad are divorced, Jess.'

'Yes, but they *could* get back together, couldn't they? There's a chance they could?'

'Well, I s'pose.' Yeah – like a bazillion trillion to one chance.

'So shall we ask her tomorrow?'

284

'Look. It's complicated, Jess. I know you mean well, but we can't just *invite* her. It's Dad's house, yeah? We'd have to get his permission first.'

'We could do that! We could ask him now.' She throws off the duvet. 'Come on!'

Leah tugs her back. 'No!'

'Why not?'

God! She was going to get all *whiny* now. 'It's not quite that simplistic, Jess. We need to be like, tactful. Choose the right moment. Look, you'd better let me do it.'

Jess snuggles her. 'Yay! You're the best, Leah. Just think – she could be here for Christmas!'

'Yeah, well, we'll see.' Leah shoves her away. 'Go back to your own room, Jess. I have to sleep. I have to keep my brain clear coz I've got double maths first thing,' she lies.

'OK!' Jess skips off like everything's sorted.

Like it's not going to end in tears. Like the answer isn't always NO.

You see what I am about here, reader. I am trying to wave my authorial wand and contrive a happy ending for the Rogers family. If only it were that simplistic. But writing a novel is a bit like choreographing tortoises. You try to round them up and point them towards the stage ready for the grand finale, only to discover that some have wandered ponderously off into a distant cabbage patch, or decided to hibernate. Will it all end in tears, despite your author's best intentions? We'll have to wait and see.

You will have inferred that it did not end in tears for Freddie and Ambrose last week, at any rate. That is to say, there were tears, but it was not the end.

Course, he texted him. Like at gone 3 a.m.? Brose came over, and Freddie was all, you're crying! Naw. I'm so so sorry. Don't be crying, Brose. C'mere. Come to bed.

And they climbed the stairs in the silent house, and Freddie's room was a mess again, but hey. Ssh. It's gonna be fine, babe. Trust me?

285

It had all been Freddie's fault, as always. Escalating some dumb thing (Brose complaining about the smell of weed) into a major fight? He was, really? Guess I'd better head into town then, find me some other company that's less judge-y. Are you cool with that, huh? Yeah, right, *trying* to escalate things? Coz Brose wasn't playing. He was all, if that's what makes you happy, Freddie.

And then he ran into Chloe and Neil, street pastoring? Gah. Pretended to be more wasted than he was, so they wouldn't like, *talk* to him? But he just knew what Neil was thinking, coz he was remembering it too? That time they got it on, only Freddie's phone rang, and they, like, came to their senses in time?

So five minutes later, there he was, in a cab heading home? Worst of both worlds – not getting any action, not feeling good about himself, either? Wa-a-ay too mad still for a climb-down, to even *begin* to think about telling Brose, so you're right – it doesn't make me happy? And he went to sleep, same thoughts going round and round: dude, the only thing that makes me happy is being with you, but I'm *so* gonna trash everything, and I have no idea why?

Then maybe 3 a.m., this weird hallucinogenic thing happened? Like that time in juvie when it was literally like in the hymn – 'I woke, the dungeon flamed with light'? This time he knew someone had been sitting there while he slept? Someone had been keeping watch, just keeping watch, and he was safe, and somehow, it was all gonna be OK? So he texted Brose.

And while he was waiting for Brose to come over, he was thinking about the tiny dude, how he'd caught him? Hey, I got you, guy. I got you. Little heart beating away. Stroking his little back, and thinking, I have *no* idea what I'm doing here. But he's yelling, he's gonna be fine.

And in a weird way, maybe I *can* be trusted, you know?

Chapter 41

'Don't get me wrong, Leah, this is the coolest den ever. But what if we get electrocuted to death? Dzzzzz! Game over!'

'Lyds, in case you haven't noticed, we're laying on a roof, not sticking our tongues into sockets.'

'Oh. Good point.'

They are up on the substation roof. It's right next to Leah's house, under a humongous beech tree. They are using their schoolbags as pillows. Nobody else knows about this place. Nobody can see them. Even if Dad comes home and looks out of his study window, he won't see them. The branches droop down and make walls and a roof. Maybe Leah could get a tent and stay up here? Then nobody would find her and make her go and live with Mum.

'We could be squirrels and this could be our drey,' she says.

'Cool! Talking squirrels, like maybe in Narnia?' says Lydia. 'We could be hiding from the Telmarines!'

'Yeah!' Leah loves how Lydia instantly gets things. Nobody else at QM plays games any more. It's like there's a *rule* against it.

There's literally no wind today. It's very quiet. Now and then a nut patters down.

'I so *wish* Wilkos would sell us fireworks,' says Lydia. 'Sparklers, even.'

'I know. Still . . .' Leah delves into her bag. 'Ta dah! Wanna Tangfastic?'

'What the—?' Lydia sits up. 'Did you pay for those?'

'Course I *paid* for them,' lies Leah.

'I didn't see you.'

'We're not exactly joined at the hip, Lydia.' Suddenly she hates the sight of the sweets. 'I could of bought them another time.'

'Yeah, but you didn't, though,' says Lydia. She says it kindly, not meanly.

'Whatever.' Leah tosses the stupid packet away on the side that isn't their garden. It lands somewhere in the undergrowth. 'I only do it to master sleight-of-hand skills. Like, very occasionally.'

'Yeah, I get that, but couldn't you learn magic tricks, instead? There are these like UNBELIEVABLE magic tricks on YouTube? This guy at a wedding—'

'FINE. I'll learn magic,' snaps Leah. God! Some people can be so judgementalist.

'And he goes up to the guests—'

Though to be fair, Lyds isn't judgementalist. She's cool. Plus she never tries to make Leah feel stupid by going Ha ha! at a mistake, or calling her a baby for not knowing stuff.

'—and then next thing, there was literally *a cross drawn on the girl's hand*? And everyone was NO! Seriously, it was *so* unbelievably awesome. We should try it.'

Leah's heart does a massive thump. She could casually mention him. Casually say his name. She flicks a beechnut shell off the roof.

'Uh, so actually, a friend of mine's – Freddie's – boyfriend, he does magic?' She clears her throat. 'So he did some at Freddie's surprise birthday party? That I went to. And it was awesome.' Leah's face is burning. But Lydia doesn't say, Ha ha, you've gone all red!

'Wait! Freddie from the cathedral choir? NO!'

'Yeah. How . . . ?'

'Who led the singing at our Leavers' service? Omigod! Why didn't you tell me you actually *know* him? I am *so* in love with him!'

Me too. She could say that. 'Yeah, well, he has a boyfriend.'

'So? I still fancy him. *Everyone* fancies him. Mum says *she* even fancies him – and she's a lesbian. Ha ha ha! What? What's the big deal? It's OK to be attracted to people, Leah.'

'I *know* it's OK,' snaps Leah. 'I'm not stupid.' Her mum's *a lesbian*? Wait. So that grumpy-face woman, Helene, who was so blah-blah-blah about everything that time Leah accidentally got Freddie into trouble, she must be like Lydia's mum's—? Wife?

'I'm attracted to like *loads* of people,' Lydia is saying. 'It's really random.'

And then – for no reason at all! – Leah starts to cry. Stupid, stupid, *stupid*. But she can't stop.

'Leah, what's wrong?' Lydia puts an arm round her shoulders. 'Did I upset you?'

'No,' chokes Leah. 'It's just. Everything's. Rubbish.' And she hiccups it all out. How she's got to move back to Cardingforth after half-term, just when finally she's happy in her life. Nobody listens to her. And Mum's acting all betrayed: *You'd rather live with your father, is that what you're saying?* And although it's dumb, she just can't make herself not be in love with you know who, and—

A car pulls up on the drive. 'Crap!' Leah wipes her nose on her sleeve. She grabs Lydia's arm. 'You can't tell *anyone* that last bit. Swear!'

'I swear.'

Jess's tiny sweet Snow White voice goes, 'Bye, Madge! Thanks, you're the best!' The car door slams.

'Quick!' They toss their schoolbags into the garden and jump down off the roof.

'Are you OK, Leah?' Lydia squeezes her arm as they hurry to the house.

'Yeah.' She wipes her nose on her sleeve again. 'Thanks. Probably it's just *puberty*. Yada-yada.'

'Hair starts sprouting in new places!' says Lydia brightly, like an infomercial. 'It's NORMAL! It's nature's way of preparing your body – TO TURN INTO A GIANT HAIRBALL!'

'WITH BOSOMS!'

Then they are literally crying with laughter.

'What's so funny?' asks Jess.

'Oh, you wouldn't understand,' gasps Leah. 'Go and get changed, coz we're going over to Lydia's. She's got to walk Dora.'

'Yay!' says Jess. 'I love Dora! I so wish we had a dog. I'm going to ask Santa for a puppy for Christmas!' She skips off.

Leah and Lydia exchange glances.

'It's OK. She's not having puppies,' says Lydia quickly. 'I'm totally, totally almost one hundred per cent certain.'

Suddenly Leah thinks of something. Oh God. Don't let us meet Chloe and Cosmo in the park. Because Jess is bound to say, 'Yay! You're Ambrose's cousin! We met you at Freddie's party!' or something dumb. Then Chloe would recognize her this time for sure.

But then Lydia makes her snort by saying, 'In other news, a giant hairball with bosoms was sighted in QM Girls today! The public are warned not to approach it!'

You will see that my rescue package for the Rogers family has gone awry. Leah was right. It's not that simplistic. Martin and Becky finally had their awkward meeting in Nero's last week, to talk about The Way Forward. They are still trapped in the binary world of break-ups, which decrees that relations must either be Amicable or Acrimonious. Of course, they both tried to be amicable, but before long, the conversation was like sticking your hand into a bag of scissors again.

Poor Becky had to stop the car in a lay-by and cry on the drive back to her parents. How, how was she ever going to cope? Even with medication, even now Mum and Dad had sorted her finances out for her. That horrible house. It smelt of misery. She knew she'd be fighting Leah every single day. *I'm not going back there. You can't make me. I'll run away.* Poor Jess was bed-wetting again. Becky had failed as a mother. But she couldn't live without them! Couldn't bear to let them go.

Poor Martin also had a little weep as he walked back to his office in St James's church. He knew he'd failed as a husband – although he'd never quite worked out what he'd done wrong. Just been the wrong person? Well, he knew it was over. He'd had to explain to Jess that Mummy wouldn't be moving back in. Leah already realized. Oh, why was it, a year after the decree absolute, that a part of him still wanted to love, cherish, protect? It was like being left with a sad little clock, wound up years before. He could hide it away in a drawer with the wedding album, but it would go on and on ticking, until it finally wound down and stopped. Without the girls in the

290

house, all he would be able to hear was that tick–tick–tick. How could he bear to be on his own all over again?

The red and gold river of Christmas merchandise is joined by an orange and black tributary. It's cobwebs and pumpkins as far as the eye can see. The fancy dress shop in Lindford is already doing a brisk trade. Homeowners are bullied into buying tubs of 'candy' for 'trick'n'treaters'. Gene suggests loading a blunderbuss with gobstoppers and discharging it at any chancers on the deanery doorstep. The dean vetoes this, but agrees to sidestep the whole issue by going out on Hallowe'en. To a Michelin Star restaurant.

Lift up your eyes. The church's new year, Advent, is in sight. Candles have been ordered. Our year in Lindchester is nearly done. Already the first fireworks are going off at dusk. A police helicopter hangs over the Abernathy estate most nights, shaking the sky.

Posters for Haydn's *Creation* have been up for some time now. This performance will be the last choral huzzah before half-term. Lindfordshire is out of sync with other regions, just to maximize childcare problems. School and choral half-term will, however, coincide with 'Employability Week' at Linden University. This is what it is called. It is not called 'Blended Learning Week' any more. Anyone referring to it as 'Blended Learning Week' will be birched behind the smoking shack by the pro vice chancellor.

Fer feck's sake. Jane knows that if she waits long enough, the wheel of pedagogical fashion will crank round again, and they'll be back to calling it plain old Half-Term. It's Tuesday, it's warm, so she's taking her Sainsbury's meal deal into the arboretum. She passes a fence groaning with foliage, and catches the rank hanky-boiling smell of ivy blossom, which is apparently the insect equivalent of crack cocaine. The air seethes with flies.

She enters the park, once again passing that blazon of a dead chivalric age, the EU flag. God, she was here right before the referendum, wasn't she? Had herself a big old prophetic migraine. The sun is glinting off the lake again. She sits on the same bench. Ah! There goes that old kingfisher. God, it's like nothing has happened. Here she is, trying the same what-if thought experiment.

What if Trump gets elected? What if *these* are the good old days, bad as they are? What if we *still* don't know we're born? She opens her sandwich. This is like in some ghastly political Groundhog Year – hah! If only we could have another try – hundreds more tries – at this nightmare which is 2016 until, chastened, we've finally learnt our lesson.

She sighs and eats her lunch. In the distance she can hear bagpipes. It's that piper outside M & S. 'Amazing Grace.' Huh. A hymn she hasn't cared for ever since she read about John Newton devoutly holding services on the deck of his slaver, *after* his conversion. 'Amazing grace, how sweet the sound, that saved a wretch like me.' Not even the tiniest twang of cognitive dissonance for you there, John?

But Jane is nothing if not ruthlessly honest. As she stares across the lake, she hears one god almighty twang. Because what about Dr Jane bleeding-heart Rossiter? Donating online to charity from the deck of her luxury cruise ship, with ninety-nine per cent of the world's population beneath her feet out of sight.

Fire, fire, fire down below. Yeah. That's what the piper should be playing.

It's Saturday night. Freddie calls round at Ambrose's coz fine, he's gonna go to the rehearsal, even if Roger's there, singing away, sharp as a fingernail down the proverbial blackboard.

'Like I keep saying to Timothy, I'd rather piss on an electric fence.'

'You've clearly never pissed on an electric fence, then,' says Brose. 'There's two hundred and twenty volts running through those babies.'

'I so have! No word of a lie. I'd be maybe five, six? My step-brothers dared me? Said it tickled? Yow! And my dad, he was zero sympathy. If they told you to jump over a cliff, would you?'

Pause.

'Freddie, just to flag this up with you – you do know your upbringing wasn't entirely normal?'

'Ha ha ha! True dat.'

They set off. Half a giant red moon slides up from behind the palace.

And you do know your dad is a real piece of work, don't you? Ambrose doesn't add. He's been trying to stay aloof from Mr May senior's machinations, ever since that confidential chat at the funeral. But he can tell he's being reeled in all the same.

Chapter 42

There are strange goings-on up on the Close. If you walk past the Song School, you will hear it. Barking, yodelling, Tarzan yells. Don't worry. It's just Mr May rehearsing the girls' choir. Their first evensong is the week after half-term, and Timothy, the Director of Music, wants to inject a little more fearlessness into their singing. They are perfectly in tune, but still making rather a timid sound unto the Lord. Freddie's task is to convey to them, by whatever means he chooses, that a bold mistake is preferable to accurate inaudibility.

How soon girls have their style cramped by fear of making a mistake. Their brothers hurl themselves at life, padded before and aft by the body armour of simply being male. The girls' choir is wading upstream against the tide of opinion that boys sing better. Let us wish them well, this little band of pioneers. It will take years to make up the lost ground.

Shall we peep in? The girls – there are fourteen of them – are not behind the tall desks decoding the Lindchester pointing. They are all in the middle of the room with Mr May, dancing. That doesn't sound like Stanford in G to me. No, I'm afraid it's 'Agadoo'. With the actions. Fourteen girls shake that pineapple tree. In a fat man voice! Werewolf voice! Cow falling over a cliff voice! STOP!

Thank goodness.

'And now . . . Train's a-coming, ladies! Woo-woo!'

The girls jump up and down and squee. They've been working on this for weeks.

'Ssh! Ready?'

And they're off. One group start chuffing. One group are the wheels. My, that's a powerful steam whistle there! Now the singing starts. "'This train is bound for glory, this train.'" Then they segue into another gospel train song. "'People get ready.'" Then back to the glory train, which chuffs off, *forte, mezzo piano, piano, pianissimo*, into the distance, with one last *Woo-woo!*

Timothy, who has come in to take the boring bit of the practice, applauds. Freddie tells the choir they are awesome. He tells them girls rock.

He walks to Brose's house. Stanford in G floats out to him across the Close. "'My soul doth magnify the Lord.'" What he wanted to say back there was, listen, don't be hating on yourselves. Don't let anyone shame you, and stop you singing and dancing and loving, you hear me? But that's maybe a bit creepy for a guy to say to young girls?

His hands are up his sleeves, like he's cold, but he's not cold. He can feel the old scars under his fingertips. That time he went too deep, and it wouldn't stop bleeding? Sitting in A & E, and the staff were all, self-harmer, drama queen, make him wait. They didn't get how it was a safety valve, a lame attempt to equalize the pressure, and make the outside match the inside. The dark inside of him where nothing was pretty at all.

Gah, why is he even going there again? Coz now? Life's good, no? He smiles. That sweet guy of his. They're heading down south so Freddie can meet his folks this half-term – hnn, could be that's what's freaking him out a little. Yeah, plus his dad, with the endless texts. *Can you call me, son. It's important.* Probably he should get onto that? Only his dad properly does his head in.

This Sunday the clocks go back. Where has the year gone? All Friday it stays grey, as though the sun hasn't ever quite risen. Sumacs and cherries blaze. There is gold above and gold underfoot as Jane mooches round the arboretum at lunchtime, thinking doomy thoughts. This is autumn weather straight from Planet Childhood, when your dad made a bonfire and it was nearly Guy Fawkes night.

Like childhood, only nowhere near cold enough. Jane can see daisies and dandelions in bloom among the fallen leaves. We are drowsing like frogs in lukewarm water, she thinks. Slowly, relentlessly, we will come to the boil. Even if we realize in time what's happening, there is nowhere left to jump, no handy Goldilocks Planet next door. So let's go ahead and expand Heathrow. Why not? It's good for the economy.

Although it is not half-term here in the diocese of Lindchester, pilgrims come from other realms where schools are shut. Tea lights flicker and prayer requests heap up at the shrine of William of Lindchester. The cathedral shop does a brisk trade.

I am aware we have not popped in here for some time. Perhaps we have been assuming that we know what merchandise a cathedral shop stocks, and are not in particular need of communion wafers or Holy Land olive wood holding crosses. More fool us. We have deprived ourselves of a range of exciting new treats: Cathedral Honey, made by the dean's own bees; boxes of locally baked cathedral Billy cakes; bottles of Lindchester Cathedral craft ale.

Happily, there is still time for amendment of life. Let us go in and buy all of the above, as well as an old-fashioned Advent calendar. Perhaps one with Bible verses instead of chocolate behind the little doors, for our greater edification in the approaching Season of Preparation and Hope.

The bell still tinkles as ever it did as we enter the shop. Small children still cluster round the pocket money section. The volunteers may look exactly the same to you as they attempt to bubble-wrap your purchase at the till. You probably still grind your teeth as they grope for the Sellotape roll that is too far away – like someone attempting a Grade 3 cross-hands piano piece – fail, and then begin the wrapping process all over again, this time with little tabs of Sellotape laboriously lined up along the counter edge in preparation.

Nothing has changed, you say? How wrong you are, reader. This cheery amateurism masks the shift towards professionalization that has overtaken the volunteer corps in Lindchester Cathedral during the last two years. One by one the various groups have all been given role (not *job*) descriptions, expected (not *obliged*) to sign an agreement (not a *contract*), and invited (not *ordered*) to participate, where appropriate, in Disclosure and Barring checks. *Or get their marching orders.*

Yes, the rot has set in here in Lindchester. It is the same everywhere, this political correctness gone mad. Dean and Chapter have swept aside generations of trust and devoted service. Gone are the happy, innocent days when the cathedral existed for the volunteers, not the other way round; and anyone at all could take unchaperoned minors into a quiet vestry without the finger of suspicion being pointed at them.

October is nearly at an end. It is Saturday night. Trains to Lindford are packed with zombies and nurses. Everywhere you look there are ashen faces dripping blood. The living dead spill out onto the streets, trailing bandages. It looks like the end of the world. Vampires and devils prowl. Perhaps hell has opened and the earth given up its dead?

The crowds that gather on the Close for the long-awaited performance of Haydn's *Creation* are not in costume – unless by some collective intuition they have all decided to come dressed up as life members of the National Trust. There was some concern voiced that the timing of the concert would prove unfortunate, since they would be competing with Hallowe'en festivities. This fear was soon dismissed. A Venn diagram showing the set of people who enjoy Cathedral Community Choir performances of Haydn, and the set of those who enjoy drinking blue kamikaze shots out of skull glasses while dressed as Donald Trump, would produce but the tiniest of intersections.

Martin brings his girls to the concert. Jess is pestering to go on the next 'Be a Chorister for a Day', because she wants to audition for the girls' choir. Martin says, 'I'll look into it and discuss it with your mother.' He waits for Leah to shout, 'How come SHE gets to do it?' But Leah says nothing. Both girls are off to Cephalonia for a half-term holiday with Granny and Granddad, to make up for their rubbish summer. And then they will move back in with their mother. Leah says nothing about

297

this, either. What's going on in her head? Is she reconciled? Martin can't tell, but he's anxious.

And 'Mrs Matt Tyler' is here! This is Jane's first experience of sitting on the front row with the chain gang, ogling the soloists' tonsils. During the interval, a select group will be invited for drinks at the deanery. They will take their eye off the time, end up speedily necking their half-finished wine, then clatter back in just as the conductor is about to raise his baton. Jane will sit through the second half cosily pished in a candlelit medieval cathedral, watching the wax form rococo stalactites and listening to gorgeous music – this Mrs Bishop caper isn't *all* bad.

Father Dominic is here with his mum, who likes a bit of Haydn. Dominic has been told his heart is fine, but he needs to go easy on caffeine and alcohol to reduce the risk of another bout of tachycardia. Dull, dull, dull! Still, it beats lying on the cathedral floor thinking you're about to meet your Maker.

The lot of lying on the cathedral floor waiting for an ambulance fell instead to the tenor soloist, James Lovatt. Twenty minutes before the concert was due to begin, he bent down to tie his laces, and his back went into spasm. Ruptured disc. Somehow he got to the floor. Whispers, flurried action. He lay behind the screened-off area in the north transept, among the instrument cases. Dimly, through his agony he heard the overture happening. Paramedics. Talking to him. Pain relief. Oh, thank God. This must be an out-of-body experience, he thought. Where was he? His part was carrying on without him, over on the other side. Uriel. 'And God saw the light was good . . .' He was floating now. 'The first of days appears . . . Chaos ends . . .' Is that me singing? But he was on a stretcher out in the night. No, that can't be me.

It was Freddie, of course. Rising to the occasion. He knew the score inside out and back to front. True, he'd been a dick about rehearsals, but it's not about deserving. As the canon chancellor (sitting on the front row with a Bible commentary hidden under his programme) could have told the precentor's wife – grace is unmerited, or it is not grace.

And Freddie just stepped out, and rode it. Spread his wings like Uriel. Like the condors riding those thermals? 'The heavens are telling the glory of God.' He could see the world spread out beneath his feet.

The cathedral is locked now. In the basket by the shrine the prayers wait to be carried to the altar in tomorrow's Eucharist.

> *Please help my son, suffering from cancer.*
> *We pray for all those in Aleppo.*
> *Please be with all refugees.*

Tomorrow is the fourth Sunday before Advent. Advent 2016. We will sing our Advent hymns, read those familiar lessons. We will pass once again from darkness into light. Advent is out there, waiting for us. Out there on the other side, after multitudes, multitudes of voters have passed through the Valley of Decision. We will know the answer by then: Trump/Clinton. Either/Or.

> I will stand at my watch-post, and station myself on the rampart;
> I will keep watch to see what he will say to me.

Pray. Pour out baskets full of prayers. Pray that we will be spared. Fire close at hand. Earthquakes. Wars, rumours of war. We can sing Haydn's *Creation*, but there's no going back to Eden. One by one the species wink out like little lights. Dead as dodos. Gone. Would that even today we knew the things that made for peace.

People get ready. Vote, pray, weep, march, campaign. Abandon your luggage. Scramble aboard before the gap's too wide and the train has gone.

This train is the 20.16, bound for Glory. Calling at Death and Judgement.

NOVEMBER

NOVEMBER

Chapter 43

ord has got out. Freddie's performance is being touted as the singing equivalent of a record-breaking standing high jump. To pull off a feat like that without any real preparation! Why, he didn't even have enough time to race home and change into his soloist's tails, let alone work on his phrasing!

There was the usual choral foundation party afterwards, back in the precentor's house. The precentor issued his customary admonition about it being Sunday tomorrow, please go easy on the salty snacks, gentlemen, they are *so* dehydrating. He burst into 'See the conquering hero comes!' as Freddie entered with Ambrose. Everyone cheered.

Freddie waved his arms, tried to explain it was no big deal. Yeah, no, no, guys, guys listen, he'd known shedloads of oratorios, like for ever? Since he was a chorister?

But the gentlemen of the choir only laughed.

'Yes, dear,' said Nigel, patting him, 'it was nothing. Like delivering babies – all in a day's work for a jobbing lay clerk.'

'Nothing to see here, folks,' muttered the sub-organist. She was lurking by the drinks table. 'Nope. Nothing at all freaky about Freddie May and his idiot savant musical memory.'

'Come, come, Iona!' said the precentor. 'We must enjoy him while we still can. He'll be off and away, applying for vocal courses before we know it.'

'Except he's got approximately two failed GCSEs to rub together.'

'I seriously doubt that will hold him back.' Giles looked across at Freddie. See the godlike youth advance, he thought. Dash it all. Never say Peter Pan has gone and decided to grow up! He wiped a sentimental tear from his eye, and poured himself another glass.

It was a champagne moment for Lindchester choral foundation, all right. (That is to say, a supermarket two-for-one Prosecco moment, times being what they are.) Even Laurence, the organist (over in his preferred corner), was looking remarkably cheerful, considering the page-turning fiasco in Part III. Yes, the concert had been triumph snatched from the jaws of mishap. Lindchester would not need to brace itself for the gleeful commiseration from other cathedrals.

Of course, thoughts were spared for poor James Lovatt, but these quickly deteriorated into competitive slipped-disc horror stories, I'm afraid. How are we to condole with others, if not by helpfully remarking 'that happened to me once, actually'?

By one in the morning, everyone had left. The salty snacks had taken their toll. The precentor reeled to his study to cast his eye over the dots for tomorrow's choral Eucharist, at which he was presiding. There had been no alternative with half-term falling when it did: All Saints was transferred to Sunday, and the Chamber Choir would be singing the traditional All Soul's Duruflé *Requiem* this year. Mere anarchy is loosed!

Uli stood in the kitchen among the champagne flutes and canape wreckage. She folded her arms and scowled. All those singing lessons Freddie had busked through. She could still hear herself saying it: *He's got to learn! Das Leben ist kein Ponyhof!* But *she*'d been the one treating life like a bloody pony farm. Schooling him like a naughty horse, reining him in, making him walk in boring little circles, when all the time he was desperate to gallop. Huh! Or prance about like a sodding Lipizzaner stallion.

Ach, Gott! She was a bad woman. She'd half-known she was being unreasonable at the time. But *grr*, she could sympathize with poor Salieri in *Amadeus*. What had he said? How *dare* God choose for his instrument a lustful, smutty, infantile boy? Something like that. She's wasted her opportunity. She should have used the time

304

to polish his German pronunciation, and turn him loose on *Winterreise*. Or start tackling Wagner, even!

As Uli stood castigating herself in the quiet kitchen, something oozed out from a tiny gap under the dresser. Her hands flew to her mouth. *Nein!* Before she could move, the creature snatched a fallen grape, stowed it away in his furry hamster chops, then squeezed back the way he had come.

Here the reader may discern the author at work, contriving happy endings again. See? Boris I is not dead after all! This is a world where small rodents may escape the claws of fate. They may establish the Republic of Free Hamsters in the floor and roof spaces of medieval canonical houses, roaming freely about the Close, knowing no boundaries. Hamsters are one thing, humans another entirely, however. That said, hamsters are tricky enough, come to think of it, as anyone who has owned one of these world-renowned escapologists will testify. So we may yet see the cathedral cat trotting round the Close with a limp mouthful of Boris.

Might it still all be all right in the end, though? For Freddie and Ambrose, for Leah and her family? For Miss Blatherwick? I am prepared to settle for all right-*ish*. I am flying by the seat of my narrative pants in this tale, having renounced the authorial luxury of going back and changing things. All I can do is keep flying, jettisoning stuff as I scan for somewhere plausible to land. *Deus ex machina* plot solutions are frowned upon, but I secretly hanker after them. I long to be reassured that some jerry-built plywood platform is even now being knocked up in the wings, ready to trundle on stage in the final scene and winch down the gods to sort the mess out. There comes a point, as we hurtle downhill with failed brakes, when we no longer object to being saved.

And so it is half-term in Lindchester. Martin has driven his girls to Birmingham International and waved them off for the week. They will be back on Saturday. He will take them to the firework display in the arboretum in the evening, then on Sunday— But he will not think about Sunday.

Over in Cardingforth Father Wendy has nipped back into Becky's house with a fresh bunch of flowers and another welcome home cake.

Father Dominic hires a Luton box van (shriek!) with a tail lift, and enlists the help of a couple of his strapping Iranian congregation members. He tries in vain to pay them. No, no – it is *honour* to them to help him. Together they drive to Mum's bungalow and load up with furniture and personal effects (Dominic has a list – though quite what 'the whatchamacallits from your Aunty Barbara' are is anyone's guess). Yes, Mother is officially moving in.

Freddie and Ambrose are also away this week. We may not follow them down to the wilds of Somerset, where Ambrose's family have farmed their acres since time out of mind; but we can at least hide in the back seat of Ambrose's car as they set off after evensong on Sunday afternoon, and eavesdrop on their conversation. You may judge for yourselves whether they are hastening together to perfect felicity.

'So, they gonna love me, your folks?'

Ambrose was silent.

'Gah! Freaking me out here, babe!'

'There *could* be a problem with that,' said Ambrose. 'They may decide to adopt you and keep you for ever.'

'Ah, you.' Freddie nudged him. 'Wish we could've taken Cosmo.'

'Plenty of dogs to borrow where we're going.'

'Wish we had a dog.'

'Labradoodle,' said Ambrose.

'Golden retriever.'

Pause.

'"Let's call the whole thang off!"' sang Freddie.

'Plenty of dogs, plenty of long walks.' Ambrose glanced at Freddie. 'Plenty of stiles . . .'

'Mmm, stiles!' sighed Freddie. Then he shook himself. 'Moving on. I'm super-excited for this week? I mean, I'm kinda nervous, obviously? And maybe a bit sad? Coz I wish I had a normal regular family for you to meet too? Ah, crap. Meant to ring my dad. Never mind.'

Good, thought Ambrose. That's one problem deferred.

'So how come you don't have the Zummerzet accent?' asked Freddie.

'I do. When I g'woam.'

'Ha ha ha! Be you gonna talk dirty to me in Wurzel, my lover?'

'Well, there won't be much else to do in the cottage. No mobile signal. No wifi. You need to brace yourself for five days without social media, babe.' And five days for me without obsessively checking the polls, the predictive websites, the early voting tallies in Florida, thought Ambrose. Probably do me good. Not forgetting five days without your dad pressurizing me. 'Think of it as a digital detox.'

'But man – five whole days? No Facebook, no Instagram, no porn?'

'Meh. I'm not much for porn.'

'Right.' Freddie started pulling at the frayed edge of his ripped jeans. 'So, uh, why's that?'

'It's all so cliché,' mourned Ambrose.

'Ha ha ha!'

'The characterization's so stereotyped, the plotlines are implausible, the narrative arc's way too predictable.'

'Narrative arc!' By now Freddie was weeping. '*Nobody* watches porn for the narrative arc!'

'No?'

'No!' He wiped his eyes. 'They just wanna see hot guys getting it on, yeah?'

Ambrose glanced at him. 'Isn't that what mirrors are for?'

'You're dirty!'

'That's how you like me.' Ah, c'mon, Freddie, he thought. You think I haven't heard the gossip? You think I'm going to stumble on those clips, and stop loving you?

Maybe not a conversation to start while driving, though.

All Souls' Day dawns. In the quiet gardens of Lindfordshire bees still buzz. A feather drifts down. The sun still toils away at the last apples. There are magpies in ones and twos. Sorrow. Joy.

Two sorrows? Or one joy? It all depends on how you look at it.

Jane looks at it as a historian. She stands on the station platform in Martonbury on Friday morning. It's happening. History. Unfurling in front of her very eyes. Idiots on Fleet Street playing Agadoo with the democracy tree. 'Enemies of the People'? What kind of an irresponsible headline is that? Don't you get how high the stakes are? This is the constitution! Parliament makes the laws, not the government. And then the 'out of touch' INDEPENDENT LEGAL FUCKING EXPERTS interpret it! These are the fucking goalposts of civilization! You can't just move them, and put them back, la la la, when you've won your little make-it-up-as-you-go-along game of Brexit. Why not just pack the cellars of Westminster with gunpowder and toss in a lighter instead?

A jet passes high overhead neatly slicing the blue. 'Sinnerman' is pounding away on a loop in her brain. Oh Jesus! The whole world is going to split in half, she thinks. There's a fault line running through it. Through the UK, through America, through us all, through every human heart.

Next Wednesday we will be looking back on it, she thinks. Looking back and asking how the fuck America let this happen. Historians like me will construct narratives. But right now, it *could* still go another way. Couldn't it? Latino voters, African Americans, women, millennials – they *could* all turn out in their thousands. Feather upon feather in the scales, vote on vote. It *could* still be OK.

If she could pray, she would. *Lord, Lord, Lord, don't you see me down here praying?* Let there be another way. So I don't have to look back and list the things that didn't happen in time.

Things like, Maria Schicklgruber did not slip on the stair and tragically miscarry. The people who might have spoken out stayed silent. The people who could have fled stayed. The briefcase with the bomb in got moved. The cattle trucks rumbled through Poland and officers were kind to their wives, their children, their dogs. Like decent people.

'Hide me. Hide me. Hide me. All on that day.'

308

Please to remember the fifth of November.
Gunpowder, treason and plot.
I see no reason why gunpowder treason
Should ever be forgot.

But for all our fireworks, have we forgotten the lessons of history? What can we do? If the foundations be destroyed, what can the righteous do? This is Saturday the fifth of November, 2016. Dusk, and the street lights just going on. Bonfire smoke. Explosions shaking the night.

Jess is already zipped up in her pink anorak ready for the firework display. Yay! Toffee apples! Sparklers! Yay!

Martin goes up to Leah's room, where she's finishing her homework, to say, 'Time to go, darling.'

Empty room. Curtain blowing. A note on the desk.

Chapter 44

I'm running away because my life is totally ruined. You and
Mum say you want what's best for me and Jess, but you never
listen to us. I am taking matters into my own hands. Goodbye.
Leah.

Martin ran to the window. 'Leah! Leah?'

A firework ripped a path up into the sky and exploded, white.
Lawn. Trees. Like an old photo. That bloody child! She'd climbed
onto the extension roof and jumped. His mind raced. Hiding in
the garden? The garage? Wasteland next door?

'Leah! Come along, please. It's time to go. Are you out there?'

Silence. Then distant crackling.

He hurtled downstairs. Jess stared up, round-eyed.

'Look, I'm afraid Leah's hiding.' Let her be hiding, let her be
safe! 'She's cross about moving back to Cardingforth. I'm afraid we
can't set off for the fireworks till— Oh, poppet, don't cry! Jessie!'
He leant down and hugged her. 'She's probably just in the garden.
Listen, I'm going to get my torch and go and find her, OK? Why
don't you watch a DVD?'

'Has she run away, Daddy?'

'What? Did she tell you she was going to?'

Jess flinched and shook her head.

'Sorry. I'm not cross with you. You can tell me, darling.' Jess
fiddled with her zip. 'This is important, sweetie. Do you have any
idea where she might have gone?'

'Um.' Jess hesitated. 'She *might* of gone to London?'

'London!' Dear Jesus! 'OK. What makes you say that?'

'She *might* of gone to seek her fortune? Like Dick Whittington?'

'Oh, sweetie!' Martin hugged her tight. 'That's a clever thought. But did she actually mention anything to you about running away, or where she might hide?'

Jess shook her head. 'Leah won't ever ever ever tell me secrets. But she tells Lydia, coz Lydia is reliable?'

'Lydia. Of course! Thanks.' Martin snatched up his phone.

Thirty minutes later, he had searched everywhere and rung everyone he could think of. His nerves groaned and twankled like a piano being shifted. He rang Leah's phone again. Answer! Answer! Nothing. Texted: *Where are you? Darling, ring me, I'm not angry*.

Jess was on the sofa, watching *Fantasia*, still in her anorak and her pink flowery wellies. He watched her staring at the screen as if she daren't take her eyes off it, daren't blink. As if this would magic Leah back. Outside, fireworks. Jess twitched at every explosion, but her eyes never wavered from the dancing mushrooms.

I can't just do nothing! thought Martin. He gnawed his fingernails. Where could she be? Think. Think! The seconds crawled past. He googled 'Reporting a missing person'. If she's not back in another thirty minutes, I'll ring 101. He searched the house again, top to bottom, in case the open window was a decoy. All the time his brain bubbled with terrified prayer. He tried not to think of that photo. First day of big school. Tried not to see it in the papers, or on Twitter. *Missing Girl*.

He stared at his phone. Do it.

Ring her. Ring the girls' mother. You can't not ring her!

Of course, Becky snatched up the welcome back cake, got in the car and drove straight there. For a moment she was on the doorstep, like a vampire that must be invited over the threshold. But then she was in.

Jess clamped on like a koala to a tree. 'Mummy, Mummy, Mummy!'

Becky reached out to Martin. They locked hands.

311

'Please can we make cinder toffee and a Second World War den under the table?' asked Jess. 'Like always?'

'Of course, darling. If your daddy . . . ?'

'Of course!' Martin blew his nose. 'Whatever you like.'

'Yay! I'll get the pillows and duvets!' Jess scampered upstairs.

'I'm so sorry!' Martin barked out a sob. He cleared his throat. 'The police are coming. It may be a while though. Here's the note.'

She read it. 'Shit.'

'I've looked everywhere! What are we going to do?'

'Ssh.' Becky gripped his hand again and shook him. 'We're going to make cinder toffee. And just . . . hold it together. Until she gets fed up and comes home. Which she will.' She bit her lips. 'Oh, what have we done, Martin? Oh God, sorry, sorry, I've been so rubbish.'

'No, no, this is my fault, not yours. I shouldn't have—'

'Oh, stop it, Martin. We've both been rubbish.'

Fireworks crackled outside. They gripped hands tighter.

'Most missing persons turn up within twenty-four hours,' he said.

She nodded. 'I know.'

Boom! Boom!

'It'll be fine,' he said. 'She'll come back.'

'Yes. She will.' But a groan, like a shout almost, broke out of her. She doubled over. 'Ah God, my baby!'

They could hear Jess coming down the stairs.

Becky straightened, blotted her eyes. Looked round her. 'Well. You've got it looking nice.'

'Thanks.'

'Right. I'll start the toffee, then.'

Keep watch, dear Lord, with those who wake, or watch, or weep this night, and give your angels charge over those who sleep.

Across the diocese of Lindchester some sleep, some wake. It sounds like war out there. Let it be over. Let it pass.

Virginia lies awake and thinks of the asylum seekers for whom this night must be terrifying.

Miss Blatherwick sleeps, shallow, fitful, fluttering at the edge of waking, like a moth at a window.

The homeless wake or sleep, cocooned in old duvets in doorways and graveyards, in Lindford and Lindchester and Renfold, in every town across the whole of the UK.

The dean lies awake and thinks of the restructure, and the finance officer who will not go quietly.

Dominic's mother sleeps in her new room, with her old things about her.

Miriam wakes with a lurch when baby Noah cries. She fumbles wildly for him in the bed. Where is he? Where am I? Then she remembers: he's in his cot. She staggers away, bouncing off furniture and doorframes. Oh God, let this stage pass. I have nothing left. She lifts him and slumps down in the chair to feed him. 'Hush little baby, don't say a word. Mama's gonna buy you a mocking bird.' Noah breaks off his guzzling and stares at her. She smiles. He smiles back. A gummy milky beam. And for one moment everything, every single thing, is swallowed up in bliss.

Martin and Becky lie in the wartime den under the kitchen table with Jess asleep between them. They listen to her soft breathing. Let Leah be safe. Let my baby be safe. Let this be over. At 1 a.m. they hear her key in the door.

Later, all four of them lie in the den as the last stray fireworks rattle the night. And for now, this little refuge is everything.

It is so cold. The first snow falls on the high places where Lindchester edges the Peaks. White water lies in dark ploughed fields. Tear-shaped leaves weep down from the silver birches.

I have built a world where the tracks are set to converge on a happy ending. A little refuge where people fall, but not to their death; where strokes and heart attacks melt into nothing; where children vanish, but then come home. I cannot even kill a hamster. Becky will move to a rented house in Lindford. They will work something out. The girls will divide their time between Mum and Dad. It will not be perfect, but it will be all right. Fear not, little flock.

But I can hear it, the gnash of slipping gears, the centre not holding. Mind the gap between the story and reality.

*

Dawn breaks on Tuesday 8 November. We are awake before America. We have gone on ahead, to see what will happen when the people choose.

Jane knows in her bones what will happen. She waits for her train, head full of cotton wool, as if the stunning blow has already landed and she is standing already in catastrophe's aftermath. It makes her think of guillotined heads in the basket, still seeing sky, lips still moving. Part of her just wants it to be over, wants that almost more than she wants Trump to lose. She is numb with having cared too much for too long. Maybe she's protecting herself? At least *this* time I saw it coming. Hah, as if believing the worst somehow second-guesses fate, and makes it not happen.

In the cathedral, the old saints totter to Morning Prayer. The retired clergy, Miss Blatherwick. The chancellor reads the Old Testament lesson: Belshazzar's Feast. The writing on the wall. All the king's wise men came in, but they could not read the writing.

The sun sets. *Keep watch, dear Lord.*

It won't happen. Because it *can't* happen, so it won't. *Probably* won't (please don't let it). The polls, the predictive websites, the early voting tallies – they all tell us it should be OK. It will be close – which will be bad enough. We will have a lot of soul-searching, a lot of work to do. There will be a nasty backlash, not doubt.

The rain falls. Tapping at every window in the diocese of Lindchester. Like something we cannot understand wanting to get in.

Dawn breaks on Wednesday 9 November. The dean of Lindchester looks out of her window. She is almost surprised to see the cathedral still standing there, among the fallen leaves. She listens. The pinging of rope on flagpole. A thin thread of wren song. Gene stands beside her, silent.

'Dover Beach,' she says. 'It feels like Dover Beach.'

'I know,' he says.

The tolerant liberal sea of democracy she has taken for granted – can they really be hearing its melancholy, long, withdrawing roar?

How uncannily the lectionary readings have fallen out this week. Yesterday the writing on the wall, today the interpretation: 'You have been weighed in the balance and found wanting.' The message that the wise in all their wisdom could not read. Project Liberalism has failed. Project Tolerance and Inclusion has failed.

'I want to hide away,' she says. 'This feels like 9/11.'

He puts his arms round her and kisses her forehead. '"Ah, love, let us be true to one another."'

'Yes,' she says. 'Yes.' And later, the Eucharist. The table where we cannot unfriend, unfollow, block or mute our brothers and sisters. Eat. Drink. Love. We are all one body. We have to hang on to one another now. At all costs.

And the days pass, as days will. Maybe it will settle down, like a shaken snowglobe of the Statue of Liberty. Like it did after the EU referendum. Sort of. In a rubbish way. Life goes on – as if nothing has changed, when everything has changed. There are people in shops and on trains talking about other things. Andy Murray's the world number one! Have you seen the John Lewis Christmas ad? They trace some continuity between before and after, as if there were no intervening catastrophe. So perhaps we are wrong?

What if half America just sent a goodbye note? *You say you want what's best for us, but you never listen. We have taken matters into our own hands.*

> Is it the best of times, is it the worst of times?
> Is it the season of Light, is it the season of Darkness?
> Is it the spring of hope, is it the winter of despair?
> Are we all going direct to Heaven, are we all going direct the other way?

It depends who you ask. But beloved, let us love. Let us throw down our weapons and be kind. Now. While we can.

'What is all this stuff, Mother?' asks Father Dominic. 'I've never even seen half of it before!'

They are sorting through a fusty old trunk.

'Oh, wedding presents, and whatnot,' she replies.

He lifts things out one by one. Napkins. A canteen of silver cutlery. Pristine Irish linen tablecloths. Box after box of embroidered pillowcases, now splotched with age.

'But you haven't even opened the packaging on these!' he says.
'Well, they're for best, aren't they?' she says. 'I was saving them.'
'For when, exactly?'

'Well, I don't know. For best.' She shrugs. 'How should I know?'
They stare at one another. 'You do know you're bonkers, don't you, Mother dear?'

'I'll give you bonkers.' She opens a flat black box. It contains six silver coffee spoons, each with a different coloured coffee bean on the handle. 'Ooh, I'd forgotten about these!'

'Exactly! Darling, if you pop your clogs now, you'll end up never having used any of it!' He picks up an armful. 'Come along. We're having tea. Best is now.'

Chapter 45

Even now, in post-Christian Britain, cathedrals draw the soul. There are times when we need to head for something far bigger and older than we are, and seek out a truth not relative to us, even while we disavow that possibility. Might there yet be a consolation we don't have to conjure up for ourselves? These ancient buildings seem to wait like vast satellite dishes, eternally tuned to some other frequency, still picking up messages from home.

Time, like an ever-rolling stream, bears us on. Already the events of last week lie behind. We are still in the canoe, shooting the next rapid, and the next, without the luxury of processing what has just happened.

Ah, maybe we should just stay off Twitter for a bit. Time out. Is that allowed? Yes, we will switch off the scary news and retreat to the safety of *Planet Earth II* (discounting the racer snakes, because we are not iguana hatchlings, after all). Let's bake cookies for one another and patch things up with kindness; until—(Until when? Until everything settles down? Until it's over and things go back to normal?)

Advent draws near. For a time and times and half a time the lectionary serves up its seasonal apocalyptic fare. Dragons, beasts, little horns speaking arrogantly, abomination of desolation, and the stars swept down from the sky. Over the centuries, these texts have been the frolicking ground of the nutter wing of the church. But this year the imagery reverberates round every news channel and social echo chamber. Like titanic organ pipes below our auditory range, we feel it vibrating up through our feet, turning the air into a shaken thunder sheet. 'There is still a vision for the appointed time; it speaks of the end.'

'Argh! It's bloody relentless!' says Giles, the precentor. 'Christ the King next Sunday.'

The canons are gathered for their weekly meeting, because life goes on. Today they are in the canon chancellor's study. Mr Happy has lit his fire. It spits gloomily in the grate. Everyone keeps their coats on.

'If only there were a pause button!' says Giles.

The treasurer strokes his chin sagely. 'So say all who live to see such times.'

'What did we ever do to you, 2016?' cries Giles. 'O, annus horribilis!'

'O anne horribilis,' corrects the chancellor. 'Vocative.'

'Shut up, Hermione,' says Giles. 'Nobody likes you.'

'*Swish* and *flick*!' says the treasurer, waving his biro like a wand. 'Expelliarmus, Annus horribilis!'

'Maybe the Queen will die?' suggests the chancellor. 'The plot so far seems to require it.'

There is a chorus of outrage. The precentor beats him round the head with a vestments catalogue. 'Unsay that, you treasonable hound!'

'Gentlemen, perhaps we can make a start?' says the dean. 'Shall I pray?'

They fall silent. In a far part of the house they hear little Noah wail. Shouts from the school playground next door. The cathedral clock. Marion breathes in. And out. The world steadies itself, recalibrates, as if governed by some hidden gyroscope that never falters.

The reader will see that the clergy Chapter of Lindchester Cathedral are already splicing levity and gallows humour into the unrelenting gloom. The bounce-back has come more swiftly than it did after Brexit – which is odd, considering how much higher the stakes are. They are aware of the oddness, but there it is. With the best will in the world, they have more pressing – if not more important – issues to deal with.

318

Yes, the statutory 'saddened and disappointed' voices that accompany any major change in cathedral life have been duly raised. I am relieved to report that the restructure will not entail too much misery. Almost all the staff whose jobs are at risk have opted for voluntary redundancy or early retirement. Crucially, Terrence Hodgeson, the cathedral administrator (such a lovely man!), was due to retire anyway next year, and is gracefully stepping down. Likewise the diocesan secretary. The way is now clear for a renewed and reformed person to take control of the rudder of the diocese. (Insert shudder here.)

But there is one major fly in the ointment. In the brave new rationalized diocese, the two current finance officers may apply for one new job. I can tell you candidly that (after a fair and transparent process) it will go to the current *diocesan* finance officer. Sara was one of Bishop Paul's stellar appointments, in the old era. She is in her early forties, and comes from a financial services background (the polite way of saying 'banker'). Many believe that she is all that stands between the diocese and ruin. There was never much hope that Duncan, the *cathedral* finance officer, would go without a fight. Just between you and me, Helene in HR has long wanted to shake Duncan loose. No love lost *there*. Like the Man from Del Monte's dark shadow, Duncan says no at every opportunity. But Duncan has his supporters, and he will see the diocese in court.

We will adhere to our code of narrative conduct, and not eavesdrop on the canons' business meeting. But I happen to know that besides the restructure, they have an ongoing safeguarding issue, fabric worries, funding applications, anxiety over the shaky start made by the girls' choir last week, and unrest among certain sections of the volunteers. The dean will dismiss the treasurer's solution (to trigger some key resignations by obliging all welcomers and stewards to wear bright yellow 'Here to Help' sashes, like John Lewis staff at Christmas).

The bishop of Barcup is in his study at home. Come the New Year, he'll have an office in William House, once the restructure's sorted. Right now, there are three archdeacons sharing his former office. The ad is about to go out for his old post. Bit of re-jigging

319

of office space is on the cards. He opens his Bible. Still likes an actual book to hang onto now and then, even though he's an iPad man in general. Had this one for yonks. Since Sunday School. Good old AV, with coloured pictures. He turns to the Psalms.

> God is our refuge and strength, a very present help in trouble.
> Therefore will not we fear, though the earth be removed,
> and though the mountains be carried into the midst of the sea.

Yep, we are deep in Psalm 46 terrain right now, thinks Matt. It's all a tad end times-y. Wars, rumours of war, earthquakes. Thank the Lord he was in for Janey when that news broke. Only an hour between the first bulletins and Danny's message from Wellington to say he was OK – but what an hour: 7.8 was a monster, all right. Tsunami alerts, the works. This was the psalm he'd ended up reading, when poor Janey shook him and yelled, 'For fuck's sake, pray he'll be OK! Pray *for* me, I can't pray!'

Never thought of it like that before. Put praying for people in a whole new light. Maybe that's one thing the Church has to offer right now? Set of coat-tails to hang onto, prayer-wise. Be still, and know that I am God. Be still, Tyler. You're just a baby bishop. You're not God. Give over. You can't sort the world out. Just pray, and keep the old powder dry.

Miss Blatherwick has also concluded that there is nothing one can do but pray. These days she prays best in the little chapel of St Michael and All Angels, surrounded by glory. All too easy to nod off in an armchair at home.

But today she nods off in the chapel, her head drooping. The morning wears away. Pools of colour creep round the floor. Angels keep watch.

'Time to get up, Barbara.'

She wakes with a start. Her father's voice! Clear as anything. Calling just as he had in childhood. Time to get up. Time to put things in order. Yes. It's high time. She's known that a while now, deep down.

It's Friday. Freddie is out running again. Mile after mile, trying to sort his head out? America. What the fuck, guys? His dad, wanting to talk money. Yeah, right. With strings. Same old. Prove-to-me-you-can-be-responsible. Gah! Fuck off fuck off fuck OFF.

Swans glide past. Whoa. Was that thunder there?

Girls' choir, ah c'mon, why so whispery? Didn't we get past that? And now Timothy's all, We have to rethink their Advent piece? Understandably. If they sing like that in a packed cathedral, nobody's gonna hear them. But to take the piece off them and score it for the whole choir, isn't that just gonna piss on the embers? He *has* to find a way of keeping the flame alive. So they believe the girls' choir train is still bound for glory?

There's Father Wendy and her dog on the opposite bank. Freddie raises a hand. She waves back. Ha, that time he tripped over Pedro? And Wendy was all, I pray for you? Aw, she's praying now. He can sense her prayer following there, like a dog at his heels. Man, he *so* wishes he had a dog! Him and Brose? Still can't agree. That week in the cottage? The best. Only, *pff*. Gone. Like it happened in a whole other world. The pre-Trump era.

He reaches the halfway point, over the bridge, and heads home. He sees the cathedral in the distance. Thunder keeps banging away. And here comes the hail – *man* it stings. Yeesh!

Suddenly, he wants to cry. Ah, everything's toxic. Brose has totally closed down, walking round like a zombie, same as he did after Brexit? And Freddie knows he can't make stuff be less shit for him? Whenever he tries, Brose just offloads on him. What is *wrong* with you, Freddie? Wake up! Don't you get how bad this is, the logic of where this ends? It ends with cattle trucks. It ends with people like you and me getting thrown off the top of buildings. Everything's fucked. We've waved off the last possible moment for doing anything about climate change. Goodbye, world.

There's only so many times Freddie can lay himself open to this, it hurts so *much*. He caught a word with Chloe, and she was like, Don't worry, hang on in there. He's an introvert, Freddie, you need to give him space to process this on his own.

Maybe it's time to try again, though? Maybe drag him to the Odeon tomorrow, see *Fantastic Beasts*? Except, how shallow is that?

Mile after mile, with the hail gritty underfoot. Mud. Leaf slime.

Then weirdly – hope? This keeps happening. Right when there is literally no reason for it, when he's walking to work or something, suddenly he's . . . glad? Out of nowhere. Like an old Christmas cactus you've given up on, then whoa, there are all these bright pink flowers? How mad is that?

Hope springs up in impossible places, like buddleia sprouting from sheer walls, from implacable concrete. Becky Rogers is flat-hunting in Lindford. Now and then Martin ventures a suggestion, or an offer of help, and Becky manages not to slap it down. On Saturday, the whole Rogers family will go to see *Fantastic Beasts and Where to Find Them*, too, to make up for missing the fireworks. Yay! Can we buy popcorn?

Once Lydia has thought *very seriously* about her behaviour, Kay has decided that they will head to the Odeon in Lindford as well. But Lydia needs to realize how much she contributed to Leah's parents' distress, by not telling anyone where Leah might be hiding. She should have mentioned the den on the substation roof. Does Lydia understand? Lydia nods and meets her mum's eye a shade too earnestly.

Oh God, I'm losing her, thinks Kay. She used to tell me everything. 'OK. Let's go then.'

Helene doesn't say a word. She doesn't need to. *That Rogers girl is a bad influence.*

I think half my little world is converging on the cinema this Saturday. Ambrose is there, in his new stripy yellow-and-black socks that Freddie promised him way back in the summer. They sit in a double seat and Ambrose cries at the end. If it could only be like that. If we could only obliviate an entire continent, wipe the slate, wave our wands and rebuild our wrecked world.

Outside the Christmas lights of Lindford swing in the wind. The street pastors walk the gum-spotted streets to seek out the lost, help up the fallen. A vicar takes homemade soup and sandwiches to the homeless people camped in his churchyard, using his mum's best wedding china.

Chapter 46

'This train is bound for glory, this train.'

It is Monday morning. Jane has an earworm. Thanks, Freddie May. That's the last time *you* come to Sunday lunch. Her train rattles on. She stares out at Lindfordshire as it whizzes by. Leaves whirl past the window. 'This train don't carry no liars, this train.' Through tunnels, under bridges, it goes; along miles of bracken-edged track, back gardens, dead willow herb.

'Don't carry nothin' but the righteous and holy!'

Well, that's me stuffed then, she thinks. Unless, of course, the act of boarding is reckoned unto us as righteousness. No ticket required. Anyone can board – so long as they're prepared to leave everything behind. No luggage on the Glory train. 'Whosoever shall seek to save his life shall lose it.' Ha, that would level the playing field between rich and poor. We have to ditch the lot and take a punt on heaven existing. There's only the conductor's word for it that this train goes right through, and comes out on the other side. Because only the conductor has gone on ahead of us to that undiscover'd country. The one traveller who has returned.

Honestly, I should be a preacher, thinks Jane. If only I hadn't jacked in the training, *I* could be a fecking bishop by now, too. She leans her head back and shuts her eyes. The world of faith is right there, like one of those parallel universes just millimetres from our own, but in a different dimension. She can almost feel it grazing her knuckles. As if she might rub against it with the back of her

323

hand, stealthily, like a stranger's fur coat in a crowd, or the wing of a huge bird. An angel's wing. White, like a swan. Cool and supple, unutterably other . . .

Her head jerks up. She scans round to see if anyone has caught her dozing. They are all deep in their own devices and desires. But we're not bound for glory, are we? According to her poet friend, Spider, we have sown postmodernism and reaped post-truth. We are bound for hell in a handbasket.

But Danny is fine. And he's coming home for Christmas. Jane draws a deep breath. Tears threaten. Dammit. Madwoman crying on train. Matt's prayer had been answered. Danny is fine. Thank you, God, who I still miss and now and then ache to believe in.

Across the diocese of Lindchester people get ready. Advent rings come out from vestry cupboards. Here and there, early Christmas trees glimmer in suburban windows, and the Lindford Rotary Club Santa sleigh has already begun ho-ho-hoing its way round the estates. *Tsk!* Undaunted, the liturgical pedants adopt their unsustainable annual stance of not singing Christmas carols until midnight on Christmas eve. The strains of 'Wachet auf' emerge from organ pipes everywhere.

The girls' choir files *sensibly* up to the triforium, to rehearse their own special part from up there (squee!). Gavin, the cathedral deputy verger, scrapes away last year's wax from the stands. Soon, soon, hundreds upon hundreds of candles. Smell of snuffed wick, hot wax. Oh yeah!

Mince pies are ordered for the post-Advent carol service bash at the deanery. Gene brings out this year's collection of plonk for the mulled wine. Supermarket Chateauneuf du Pape, mainly – hostess gifts from guests who don't know any better, bless their Marks and Sparks cotton socks.

Archdeacon Bea has been busy making sheep for the Messy Nativity animal trail around the shop windows of Martonbury. While she knits, she prays, calling to mind the clergy and churches under her care. She sometimes visualizes her prayers as birds. White knitted doves that take flight on purly wings and speed off to perch on a spire, or a shoulder, or perhaps on a hospital bedhead, and silently bestow a blessing.

Perhaps one such prayer roosts in the bedroom of the rector of Risley Hill. Laurie wakes with lurch, as if the Second Coming has happened and he's been left behind. Poor Laurie comes from a hellfire Nonconformist background, and at 3 a.m. his brain still defaults to damnation.

Julie snores beside him, on her back, mouth open. He can smell the vodka. Who are we kidding? he thinks. She's an alcoholic. She has not been healed. She's a drunk and I'm a sham. He's all glossy surface, no substance. His ministry began so well! Solid foundations, praising God, enjoying favour, the Lord adding daily to their number those who were being saved. But now, ah, for years now, he's been building with straw. One match, that's all it would take. He can't go on like this. Fending off worried church members. Hunting down the bottles, disposing of the empties. Hiding her car keys. Never confronting her.

In case she confronts him.

Except she can't confront him because she doesn't know. Nobody knows. He deletes his browsing history each time in a panicked sweat of repentance. Sometimes he lasts months. But then he finds a reason. He needs to do some research, yes? To help him understand the struggles that teenage boys and young men face in this digital age. But each time he craves a harder hit. More degrading, more extreme.

Younger.

Delete! (Can you ever really delete it, or is it always there, some-where, each keystroke saved on the hard drive for the police to find?)

This is not him, even! He has *no* interest in teenage girls, young teenage girls. He has never once been unfaithful to Julie. Never even touched another woman inappropriately – despite the rumours and false accusations.

His advent sermon is ready. Judgement is not something to fear, amen? Say to the anxious, be strong, fear not, your God is coming with judgement – yes, but coming with judgement *to save you*! Our God is a God of gentleness, praise him. Fear not.

Oh, then why is he so afraid?

Clear history. The last hour. Today. Today and yesterday. All time. Clear. Clear. For once and for all, please, Lord. Wash me, and I shall be whiter than snow. Please.

I was not expecting to feel sorry for the dodgy vicar of Risley Hill. But then, I didn't know the whole story. He is not the only one of my characters who is afraid of being found out. Lydia still quakes when she thinks of her guilty secret. Even though she's almost one hundred and fifty per cent certain it's OK. Because they'd know by now, if—Surely?

'*No*, Dora.'

The dog froze, caught in the very act, fleece throw in mouth.

Both Kay and Helene laughed.

'Did you ever see such a picture of guilt?' asked Kay. She rescued the throw, folded it and draped it on a chair back. 'Whatever's got into her?'

'Maybe she's broody?' said Helene.

'Are you broody, girl?' Kay bent down and rubbed the dog's ears. 'Aw, sorry, Dora-nora. We can't let you make puppies now. Maybe next year, hmm?'

Lydia hovered from the doorway. Shitake mushrooms! ACT NORMAL!!! She wandered to the table and scooped up her dinner money. 'So, off-to-school-now-Mum-bye!'

Outside on the street, Lydia strolled and whistled casually. She gave a naturalistic wave to Mum, who was watching out of the window. Good thing Lydia was so good at drama, and could pull off super relaxed like this, to avoid arousing suspicion. She got out her phone to text Leah: *SHIIIIIIIITTTTTTTT!!!!!!! NOOOOOO!!!! Think Dora probs pregnant!!!!!*

'Uh-oh,' said Kay. '*Now* what's she up to?'

'Checked your cocktail ciggies, recently?' asked Helene. 'Or have they moved on to the drinks cabinet?'

'Oh God, I hope not.'

Dora let out a long doggy sigh and slumped in her basket.

Cold nights. Frost winks on pavements like an infinity of tiny stars, a universe of stars under our feet as we hurry home. If we escape the orange smudge of towns there are stars above us too. Stars of wonder, whole realms of glory. Sleepers, awake! It will come upon a midnight clear. There will be angels bending near the earth. But once again, man at war with man will not hear the love song that they bring.

Miss Blatherwick is getting ready. Since that episode of nodding off in the chapel of St Michael, she has been brisk with herself. Shilly-shallying is selfish. Her friends are worried for her. (Dear Freddie! Offering to drive her to the doctor, fretting over her.) And who knows, this too may turn out to be nothing serious.

Her copy of *Adam Bede* waits on the coffee table, with the bookmark still only halfway through. It is not Miss Blatherwick's custom to abandon books. Perhaps it had become too associated with waiting rooms and tests, and whatnot, and hence one's reluctance? She picks it up and puts it in her handbag and sets off for the GP's, and then to her solicitor's. I would like to finish it, she thinks.

'You're planning on asking him?' Iona rolls her eyes. 'You're mad, Timothy. Just tell him on the night, like last time.'

'That was a one-off,' says the director of music. 'It's not fair to spring it on him. He needs time to prepare.'

'Prepare? It's *Messiah*, for God's sake. Bet you he's got every single note filed away in his freaky memory. He could probably sing the timpani part. Or burp it. Did you know he's been teaching the girls to burp? Nice.'

'Well, anyway, I'm asking him,' says Timothy. 'Giles agrees.'

'Good. Excellent plan. Give him maximum scope for self-sabotage.' Iona stomps off to the organ loft to practise.

'Well, I trust him not to do that,' Timothy calls after her.

The door slams.

His entire whole life Freddie has known he can't be trusted. Fucking stuff-up was inevitable. In fact, it actually made sense to proactively fuck stuff up, just to get it out of the way? But recently he's been all, Whoa, whoa, whoa. Can we get a reality check here? This is a thought, not a fucking law of nature. It's not gravity. It's not every-action-has-an-equal-and-opposite-reaction. I mean, who says I can't be trusted?

Yeah, yeah.

My dad.

Gah, does it *have* to come back to his dad? Like he's endlessly rehearsing this same textbook gay cliché? (*The list of father figures who have betrayed your trust.*) No denying he's trapped in his own counter-suggestibility, though, his Pavlovian 'fuck you, Dad' reflex. Problem is, what happens when what his dad wants, is actually what Freddie wants – only he can't admit it, coz no way is he giving his dad that satisfaction?

Like, Dad 'approves of Ambrose'. Finally, you're in a 'stable relationship', son!

Except, *is* it stable, though? Ah, maybe he's catastrophizing again? But Brose is still really down, and Freddie's starting to freak out that maybe it's not just the whole Trumpocalypse State of the World thang, it's actually Brose getting cold feet? Coz that week in Somerset, they were just begi-i-inning to float the moving-in-together idea? But now, nu–uh. Silence. And whenever he wants to raise it, he kind of can't, coz it sounds all self-obsessed and needy?

Oh God – what if it's over?

Gah, stop that. No time for it right now. Gotta rehearse the girls for Sunday. Will it work, his idea? It's a bit left field. Ah, let that be all right. Please.

Advent arrives. Fidel Castro dies. We should be thinking about this. Pondering the Bay of Pigs, having a reaction. Tomorrow and tomorrow and tomorrow. There's no slack. Everything is speeding up. Has it always been like this – history, one damn thing after another – and we never noticed? Didn't we once spend hours over the Sunday papers? Not just snatch news scraps on the hoof, always intending to digest it later?

What if it's over – the life we love, the world we know?

Get thee up onto a high mountain, bringer of good tidings. If ever we needed good news, we need it now. *Be not afraid.*

＊

The girls wait high up in the triforium. Their candles flicker in the dark, lighting their faces. The cathedral is packed. In the nave below the choir sings: 'This train is bound for glory.' 'People get ready.' The girls watch Freddie for the signal. The song trails off down below, a final whistle.

Then Freddie sings. His voice rings out like the archangel's:

"'The trumpet sounds within my soul . . .'"

And the girls reply:

"'I ain't got long to stay here.'"

DECEMBER

Chapter 47

December. Here and there light shines in the windows of early risers. The dean makes her first cup of coffee. No matter how early Marion gets up to pray, when she looks across the Close, there is already a light on in the bishop's study.

Yes, the bishop is at prayer. Or rather, he is gathering his thoughts, calming his soul, in preparation. He can see the cathedral Christmas tree standing shadowy in the faint glow of the Narnian streetlamps. Logs from last year's tree are stacked and waiting beside the drawing-room fireplace. Hand-chopped by the lovely Freddie May. A year ago, Freddie could barely bring himself to talk to us, bless him. Sonya was praying fervently for a melting of heart. Well, they are further on now. It's been several months since the last diatribe.

The bishop winces. He can only hope and pray his predecessor's letter to the House of Bishops doesn't get leaked. Steve has the utmost respect for Paul Henderson – and indeed, for anyone who finds themselves same-sex attracted, yet at huge personal cost, chooses not to act upon it. But he rather questions the wisdom of Paul's intervention in the debate.

He smiles. Well, there's one from the depths of chorister memory. A thousand Christmas lights. Yes, let this dark earth be bright once again.

Yes, Christmas in the dorm. The wild excitement. Who'd get picked for 'Once in royal'? Sugar mice. *Look and Learn* annual. View-master!

So tempting to believe that was a lost age of innocence and simplicity. To edit out the chilblains, the Cold War, the systemic sexism and casual racism. Tempting, too, to think of 2016 as an unprecedented disaster; while for huge swathes of the world – and of his diocese – this year seems to herald a bright new dawn, not the end of the world. Listen, *listen* to this voice – this is Steve's plea. Listen to the poor, the marginalized, the frightened, the patriotic. The Other. These people aren't all racist bigots. He tries to believe this.

Ah, how fractured everything is. Why is it *so* impossible to entertain the other view? It's not the duck/rabbit picture, where you can see it both ways. No, it's more like the dress that went viral. He remembers his frank disbelief when Sonya maintained it was blue and black. No matter how hard he tried – squinting, holding it at arm's length – it refused to be anything but white and gold.

He tries to focus: Advent. 'Light and life to all he brings, Risen with healing in his wings.' Even so, come Lord Jesus! Except: 'Woe unto you that desire the day of the LORD! The day of the LORD is darkness, and not light.' So, which is it – light, or darkness? Both strands run through the Gospel. That urgent either/or – sheep/goat, wheat/chaff, wise/foolish, in/out. Yet at the same time, there's the unceasing all-embracing compassion of our God, who wills not the death of a sinner.

Steve finishes his coffee. Come on, gather those rambling thoughts, Pennington. The day is at hand.

There is another bishop praying in the diocese of Lindchester this Monday morning. Unlike Steve, the bishop of Barcup is a firm believer in keeping the old powder dry as a back-up to trusting God. Matt is not inclined simply to hope the former bishop of Lindchester's letter goes away. Nope, they need to get the diocesan comms officer on board ASAP. Probably good to catch a quiet word with young tartypants at some stage, so he's not blindsided if the thing goes tits-up. Which it easily could. There's at least one journo out there with a serious axe to grind.

Matt rubs his head and face. Great. As they haven't got enough crapola hitting the fan, with the restructure fun and games kicking off. Local press have got hold of it now. Duncan, the finance officer, has made the connection between the HR officer and the archdeacon of Lindford and is crying foul. Obviously, Matt's confident Helene kept the processes squeaky clean – transparency, avoiding conflict of interest, Kay stepping out of various meetings – but things look set to get pretty personal if it comes to a tribunal.

No offence, 2016, but Matt will be glad to see the back of you. Just to round it off, he's in the domestic doghouse. Today is their second wedding anniversary. Janey got him a swanky Egyptian cotton dressing gown, *but he forgot*. Head-desk. Schoolboy error. It turns out, cotton buds from the bathroom do *not* make an acceptable second anniversary present, even if they've been gift-wrapped. Funny that. Diary's chocka, so he can't even scramble a posh restaurant booking, then pretend he had a surprise lined up all along. Still, Janey's granted him a one week 'exceptional factors' extension. (The exceptional factor being 'you're a dickhead, Tyler'.)

The sun comes up over a white landscape. Earth stands hard as iron. Roofs and railings have grown a white pelt overnight. High above and silent, vapour trails are darts of light in the blue. All Lindfordshire is silver-white in the low sunshine – white twigs, white plumes on dead buddleia, and splashes of gold where sunshine glows through the remaining oak leaves. Light-gilt sheep graze in the frost. A turbine turns, turns. Pigeons sit hunched on branches and youngsters pull up their fur-trimmed coat hoods.

Neil, on the fast train to London, wonders if the time has come to stop dividing his life in half. Should he sell the agency, set up something new nearer to home? Aye, this is home now, out here in the boonies with Ed. Two years today they've been civil partnered, can you credit it? And maybe next year, General Synod willing, they can finally get married. Not holding his breath *there*, mind you. He stares as Lindfordshire whizzes by. Light races along the rails and the rain-filled tractor ruts. Well? I'm open to suggestions, pal. What do you want me to do?

Jane stamps her feet on Martonbury station platform. Her breath smokes. She grins. Cotton buds! Dickhead.

*

Freddie jogs down the hill towards Vespas. His heart is singing and he's almost, almost airborne? Seriously, another second and his feet are gonna literally leave the ground? Does he fancy soloing in *Messiah*? HELL YEAH! Headlining with Andy, ha ha ha, bring it! Man, must be some jinx on tenors lined up to sing in Lindchester, though. First James Lovatt, next wossname. Vocal cord nodules? Eesh. So yeah, now it's Freddie? Probs better watch out he doesn't fall under a bus, yeah? Giles and Timothy, they must really trust him? Awesome.

'Comfort, comfort ye my people . . .'

Plus the little dude's christening a week on Sunday? Aw.

And Brose. Freddie laughs. All ri-i-ight.

Yes, all is well again between Freddie and Ambrose. It came to Freddie last week that he was forever waiting for Ambrose to act the grown-up? Sort stuff out, you know? What if, maybe, it was down to Freddie? So, long story short, he Whatsapped him.

FREDDIE	Babe, what's a man gotta do to get some *croquembouche* round here??????
AMBROSE	Where's my owl?
FREDDIE	???
AMBROSE	You promised me an owl. No owl, no *croquembouche*.
FREDDIE	LOL Wait . . . I'm on it. (Pause.)
FREDDIE	There you go.
AMBROSE	Um. Pretty sure that's not an owl . . .
FREDDIE	No?
AMBROSE	Maybe bring it round and let me check it over?
FREDDIE	LMAO. On my way . . .

I believe now would be a good moment for me to delve in my narrative toolkit and select the strategy of ellipsis. I do this to spare your blushes – or else to allow you time to bring your own feverish imagination to bear. That is entirely a matter for you.

Afterwards.

'Dude, so are we . . . OK?'

'Hope so. Sorry I've been such lousy company, Freddie.'

'Yeah, look, listen, uh, there's not . . . something else going on?'
Silence. Ambrose closed his eyes.

'Shit!' Freddie's heart thundered. 'I'm dumped?'

'What?' His eyes popped wide open again. 'No. No! Why would
you think that?' He grabbed a pillow and hit him.

'Gah, dude, I don't know?' Freddie fended him off. 'Only c'mon,
when you go all silent on me, I'm like— Hey! Are you crying?
Aw, babe.'

'I'm fine. Sorry. Give me a moment?'

'Sure.' Outside the clock chimed, and tiny, like it was a long way
off, a robin singing outside the window?

'OK. It's just, Freddie, you have to understand, right now it feels
like you're the only good thing that's happened in this whole
nightmare year?' He wiped his eyes. 'But look, I've got a confession.
Ah, I should've told you this ages ago.'

'Shit! You're married!'

'What? No! What is *wrong* with you?'

'Sorry!' Freddie wrapped his arms round his head. 'Stop that!'

'Then stop second-guessing me!'

'Yeah? Then just *tell* me what it is already!'

Turned out to be his dad? Trying to co-opt Ambrose, get him on
board with his schemes for Freddie's future? Brose was all, I
should've told him no right at the start. (Ha, like that would've
made a difference!) But it was the funeral, Ambrose didn't like to
sound rude, wanted to make a good impression. And then little by
little – with everything sounding so reasonable at every stage – he
found himself being drawn in deeper.

Yeah, sounded about right. Vintage dad. Freddie was all, Hey,
don't beat yourself up, babe. Once he starts, you have to be fucking
Houdini to escape.

So basically, now Freddie was 'finally showing signs of settling
down', if Ambrose was happy to 'act as his financial advisor',
Freddie's dad was now prepared to advance Freddie the same

amount his stepbrothers and sisters all inherited from their grand-father. It would be simpler all round if Ambrose just allowed Freddie believe Granddad had changed his mind about his will . . .

Wow. Nice, Dad. Course, Freddie sent him a text telling him to back the fuck off. *1. Please do NOT discuss me with my boyfriend behind my back. Not OK. 2. I am not expecting any money from Gramps. 3. I do not need or want any money from you tnx. End of.*

Yeah, right. When was it ever the end of anything with Dad? He'd find another way.

All set for Christmas? we ask one another. Secret Santas that nobody really wants are organized in offices. Advent rings go up on doors, cards drop on mats. (Daring thought – has the time come for not sending any?) Queues lengthen in the Post Office as the threat of a strike looms.

In Lindford, a woman gets the keys to her new flat. She lets herself in and stands in the bare sitting room, and imagines Christmas differently this year.

Elsewhere, a woman phones her GP. The receptionist asks: 'Is it an emergency?' And because she doesn't like to make a fuss, she says', 'Not really'. She is given an appointment for next week.

Elsewhere again, a woman weaves as she drives along the country road to Risley Hill. Ah, there it is. She knew it would come in the end. The blue light flashing in her rear-view mirror. She pulls over, switches the engine off and closes her eyes. Waits for the knock on the window.

At the same moment, a nine-year-old is writing her letter to Santa. *What Leah and me would really really like is a puppy!* She draws a puppy and sprinkles glitter. Glitter puppy! Yay!

Talking of puppies, Chloe rings her cousin Ambrose to wail.

'Oh God! Remember that dog Cosmo raped? Well, I ran into her owner in the arboretum. Argh! It's only the new archdeacon! Kay? I was *mortified*! Apparently, those little monkeys never breathed a word! But I gave them my card, I said. Didn't they tell you? Kay did not know a *thing* about it! Ha ha ha! Oh, I shouldn't laugh, but how could she not have spotted her dog's expecting any day now? I mean, it's *obvious*! Oh, I feel terrible! Should I offer to take one of the puppies?'

Silence.

'Well, *say* something, useless!' urges Chloe. 'Is it my responsibility to help? Should I offer cash, maybe?'

'Don't ask me. You're the lawyer.'

'Oh, thanks!'

'What breed of dog?'

'What difference does *that* make?' cries Chloe. 'Golden retriever.'

'No! You're kidding me!' Ambrose laughs. 'Golden labradoodle puppies?'

'Yes, I guess. If that's what they're called.'

He laughs again. 'Well, that's Christmas sorted. Put me down for one.'

Chapter 48

ow to help your dog whelp (with pictures). Kay and Helene did some panicked research. *The average number of pups in a litter is approximately eight.* Eight! *But litters can vary from four, with fifteen being the largest known!* FIFTEEN! Help!

I'm afraid Kay was *very disappointed* with Lydia when the truth came out. Irresponsibly leaving poor Dora unattended like that! Lydia (defenceless against maternal disappointment) tearfully deflected the lion's share of the blame onto Leah, whereupon Kay got on the phone to Martin to complain.

It was greatly to Martin's credit that he took it on the chin. He did not remark that if this was the worst her precious daughter got up to, then frankly, Kay should count her blessings. Nor did he retaliate by reminding her that *Lydia* knew all about Leah's hiding place on top of the electrical substation, the night Leah went missing.

His mildness was rewarded. A couple of hours later Kay rang again to apologize. Martin, being English, apologized straight back, and offered to bring round the box from Becky's new washing machine (he had also done some internet research), if that would be helpful?

'Yes! That's so kind!' said Kay. 'Oh help, the timing's a *nightmare!* You don't want a puppy, do you?'

'Er, not really – but I'll ask around, if you like.'

It came upon the midnight clear, in a large cardboard box in the corner of the dining room, when the human fuss had died down and the house was quiet. Light from a table lamp shone golden on Dora's nest. Yes, it was time.

Upstairs, the humans slept through it all.

Helene was first down the next morning. She heard the squeaks as she headed to the kitchen. She hesitated. It seemed unfair – she wasn't really a dog person. Call Kay and Lydia to share the moment? No. Better to check it out first.

Dora lay sleeping. Beside her, one, two, three, four, five puppies. All alive and well. Good. OK. Five was manageable. Helene gave herself permission to breathe. Bedding needed changing, but no dead pups to deal with before Lydia got up.

Helene stood a moment watching. They were lined up like sausages, blind as moles, feeding away. Toffee coloured. Big heads, little baldy pink ears. They looked half-finished. Dora opened a sleepy eye.

'Well, many congratulations, Dora. That's a considerable achievement.' Good grief! She sounded like she was about to announce a performance-related pay increment.

Dora wagged her tail once in acknowledgement.

What do you know? I'm welling up, thought Helene. She squatted down and stroked the dog's head. Well done.

'Aren't they just ridonkulously CUTE?' whispered Lydia in registration.

'Yeah, yeah, they're cute.' Miss Dutton kept glancing their way. But Lydia was totally obliviated, as per usual. 'Shh.'

'So we tied different coloured ribbons round their necks? And I've given them all names? That's Toffee, and Butterscotch – he's secretly my favourite? Taffy, Caramel, and I was going to call this one Fudge? Only Mum's like, that sounds like the F-word? So we went with Honeycomb—'

'Lydia Redfern! Is that a phone?'

See? Told you, thought Leah.

'Sorry, Miss Dutton, only I was just showing Leah something super-exciting?'

'Well, if it's super-exciting, perhaps you'd like to share it with the whole class?'

'Cool!' Lydia leapt up. 'So my dog's had puppies?'

Leah yanked on her blazer. God, she could be dumb sometimes.

But Miss Dutton only went, 'OOH! Let's see!'

Then everyone had to look, and the entire whole class went, aw, puppies! I *so* want one? Even Miss Dutton was totally under the Puppyarmus jinx – she had a pug. And all she did was tell Lydia to put her phone away in class in future.

'I don't get why you're not excited,' whispered Lydia. 'Is everything OK?'

'Course I'm excited. I'm just not a publicly demonstrative person.'

But secretly she thought the puppies looked kind of icky, a bit like foetuses still? Plus she kept thinking of The Very Disappointing Incident, and how she and Lydia googled it when they got back to Lydia's. They were all NOOOO! It *swells up* and they get *locked together*? Gross!

That was just dogs, obviously. You'd have to be pretty babyish to think that happened with humans, wouldn't you, ha ha! Leah nearly mentioned that to Lydia at the time, only then she didn't.

There you are, reader. I bring you puppies, like the Balm of Gilead, to heal the sin-sick soul. All manner of thing shall be well. We will now wave off the excited girls of QM and take wing to a different part of Lindford.

It is a while since we paid a visit to Poundstretcher University. Look at that. Dr Jane Rossiter has a bunch of red roses in a beer glass on her office desk. If you peer closely you will spot that it is actually a dozen red cotton handkerchiefs cunningly fashioned into long-stemmed roses.

Matt had produced them with a flourish at breakfast.

'You can never have too many hankies, Jane.'

'Actually, you can,' said Jane. 'Just to head off another flamboyant romantic gesture, a thousand hankies would be *way* too many.'

'Duly noted. Um, are you still pissed at me, by any chance?'

'No, and I wasn't at the time, really,' she admitted. 'I just wanted you to sweat a bit.'

Silence.

'The old antennae are still registering pissed,' said Matt.

'Yes, well, you weren't to know, but when I was five, I was made to stand in the playground with a label round my neck,' she told him. '"I did not bring a clean hanky to school."'

'Really? Pretty Dickensian.'

'I've not been a huge hanky fan since then.'

He put his arms round her. 'Come on, Janey. What's up really?'

'Bollocks. Fine. Danny wants to meet his English rellies while he's over here,' she said. 'Wants to get a better sense of his roots. I can't not oblige, can I?'

He hugged her tighter and said nothing. Matt knew a rhetorical question when one bit him on the backside.

'Oh well,' said Jane. 'Thanks for these, anyway.' She sniffed the hanky roses. 'They appear to be the scentless kind.'

'I thought about spraying them with Febreze,' said Matt. 'I got you something else paper as well.' He produced an envelope. 'Tickets for *Messiah* this Saturday.'

She narrowed her eyes. 'Did you buy these?'

He took a prudent step back. 'Yes. Yes, I did.'

'No, you didn't! You were comped them, you lying toad. Grr. Don't bloody tell me I'm meant to sit on the front row again, like a good little bishop's wifey? I am!'

'Oh, please come, Janey. Freddie's singing again . . .'

She smacked him round the head with her bouquet.

'Ow. Can I take that as a yes, then?'

'Yes, you wheedling bastard.'

If you wander the streets of any town in Lindfordshire and nose through house windows, you will glimpse people trimming their Christmas trees. It is wall-to-wall carol services in the cathedral now. Bars and restaurants bristle with red felt antlers and bonhomie as office dos get under way. In Lindford marketplace the garden shed Christmas market goes up again. Shoppers get snockered on Glühwein and impulse-buy festive jumpers. The piper still pipes outside Marks & Spencer, and the backdrop of seasonal dread descends: how on earth will we fit everything in?

On Thursday Matt got into his Mini and headed for the Close. Emergency troubleshooting meeting re the restructure. Needed to catch a word with Bea about the Risley Hill situation, too. Pretty grim news about Julie's drink-driving charge, but it sounded like Laurie was ready to ask for help at last.

Matt parked up and rang the treasurer's bell, on the off-chance young tartypants hadn't left for work yet.

Just in the chuffing nick of time, as it turned out.

'Hi, Freddie. Got a moment?'

'Oh God.' Freddie was in his Vespas Breton shirt. 'What is it?'

'What's what?'

'Dude, you tell me. I literally just this minute get a tweet off Roderick Fallon? Plus this unknown number keeps calling from London?'

Dang. Matt shouldered himself in. 'Everything's fine.'

'Bull*shit*. If everything's fine, why are you here?' Freddie was white. 'Ah nuts. I know what this is. *Shit*. Just when my life's on track—'

'Hold on. Cool your jets,' said Matt. 'Can we go somewhere private?'

They went through to the treasurer's sitting room. Freddie was shaking.

'It's Paul, isn't it? It is! Shit! How? Fuck! Matt, I swear, I told literally *no one*, not my mentor, not even Brose? Oh God oh God oh God. I do *not* need this right now? I mean, Miss B's in hospital? *Messiah*, little dude's christening, girls' choir, plus work—'

'Whoa, whoa, whoa.' Matt put a hand on his arm. 'Can we sit?'

They sat. Freddie sucked in air. Hugged himself. 'Sorry, man. Go ahead.'

So Matt explained about Paul's letter. 'Don't worry, absolutely no specifics. He just describes his personal journey. In the abstract, if you like.' Matt paused. Taking it OK so far. 'But it sounds like

344

someone's leaked it to Fallon. Relax. He's just putting out feelers.'

''K. So if I lay low?'

'Yep, my best guess is it'll blow over.'

Freddie slumped and began to tug at his hair. 'Gah. Hate this. Is it *never* gonna go away?'

'I wish I knew, Freddie,' said Matt. 'The bishops will be bombarded with letters from all sides ahead of next General Synod. I wish Paul hadn't waded in, but he has. Didn't want you to be blindsided.'

'Cheers.'

For a second, Matt was tempted to leave it there, sidestep the potential meltdown. But what if Freddie got sight of the letter from some other quarter? Deep breath. 'So, Paul's basically adding his voice to the debate by coming out as same-sex attracted, but choosing to be in a heterosexual marriage.'

'Say *what*?' Freddie reared up. '*Same-sex attracted?* Paul Henderson is fucking capital letters G.A.Y. He needs to add his voice by coming out as a full-on ass hunter!'

Matt raised his hands. 'Would it help to read the letter?'

'NO! Do *not* try and make me empathize here, Matt!'

'OK.'

'Get *him* to empathize! Didn't he even *think* how this would make me feel? My sexuality is deviant, it's not valid, it doesn't even *exist*. I'm nothing. What we had was nothing. Just one big sinful mistake. So rub me out, go ahead! Make like it never happened!'

'I hear you, Freddie,' said Matt. 'But come on, this is *Paul*. We both know you'll never be nothing to him. He thinks he's protecting you.'

'Ah, nuts. No fair, Matt, I *said* don't make me empathize. Oh God, now I'm crying.' Freddie wiped his eyes on his sleeve. 'Yeah but no, if he cares, Matt, if he's so big on *protecting* me, then maybe don't fuck me when my head's all over the place, and all I need is for him to – gah, *hate* this cliché shit – be like a father to me? Part of me thinks that.'

Matt stared. 'Only *part* of you thinks that? Freddie, one hundred per cent of you should think it.'

'Yeah, no, I know I'm a total whore – well, I was, now not so much? But still. Don't you think he was of out of order?'

'Yes! Total dereliction of duty and betrayal of pastoral trust. It's a no-brainer. And he'd be the first to admit it.' Matt gripped Freddie's shoulders. 'Look at me. Freddie, I've said it all along: you were not to blame.'

You were not to blame. Thinking back, it was like, that was the hinge? Something kind of small, only everything turned on it?

Couple of years ago – hell, a couple of months even – the Paul thang would've put him in a total tailspin? Right now he'd be flaking on *Messiah*, giving Brose the run-around, trashing everything? Because for his entire whole life up till now, he'd believed it was *always* all his fault? But suddenly, he can step back? He can be all, you are not the centre of the fucking universe, Freddie May. Get over yourself, already. Or maybe, stop beating up on your poor self?

Weirdly? It felt like spring-cleaning. Like he was cleaning his head out. Kind of seasonal, no?

> The voice of him that crieth in the wilderness; prepare ye the way of the LORD; make straight in the desert a highway for our God.

Yeah, he was totally gonna *ace* that sucker. With a bit of luck and Miss B would be out of hospital to hear him? He jogged across to the Song School in the dark to rehearse.

Up in Lindford General Hospital a copy of *Adam Bede* lies on a bedside locker, with a bookmark three-quarters of the way through.

Chapter 49

Children count the number of sleeps till *He* comes, the all-seeing all-knowing one, with his inventory of acts and omissions. He will come like a thief in the night into all the bedrooms of Christendom to judge everyone according to their deeds.

A grey Monday dawns. Cold drizzle falls across the diocese of Lindchester. Heads down and hurry through the streets, people. Less than two weeks, and so much still to be got through! The cards still to send, the presents to buy and wrap. God, let this horrible year end!

Here and there, in garden or park or hedgerow, nature decks itself. Bright, bright leaves, like gold to crown him again. The holly and the ivy. White as milk, black as coal, red as blood. The shortest day approaches. The year's hinge. Something small, but everything turns on it. Gulls gather at the landfill. A lone magpie blurs past. Moles turn up inky earth along the road edge. Every single moment could be a hinge. It is not yet too late. It could still all go either way. If only we could stay awake, if only we knew the things that make for peace.

All that remains now is gratitude, thinks Miss Blatherwick. She is home, and this is where she plans to stay – if that proves practicable.

Ah, so much to be grateful for. It will soon be light. She lies in her bed, propped up on many cushions. It reminds her of the war,

347

sleeping downstairs. (Dear Freddie! Manhandling her bed down that awkward staircase with Ambrose. Arranging a rota of friends to pop in during the day.) Childhood nights, lying under the big oak table, pillow, eiderdown, listening to the bombers droning over Kent to London. Death passing by overhead.

Time to get up, Barbara. It's her father's voice again.

Gratitude. Yes. The privilege of still having time. Time for amendment of life. Pondering one's last words. And to die in peace. How blessed we are. Miss Blatherwick's prayers have been poured out again for the trapped souls in Aleppo. Those last anguished farewell messages. Burning buses.

Time to get up, Barbara. She rouses herself, folds back the covers, then manoeuvres her legs over the edge of the bed and looks about her little world. Beside her are all life's special treats: her wireless, Lucozade, chocolate Bath Olivers, a bowl of satsumas. And a good novel. *Adam Bede.* There might yet be time to finish that.

She gets to her feet. Creation, preservation, all the blessings of this life. Not least, she thinks with a smile, the inconvenience of a downstairs bathroom suddenly becoming a boon! She draws back the sitting-room curtains. Later she might open the French windows too, and sit in her armchair – or perhaps lie in bed if she is tired – and read, or watch the birds at the feeder. It will be like an old-fashioned sanatorium. Fresh air.

Slowly, slowly. No rush any more. She reaches the bathroom. Sliver of lily of the valley soap. This bar should see her out. The pain is manageable. And when it proves unmanageable, there will be pain relief. A nurse will come towards the end. A few months, the consultant said – but she rather doubts it will be that long. It makes her smile, remembering how she cast her eyes down and thanked him for the diagnosis – as though he were announcing that she'd passed an important examination with flying colours! But perhaps she has? Eighty-one years of being herself, to the very best of her ability. Not a Nobel achievement, to be sure, but nobody *else* could have gained a qualification in being Barbara Blatherwick. One had sensed that behind those superficial symptoms something else had been waiting all along. To be told its name – *pancreatic cancer* – felt akin to learning who that stranger was, whom one glimpsed everywhere, but couldn't quite place. Ah, so it's *you*, is it? I am not so afraid of you, after all.

Slowly, slowly. Back to the sitting room. She puts on her ankle-length housecoat. I'm glad I kept you all these years, she thinks. Dove grey wool, navy blue piping. Handmade on Mother's Singer sewing machine. Perfect for those draughty Cambridge corridors. Bright young undergraduates. (Am I really the last of the gang?)

She lowers herself into the chair and arranges the grey folds. Someone will call soon and make her a cup of English breakfast tea. Someone from Freddie's rota. In a moment, she will reach for *Adam Bede*. She closes her eyes. The cathedral clock chimes. Not long now. Not many more sleeps.

'Dude, I'm just not coping.'

They are standing in the hallway of Ambrose's house in Vicars' Court.

'Hey.' Ambrose gathers him in. 'I've got you.'

'Ah, God.' He rests his head on Ambrose's shoulder. 'Sorry. But it's like she's my real mum, you know? I owe her like *everything*? She literally bailed me out a couple of times? *Literally* literally, as in police? Plus she was there for me at the trial, came to visit me in Young Offenders, when I had nobody else? Mum was stuck in Argentina, and my dad? Having his tough-love phase. "I am not going to be an enabler, son, you've got to learn." All that shite. So you get why I won't take his money? I know he'd bankroll a Masters course in a heartbeat? But nu-uh. Always got strings attached. Always the control-freaky strings with my dad? Man. Sorry. Why'm I venting about my dad here? Ah, *really* don't wanna go to work.' He wipes his eyes. 'Maybe call in sick? Go and sit with her?'

'She'd just send you packing, Freddie.'

'Yeah.' He takes a deep breath. ''K. Thanks, babe.'

Ambrose picks up his bag. 'Listen, want to come and get a Christmas tree with me after work?'

'You bet! Awesome! What about presents?'

'Well, I'm hoping Santa's going to bring me an owl . . .'

'Excuse me?' Freddie tweaks him. 'You've already had yourself a whole owlery, Mister. Plus I gave you the bee socks, remember?'

'Yeah, you talk big, but where's my hot-air balloon?' asks Ambrose. 'Where's my peach tree?'

'"You better not pout..."' sings Freddie. Nuts! Forgot I said peach tree.

Ambrose laughs and shuts his door behind them. The Christmas wreath jiggles. A pause. A pause in which both of them nearly say it. *We should move in together properly*.

'Hnn. Cool wreath, dude.'

'Thanks.'

They set off across the Close. They will walk hand in hand until they reach the big archway. Beyond it lies the gauntlet of *I don't care what they do in private* glares, or *Aw bless!* smiles, or neutral glances that note them, and slide away.

'Just can't believe she's really gonna die? I mean, I know we all are, but.'

'I know, babe.' Ambrose squeezes his hand. 'Still, nice that you get to look after her. Maybe?'

'Full circle. Yeah.'

They unclasp hands and walk side by side down the hill, not a gay couple, just a couple of guys, unremarkable, invisible.

A rumbling. The whole office was shaking. Lateral movement. Crap! Not good. Top of a 1960s tower block in an earthquake. Jane leapt up and legged it down the stairs. It wasn't the Abernathy building after all, it was home. She could hear things falling. Glass smashing.

'Matt! Matt!' The shaking stopped. Silence. 'Is anything broken?' she called. She looked out of the window. Of course. It was their dacha by the lake. She watched the quake ripples slide quietly across the water.

Jane opened her eyes. Dark. In the distance, a train. Matt was snoring again. No wonder she was dreaming of bloody earthquakes. In a moment, she'd get up. Nicking off work today to go to the airport and get her baby. Then next week – joy of joys – a trip down the rutted road of memory lane, to visit the rellies she hadn't seen since Mum's funeral.

The train dwindled away. Everything was calm. As if the lake was really there, just outside the window, and nothing was broken after all.

350

*

Oh, there is so much still to do, and so little time. We are in the home straight now. The great O's of Advent are upon us. O Wisdom! O Lord! What will become of all my characters? I should have plotted and schemed better. Never mind. I can always renege on my promise not to go back and change things. Am I not the author? This is post-truth fiction. I can bring back Bowie and Snape, edit out Brexit. I can hack into the hackers, undo the Russian interference in the US election, appoint Hillary. I can turn back the clock, re-run the bad choices, delete every atrocity, right all wrongs, feed the hungry, wipe away every tear.

I can still undo it all. I can still fix it.

But who will fix our poor world? What if this year is the hinge on which it all turns – from best of times to worst of times? What if we are watching in hyper-real slow motion as the earth catches fire? Why are we powerless to stop it?

Heads down and hurry home, people. Past the bundles in doorways, the tents huddled under flyovers, as trains rumble past above us and planes fly overhead. All through the night – trains, planes, trains, planes. The sound weaves itself into our dreams as we fall asleep fretting over our To Do lists. Earthquake. Fire. Famine. The end of the world. Dickens' tumbrils rumbling over our souls. 'Crush humanity out of shape once more, under similar hammers, and it will twist itself into the same tortured forms.'

Term ends. The 4x4s clot the Close, collecting the Ollies and Ellies. Only the choristers remain. Don't be sad for them. You should see the treats that will cram their young lives! The school minibus has already whisked them off to Lindford to watch *Fantastic Beasts and Where to Find Them* (rather than – as advertised – *Fantastic Breasts and Where to Find Them*. Always proofread carefully, Mr Director of Music!). The magic is ramped up this year by the appearance of Mr Hardman at the chorister Christmas party, to perform real magic tricks! And the appearance of Mr May to do his horrible and COMPLETELY VERBOTEN Tuvan throat singing.

The littlest choristers gaze up at these two magicians, these inhabitants of the impossibly glamorous realm of adulthood, out

351

there beyond the voice change, where they ache to be. A place where you can do exactly what you want! Where Free Cash comes out of a hole in the wall, and nobody tells you when to go to bed. But, oh, the unimaginable number of evensongs and school terms and sports days and exams they must get through first.

Freddie looks down at the littlies and remembers. Man, seems like just a second ago. Crushing on the older boys, desperate to be loved, to be noticed, and Christmas still all magical?

Talking of magicians and crushing on the older boys, we cannot bid farewell to Lindchester without a final glimpse of Dr Prospero Jacks. This tale – this life! – is strewn with turning points. I won't lie to you and pretend that a certain notion did not flit across Andrew's mind when he came to sing *Messiah*. He saw how blissful his former protégé was with Long Lankin, and it occurred to him that it might be interesting to flex his powers . . . But no. Oh, the rose gardens we never enter.

Instead, Andrew made himself useful by brokering an introduction to the contralto – a hugely well-connected opera singer, and visiting professor of singing at an eminent institution. Andrew had called in some long-standing favours and lured her to the provinces with this very introduction in mind. How fortuitous that Freddie was now soloing. I am happy to report that there were only one or two points when the mask slipped, and Madeleine Darling's expression betrayed her feelings about the choir behind her; just a couple of moments when she looked as Gene might, had he accidentally sipped a glass of warm white at a cathedral bash.

And so Andrew enjoyed the chaste consolations of being kind. He was even able to offer timely counsel after the rehearsal. He could discern that La Madeleine was thinking 'Meh' to Freddie's performance so far.

'Uh. Can I ask you something, Andrew?'

'Of course.'

'So I'm thinking that went OK, but kind of . . . static, you know? Thing is, I've still got plenty in reserve, voice-wise?'

'And you're wondering whether to tap into it?'

'Yeah.' Freddie tugged his hair. 'Only I'm worried everyone's all, No showboating, it's not all about you? It's an oratorio, not Covent fucking Garden.'

'More's the pity,' said Andrew. 'What's your instinct, as an artist?'

'Hnn.' Freddie thought. 'To risk it? Never hold back. Risk everything, every time, coz you never know what's round the corner?'

Andrew smiled. 'O wise young judge.'

Even the unmusical sensed something was happening. The canon chancellor looked up from his hidden Bible commentary and stared. The most jaded of *Messiah* scorners felt a tingle.

Every valley shall be exal – – – – – –

Go, Freddie! On the front row, Jane clocked a spot of soloist inter-action: the snooty bass smiled. He turned to the tall strapping Brunhilde of a contralto, and raised an eyebrow.

– – – – alted!

Bloody hell. The contralto tilted her head in acknowledgement.

I wish Miss Blatherwick could have been there to hear her boy enter his glory. But she has been to her last *Messiah*. She has been to her last choral evensong, too, and her last carol service. She had intended to notice them, savour them while they were happening, but they had slipped past. You never know what's round the corner.

But if Miss Blatherwick cannot come to the carols, the carols will come to her. On Wednesday evening, a little band of singers gathers in her garden beside her poor stunted apple tree. It is the solstice. Longest darkest day. O Dayspring! True, the nights will shorten from now on, but it will not feel that way. Rain patters.

Sonya, whose turn it is to sit with her, draws back the sitting-room curtain and opens the French windows a crack. Miss Blatherwick sees the torch-lit faces.

'Here is the little door.' Ah now, her favourite!

A little door, a tiny hinge. But to think what turned on it.

*

'We need not wander more . . .' Freddie jogs home by himself in the rain to the treasurer's. Don't hold back. Give it everything. Coz you never know.

His heart is going *mental*. Seriously. *Allegro, presto*. Gah, *prestissimo!* Any second his phone's gonna buzz? Coz in a second Brose is gonna find it. Post-it over the keyhole. *OWL*. Arrow pointing.

Freddie leans his forehead on the treasurer's door. Hands shaking wa-a-ay too much to get the key in. Oh God oh God oh God. Right about now Brose will see it perched there on the wreath, little tennis ball Scops owl? He'll be laughing. Then he'll see the tiny scroll tied to its leg? Maybe now he's unrolling it? Reading the message:

Marry me?

Chapter 50

Somehow, Freddie got the door open. He sat on the stairs, knees jittering. Hours passed. Every minute was full of hours. Yes or no? Text me! Text me! The treasurer's house was silent. Only the radiators ticking. The cathedral clock chimed. Quarter to. Brose *had* to be home by now, surely?

Shit. Had he called it wrong? Maybe Brose wanted to propose to *him*, maybe he couldn't handle Freddie taking the initiative? Oh God, bet he had a plan of his own! That would be so like him. And now Freddie had managed to fuck it up.

Unless Brose was all, wow, um, let's try living together first, Freddie, see how that goes. We can't even decide what breed of dog to get. *Way* too soon to be talking about getting married.

What if the answer was no? Oh God, what if *that* was why he'd never raised the whole moving in together thang again? He'd decided Freddie wasn't a keeper, too high maintenance, too much kink going on – only now with Miss B and everything, he was gonna let him down gently?

Whoa, whoa, whoa, wait up a minute here. Maybe it's *none* of these scenarios? Maybe it's all fine and there's some totally normal explanation, like Brose went for a walk, or swang by someone's house for a drink? Freddie took a deep breath. Rolled his shoulders. Looked at his phone. 7.50. If he hasn't texted by 8 p.m., I'll go over there, see what's going on. Better to know the truth, yeah? He hugged himself and shivered. This is why we went with tonight, remember, not Plan A, Christmas Day? Miss B's suggestion. Her point was, so Christmas won't be ruined?

Ah, fuck this. Need a beer. Freddie grabbed the bannister, hauled himself to his feet and headed to the kitchen.

He saw it immediately. Playing card stuck to the fridge. Ba-doom! went his heart. How the—? When did—? He raced across. Please, please be the two of hearts? He peeled it off, turned it over. Ace of diamonds. And the words: *Check your back pocket.*

NO! Omigod, omigod! He shoved a hand in his jeans pocket. Pulled out a ring! Only *an actual diamond solitaire*? Tap at the kitchen window. He looked up. There was Brose, laughing. Holding the little owl. And nodding. Yes! Yes! Yes!

Ambrose had found the little owl before setting off to sing carols for Miss B. He'd had it in his coat pocket all the time they stood in her garden. Totty was in on the plan. She'd let him in so he could stick the card on the fridge, and stow the champagne. Then she and Philip tactfully went out for the evening. It was far too good a plan to waste – although Ambrose was *burning* to say yes. Patient as an ox, he held his tongue, stalked Freddie home, and then had rather a long cold wait outside the treasurer's kitchen window, while Freddie sat on the stairs catastrophizing. But it was worth the wait, I think.

Afterwards (as we say in the trade) Ambrose lay in bed admiring his fiancé, who lay admiring his ring. Neither of them could stop smiling.

'So tell me about this bad boy?'

'Well, it's vintage, obviously.' Ambrose poured more champagne. 'Russian, early twentieth century.'

'Aw, man, you didn't spend a fortune here, did you?'

'Um, you *probably* don't want to know, Freddie.'

'I *so* want to know!'

He sighed. 'Fine then. I won it in a card game.'

'Say *what*?'

'In St Petersburg, 2011. A young Russian aristocrat staked it, and lost. Apparently, it was a family heirloom.' Ambrose covered his face with a hand. 'I found out later he shot himself.'

'Omigod! Seriously?'

'Yes.' Pause. He removed his hand. Grinned. 'Nah, I bought it online.'

'Doh!' Ambrose fended him off, laughing. 'You are *so* mean to me!' Freddie went back to admiring. 'Oh yeah. Girl's best friend. Want me to buy you one, too?'

'Very happy with my owl.'

'Yeah, you're all about owls, I noticed that. Can't wait to show Miss B.'

'She's seen it,' said Ambrose. 'Gave it her seal of approval.'

'No way! You told her?'

'I wanted her advice. About when would be a good time to ask you.'

'And she said today? That's what she told me too! Ha ha ha! Miss B – what a legend.'

They fell silent.

'Hey,' said Ambrose. 'It's OK to be sad.'

'Don't wanna be sad tonight!' But a sob escaped. 'Ah, you saw how she looked? Man, didn't think it would be so fast, you know?'

Ambrose gathered him in. 'I know.'

Over on the other side of the Close, Miss Blatherwick smiled as she drifted in and out of sleep. Gratitude. Gratitude. All those prayers. That little lost six-year-old. To know he will be fine. A dear someone for him. Blessings. Yes.

Three days to Christmas Eve. Lindfordshire is awash with lists. Present lists. Card lists. Wish lists. To Do lists. Foodbank Donation lists. Self-Care for Coping with Stress at Christmas lists. The whole of life is on a list somewhere.

Archdeacon Kay has a list. A top-secret list of people who will be getting a puppy for Christmas. Or rather, the promise of one – the pups won't be ready to leave mum until they are eight weeks old. Poor Lydia is already breaking her heart at the thought of saying goodbye to Butterscotch.

Freddie is on that list – though he has no idea.

Becky is on that list. Yay! Ssh! Lydia is *not* to tell Leah! (Lydia has told Leah, obvs, but that's OK, because Leah promised not to tell Jess.)

Father Dominic is *not* on that list. He is not *completely* mad! He has Mother, for heaven's sake! He is not about to saddle himself with another dependent relative. *Stop* showing me puppy pics, Chloe!

Father Ed is on the list. Neil thinks he doesn't know. Ed feigns ignorance, but he smiles, because it tells him Neil really is going to sell the business, buy a disused chapel to do up, and settle here in the boonies at last.

That leaves one puppy unaccounted for. Lydia has not begged and wept in vain. Ssh! Don't tell her.

And as every child knows, Santa has a list. Double-checked. Oh, he knows which you are – naughty or nice. He's been watching you. There will be a reckoning.

Tick.

Tick.

Tick.

The minutes, the hours, the days pass. The To Do lists get scaled down. Let us spare a thought for single people in this frenzy of coupledom and family fun, and pop in on Father Dominic and Mother Virginia.

They are saying Morning Prayer together in church on Christmas Adam. This is the feast that comes before Christmas Eve. Virginia – with her benighted Evangelical background, bless! – briefly falls for this. But she will shortly have her revenge.

Just as he is about to begin the Canticle, Dominic's tachycardia starts up. Virginia has been told the drill. The office is suspended as he performs the Valsalva manoeuvre – a glamorous matter of 'holding your nose, closing your mouth and trying to exhale hard while straining as if you were on the toilet'. It doesn't work. He nips to the church loo and tries dashing cold water on his face. This doesn't work either.

Virginia hovers. 'Is there anything I can do?'

'It will stop by itself,' he gasps. 'Eventually. Like hiccups. Sorry about this.'

They sit and wait in the vestry. Pigeon shadows sail past the window.

'While we're here,' says Virginia, 'You need to know we have a really serious safeguarding issue. A live one, not historic. It's a PCC member. I've involved the police, obviously.'

'No! Oh my God!' says Dominic. 'Who?'

'Oh, nobody. Did it work?' she asks brightly. 'The shock. You said it was like hiccups.'

'Oh!' Dominic clutches his heart. '*Outrageous!* Yes, it did. But that's *very* naughty of you, Mother Gin!'

Virginia laughs till she cries. Dominic remembers discussing her with Matt before she was appointed. Not a barrel of laughs, indeed! They giggle and bat one another weakly. Stop it! *You* stop it!

In the end, Dominic wipes his eyes. 'Oh dear. I need a cigarette. I feel as if we ought to get married now.'

'Don't be ridiculous!' whimpers Virginia.

'Well, let's at least do Christmas together,' he says. 'I know! We could have it in church. Let's invite the guys in the graveyard. Round up all the waifs and strays.'

'Yes! Like in *Rev*,' says Virginia.

'Exactly!' Only without the utter failure and church closure, preferably, thinks Dominic.

The last two days of Advent are here. Hurry, hurry! Do those things that you ought to have done. Put a penny in the old man's hat. Be kind. Mend fences and bridges. Make straight the way for God within.

Jane has taken Danny to meet the long-lost rellies. Three-hour motorway journey of sweaty palms and skittering pulse – only to find the grudge they all held existed only in Jane's head. Nobody had been judging her all these years for refusing to move back and look after her dying mother. Or for shaking the dust off her stilettos and getting out in the first place.

'Maybe you were judging yourself, eh,' suggested Danny. 'Coz you felt guilty?'

Jane had already worked this out, thank you very much. It was a sign of her immense maturity that she didn't smack him round the bonce. That, and the fact that all too soon she'd be driving him to Heathrow again. Ah, Jesus! Why does life have to be one long process of saying goodbye?

All around the diocese there are baking smells. It has always been that kind of a place. Traditional. Homely. Open fires and secret kindness. The big wheel of good taste turns and suddenly Lindchester is bang on trend. Is there a more *hygge* place outside Denmark on God's green earth?

Becky bakes star cookies. She drives back to Cardingforth and gives them to Wendy to say thank you for everything. She tells her about the new flat, the new puppy, and that Jess will audition for the cathedral girls' choir in the New Year. Yes, Leah is OK with that. Grandma and Granddad will contribute to Jess's school fees, and set aside the same amount for when Leah goes to university. (Plus anyway, Leah never wanted to be in some lame choir in the first place.)

On the way back to Lindford Becky sings in the car. I won't ever have to see this place again. Thank you, thank you. On Christmas morning, she will join the girls and their father at his place, and she will cook the dinner. And it will be all right. Not perfect − she's done with perfect − but all right.

After Becky has gone, Wendy creaks down onto the kitchen floor − *oof!* − and strokes Pedro. 'Well, she seems much happier, doesn't she? I'm glad she's getting a dog. Everyone should have a dog, shouldn't they, boy?'

Pedro lies in the same patch where Lulu breathed her last. Sunshine falls across the floor. Could it really be three years ago? Oh, Lulu. Heaven − the place where every animal you've loved comes running to greet you. That's what they said. Wendy does not know. There must be some scooping up, though. All the beloved animals, all the places, all the people. Surely nothing loved can be lost for ever − but how this can be, she cannot imagine, only trust.

The vicarage in Risley Hill is empty this Christmas. Laurie is on sick leave. Julie is spending some time at a private rehab centre. The bishop of Barcup has a discretionary fund for these things. That is the story. In fact, the bishop of Barcup was approached by an anonymous benefactor, who had made a couple of wee (ahem) lifestyle changes this year, and found himself with extra funds as a result. The benefactor also took the opportunity to give the bishop a case of Nyetimber to apologize for hating him. And maybe in the New Year he can catch a word with him about reader training?

'Twas the night before Christmas, and all through the house not a creature was stirring, except for a hamster. Boris II rustles in his sawdusty bed, safe in his cage on the precentor's kitchen table. He does not see Boris I skimming across the floor, chops bulging with stolen Stollen (Ulrika has been baking too). Does Boris I bow the knee? Folklore has all animals doing obeisance on Christmas Eve. I wish I could tell you that Amadeus, the cathedral cat, displayed such piety. Gavin, the deputy verger, has twice removed him from the manger, and replaced the evicted Christ child.

Listen. The cathedral organ plays softly. Tonight the central white candle on the wreath will be lit. The chamber choir gathers to rehearse for the midnight.

Out in the holy night the street pastors raise the fallen and seek the lost. Churches open their halls to the homeless. In the side aisle of Lindford parish church, Dominic and his mum lay a big table with her best wedding china and the unused silver and pristine Irish linen tablecloths.

'However many are coming?' she asks.

'We'll have to wait and see,' he replies. 'Mother Gin's been into the highways and byways and compelled them to come in.'

'But what if we run out of turkey?'

'Pooh! Sufficient unto the day are the turkeys thereof, Mother.'

And so the dark night wakes, the glory breaks, and Christmas comes once more. My story is nearly done. My tortoises are assembled, and we are poised at least to nod in the direction of perfect felicity as 2016 draws to a close. Is that not what we want – for the year to end tidily like a novel? And then for a fresh volume to start, full of possibility and hope, where anything could still happen, and it might yet be all right?

Across the diocese of Lindchester, across the nation, people come to church. They come to the crib service, the midnight, the Christmas Day Eucharist. In this dark year, they come in their hundreds, their thousands. They come to village churches, to high street churches, to cathedrals and chapels and café churches on housing estates. Because where else is there? Dear old C of E – quintessence of *hygge*! Maybe there is still an ancient homing device in us all. Maybe a chorus of wartime wirelesses has crackled to life in the cobwebby attics of our post-truth land: 'O come, let us adore him.'

Children wake while it's still dark. He's been! He's been! Bulging stockings. Heaps under trees. Did a single child, however naughty, find a lump of coal? A switch? No! Santa is all-merciful. As always, there are perfect gifts (puppies, peach trees in terracotta pots, hot-air balloon vouchers). There are perfectly acceptable gifts (booze and food, cash and vouchers). And there are perfect-for-the-present-drawer gifts (remember to remove the gift tag from Aunty Brenda).

And here we are, wine-flushed and paper crown askew, looking back on Christmas.

St Stephen. St John. Holy Innocents. This week of in-between-ness passes swiftly. Miss Blatherwick is fading fast. She knows it. The nurse is with her now. There is a race against the clock to finish *Adam Bede*. One by one they come – in response to Freddie's Facebook plea. They sit at her bedside and read a chapter to her, just as she once read to them. Former pupils, in whose thickening middle-aged bodies the piping choristers of yesteryear are concealed. Who would have thought Miss B had so many boys?

I cannot tell you how much Miss Blatherwick absorbs of George Eliot's plot. There's Hester and that ne'er-do-well. Love triangles. Adam. Dinah Morris. But strands from other stories keep weaving themselves in. It's the dratted morphine. There is to be a wedding. A father handing over a bequest. Something about a puppy. No, that's the real world. How will it all end? Will she be frightened?

All of Lindfordshire is locked down in frost. Ice feathers out across standing water. Fog lurks knee-high in fields. The sun floats up, vast as a harvest moon, gilding all the east-facing windows, burnishing every brick. Willows blaze like polished copper.

Freddie is out running before dawn. Mile after mile. He presses his thumb across his ring finger. Feels the diamond. Clenches his fist. Why does it have to be this way, happy and sad all tangled up in a mess like this? It hurts so much. He makes himself think about the miracle puppy instead. Golden labradoodle! Cosmo – lad! Ha ha ha! So maybe in the New Year things will be better? Dog-walking with Brose.

Ah, don't be wishing it gone. Oh God, Miss B – what will I do without you? Never not gonna need your wisdom. And now his dad? Only sending a congratulations card and a ridonkulous cheque? Gah! Can't throw it back in his face, but can't let him think he's won? Miss B was all, he loves you, Freddie. In his own way. Right, in his own strings-attached control-freaky way. Emotional blackmail, same old. See this cheque? I love you *this* much. Now prove you love me back, son. Be what I want you to be. Like I haven't *always* loved you anyway, Dad. If only you'd paid attention to the fact.

He rounds a bend, then, whoa! The sun comes floating up through the trees, like this massive Chinese lantern? Makes him think of Brose again. Him and me, floating up in a hot-air balloon next summer? Yeah. Just hanging in mid-air over it all, looking down? Like the condors kicking back on the thermals. Maybe all this will look kinda small from up there? Ah, I am so small. I am *so* small.

It is New Year's Eve once more. Softly, softly, the needles fall from Christmas trees all across the diocese. The nice Chablis has all gone again, and only the coconut ones rattle round the plastic sweet tub. Before long, the pall of back-to-work dread will descend. We will ache for a fresh start, to be made over anew, repurposed, upcycled, saved. But tonight there will be partying.

This year in the deanery there is a three-in-one trinity of parties. Historically on the Close, the bishop and dean have held rival celebrations. However, in this year of restructuring Steve and Marion have amalgamated their unwieldy gatherings into one manageable do. This much is known to all. But tonight is also a surprise engagement party – known to all except Freddie and Ambrose. This was the brainchild of Ulrika and Iona. Whether it sprang from a vague guilt about being a bit mean to Mr May for so long, I leave to the reader to determine. They have gathered as many of the couple's loved ones as possible. Let us sneak into the deanery behind the lay clerks and snoop.

There is a hiatus before the happy pair arrive, in which rather a lot of Gene's champagne, vodka and caviar is consumed. The generous Blatherwick Bequest to the Choral Foundation (still a secret) is openly discussed. The lay clerks race clockwork nuns. Kat, the bishop's EA, takes on Neil in a fiercely contested tennis ball keepy-uppy challenge in the hallway – and wins. Aye, but only coz he let her. Ed and Dominic dotingly compare puppy pics. Gene attempts to provoke the bishop by riffing on the lamentable mission creep of Evangelical management-itis in the Church. The bishop replies that if Gene has an alternative oar to hand, then by all means start paddling. The church canoe is hurtling downstream, brother, but there might still be time to turn it round before the Falls. Gene's answer – if he has one – is quelled by a stern glance from the dean. He raises his hands. He has promised to behave.

Jane, too, has promised to behave.

'I bet Jen would've made a better bishop's wife,' she grumbled in the car.

'Probably,' agreed Matt. 'But you have one definite advantage.'

'Yeah, point taken. I'm still alive.'

'Mind you, if she'd still been alive when I nearly ran you over in that alley,' said Matt, 'I might've had my work cut out.'

Jane laughed her filthy laugh. 'Ooh, you bad bishop.'

'Ew. Get a room, you guys,' said Danny from the back seat.

Archdeacon Bea has made no promise to behave. She spends time talking to Sonya, who has just come from reading to Miss Blatherwick. Sonya explains about the great *Adam Bede* readathon.

'Ah, bless her,' said Bea. 'So she's not in a hospice?'

'—piss. No, she's at home.'

364

The bishop of Barcup, standing nearby, does a nose trick with his champagne.

But wait! A text has arrived from the nurse. All done.

Yes, the final chapter and the epilogue is finished. The last words have been read: "'Come in, Adam, and rest; it has been a hard day for thee.'" The book has been closed and put down. Freddie and Ambrose are on their way over now. Miss B sent them packing, because she's in on the secret, of course.

Positions, people!

Iona seats herself at the deanery piano. The door opens. A drunken chorus of 'Congratulations' bursts out. Aw, you guys!

Then ta-dah! Leah and Jess wheel in a trolley with another *even bigger croquembouche*, which they'd spent all afternoon helping Uli to make. It fizzes with sparklers, and leans like the Tower of Pisa – but not bloody bad for a first attempt, *ja*? There are cheers, tears, and popping corks. Naw, you GUYS!

And now it is nearly midnight. As is traditional, the revellers will gather at the cathedral's west front, around the Christmas tree. They will drink champagne, and caterwaul 'Auld Lang Syne' as Great Tom tolls twelve. Here they come now. Some of the non-designated drivers are staggering a little, I fear.

Jane clutches at Gene's arm.

'Oopsy-daisy, Maisie!' he says.

Her promise lapses. She launches her final rant of the year. 'Farewell 2016! Don't forget to write. And helloooo 2017! The rough beast slouches towards Washington to be born.'

'Oh, don't worry,' says Gene. 'America just needs to get shit-faced for four years. It'll learn.'

'Not before we all get obliterfried.' She grips his arm. 'It's the end of the world.'

'Oh, it always is, Mrs Bishop. It always is. Ah, look!'

Everyone looks. A red Chinese lantern sails past high above the spire.

Where will it come down? wonders Marion. We're not meant to let them off any more. They set fire to things. Kill livestock. Oh Lord, the far-off unimagined consequences of our actions. Cities burning. Dead children. Even now, as we stand here. And yet, we are still standing here. Together, in spite of everything. In spite of the storms ahead. The employment tribunals. General Synod. The Anglican Communion hanging by a thread.

She turns to Bishop Steve. 'Well, we're still here.'

'Yes,' he says. He sees Freddie, hovering as though he has something to say. But he doesn't speak. So Steve says, 'Congratulations.'

'Thanks.'

'And you finished the book! If memory serves, the galloping horseman gets there at the eleventh hour, with a hard-won release from death?'

'Yeah.'

'And they get married and lived happily ever after?'

'Yeah.' He sobs once, then reins it back in.

'Bless you.' Steve puts an arm round his shoulders. 'Come on. Awkward Evangelical man-hug.'

Freddie smiles through his tears. Leans on him. 'Thanks, Steve.'

Any minute now we'll be looking back on it. The final second will tick past. Everything is poised. Everything always is. Best of races, worst of races. We are so small. We cannot scramble out of our finitude and be sure how it will end. We cannot escape from the brackets and check the formula. Is there a plus against us, or a minus?

'Nearly time,' says the nurse. 'Would you like me to open the window?'

Miss Blatherwick stares. The nurse's face looks odd. Like a rather interesting Picasso. There is something urgent. A plane going down. A message from Freddie. But no. That was a long time ago.

The nurse squeezes her hand. 'I'll open it. Then we'll hear it strike midnight.'

Fireworks. They'll all be there, waiting. Come in and rest; it has been a hard day for thee. Aha, she thinks. So this is what it's like. Father's voice. Time to get up, Barbara. Good. I had been so afraid.

They are counting down. Ten. Nine. Eight. The chimes start.

The nurse looks at her watch.

Love, thinks Miss Blatherwick. That's all. Love.

Cheering. And there's Great Tom tolling out. Love. Love. Love.

'Happy New Year, Barbara.' The nurse takes her hand and bends close. 'Did you say something, my dear?'

Miss Blatherwick breathes out her last word: 'Love.'

THE END

Acknowledgements

I would like to thank everyone who read *Realms of Glory* as it unfolded during 2016. I am grateful for your company along the way, and for your feedback and comments. An especial thank you to everyone in Liverpool Cathedral, to my colleagues in the Manchester Writing School, and to my friends and family. Without your support, the challenge of chronicling this strange year in real time would have proved impossible.